Calvary Alley

by

Alice Hegan Rice

Double 9
BOOKS

Calvary Alley
by Alice Hegan Rice

Copyright © 2023

All Rights reserved.

ISBN: 978-93-60465-50-6

Published by

DOUBLE 9 BOOKS

2/13-B, Ansari Road
Daryaganj, New Delhi – 110002
info@double9books.com
www.double9books.com
Tel. 011-40042856

ABOUT THE AUTHOR

ALICE HEGAN RICE was an American author who was born January 11, 1870, and died February 10, 1942. Her birth name was Alice Caldwell Hegan. Four movies and a play were made from her 1901 book Mrs. Wiggs of the Cabbage Patch. She was born in Shelbyville, Kentucky, on January 11, 1870. Her parents were Samuel Watson Hegan and Sallie P. Hegan. When she was a child, she would make up stories on the spot to keep her family entertained. As a student, it was clear that writing was her best subject. She was so good at writing that a piece she sent in when she was 15 years old was read by the newspaper. Rice grew up in a pretty good family, but when she went to a Sunday School mission in the "Cabbage Patch," a slum in Louisville, her views on life changed. A group of troublesome boys stopped the mission, but Rice was able to calm things down by telling them a story she had just read. She kept telling them crazy stories about pirates and gangsters for the rest of the mission. She learned about poor and people who don't have much through this experience.

CONTENTS

CHAPTER I
THE FIGHT

You never would guess in visiting Cathedral Court, with its people's hall and its public baths, its clean, paved street and general air of smug propriety, that it harbors a notorious past. But those who knew it by its maiden name, before it was married to respectability, recall Calvary Alley as a region of swarming tenements, stale beer dives, and frequent police raids. The sole remaining trace of those unregenerate days is the print of a child's foot in the concrete walk just where it leaves the court and turns into the cathedral yard.

All the tired feet that once plodded home from factory and foundry, all the unsteady feet that staggered in from saloon and dance-hall, all the fleeing feet that sought a hiding place, have long since passed away and left no record of their passing. Only that one small footprint, with its perfect outline, still pauses on its way out of the alley into the great world beyond.

At the time Nance Molloy stepped into that soft concrete and thus set in motion the series of events that was to influence her future career, she had never been told that her inalienable rights were life, liberty, and the pursuit of happiness. Nevertheless she had claimed them intuitively. When at the age of one she had crawled out of the soap-box that served as a cradle, and had eaten half a box of stove polish, she was acting in strict accord with the Constitution.

By the time she reached the sophisticated age of eleven her ideals had changed, but her principles remained firm. She did not stoop to beg for her rights, but struck out for them boldly with her small bare fists. She was a glorious survival of that primitive Kentucky type that stood side by side with man in the early battles and fought valiantly for herself.

On the hot August day upon which she began to make history, she stood in the gutter amid a crowd of yelling boys, her feet far apart, her hands full of mud, waiting tensely to chastise the next sleek head that dared show itself above the cathedral fence. She wore a boy's shirt and a ragged brown skirt that flapped about her sturdy bare legs. Her matted hair was bound in two disheveled braids around her head and secured with a piece of shoe-string.

Her dirty round face was lighted up by a pair of dancing blue eyes, in which just now blazed the unholy light of conflict.

The feud between the Calvary Micks and the choir boys was an ancient one, carried on from one generation to another and gaining prestige with age. It was apt to break out on Saturday afternoons, after rehearsal, when the choirmaster had taken his departure. Frequently the disturbance amounted to no more than taunts and jeers on one side and threats and recriminations on the other, but the atmosphere that it created was of that electrical nature that might at any moment develop a storm.

Nance Molloy, at the beginning of the present controversy, had been actively engaged in civil warfare in which the feminine element of the alley was pursuing a defensive policy against the marauding masculine. But at the first indication of an outside enemy, the herd instinct manifested itself, and she allied herself with prompt and passionate loyalty to the cause of the Calvary Micks.

The present argument was raging over the possession of a spade that had been left in the alley by the workmen who were laying a concrete pavement into the cathedral yard.

"Aw, leave 'em have it!" urged a philosophical alleyite from the top of a barrel. "Them ole avenoo kids ain't nothin'!—We could lick daylight outen 'em if we wanted to."

"Ye-e-e-s you could!" came in a chorus of jeers from the fence top, and a brown-eyed youth in a white-frilled shirt, with a blue Windsor tie knotted under his sailor collar, added imperiously, "You get too fresh down there, and I'll call the janitor!"

This gross breach of military etiquette evoked a retort from Nance that was too inelegant to chronicle.

"Tomboy! tomboy!" jeered the brown-eyed youth from above. "Why don't you borrow some girls' clothes?"

"All right, Sissy," said Nance, "lend me yours."

The Micks shrieked their approval, while Nance rolled a mud ball and, with the deadly aim of a sharpshooter, let it fly straight at the white-frilled bosom of her tormentor.

"Soak it to her, Mac," yelled the boy next to him, "the kid's got no business butting in! Make her get out of the way!"

"Go on and make me!" implored Nance.

"I will if you don't stand back," threatened the boy called Mac.

Nance promptly stepped up to the alley gate and wiggled her fingers in a way peculiarly provocative to a juvenile enemy.

"Poor white trash!" he jeered. "You stay where you belong! Don't you step on our concrete!"

"Will if I want to. It's my foot. I'll put it where I like."

"Bet you don't. You're afraid to."

"I ain't either."

"Well, *do* it then. I dare you! Anybody that would take a—"

In a second Nance had thrust her leg as far as possible between the boards that warned the public to keep out, and had planted a small alien foot firmly in the center of the soft cement.

This audacious act was the signal for instant battle. With yells of indignation the choir boys hurled themselves from the fence, and descended upon their foes. Mud gave place to rocks, sticks clashed, the air resounded with war cries. Ash barrels were overturned, straying cats made flying leaps for safety, heads appeared at doorways and windows, and frantic mothers made futile efforts to quell the riot.

Thus began the greatest fight ever enjoyed in Calvary Alley. It went down in neighborhood annals as the decisive clash between the classes, in which the despised swells "was learnt to know their places onct an' fer all!" For ten minutes it raged with unabated fury, then when the tide of battle began to set unmistakably in favor of the alley, parental authority waned and threats changed to cheers. Old and young united in the conviction that the Monroe Doctrine must be maintained at any cost!

In and out of the subsiding pandemonium darted Nance Molloy, covered with mud from the shoestring on her hair to the rag about her toe, giving and taking blows with the best, and emitting yells of frenzied victory over every vanquished foe. Suddenly her transports were checked by a disturbing sight. At the end of the alley, locked in mortal combat, she beheld her arch-enemy, he of the brown eyes and the frilled shirt, whom the boys called Mac, sitting astride the hitherto invincible Dan Lewis, the former philosopher of the ash barrel and one of the acknowledged leaders of the Calvary Micks.

It was a moment of intense chagrin for Nance, untempered by the fact that Dan's adversary was much the bigger boy. Up to this time, the whole affair had been a glorious game, but at the sight of the valiant Dan lying helpless on his back, his mouth bloody from the blows of the boy above him, the comedy changed suddenly to tragedy. With a swift charge from the rear, she flung herself upon the victor, clapping her mud-daubed hands about his eyes and dragging him backward with a force that sent them both rolling in the gutter.

Blind with fury, the boy scrambled to his feet, and, seizing a rock, hurled it with all his strength after the retreating Dan. The missile flew wide of its mark and, whizzing high over the fence, crashed through the great rose window that was the special pride of Calvary Cathedral.

The din of breaking glass, the simultaneous appearance of a cross-eyed policeman, and of Mason, the outraged janitor, together with the horrified realization of what had happened, brought the frenzied combatants to their senses. Amid a clamor of accusations and denials, the policeman seized upon two culprits and indicated a third.

"You let me go!" shrieked Mac. "My father'll make it all right! Tell him who I am, Mason! Make him let me go!"

But Mason was bent upon bringing all the criminals to justice.

"I'm going to have you all up before the juvenile court, rich and poor!" he declared excitedly. "You been deviling the life out of me long enough! If the vestry had 'a' listened at me and had you up before now, that window wouldn't be smashed. I told the bishop something was going to happen, and he says, 'The next time there's trouble, you find the leaders and swear out a warrant. Don't wait to ask anybody!'"

By this time every window in the tenement at the blind end of the alley had been converted into a proscenium box, and suggestions, advice, and incriminating evidence were being freely volunteered.

"Who started this here racket, anyhow?" asked the policeman, in the bored tone of one who is rehearsing an oft-repeated scene.

"I did," declared Nance Molloy, with something of the feminine gratification Helen of Troy must have felt when she "launched a thousand ships and burnt the topless towers of Ilium."

"You Nance!" screamed a woman from a third-story window. "You know you never done no such a thing! I was settin' here an' seen ever'thing that happened; it was them there boys."

"So it was you, Dan Lewis, was it?" said the policeman, recognizing one of his panting victims, the one whose ragged shirt had been torn completely off, leaving his heaving chest and brown shoulders bare. "An' it ain't surprised, I am. Who is this other little dude?"

"None of your business!" cried Mac furiously, trying to wrench himself free. "I tell you my father will pay for the darned old window."

"Aisy there," said the policeman. "Does anybody know him?"

"It's Mr. Clarke's son, up at the bottle works," said Mason.

"You let me go," shrieked the now half-frantic boy. "My father 'll make you pay for this. You see if he don't!"

"None o' your guff," said the policeman. "I ain't wantin' to keep you now I got your name. Onny more out o' the boonch, Mr. Mason?"

Mason swept a gleaning eye over the group, and as he did so he spied the footprint, in the concrete.

"Who did that?" he demanded in a fresh burst of wrath.

Those choir boys who had not fled the scene gave prompt and incriminating testimony.

"No! she never!" shouted the woman from the third floor, now suspended half-way out of the window. "Nance Molloy was up here a-washin' dishes with me. Don't you listen at them pasty-faced cowards a-puttin' it off on a innercent little girl!"

But the innocent little girl had no idea of seeking refuge in her sex. Hers had been a glorious and determining part in the day's battle, and the distinction of having her name taken down with those of the great leaders was one not to be foregone.

"I did do it," she declared excitedly. "That there boy dared me to. Ketch me takin' a dare offen a avenoo kid!"

"What's your name, Sis?" asked the policeman.

"Nance Molloy."

"Where do you live?"

"Up there at Snawdor's. That there was Mis' Snawdor a-yellin' at me."

"Is she yer mother?"

"Nope. She's me step."

"And yer father?"

"He's me step too. I'm a two-step," she added with an impudent toss of the head to show her contempt for the servant of the law, a blue-coated, brass-buttoned interloper who swooped down on you from around corners, and reported you at all times and seasons.

By this time Mrs. Snawdor had gotten herself down the two flights of stairs, and was emerging from the door of the tenement, taking down her curl papers as she came. She was a plump, perspiring person who might have boasted good looks had it not been for two eye-teeth that completely dominated her facial landscape.

"You surely ain't fixin' to report her?" she asked ingratiatingly of Mason. "A little 'leven-year-ole orphin that never done no harm to nobody?"

"It's no use arguing," interrupted Mason firmly. "I'm going to file out a warrant against them three children if it's the last act of my mortal life. There ain't a boy in the alley that gives me any more trouble than that there little girl, a-throwin' mud over the fence and climbing round the coping and sneaking into the cathedral to look under the pews for nickels, if I so much as turn my back!"

"He wants the nickels hisself!" cried Nance shrilly, pushing her nose flat and pursing her lips in such a clever imitation of the irate janitor that the alley shrieked with joy.

"You limb o' Satan!" cried Mrs. Snawdor, making a futile pass at her. "It's a God's mericle you ain't been took up before this! And it's me as 'll have the brunt to bear, a-stoppin' my work to go to court, a-lying to yer good character, an' a-payin' the fine. It's a pity able-bodied men like policemens an' janitors can't be tendin' their own business 'stid of comin' interferin' with the family of a hard-workin' woman like me. If there's any justice in this world it ain't never flowed in my direction!"

And Mrs. Snawdor, half dragging, half pushing Nance, disappeared into the dark entrance of the tenement, breathing maledictions first against her charge, then against the tyranny of the law.

CHAPTER II
THE SNAWDORS AT HOME

If ever a place had a down-at-heel, out-of-elbow sort of look, it was Calvary Alley. At its open end and two feet above it the city went rushing and roaring past like a great river, quite oblivious of this unhealthy bit of backwater into which some of its flotsam and jetsam had been caught and held, generating crime and disease and sending them out again into the main current.

For despite the fact that the alley rested under the very wing of the great cathedral from which it took its name, despite the fact that it echoed daily to the chimes in the belfry and at times could even hear the murmured prayers of the congregation, it concerned itself not in the least with matters of the spirit. Heaven was too remote and mysterious, Hell too present and prosaic, to be of the least interest. And the cathedral itself, holding out welcoming arms to all the noble avenues that stretched in leafy luxury to the south, forgot entirely to glance over its shoulder at the sordid little neighbor that lay under the very shadow of its cross.

At the blind end of the alley, wedged in between two towering warehouses, was Number One, a ramshackle tenement which in some forgotten day had been a fine old colonial residence. The city had long since hemmed it in completely, and all that remained of its former grandeur were a flight of broad steps that once boasted a portico and the imposing, fan-shaped arch above the doorway.

In the third floor of Number One, on the side next the cathedral, dwelt the Snawdor family, a social unit of somewhat complex character. The complication came about by the paterfamilias having missed his calling. Mr. Snawdor was by instinct and inclination a bachelor. He had early in life found a modest rut in which he planned to run undisturbed into eternity, but he had been discovered by a widow, who was possessed of an initiative which, to a man of Snawdor's retiring nature, was destiny.

At the time she met him she had already led two reluctant captives to the hymeneal altar, and was wont to boast, when twitted about the fact, that "the Lord only knew what she might 'a' done if it hadn't been fer them eye-teeth!" Her first husband had been Bud Molloy, a genial young Irishman who good-naturedly allowed himself to be married out of gratitude for her care of his motherless little Nance. Bud had not lived to repent the act; in less than a month he heroically went over an embankment with his engine, in one of those fortunate accidents in which "only the engineer is killed."

The bereft widow lost no time in seeking consolation. Naturally the first person to present himself on terms of sympathetic intimacy was the undertaker who officiated at poor Bud's funeral. At the end of six months she married him, and was just beginning to enjoy the prestige which his profession gave her, when Mr. Yager also passed away, becoming, as it were, his own customer. Her legacy from him consisted of a complete embalming outfit and a feeble little Yager who inherited her father's tendency to spells.

Thus encumbered with two small girls, a less sanguine person would have retired from the matrimonial market. But Mrs. Yager was not easily discouraged; she was of a marrying nature, and evidently resolved that neither man nor Providence should stand in her way. Again casting a speculative eye over the field, she discerned a new shop in the alley, the sign of which announced that the owner dealt in "Bungs and Fawcetts." On the evening of the same day the chronic ailment from which the kitchen sink had suffered for two years was declared to be acute, and Mr. Snawdor was called in for consultation.

He was a timid, dejected person with a small pointed chin that trembled when he spoke. Despite the easy conventions of the alley, he kept his clothes neatly brushed and his shoes polished, and wore a collar on week days. These signs of prosperity were his undoing. Before he had time to realize what was happening to him, he had been skilfully jolted out of his rut by the widow's experienced hand, and bumped over a hurried courtship into a sudden marriage. He returned to consciousness to find himself possessed of a wife and two stepchildren and moved from his small neat room over his shop to the indescribable disorder of Number One.

The subsequent years had brought many little Snawdors in their wake, and Mr. Snawdor, being thus held up by the highwayman Life, ignominiously surrendered. He did not like being married; he did not enjoy being a father; his one melancholy satisfaction lay in being a martyr.

Mrs. Snawdor, who despite her preference for the married state derived little joy from domestic duties, was quite content to sally forth as a wage-earner. By night she scrubbed office buildings and by day she slept and between times she sought diversion in the affairs of her neighbors.

Thus it was that the household burdens fell largely upon Nance Molloy's small shoulders, and if she wiped the dishes without washing them, and "shook up the beds" without airing them, and fed the babies dill pickles, it was no more than older housekeepers were doing all around her.

Late in the afternoon of the day of the fight, when the sun, despairing of making things any hotter than they were, dropped behind the warehouse, Nance, carrying a box of crackers, a chunk of cheese, and a bucket of beer, dodged in and out among the push-carts and the barrels of the alley on her way home from Slap Jack's saloon. There was a strong temptation on her part to linger, for a hurdy-gurdy up at the corner was playing a favorite tune, and echoes of the fight were still heard from animated groups in various doorways. But Nance's ears still tingled from a recent boxing, and she resolutely kept on her way until she reached the worn steps of Number One and scurried through its open doorway.

The nice distinction between a flat and a tenement is that the front door of one is always kept closed, and the other open. In this particular instance the matter admitted of no discussion, for there was no front door. The one that originally hung under the fan-shaped Colonial arch had long since been kicked in during some nocturnal raid, and had never been replaced.

When the gas neglected to get itself lighted before dark at Number One, you had to feel your way along the hall in complete darkness, until your foot struck something; then you knew you had reached the stairs and you began to climb. It was just as well to feel along the damp wall as you went, for somebody was always leaving things on the steps for people to stumble over.

Nance groped her way cautiously, resting her bucket every few steps and taking a lively interest in the sounds and smells that came from behind the various closed doors she passed. She knew from the angry voices on the first floor that Mr. Smelts had come home "as usual"; she knew who was having sauerkraut for supper, and whose bread was burning.

The odor of cooking food reminded her of something. The hall was dark and the beer can full, so she sat down at the top of the first flight and, putting her lips to the foaming bucket was about to drink, when the door behind her opened and a keen-faced young Jew peered out.

"Say, Nance," he whispered curiously, "have they swore out the warrant on you yet?"

Nance put down the bucket and looked up at him with a fine air of unconcern.

"Don't know and don't keer!" she said. "Where was you hidin' at, when the fight was goin' on?"

"Getting my lessons. Did the cop pinch the Clarke guy?"

"You betcher," said Nance. "You orter seen the way he took on! Begged to beat the band. Me and Danny never. Me and him—"

A volley of curses came from the hall below, the sound of a blow, followed by a woman's faint scream of protest, then a door slammed.

"If I was Mis' Smelts," said Nance darkly, with a look that was too old for ten years, "I wouldn't stand for that. I wouldn't let no man hit me. I'd get him sent up. I—"

"You walk yourself up them steps, Nance Molloy!" commanded Mrs. Snawdor's rasping voice from the floor above. "I ain't got no time to be waitin' while you gas with Ike Lavinsky."

Nance, thus admonished, obeyed orders, arriving on the domestic hearth in time to prevent the soup from boiling over. Mr. Snawdor, wearing a long apron and an expression of tragic doom, was trying to set the table, while over and above and beneath him surged his turbulent offspring. In a broken rocking-chair, fanning herself with a box-top, sat Mrs. Snawdor, indulging herself in a continuous stream of conversation and apparently undisturbed by the uproar around her. Mrs. Snawdor was not sensitive to discord. As a necessary adjustment to their environment, her nerves had become soundproof.

"You certainly missed it by not being here!" she was saying to Mr. Snawdor. "It was one of the liveliest mix-ups ever I seen! One of them rich boys bust the cathedral window. Some say it'll cost over a thousan' dollars to git it fixed. An' I pray to God his paw'll have to pay every cent of it!"

"Can't you make William J. and Rosy stop that racket?" queried Mr. Snawdor, plaintively. The twins had been named at a time when Mrs. Snawdor's loyalty was wavering between the President and another distinguished statesman with whom she associated the promising phrase, "free silver." The arrival of two babies made a choice unnecessary, and, notwithstanding the fact that one of them was a girl, she named them William J. and Roosevelt, reluctantly abbreviating the latter to "Rosy."

"They ain't hurtin' nothin'," she said, impatient of the interruption to her story. "I wisht you might 'a' seen that ole fool Mason a-lordin' it aroun', an' that little devil Nance a-takin' him off to the life. Everybody nearly died a-laughin' at her. But he says he's goin' to have her up in court, an' I ain't got a blessed thing to wear 'cept that ole hat of yours I trimmed up. Looks like a shame fer a woman never to be fixed to go nowhere!"

Mr. Snawdor, who had been trying ineffectually to get in a word, took this remark personally and in muttering tones called Heaven to witness that it was none of his fault that she didn't have the right clothes, and that it was a pretty kind of a world that would keep a man from gettin' on just because he was honest, and—

"Oh, shut up!" said Mrs. Snawdor, unfeelingly; "it ain't yer lack of work that gits on my nerves; it's yer bein' 'round. I'd pay anybody a quarter a week to keep yer busy!"

Nance, during this exchange of conjugal infelicities, assisted by Lobelia and Fidy, was rescuing sufficient dishes from the kitchen sink to serve for the evening meal. She, too, was finding it difficult to bring her attention to bear on domestic matters after the exciting events of the afternoon.

"An' he says to me,"—she was recounting with dramatic intensity to her admiring audience—"he says, 'Keep offen that concrete.' An' I says, 'It'll take somebody bigger'n you to make me!'"

Now, of course, we know that Nance never said that, but it was what she wished she had said, which, at certain moments in life, seems to the best of us to be quite the same thing.

"Then what?" said Fidy, with a plate suspended in air.

"Then," said Nance with sparkling eyes, "I sticks my foot right in the middle of their old concrete, an' they comes pilin' offen the fence, an' Dan Lewis he—"

"You Nance!" came in warning tones from the other room, "you shet your head an' git on with that supper. Here comes your Uncle Jed this minute!"

At this announcement Nance dropped her dish towel, and dashing to the door flung herself into the arms of a short, fat, baldheaded man who had just come out of the front room across the hall.

"Easy there!" warned the new-comer. "You ain't aimin' to butt the engine clean offen the track, air yer?"

Nance got his arm around her neck, and her arm around his knees, and thus entwined they made their way to the table.

Uncle Jed Burks, uncle by courtesy, was a boarder by day and a gate-tender by night at the signal tower at the railroad crossing. On that day long ago when he had found himself a widower, helpless in the face of domestic problems, he had accepted Mrs. Snawdor's prompt offer of hospitality and come across the hall for his meals. At the end of the week he had been allowed to show his gratitude by paying the rent, and by the end of the month he had become the chief prop of the family. It is difficult to conceive of an Atlas choosing to burden himself with the world, but there are temperaments that seek responsibilities just as there are those, like Mr. Snawdor, who refuse them.

Through endless discomforts, Uncle Jed had stayed on, coaxing Mr. Snawdor into an acceptance of his lot, helping Mrs. Snawdor over financial difficulties, and bestowing upon the little Snawdors the affection which they failed to elicit from either the maternal or the paternal bosom. And the amazing thing was that Uncle Jed always thought he was receiving favors instead of conferring them.

"What's this I hear about my little partner gittin' into trouble?" he asked, catching Nance's chin in his palm and turning her smudged, excited face up to his.

Nance's eyes fell before his glance. For the first time since the fight her pride was mingled with misgiving. But when Mrs. Snawdor plunged into a fresh recital of the affair, with evident approval of the part she had played, her self-esteem returned.

"And you say Mason's fixin' to send her up to the juvenile court?" asked Uncle Jed gravely, his fat hand closing on her small one.

"Dan Lewis has got to go too!" said Nance, a sudden apprehension seizing her at Uncle Jed's solemn face.

"Oh, they won't do nothin' to 'em," said Mrs. Snawdor, pouring hot water over the coffee grounds and shaking the pot vigorously. "Everybody knows it was the Clarke boy that bust the window. Clarke's Bottle Works' son, you know, up there on Zender Street."

"Was it the Clarke boy and Dan Lewis that started the fracas?" asked Uncle Jed.

"No, it was me!" put in Nance.

"Now, Nance Molloy, you lemme hear you say that one time more, an' you know what'll happen!" said Mrs. Snawdor, impressively. "You're fixin' to make me pay a fine."

"I'm mighty sorry Dan Lewis is mixed up in it," said Uncle Jed, shaking his head. "This here's his second offense. He was had up last year."

"An' can you wonder?" asked Mrs. Snawdor, "with his mother what she is?"

"Mrs. Lewis ain't a bad looker," Mr. Snawdor roused himself to observe dejectedly.

His wife turned upon him indignantly. "Well, it's a pity she ain't as good as her looks then. Fer my part I can't see it's to any woman's credit to look nice when she's got the right kind of a switch and a good set of false teeth. It's the woman that keeps her good looks without none of them luxuries that orter be praised."

"Mrs. Lewis ain't done her part by Dan," said Uncle Jed, seating himself at the red-clothed table.

"I should say she ain't," Mrs. Snawdor continued. "I never seen nothin' more pathetical than that there boy when he was no more than three years old, a-tryin' to feed hisself outer the garbage can, an' her a comin an' a goin' in the alley all these years with her nose in the air, too good to speak to anybody."

"Dan don't think his mother's bad to him," said Nance. "He saved up his shoe-shine money an' bought her some perfumery. He lemme smell it."

"Oh, yes!" said Mrs. Snawdor, "she's got to have her perfumery, an' her feather in her hat, an' the whitewash on her face, no matter if Dan's feet are on the groun', an' his naked hide shinin' through his shirt."

"Well, I wish him an' this here little girl wasn't mixed up in this business," repeated Uncle Jed. "Courts ain't no place fer children. Seems like I can't stand fer our little Nance to be mixin' up with shady characters."

Nance shot an apprehensive glance at him and began to look anxious. She had never seen Uncle Jed so solemn before.

"You jes' remember this here, Nancy," went on the signalman, who could no more refrain from pointing a moral when the chance presented itself, than a gun can help going off when the trigger is pulled; "nothin' good ever comes from breakin' laws. They wouldn't a-been made into laws if they wasn't fer our good, an' even when we don't see no reason in keepin' 'em, we ain't got no more right to break through than one of them engines up at the crossing's got a right to come ahead when I signals it from the tower to stop. I been handin' out laws to engines fer goin' on thirty year, an' I never seen one yet that bust over a law that didn't come to grief. You keep on the track, Sister, an' watch the signals an' obey orders an' you'll find it pays in the end. An' now, buck up, an' don't be scared. We'll see what we can do to git you off."

"Who's skeered?" said Nance, with a defiant toss of her head. "I ain't skeered of nothin'."

But that night when Mrs. Snawdor and Uncle Jed had gone to work, and Mr. Snawdor had betaken himself out of ear-shot of the wailing baby, Nance's courage began to waver. After she had finished her work and crawled into bed between Fidy and Lobelia, the juvenile court, with its unknown terrors, rose before her. All the excitement of the day died out; her pride in sharing the punishment with Dan Lewis vanished. She lay staring up into the darkness, swallowing valiantly to keep down the sobs, fiercely resolved not to let her bed-fellows witness the break-down of her courage.

"What's the matter, Nance?" asked Fidy.

"I'm hot!" said Nance, crossly. "It feels like the inside of a oven in here!"

"I bet Maw forgot to open the window into the shaft," said Fidy.

"Windows don't do no good," said Nance; "they just let in smells. Wisht I was a man! You bet I would be up at Slap Jack's! I'd set under a 'lectric fan, an' pour cold things down me an' listen at the 'phoney-graf ever' night. Hush! Is that our baby?"

A faint wail made her scramble out of bed and rush into the back room where she gathered a hot, squirming bundle into her arms and peered anxiously into its wizened face. She knew the trick babies had of dying when the weather was hot! Two other beloved scraps of humanity had been taken away from her, and she was fiercely determined to keep this one. Lugging the baby to the window, she scrambled over the sill.

The fire-escape was cluttered with all the paraphernalia that doubles the casualty of a tenement fire, but she cleared a space with her foot and sat down on the top step. Beside her loomed the blank warehouse wall, and from the narrow passage-way below came the smell of garbage. The clanging of cars and the rumbling of trucks mingled with the nearer sounds of whirring sewing machines in Lavinski's sweat-shop on the floor below. From somewhere around the corner came, at intervals, the sharp cry of a woman in agony. With that last sound Nance was all too familiar. The coming and going of a human life were no mystery to her. But each time the cry of pain rang out she tried in vain to stop her ears. At last, hot, hungry, lonesome, and afraid, she laid her dirty face against the baby's fuzzy head and they sobbed together in undisturbed misery.

When at last the child fell into a restless sleep, Nance sat patiently on, her small arms stiffening under their burden, and her bare feet and legs smarting from the stings of hungry mosquitos.

By and by the limp garments on the clothes line overhead began to stir, and Nance, lifting her head gratefully to the vagrant breeze, caught her breath. There, just above the cathedral spire, white and cool among fleecy clouds, rose the full August moon. It was the same moon that at that moment was turning ocean waves into silver magic; that was smiling on sleeping forests and wind-swept mountains and dancing streams. Yet here it was actually taking the trouble to peep around the cathedral spire and send the full flood of its radiance into the most sordid corners of Calvary Alley, even into the unawakened soul of the dirty, ragged, tear-stained little girl clasping the sick baby on Snawdor's fire-escape.

Something in Nance responded. Her tense muscles relaxed; she forgot to cry. With eyes grown big and wistful, she watched the shining orb. All the bravado, the fear, and rebellion died out of her, and in hushed wonder she got from the great white night what God in heaven meant for us to get.

CHAPTER III
THE CLARKES AT HOME

While the prodigal son of the house of Clarke was engaged in breaking stained-glass windows in Calvary Alley, his mother was at home entertaining the bishop with a recital of his virtues and accomplishments. Considering the fact that Bishop Bland's dislike for children was notorious, he was bearing the present ordeal with unusual fortitude.

They were sitting on the spacious piazza at Hill-crest, the country home of the Clarkes, the massive foundation of which was popularly supposed to rest upon bottles. It was a piazza especially designed to offset the discomforts of a Southern August afternoon and to make a visitor, especially if he happened to be an ecclesiastical potentate with a taste for luxury, loath to forsake its pleasant shade for the glaring world without.

"Yes, yes," he agreed for the fourth time, "a very fine boy. I must say I give myself some credit for your marriage and its successful result."

Mrs. Clarke paused in her tea-pouring and gazed absently off across the tree tops.

"I suppose I ought to be happy," she said, and she sighed.

"Every heart knoweth its own—two lumps, thank you, and a dash of rum. I was saying—Oh, yes! I was about to remark that we are all prone to magnify our troubles. Now here you are, after all these years, still brooding over your unfortunate father, when he is probably long since returned to France, quite well and happy."

"If I could only be sure. It has been so long since we heard, nearly thirteen years! The last letter was the one you got when Mac was born."

"Yes, and I answered him in detail, assuring him of your complete recovery, and expressing my hope that he would never again burden you until with God's help he had mastered the sin that had been his undoing."

Mrs. Clarke shook her head impatiently.

"You and Macpherson never understood about father. He came to this country without a friend or a relation except mother and me. Then she died, and he worked day and night to keep me in a good boarding-school, and to give me every advantage that a girl could have. Then his health broke, and he couldn't sleep, and he began taking drugs. Oh, I don't see how anybody could blame him, after all he had been through!"

"For whatever sacrifices he made, he was amply rewarded," the bishop said. "Few fathers have the satisfaction of seeing their daughters more successfully established in life."

"Yes, but what has it all come to for him? Made to feel his disgrace, aware of Macpherson's constant disapproval—I don't wonder he chose to give me up entirely."

"It was much the best course for all concerned," said the bishop, with the assured tone of one who enjoys the full confidence of Providence. "The fact that he had made shipwreck of his own life was no reason for him to make shipwreck of yours. I remember saying those very words to him when he told me of Mr. Clarke's attitude. Painful as was your decision, you did quite right in yielding to our judgment in the matter and letting him go."

"But Macpherson ought not to have asked it of me. He's so good and kind and good about most things, that I don't see how he could have felt the way he did about father."

The bishop laid a consoling hand on her arm.

"Your husband was but protecting you and himself against untold annoyance. Think of what it would have meant for a man of Mr. Clarke's position to have a person of your father's habits a member of his household!"

"But father was perfectly gentle and harmless—more like an afflicted child than anything else. When he was without an engagement he would go for weeks at a time, happy with his books and his music, without breaking over at all."

"Ah, yes! But what about the influence of his example on your growing son? Imagine the humiliation to your child."

Mrs. Clarke's vulnerable spot was touched.

"I had forgotten Mac!" she said. "He must be my first consideration, mustn't he? I never intend for him to bear any burden that I can bear for him. And yet, how father would have adored him, how proud he would have been of his voice! But there, you must forgive me for bringing up this painful subject. It is only when I think of father getting old and being ill, possibly in want, with nobody in the world—"

"Now, now, my dear lady," said the bishop, "you are indulging in morbid fancies. Your father knows that with a stroke of the pen he can procure all the financial assistance from you he may desire. As to his being unhappy, I doubt it extremely. My recollection of him is of a very placid, amiable man living more in his dreams than in reality."

Mrs. Clarke smiled through her tears.

"You are quite right. He didn't ask much of life. A book in his hand and a child on his knee meant happiness for him."

"And those he can have wherever he is," said her spiritual adviser. "Now I want you to turn away from all these gloomy forebodings and leave the matter entirely in God's hands."

"And you think I have done my duty?"

"Assuredly. It is your poor father who has failed to do his. You are a model wife and an almost too devoted mother. You are zealous in your work at the cathedral; you—"

"There!" said Mrs. Clarke, smiling, "I know I don't deserve all those compliments, but they do help me. Now let's talk of something else while I give you a fresh cup of tea. Tell me what the board did yesterday about the foreign mission fund."

The bishop, relieved to see the conversation drifting into calmer waters, accepted the second cup and the change of topic with equal satisfaction. His specialty was ministering to the sorrows of the very rich, but he preferred to confine his spiritual visits to the early part of the afternoon, leaving the latter part free for tea-drinking and the ecclesiastical gossip so dear to his heart.

"Well," he said, leaning back luxuriously in his deep willow chair, "we carried our point after some difficulty. Too many of our good directors take refuge in the old excuse that charity should begin at home. It should, my dear Elise, but as I have said before, it should not end there!"

Having delivered himself of this original observation, the bishop helped himself to another sandwich.

"The special object of my present visit," he said, "aside from the pleasure it always gives me to be in your delightful home, is to interest you and your good husband in a mission we are starting in Mukden, a most ungodly place, I fear, in Manchuria. A thousand dollars from Mr. Clarke at this time would be most acceptable, and I shall leave it to you, my dear lady, to put the matter before him, with all the tact and persuasion for which you are so justly noted."

Mrs. Clarke smiled wearily.

"I will do what I can, Bishop. But I hate to burden him with one more demand. Since he has bought these two new factories, he is simply worked to death. I get so cross with all the unreasonable demands the employees make on him. They are never satisfied. The more he yields, the more they demand. It's begging letters, petitions, lawsuits, strikes, until he is driven almost crazy."

The whirr of an approaching motor caused them both to look up. A grizzled man of fifty got out and, after a decisive order to the chauffeur, turned to join them. His movements were quick and nervous, and his eyes restless under their shaggy gray brows.

"Where's the boy?" was his first query after the greetings were over.

"He went to choir practice. I thought surely he would come out with you. Hadn't we better send the machine back for him?"

"We were just speaking of that fine lad of yours," said the bishop, helping himself to yet another sandwich. "Fine eyes, frank, engaging manner! I suppose he is too young yet for you to be considering his future calling?"

"Indeed he isn't!" said Mrs. Clarke. "My heart is set on the law. Two of his Clarke grandfathers have been on the bench."

Mr. Clarke smiled somewhat grimly.

"Mac hasn't evinced any burning ambition in any direction as yet."

"Mac is only thirteen," said Mrs. Clarke with dignity; "all of his teachers will tell you that he is wonderfully bright, but that he lacks application. I think it is entirely their fault. They don't make the lessons sufficiently interesting; they don't hold his attention. He has been at three private schools, and they were all wretched. You know I am thinking of trying a tutor this year."

"I want her to send him to the public schools," Mr. Clarke said with the air of detached paternity peculiar to American fathers. "I went to the public schools. They gave me a decent start in life; that's about all you can expect of a school."

"True, true," said the bishop, his elbows on the arms of his chair, and his fingers tapping each other meditatively. "I am the last person to minimize the value of the public schools, but they were primarily designed, Mr. Clarke, neither for your boy, nor mine. Their rules and regulations were designed expressly for the children of the poor. I was speaking on this subject only yesterday to Mrs. Conningsby Lee. She's very indignant because her child was forced to submit to vaccination at the hands of some unknown young physician appointed by the city.

"I should feel like killing any one who vaccinated Mac without my consent!" exclaimed Mrs. Clarke, "but I needn't worry. He wouldn't allow it. Do you know we have never been able to persuade that child to be vaccinated?"

"And you don't propose for the State to do what you can't do, do you?" Mr. Clarke said, pinching her cheek.

"What Mrs. Clarke says is not without weight," said the bishop, gallantly coming to her rescue. "There are few things upon which I wax more indignant than the increasing interference of the State with the home. This hysterical agitation against child labor, for instance; while warranted in exceptional cases, it is in the main destructive of the formation of the habit of industry which cannot be acquired too young. When the State presumes to teach a mother how to feed her child, when and where to educate it, when and where to send it to work, the State goes too far. There is nothing more dangerous to the family than the present paternalistic and pauperizing trend of legislation."

"I wish you would preach that to the factory inspectors," said Mr. Clarke, with a wry smile. "Between the poor mothers who are constantly trying to get the children into the factory, and the inspectors who are trying to keep them out, I have my hands full."

"A mother's love," said the bishop, who evidently had different rules for mothers and fathers, "a mother's intuition is the most unerring guide for the conduct of her child; and the home, however humble, is its safest refuge."

Mrs. Clarke glanced anxiously down the poplar-bordered driveway. Her mother's intuition suggested that as it was now five-thirty, Mac must have been engaged in some more diverting pastime than praising the Lord with psalms and thanksgiving.

"Your theory then, Bishop," said Mr. Clarke, who was evincing an unusual interest in the subject, "carried to its legitimate conclusion, would do away with all state interference? No compulsory education or child-labor laws, or houses of correction?"

"Oh, I don't think the bishop means that at all!" said Mrs. Clarke. "But he is perfectly right about a mother knowing what is best for her child. Take Mac, for instance. Nobody has ever understood him, but me. What other people call wilfulness is really sensitiveness. He can't bear to be criticized, he—"

The sudden appearance of a limping object skirting the bushes caused her to break off abruptly.

"Who on earth is that over there beyond the fountain?" she asked. "Why, upon my word, it's Mac!—Mac!" she called anxiously. "Come here!"

The boy shamefacedly retraced his steps and presented himself on the piazza. His shoes and stockings were covered with mud; the frills on his shirt were torn and dirty; one eye was closed.

"Why, my darling child!" cried his mother, her listless, detached air giving place to one of acute concern, "you've been in an accident!"

She had flown to him and enveloped him, mud and all, in her gauzy embrace—an embrace from which Mac struggled to escape.

"I'm all right," he insisted impatiently. "Those kids back of the cathedral got to bothering us, and we—"

"You mean those rowdies in the alley of whom Mason is always complaining?" demanded the bishop, sternly.

"Yes, sir. They were throwing rocks and stepping on the new walk—"

"And you were helping the janitor keep them out?" broke in Mrs. Clarke. "Isn't it an outrage, Bishop, that these children can't go to their choir practice without being attacked by those dreadful ruffians?"

"You are quite sure you boys weren't to blame?" asked Mr. Clarke.

"Now, Father!" protested his wife, "how can you? When Mac has just told us he was helping the janitor?"

"It is no new thing, Mr. Clarke," said the bishop, solemnly shaking his head. "We have had to contend with that disreputable element back of us for years. On two occasions I have had to complain to the city authorities. A very bad neighborhood, I am told, very bad indeed."

"But, Mac dearest," pursued his mother anxiously as she tried to brush the dried mud out of his hair. "Were you the only boy who stayed to help Mason keep them out?"

Mac jerked his head away irritably.

"Oh! It wasn't that way, Mother. You see—"

"That's Mac all over," cried Mrs. Clarke. "He wouldn't claim any credit for the world. But look at the poor child's hands! Look at his eye! We must take some action at once. Can't we swear out a warrant or something against those hoodlums, and have them locked up?"

"But, Elise," suggested Mr. Clarke, quizzically, "haven't you and the bishop just been arguing that the State ought not to interfere with a child? That the family ties, the mother's guidance—"

"My dear Mr. Clarke," interrupted the bishop, "this, I assure you, is an exceptional case. These young desperados are destroying property; they are lawbreakers, many of them doubtless, incipient criminals. Mrs. Clarke is quite right; some action must be taken, has probably been taken already. The janitor had instructions to swear out a warrant against the next offender who in any way defaced the property belonging to the cathedral."

It was at this critical point that the telephone rang, and a maid appeared to say that Mr. Clarke was wanted. The bishop took advantage of the interruption to order his carriage and make his adieus.

"You may be assured," he said at parting, "that I shall not allow this matter to rest until the offenders are brought to justice. Good-by, good-by, my little man. Bear in mind, my dear Elise, that Mukden matter. Good-by."

"And now, you poor darling!" said Mrs. Clarke in a relieved tone, as she turned her undivided attention on her abused son, "you shall have a nice hot bath and a compress on the poor eye, and whatever you want for your dinner. You are as white as a sheet, and still trembling! You poor lamb!"

Mr. Clarke met them at the drawing-room door:

"Mac!" he demanded, and his face was stern, "did you have anything to do with the breaking of the big window at the cathedral?"

"No, sir," Mac faltered, kicking at the newel post.

"You didn't even know it was broken?"

"Oh, everybody was throwing rocks, and that old, crazy Mason—"

"But I thought you were helping Mason?"

"I was—that is—those alley micks—"

"That will do!" his father said angrily. "I've just been notified to have you at the juvenile court next Friday to answer a charge of destroying property. This is a nice scrape for my son to get into! And you didn't have the grit to tell the truth. You lied to me! You'll go to bed, sir, without your dinner!"

Mrs. Clarke's eyes were round with indignation, and she was on the point of bursting into passionate protest when a warning glance from her husband silenced her. With a sense of outraged maternity she flung a protective arm about her son and swept him up the stairs.

"Don't make a scene, Mac darling!" she whispered. "Mother knows you didn't do it. You go up to bed like a little gentleman, and I'll slip a tray up to you and come up myself the minute dinner is over."

That night when the moon discovered Nance Molloy in Calvary Alley, it also peeped through the window at Mac Clarke out at Hillcrest. Bathed, combed, and comforted, he lay in a silk-draped bed while his mother sat beside him fanning him. It would be pleasant to record that the prodigal had confessed his sins and been forgiven. It would even be some comfort to state that his guilty conscience was keeping him awake. Neither of these facts, however, was true. Mac, lying on his back, watching the square patch of moonlight on the floor, was planning darkest deeds of vengeance on a certain dirty, tow-headed, bare-legged little girl, who had twice got the better of him in the conflict of the day.

CHAPTER IV
JUVENILE COURT

The goddess of justice is popularly supposed to bandage her eyes in order to maintain an impartial attitude, but it is quite possible that she does it to keep from seeing the dreary court-rooms which are supposed to be her abiding place.

On the hot Friday morning following the fight, the big anteroom to the juvenile court, which was formerly used for the police court, was just as dirty and the air just as stale as in mid-winter, when the windows were down and the furnace going.

Scrub women came at dawn, to be sure, and smeared its floors with sour mops, and occasionally a janitor brushed the cobwebs off the ceiling, but the grime was more than surface deep, and every nook and cranny held the foul odor of the unwashed, unkempt current of humanity that for so many years had flowed through it. Ghosts of dead and gone criminals seemed to hover over the place, drawn back through curiosity, to relive their own sorry experiences in the cases of the young offenders waiting before the bar of justice.

On the bench at the rear of the room the delegation from Calvary Alley had been waiting for over an hour. Mrs. Snawdor, despite her forebodings, had achieved a costume worthy of the occasion, but Uncle Jed and Dan had made no pretense at a toilet. As for Nance, she had washed her face as far east and west as her ears and as far south as her chin; but the regions beyond were unreclaimed. The shoe-string on her hair had been replaced by a magenta ribbon, but the thick braids had not been disturbed. Now that she had got over her fright, she was rather enjoying the novelty and excitement of the affair. She had broken the law and enjoyed breaking it, and the cop had pinched her. It was a game between her and the cop, and the cop had won. She saw no reason whatever for Uncle Jed and Dan to look so solemn.

By and by a woman in spectacles took her into a small room across the hall, and told her to sit on the other side of the table and not to shuffle her feet. Nance explained about the mosquito bites, but the lady did not listen.

"What day is this?" asked the spectacled one, preparing to chronicle the answers in a big book.

"Friday," said Nance, surprised that she could furnish information to so wise a person.

"What day of the month?"

"Day before rent day."

The corner of the lady's mouth twitched, and Nance glanced at her suspiciously.

"Can you repeat these numbers after me? Four, seven, nine, three, ten, six, fourteen."

Nance was convinced now that the lady was crazy, but she rattled them off glibly.

"Very good! Now if the little hand of your clock was at twelve, and the big hand at three, what time would it be?"

Nance pondered the matter deeply.

"Five after twelve!" she answered triumphantly.

"No; try again."

Nance was eager to oblige, but she had the courage of her convictions and held her point.

"Wouldn't it be a quarter past?" suggested the examiner.

"No, ma'am, it wouldn't. Our clock runs ten minutes slow."

The grave face behind the spectacles broke into a smile; then business was resumed.

"Shut your eyes and name as many objects as you can without stopping, like this: trees, flowers, birds. Go ahead."

"Trees, flowers, birds, cats, dogs, fight, barrel, slop, mud, ashes."

"Go on, quicker—keep it up. Nuts, raisins, cake—"

"Cake, stove, smoke, tub, wash-board, scrub, rag, tub, stove, ashes."

"Keep it up!"

"I dunno no more."

"We can't get beyond ashes, eh?" said the lady. "Now suppose you tell me what the following words mean. Charity?"

"Is it a organization?" asked Nance doubtfully.

"Justice?"

"I dunno that one."

"Do you know what God is?"

Nance felt that she was doing badly. If her freedom depended on her passing this test, she knew the prison bars must be already closing on her. She no more knew what God is than you or I know, but the spectacled lady must be answered at any cost.

"God," she said laboriously, "God is what made us, and a cuss word."

Many more questions followed before she was sent back to her place between Uncle Jed and Mrs. Snawdor, and Dan was led away in turn to receive his test.

Meanwhile Uncle Jed was getting restless. Again and again he consulted his large nickel-plated watch.

"I ought to be getting to bed," he complained. "I won't get more 'n four hours' sleep as it is."

"Here comes the Clarke boy!" exclaimed Nance, and all eyes were turned in the direction of the door.

The group that presented itself at the entrance was in sharp contrast to its surroundings. Mac Clarke, arrayed in immaculate white, was flanked on one side by his distinguished-looking father and on the other by his father's distinguished-looking lawyer. The only evidence that the aristocratic youth had ever come into contact with the riffraff of Calvary Alley was the small patch of court-plaster above his right eye.

"Tell the judge we are here," said Mr. Clarke briskly to his lawyer. "Ask him to get through with us as soon as possible. I have an appointment at twelve-thirty."

The lawyer made his way up the aisle and disappeared through the door which all the morning had been swallowing one small offender after another.

Almost immediately a loud voice called from the platform:

"Case of Mac Clarke! Nance Molloy! Dan Lewis!" And Nance with a sudden leap of her heart, knew that her time had come.

In the inner room, where the juvenile cases had a private hearing, the judge sat at a big desk, scanning several pages of type-written paper. He was a young judge with a keen, though somewhat weary, face and eyes, full of compassionate knowledge. But Nance did not see the judge; her gaze was riveted upon her two arch enemies: Mason, with his flat nose and pugnacious jaw, and "Old Cock-eye," the policeman who looked strangely unfamiliar with his helmet off.

"Well, Mr. Mason," said the judge when the three small offenders had been ranged in front of the desk, with the witnesses grouped behind them, "I'll ask you to tell me just what took place last Saturday afternoon at the cathedral."

Mason cleared his throat and, with evident satisfaction, proceeded to set forth his version of the story:

"I was sweeping out the vestibule, your Honor, when I heard a lot of yelling and knew that a fight was on. It's that away every Saturday afternoon that I ain't on the spot to stop it. I run down through the cathedral and out to the back gate. The alley was swarming with a mob of fighting, yelling children. Then I see these two boys a-fighting each other up at the end of the alley, and before I can get to 'em, this here little girl flings herself between 'em, and the big boy picks up a rock and heaves it straight th'u the cathedral window."

"Well, Mac," said the judge, turning to the trim, white-clad figure confronting him—a figure strangely different from the type that usually stood there. "You have heard what the janitor charges you with. Are you guilty?"

"Yes, sir," said Mac.

"The breaking of the window was an accident?"

Mac glanced quickly at his father's lawyer, then back at the judge.

"Yes, sir."

"But you were fighting in the alley?"

"I was keeping the alley boys out of the cathedral yard."

"That's a lie!" came in shrill, indignant tones from the little girl at his elbow.

"There seems to be some difference of opinion here," said the judge, putting his hand over his mouth to repress a smile at the vehemence of the accusation. "Suppose we let this young lady give her version of it."

Nance jerking her arm free from Mrs. Snawdor's restraining hand, plunged breathlessly into her story.

"He was settin' on the fence, along with a parcel of other guys, a-makin' faces an' callin' names long afore we even took no notice of 'em."

"Both sides is to blame, your Honor," interposed Mason, "there ain't a day when the choir rehearses that I don't have to go out and stop 'em fighting."

"Well, in this case who started the trouble?" asked the judge.

Mrs. Snawdor clutched at Nance, but it was too late.

"I did," she announced.

The judge looked puzzled.

"Why, I thought you said the choir boys began it by sitting on the fence and making faces and calling names."

"Shucks," said Nance, contemptuously, "we kin beat 'em makin' faces an' callin' names."

"Well, how did you start the fight?"

"That there big boy dared me to step in the concrete. Didn't you now?"

Mac stood looking straight ahead of him and refused to acknowledge her presence.

"It strikes me," said the judge, "that you choir boys could be better employed than in teasing and provoking the children in the alley. What do you think, Mac?"

Mac had been provided with no answer to this question, so he offered none.

"Unfortunately," the judge continued, "it is the fathers of boys like you who have to take the punishment. Your father will have to pay for the window. But I want to appeal to your common sense and your sense of justice. Look at me, Mac. You have had advantages and opportunities beyond most boys. You are older than these children. Don't you think, instead of using your influence to stir up trouble and put us to this annoyance and expense, it would be much better for you to keep on your side of the fence and leave these people back of the cathedral alone?"

"Yes, sir," said Mac, perfunctorily.

"And you promise me to do this?"

"Yes, sir."

"We will give you a chance to make your promise good. But remember your name is on our record; if there is any more trouble whatever, you will hear from us. Mr. Clarke, I look to you to see that your son behaves himself. You may step aside please. And now, boy, what is your name?"

"Dan Lewis."

"Oh, yes. I think we have met before. What have you to say for yourself?"

The shoeless, capless, unwashed boy, with his ragged trousers hitched to his shoulders by one suspender, frowned up at the judge through a fringe of tumbled hair.

"Nothin'," he said doggedly.

"Where do you live?"

"I live at home when me maw's there."

"Where is she now?"

This question caused considerable nudging and side-glancing on the part of Mrs. Snawdor.

"She's went to the country," said Dan.

"Is your father living?"

"I dunno."

"Did you go to school last year?"

"No."

"Why not?"

"Didn't have no shoes."

"Does your mother work?"

This question brought more nudges and glances from Mrs. Snawdor, none of which were lost on the boy.

"Me mother don't have to work," he said defiantly. "She's a lady."

The judge cleared his throat and called Mrs. Snawdor sharply to order.

"Well, Dan," he said, "I am sorry to see you back here again. What were you up for before?"

"Chuckin' dice."

"And didn't I tell you that it would go hard with you if you came back?"

"Yes, sir, but I never chucked no more dice."

"And I suppose in spite of the way your mouth is bruised, you'll tell me you weren't mixed up in this fight?"

The boy stood staring miserably at the wall with eyes in which fear and hurt pride struggled for mastery.

"Yer Honor!" the policeman broke in. "It's three times lately I've found him sleepin' in doorways after midnight. Him and the gang is a bad lot, yer

Honor, a scrappin' an' hoppin' freights an' swipin' junk, an' one thing an' another."

"I never swiped no junk," Dan said hopelessly, "I never swiped nothink in my life."

"Is there no definite charge against this boy?"

"Well, sir," said Mason, "he is always a-climbin' up the steeple of the cathedral."

Dan, sullen, frightened, and utterly unable to defend himself, looked from the officer to the janitor with the wide, distrustful eyes of a cornered coyote.

Suddenly a voice spoke out in his behalf, a shrill, protesting, passionate voice.

"He ain't no worser nor nobody else! Ast Mammy, ast Uncle Jed! He's got to sleep somewheres when his maw fergits to come home! Ever'body goes an' picks on Danny 'cause he ain't got nobody to take up fer him. 'T ain't fair!" Nance ended her tirade in a burst of tears.

"There, there," said the judge, "it's going to be fair this time. You stop crying now and tell me your name?"

"Nance Molloy," she gulped, wiping her eyes on her sleeve.

"How old are you?"

"'Leven, goin' on twelve."

"Well, take that gum out of your mouth and stop crying."

He consulted his papers and then looked at her over his glasses.

"Nancy," he said, "are you in the habit of slipping into the cathedral when the janitor is not around?"

"Yes, sir."

"What for?"

"Lookin' at the pretties, an' seein' if there's any nickels under the seats."

"You want to buy candy, I suppose?"

"No, sir, a bureau."

Even the tired-looking probation officer looked up and smiled.

"What does a little girl like you want with a bureau?" asked the judge.

"So's I won't have to keep me duds under the bed."

"That's a commendable ambition. But what about these other charges; truancy from school, fighting with the boys, throwing mud, and so on?"

"I never th'ow mud, 'ceptin' when I'm th'owin' back," explained Nance.

"A nice distinction," said the judge. "Is this child's mother present?"

Mrs. Snawdor, like a current that has been restrained too long, surged eagerly forward, and overflowed her conversational banks completely.

"Well, I ain't exactly her mother, but I'm just the same as her mother. You ast anybody in Calvary Alley. Ast Mr. Burks here, ast Mrs. Smelts what I been to her ever since she was a helpless infant baby. When Bud Molloy lay dyin' he says to the brakeman, 'You tell my wife to be good to Nance,'"

"So she's your stepchild?"

"Yes, sir, an' Bud Molloy was as clever a man as ever trod shoe-leather. So was Mr. Yager. Nobody can't say I ever had no trouble with my two first. They wasn't what you might call as smart a man as Snawdor, but they wasn't no fool."

It was a peculiarity of Mrs. Snawdor's that she always spoke of her previous husbands as one, notwithstanding the fact that the virtues which she attributed to them could easily have been distributed among half a dozen.

"Well, well," said the judge impatiently, "what have you to say about the character of this little girl?"

Mrs. Snawdor shifted her last husband's hat from the right side of her head to the left, and began confidentially:

"Well I'll tell you, Jedge, Nance ain't so bad as whut they make her out. She's got her faults. I ain't claimin' she ain't. But she ain't got a drop of meanness in her, an' that's more than I can say for some grown folks present." Mrs. Snawdor favored Mr. Mason with such a sudden and blighting glance that the janitor quailed visibly.

"Do you have trouble controlling her?" asked the judge.

"Nothin' to speak of. She's a awful good worker, Nance is, when you git her down to it. But her trouble is runnin'. Let anything happen in the alley, an' she's up an' out in the thick of it. I'm jes' as apt to come home an' find her playin' ball with the baby in her arms, as not. But I don't have to dress her down near as often as I used to."

"Then you wouldn't say she was a bad child?"

Mrs. Snawdor's emphatic negative was arrested in the utterance by Mr. Mason's accusing eye.

"Well, I never seen no child that was a angel," she compromised.

"Does Nancy go to school?" the judge asked.

"Well, I was threatenin' her the other day, if she didn't behave herself, I was goin' to start her in again."

"I ain't been sence Christmas," volunteered Nance, still sniffling.

"You shet yer mouth," requested Mrs. Snawdor with great dignity.

"Why hasn't she been to school since Christmas?" the judge proceeded sternly.

"Well, to tell you the truth, it was on account of Mr. Snawdor. He got mad 'bout the vaccination. He don't believe in it. Says it gives you the rheumatism. He's got a iron ring on ever' one of the childern. Show yours to the jedge, Nance! He says ef they has to vaccinate 'em to educate 'em, they ain't goin' to de neither one."

"But don't you know that we have compulsory education in this State? Hasn't the truant officer been to see you?"

Mrs. Snawdor looked self-conscious and cast down her eyes.

"Well, not as many times as Snawdor says he has. Snawdor's that jealous he don't want me to have no gentlemen visitors. When I see the truant officer or the clock-man comin', I just keep out of sight to avoid trouble."

The judge's eyes twinkled, then grew stern. "In the meanwhile," he said, "Nancy is growing up in ignorance. What sort of a woman are you to let a child go as ragged and dirty as this one and to refuse her an education?"

"Well, schools ain't what they wuz when me an' you wuz young," Mrs. Snawdor said argumentatively. "They no more'n git a child there than they want to cut out their palets or put spectacles on her. But honest, Judge, the truth of it is I can't spare Nance to go to school. I got a job scrubbin' four nights in the week at the post-office, an' I got to have some help in the daytime. I leave it to you if I ain't."

"That's neither here nor there," said the judge. "It is your business to have her at school every morning and to see that she submits to the regulations. You are an able-bodied woman and have an able-bodied husband. Why don't you move into a decent house in a decent neighborhood?"

"There ain't nothin' the matter with our neighborhood. If you'd jes' git 'em to fix the house up some. The roof leaks something scandalous."

"Who is your landlord?"

"Well, they tell me *he* is," said Mrs. Snawdor, pointing a malicious finger at Mr. Clarke. This *coup d'etat* caused considerable diversion, and the judge had to call the court sharply to order.

"Is that your husband in the rear of the room?" he asked Mrs. Snawdor.

"Law, no; that's Mr. Burks, our boarder. I begged Snawdor to come, but he's bashful."

"Well, Mr. Burks, will you step forward and tell us what you know of this little girl?"

Uncle Jed cleared his throat, made a pass at the place where his front hair used to be, and came forward.

"Have you known this child long?" asked the judge.

"Eleven years, going on twelve," said Uncle Jed, with a twinkle in his small eyes, "me an' her grandpa fought side by side in the battle of Chickasaw Bluffs."

"So she comes of fighting stock," said the judge. "Do you consider her incorrigible?"

"Sir?"

"Do you think her stepmother is able to control her?"

Uncle Jed looked a trifle embarrassed.

"Well, Mrs. Snawdor ain't whut you might say regular in her method. Sometimes she's kinder rough on Nance, and then again she's a heap sight too easy."

"That's a God's truth!" Mrs. Snawdor agreed fervently from the rear.

"Then you do not consider it altogether the child's fault?"

"No, sir, I can't say as I do. She jes' gits the signals mixed sometimes, that's all."

The judge smiled.

"So you think if she understood the signals, she'd follow them?"

Uncle Jed's face became very earnest as he laid his hand on Nance's head.

"I believe if this here little lass was to once git it into her head that a thing was right, she'd do it if it landed her where it landed her paw, at the foot of a forty-foot embankment with a engine a-top of her."

"That's a pretty good testimony to her character," said the judge. "It's our business, then, to see that she gets more definite instructions as to the traffic laws of life. Nance, you and Dan step up here again."

The children stood before him, breathing hard, looking him straight in the face.

"You have both been breaking the law. It's a serious thing to be up in court. It is usually the first step on the down grade. But I don't believe either of you have been wholly to blame. I am going to give you one more chance and put you both on probation to Mrs. Purdy, to whom you are to report once a week. Is Mrs. Purdy in the room?"

An elderly little lady slipped forward and stood behind them with a hand on the shoulder of each. Nance did not dare look around, but there was something comforting and reassuring in that fat hand that lay on her shoulder.

"One more complaint against either of you," cautioned the judge impressively, "and it will be the house of reform. If your families can't make you behave, the State can. But we don't want to leave it to the family or the State; we want to leave it to you. I believe you can both make good, but you'll have to fight for it."

Nance's irregular features broke into a smile. It was a quick, wide smile and very intimate.

"Fight?" she repeated, with a quizzical look at the judge. "I thought that was what we was pinched fer."

CHAPTER V
ON PROBATION

For a brief period Nance Molloy walked the paths of righteousness. The fear of being "took up" proved a salutary influence, but permanent converts are seldom made through fear of punishment alone. She was trying by imitation and suggestion to grope her way upward, but the light she climbed by was a borrowed light which swung far above her head and threw strange, misleading shadows across her path. The law that allowed a man to sell her fire-crackers and then punished her for firing them off, that allowed any passer-by to kick her stone off the hop-scotch square and punished her for hurling; the stone after him, was a baffling and difficult thing to understand.

At school it was no better. The truant officer said she must go every day, yet when she got there, there was no room for her. She had to sit in the seat with two other little girls who bitterly resented the intrusion.

"You oughtn't to be in this grade anyhow!" declared one of them. "A girl ought to be in the primer that turns her letters the wrong way."

"Well, my letters spell the words right," said Nance hotly, "an' that's more'n yours do, Pie-Face!"

Whereupon the girl stuck out her tongue, and Nance promptly shoved her off the end of the seat, with the result that her presence was requested in the office at the first recess.

"If you would learn to make your letters right, the girls would not tease you," said the principal, kindly. "Why do you persist in turning them the wrong way?"

Now Nance had learned to write by copying the inscriptions from the reverse side of the cathedral windows, and she still believed the cathedral was right. But she liked the principal and she wanted very much to get a good report, so she gave in.

"All right," she said good-naturedly, "I'll do 'em your way. An' ef you ketch me fightin' agin, I hope you'll lick hell outen me!"

The principal, while decrying its forcible expression, applauded her good intention, and from that time on took special interest in her.

Nance's greatest drawback these days was Mrs. Snawdor. That worthy lady, having her chief domestic prop removed and finding the household duties resting too heavily upon her own shoulders, conceived an overwhelming hatred for the school, the unknown school-teacher, and the truant officer, for whom she had hitherto harbored a slightly romantic interest.

"I ain't got a mite of use for the whole lay-out," she announced in a sweeping condemnation one morning when Nance was reminding her for the fourth time that she had to have a spelling book. "They' re forever wantin' somethin'. It ain't no use beginnin' to humor 'em. Wasn't they after me to put specs on Fidy last week? I know their tricks, standin' in with eye-doctors an' dentists! An' here I been fer goin' on ten years, tryin' to save up to have my own eye-teeth drawed an' decent ones put in. Snawdor promised when we got married that would be his first present to me. Well, if I ever get 'em, they *will* be his first present."

"Teacher says you oughtn't to leave the milk settin' uncovered like that; it gits germans in it," said Nance.

"I'd like to know whose milk-can this is?" demanded Mrs. Snawdor indignantly. "You tell her when she pays fer my milk, it 'll be time enough fer her to tell me what to do with it. You needn't be scurryin' so to git off. I'm fixin' to go to market. You'll have to stay an' 'tend to the children 'til I git back."

"But I'm tryin' to git a good report," urged Nance. "I don't want to be late."

"I'll send a excuse by Fidy, an' say you 're sick in bed. Then you kin stay home all day an' git the house cleaned up."

"Naw, I won't," said Nance rebelliously, "I ain't goin' to miss ag'in."

"You're goin' to shut up this minute, you sass-box, or I'll take you back to that there juvenile court. Git me a piece o' paper an' a pencil."

With great effort she wrote her note while Nance stood sullenly by, looking over her shoulder.

"You spelled teacher's name with a little letter," Nance muttered.

"I done it a-purpose," said Mrs. Snawdor vindictively, "I ain't goin' to spell her with a capital; she ain't worth it."

Nance would undoubtedly have put up a more spirited fight for her rights, had she not been anxious to preserve peace until the afternoon. It was the day appointed by the court for her and Dan Lewis to make their first report to Mrs. Purdy, whose name and address had been given them on a card. She had washed her one gingham apron for the occasion, and had sewed up the biggest rent in her stockings. The going forth alone with Dan on an errand of any nature was an occasion of importance. It somehow justified those coupled initials, enclosed in a gigantic heart, that she had surreptitiously drawn on the fence.

After her first disappointment in being kept at home, she set about her task of cleaning the Snawdor flat with the ardor of a young Hercules attacking the Augean stables. First she established the twins in the hall with a string and a bent pin and the beguiling belief that if they fished long enough over the banister they would catch something. Next she anchored the screaming baby to a bedpost and reduced him to subjection by dipping his fingers in sorghum, then giving him a feather. The absorbing occupation of plucking the feather from one sticky hand to the other rendered him passive for an hour.

These preliminaries being arranged, Nance turned her attention to the work in hand. Her method consisted in starting at the kitchen, which was in front, and driving the debris back, through the dark, little, middle room, until she landed it all in a formidable mass in Mrs. Snawdor's bedroom at the rear. This plan, pursued day after day, with the general understanding that Mrs. Snawdor was going to take a day off soon and clean up, had resulted in a condition of indescribable chaos. As Mr. Snawdor and the three younger children slept in the rear room at night, and Mrs. Snawdor slept in it the better part of the day, the hour for cleaning seldom arrived.

To-day as Nance stood in the doorway of this stronghold of dirt and disorder, she paused, broom in hand. The floor, as usual, was littered with papers and strings, the beds were unmade, the wash-stand and dresser were piled high with a miscellaneous collection, and the drawers of each stood open, disgorging their contents. On the walls hung three enlarged crayons of bridal couples, in which the grooms were different, but the bride the same. On the dusty window sill were bottles and empty spools, broken glass chimneys, and the clock that ran ten minutes slow. The debris not only filled the room, but spilled out into the fire-escape and down the rickety iron ladders and flowed about the garbage barrels in the passage below.

It was not this too familiar scene, however, that made Nance pause with her hand on the door-knob and gaze open-mouthed into the room. It was the sight of Mr. Snawdor sitting on the side of the bed with his back toward her, wiping his little red-rimmed eyes on a clean pocket handkerchief, and patting his trembling mouth with the hand that was not under the quilt.

Heretofore Nance had regarded Mr. Snawdor as just one of the many discomforts with which the family had to put up. His whining protests against their way of living had come to be as much a matter of course as the creaking door or the smoking chimney. Nobody ever thought of listening to what he was saying, and everybody pushed and ordered him about, including Nance, who enjoyed using Mrs. Snawdor's highhanded method with him, when that lady was not present.

But when she saw him sitting there with his back to her, crying, she was puzzled and disturbed. As she watched, she saw him fumble for something under the quilt, then lift a shining pistol, and place the muzzle to his thin, bald temple. With a cry of terror, she dashed forward and knocked the weapon from his hand.

"You put that down!" she cried, much as she would have commanded William J. to leave the butcher knife alone. "Do you want to kill yerself?"

Mr. Snawdor started violently, then collapsing beside the bed, confessed that he did.

"What fer?" asked Nance, terror giving way to sheer amazement.

"I want to quit!" cried Mr. Snawdor, hysterically. "I can't stand it any longer. I'm a plumb failure and I ain't goin' to ever be anything else. If your maw had taken care of what I had, we wouldn't have been where we are at. Look at the way we live! Like pigs in a pen! We're nothing but pore white trash; that's what we are!"

Nance stood beside him with her hand on his shoulder. Poor white trash! That was what the Clarke boy had called her. And now Mr. Snawdor, the nominal head of the family, was acknowledging it to be true. She looked about her in new and quick concern.

"I'm going to clean up in here, too," she said. "I don't keer whut mammy says. It'll look better by night; you see if it don't."

"It ain't only that—" said Mr. Snawdor; then he pulled himself up and looked at her appealingly. "You won't say nuthin' about this mornin', will you, Nance?"

"Not if you gimme the pistol," said Nance.

When he was gone, she picked up the shining weapon and gingerly dropped it out on the adjoining roof. Then her knees felt suddenly wobbly, and she sat down. What if she had been a minute later and Mr. Snawdor had pulled the trigger? She shivered as her quick imagination pictured the scene. If Mr. Snawdor felt like that about it, there was but one thing to do; to get things cleaned up and try to keep them so.

Feeling very important and responsible, she swept and straightened and dusted, while her mind worked even faster than her nimble hands. Standards are formed by comparisons, and so far Nance's opportunity for instituting comparisons had been decidedly limited.

"We ain't pore white, no such a thing!" she kept saying to herself. "Our house ain't no worser nor nobody else's. Mis' Smelts is just the same, an' if Levinski's is cleaner, it smells a heap worse."

Dinner was over before Mrs. Snawdor returned. She came into the kitchen greatly ruffled as to hair and temper from having been caught by the hook left hanging over the banisters by William J.

"Gimme the rocker!" she demanded. "My feet hurt so bad I'd just like to unscrew 'em an' fling 'em in the dump heap."

"Where you been at?" asked Uncle Jed, who was cutting himself a slice of bread from the loaf.

"I been down helpin' the new tenant move in on the first floor."

"Any childern?" asked Nance and Lobelia in one breath.

"No; just a foreign-lookin' old gentleman, puttin' on as much airs as if he was movin' into the Walderastoria. Nobody knows his name or where he comes from. Ike Lavinski says he plays the fiddle at the theayter. Talk about your helpless people! I had to take a hand in gettin' his things unloaded. He liked to never got done thankin' me."

Mr. Snawdor, who had been sitting in dejected silence before his untouched food, pushed his plate back and sighed deeply.

"Now, fer heaven sake, Snawdor," began his wife in tones of exasperation, "can't I do a kind act to a neighbor without a-rufflin' yer feathers the wrong way?"

"I cleaned up yer room while you was gone," said Nance, eager to divert the conversation from Mr. Snawdor. "Uncle Jed an' me carried the trash down an' it filled the ash barrel clean up to the top."

"Well, I hope an' pray you didn't throw away my insurance book. I was aimin' to clean up, myself, to-morrow. What on earth's the matter with Rosy Velt?"

Rosy, who had been banished to the kitchen for misbehavior, had been conducting a series of delicate experiments, with disastrous results. She had been warned since infancy never to put a button up her nose, but Providence having suddenly placed one in her way, and at the same time engaged her mother's attention elsewhere, the opportunity was too propitious to be lost.

Nance took advantage of her stepmother's sudden departure to cheer up Mr. Snawdor.

"We're gittin' things cleaned up," she said, "I can't work no more to-day though, 'cause I got to report to the lady."

"Ain't you goin' to slick yerself up a bit?" asked Uncle Jed, making a futile effort to smooth her hair.

"I have," said Nance, indignantly, "Can't you see I got on a clean apron?"

Uncle Jed's glance was not satisfied as it traveled from the dirty dress below the apron to the torn stockings and shabby shoes.

"Why don't you wear the gold locket?" suggested Mrs. Snawdor, who now returned with Rosy in one hand and the button in the other.

The gold locket was the one piece of jewelry in the family and when it was suspended on a black ribbon around Nance's neck, it filled her with a sense of elegance. So pleased was she with its effect that as she went out that afternoon, she peeped in on the new tenant in the hope that he would notice it. She found him leaning over a violin case, and her interest was fired at once.

"Can you play on the fiddle?" she demanded.

The small, elderly man in the neat, black suit lifted his head and smiled at her over his glasses.

"Yes, my little friend," he said in a low, refined voice, "I will play for you to dance sometime. You would like that? Yes?"

Nance regarded him gravely.

"Say, are you a Polock or a Dago?" she asked.

He gave an amused shrug.

"I am neither. My name is Mr. Demorest. And you are my little neighbor, perhaps?"

"Third floor on the right," said Nance, adding in a business-like tone, "I'll be down to dance to-night."

She would have liked very much to stay longer, for the old gentleman was quite unlike any one she had ever talked to before, but the card in her hand named the hour of two, and back of the card was Mrs. Purdy, and back of Mrs. Purdy the juvenile court, the one thing in life so far whose authority Nance had seen fit to acknowledge.

CHAPTER VI
BUTTERNUT LANE

At the corner Dan Lewis stood aside like a deposed chieftain while his companions knelt in an excited ring, engrossed in a game sanctioned by custom and forbidden by law. Even to Nance's admiring eye he looked dirtier and more ragged than usual, and his scowl deepened as she approached.

"I ain't goin'," he said.

"Yes, you are, too. Why not?" said Nance, inconsequently.

"Aw, it ain't no use."

"Ain't you been to school?"

"Yep, but I ain't goin' to that lady's house. I ain't fit."

"You got to go to take me," said Nance, diplomatically. "I don't know where Butternut Lane's at."

"You could find it, couldn't you?"

Nance didn't think she could. In fact she developed a sudden dependence wholly out of keeping with her usual self-reliance.

This seemed to complicate matters for Dan. He stood irresolutely kicking his bare heels against the curb and then reluctantly agreed to take her as far as Mrs. Purdy's gate, provided nothing more was expected of him.

Their way led across the city to a suburb, and they were hot and tired before half the distance was covered. But the expedition was fraught with interest for Nance. After the first few squares of sullen silence, Dan seemed to forget that she was merely a girl and treated her with the royal equality usually reserved for boys. So confidential did they become that she ventured to put a question to him that had been puzzling her since the events of the morning.

"Say, Dan, when anybody kills hisself, is it murder?"

"It's kinder murder. You wouldn't ketch me doin' it as long as I could get something to eat."

"You kin always git a piece of bread," said Nance.

"You bet you can't!" said Dan with conviction. "I ain't had nothin' to eat myself since yisterday noon."

"Yer maw didn't come in last night?"

"I 'spec' she went on a visit somewhere," said Dan, whose lips trembled slightly despite the stump of a cigarette that he manfully held between them.

"Couldn't you git in a window?"

"Nope; the shutters was shut. Maybe I don't wisht it was December, an' I was fourteen!"

"Sammy Smelts works an' he ain't no older'n me," said Nance. "You kin git a fake certificate fer a quarter."

Dan smiled bitterly.

"Where'm I goin' to git the quarter? They won't let me sell things on the street, or shoot craps, or work. Gee, I wisht I was rich as that Clarke boy. Ike Lavinski says he buys a quarter's worth of candy at a time! He's in Ike's room at school."

"He wasn't there yesterday," said Nance. "Uncle Jed seen him with another boy, goin' out the railroad track."

"I know it. He played hookey. He wrote a excuse an' signed his maw's name to it. Ike seen him do it. An' when the principal called up his maw this mornin' an' ast her 'bout it, she up an' said she wrote it herself."

Nance was not sure whether she was called upon to admire the astuteness of Mac or his mother, so she did not commit herself. But she was keenly interested. Ever since that day in the juvenile court she had been haunted by the memory of a trim, boyish figure arrayed in white, and by a pair of large brown eyes which disdainfully refused to glance in her direction.

"Say, Dan," she asked wistfully, "have you got a girl?"

"Naw," said Dan disdainfully, "what do I keer about girls?"

"I don't know. I thought maybe you had. I bet that there Clarke boy's got two or three."

"Let him have 'em," said Dan; then, finding the subject distasteful, he added, "what's the matter with hookin' on behind that there wagon?" And suiting the action to the word, they both went in hot pursuit.

After a few jolting squares during which Nance courted death with her flying skirts brushing the revolving wheels, the wagon turned into a side street, and they were obliged to walk again.

"I wonder if this ain't the place?" she said, as they came in sight of a low, white house half smothered in beech-trees, with a flower garden at one side, at the end of which was a vine-covered summer-house.

"Here's where I beat it!" said Dan, but before he could make good his intention, the stout little lady on the porch had spied them and came hurrying down the walk, holding out both hands.

"Well, if here aren't my probationers!" she cried in a warm, comfortable voice which seemed to suggest that probationers were what she liked best in the world.

"Let me see, dear, your name is Mac?"

"No, ma'am, it's Dan," said that youth, trying to put out the lighted cigarette stump which he had hastily thrust into his pocket.

"Ah! to be sure! And yours is—Mary?"

"No, ma'am, it's Nance."

"Why, of course!" cried the little lady, beaming at them, "I remember perfectly."

She was scarcely taller than they were as she walked between them, with an arm about the shoulder of each. She wore a gray dress and a wide white collar pinned with a round blue pin that just matched her round blue eyes. On each side of her face was a springy white curl that bobbed up and down as she walked.

"Now," she said, with an expectant air, when they reached the house. "Where shall we begin? Something to eat?"

Her question was directed to Dan, and he flushed hotly.

"No, ma'am," he said proudly.

"Yes, ma'am," said Nance, almost in the same breath.

"I vote 'Yes,' too; so the ayes have it," said Mrs. Purely gaily, leading them through a neat hall into a neat kitchen, where they solemnly took their seats.

"My visitors always help me with the lemonade," said the purring little lady, giving Nance the lemons to roll, and Dan the ice to crack. Then as she fluttered about, she began to ask them vague and seemingly futile questions about home and school and play. Gradually their answers grew from monosyllables into sentences, until, by the time the lemonade was ready to serve, Nance was completely thawed out and Dan was getting soft around the edges. Things were on the way to positive conviviality when Mrs. Purdy suddenly turned to Nance and asked her where she went to Sunday school.

Now Sunday school had no charms for Nance. On the one occasion when curiosity had induced her to follow the stream of well-dressed children into the side door of the cathedral, she had met with disillusion. It was a place where little girls lifted white petticoats when they sat down and straightened pink sashes when they got up, and put nickels in a basket. Nance had had no lace petticoat or pink sash or nickel. She showed her discomfort by misbehaving.

"Didn't you ever go back?" asked Mrs. Purdy.

"Nome. They didn't want me. I was bad, an' the teacher said Sunday school was a place for good little girls."

"My! my!" said Mrs. Purdy, "this will never do. And how about you, Dan? Do you go?"

"Sometimes I've went," said Dan. "I like it."

While this conversation was going on Nance could not keep her eyes from the open door. There was more sky and grass out there than she had ever seen at one time before. The one green spot with which she was familiar was the neat plot of lawn on each side of the concrete walk leading into the cathedral, and that had to be viewed through a chink in the fence and was associated with the words, "Keep Out."

When all the lemonade was gone, and only one cookie left for politeness, Mrs. Purdy took them into the sitting-room where a delicate-looking man sat in a wheel-chair, carving something from a piece of wood. Nance's quick eyes took in every detail of the bright, commonplace room; its gay, flowered carpet and chintz curtains, its "fruit pieces" in wide, gold frames, and its crocheted tidies presented a new ideal of elegance.

There was a music-box on the wall in which small figures moved about to a tinkling melody; there were charm strings of bright colored buttons, and a spinning-wheel, and a pair of bellows, all of which Mrs. Purdy explained at length.

"Sister," said the man in the chair, feebly, "perhaps the children would like to see my menagerie."

"Why, dearie, of course they would," said Mrs. Purdy, "Shall I wheel you over to the cabinet?"

"I'll shove him," said Dan, making his first voluntary remark.

"There now!" said Mrs. Purdy, "see how much stronger he is than I am! And he didn't jolt you a bit, did he, dearie?"

If the room itself was interesting, the cabinet was nothing short of entrancing. It was full of carved animals in all manner of grotesque positions.

And the sick gentleman knew the name of each and kept saying such funny things about them that Nance laughed hilariously, and Dan forgot the prints of his muddy feet on the bright carpet, and even gave up the effort to keep his hand over the ragged knee of his pants.

"He knows all about live animals, too," chirped Mrs. Purdy. "You'll have to come some day and go over to the park with us and see his squirrels. There's one he found with a broken leg, and he mended it as good as new."

The sun was slipping behind the trees before the children even thought of going home.

"Next Friday at three!" said Mrs. Purdy, cheerily waving them good-by. "And we are going to see who has the cleanest face and the best report."

"We sure had a good time," said Nance, as they hurried away through the dusk. "But I'll git a lickin' all right when I git home."

"I liked that there animal man," said Dan slowly, "an' them cookies."

"Well, whatever made you lie to the lady 'bout bein' hungry?"

"I never lied. She ast me if I wanted her to give me somethin' to eat. I thought she meant like a beggar. I wasn't goin' to take it that way, but I never minded takin' it like—like—company."

Nance pondered the matter for a while silently; then she asked suddenly:

"Say, Dan, if folks are borned poor white trash, they don't have to go on bein' it, do they?"

CHAPTER VII
AN EVICTION

The three chief diversions in Calvary Alley, aside from fights, were funerals, arrests, and evictions. Funerals had the advantage of novelty, for life departed less frequently than it arrived: arrests were in high favor on account of their dramatic appeal, but the excitement, while intense, was usually too brief to be satisfying; for sustained interest the alley on the whole preferred evictions.

The week after Nance and Dan had reported to Mrs. Purdy, rumor traveled from house to house and from room to room that the rent man was putting the Lewises out. The piquant element in the situation lay in the absence of the chief actor. "Mis' Lewis" herself had disappeared, and nobody knew where she was or when she would return.

For many years the little cottage, sandwiched between Mr. Snawdor's "Bung and Fawcett" shop and Slap Jack's saloon had been the scandal and, it must be confessed the romance of the alley. It stood behind closed shutters, enveloped in mystery, and no visitor ventured beyond its threshold. The slender, veiled lady who flitted in and out at queer hours, and whom rumor actually accused of sometimes arriving at the corner in "a hack," was, despite ten years' residence, a complete stranger to her neighbors. She was quiet and well-behaved; she wore good clothes and shamefully neglected her child. These were the meager facts upon which gossip built a tower of conjecture.

As for Dan, he was as familiar an object in the alley as the sparrows in the gutter or the stray cats about the garbage cans. Ever since he could persuade his small legs to go the way he wanted them to, he had pursued his own course, asking nothing of anybody, fighting for his meager rights, and becoming an adept in evading the questions that seemed to constitute the entire conversation of the adult world. All that he asked of life was the chance to make a living, and this the authorities sternly forbade until he should reach that advanced age of fourteen which seemed to recede as he approached. Like most of the boys in the gang, he had been in business since he was six; but it was business that changed its nature frequently and had to be transacted under great difficulty. He had acquired proficiency as a crap-shooter only to find that the profession was not regarded as an honorable one; he had invested heavily in pins and pencils and tried to peddle them out on the avenue, only to find himself sternly taken in hand by a determined lady who talked to him about minors and street trades. Shoe-shining had been tried; so had selling papers, but each of these required capital, and Dan's appetite was of such a demanding character that the acquisition of capital was well nigh impossible.

From that first day when the truant officer had driven him into the educational fold, his problems had increased. It was not that he disliked school. On the contrary he was ambitious and made heroic efforts to keep up with the class; but it was up-hill work getting an education without textbooks. The city, to be sure, furnished these to boys whose mothers applied for them in person, but Dan's mother never had time to come. The cause of most of his trouble, however, was clothes; seatless trousers, elbowless coats, brimless hats, constituted a series of daily mortifications which were little short of torture.

Twice, through no fault of his own, he had stood alone before the bar of justice, with no voice lifted in his behalf save the shrill, small voice of Nance Molloy. Twice he had been acquitted and sent back to the old hopeless environment, and admonished to try again. How hard he had tried and against what odds, surely only the angel detailed to patrol Calvary Alley has kept any record.

If any doubts assailed him concerning the mother who took little heed of his existence, he never expressed them. Her name rarely passed his lips, but he watched for her coming as a shipwrecked mariner watches for a sail. When a boy ponders and worries over something for which he dares not ask an explanation, he is apt to become sullen and preoccupied. On the day that the long-suffering landlord served notice, Dan told no one of his mother's absence. Behind closed doors he packed what things he could, clumsily tying the rest of the household goods in the bedclothes. At noon the new tenant arrived and, in order to get his own things in, obligingly assisted in moving Dan's out. It was then and then only that the news had gone abroad.

For three hours now the worldly possessions of the dubious Mrs. Lewis had lain exposed on the pavement, and for three hours Dan had sat beside them keeping guard. From every tenement window inquisitive eyes watched each stage of the proceeding, and voluble tongues discussed every phase of the situation. Every one who passed, from Mr. Lavinski, with a pile of pants on his head, to little Rosy Snawdor, stopped to take a look at him and to ask questions.

Dan had reached a point of sullen silence. Sitting on a pile of bedclothes, with a gilt-framed mirror under one arm and a flowered water pitcher under the other, he scowled defiance at each newcomer. Against the jeers of the boys he could register vows of future vengeance and console himself with the promise of bloody retribution; but against the endless queries and insinuations of his adult neighbors, he was utterly defenseless.

"Looks like she had ever'thing fer the parlor, an' nothin' fer the kitchen," observed Mrs. Snawdor from her third-story window to Mrs. Smelts at her window two floors below.

"I counted five pairs of curlin' irons with my own eyes," said Mrs. Smelts, "an' as fer bottles! If they took out one, they took out a hunderd."

"You don't reckon that there little alcohol stove was all she had to cook on, do you?" called up Mrs. Gorman from the pavement below.

"Maybe that's what she het her curlin' irons on!" was Mrs. Snawdor's suggestion, a remark which provoked more mirth than it deserved.

Dan gazed straight ahead with no sign that he heard. However strong the temptation was to dart away into some friendly hiding place, he was evidently not going to yield to it. The family possessions were in jeopardy, and he was not one to shirk responsibilities.

Advice was as current as criticism. Mrs. Gorman, being a chronic recipient of civic favors, advocated an appeal to the charity organization; Mrs. Snawdor, ever at war with foreign interference, strongly opposed the suggestion, while Mrs. Smelts with a covetous eye on the gilt mirror under Dan's arm, urged a sidewalk sale. As for the boy himself, not a woman in the alley but was ready to take him in and share whatever the family larder provided.

But to all suggestions Dan doggedly shook his head. He was "thinkin' it out," he said, and all he wanted was to be let alone.

"Well, you can't set there all night," said Mrs. Snawdor, "if yer maw don't turn up by five o'clock, us neighbors is goin' to take a hand."

All afternoon Dan sat watching the corner round which his mother might still appear. Not a figure had turned into the alley, that he had not seen it, not a clanging car had stopped in the street beyond, that his quick ear had not noted.

About the time the small hand of the cathedral clock got around to four, Nance Molloy came skipping home from school. She had been kept in for a too spirited resentment of an older girl's casual observation that both of her shoes were for the same foot. To her, as to Dan, these trying conventions in the matter of foot-gear were intolerable. No combination seemed to meet the fastidious demands of that exacting sixth grade.

"Hello, Dan!" she said, coming to a halt at sight of the obstructed pavement. "What's all this for?"

"Put out," said Dan laconically.

"Didn't yer maw never come back?"

"Nope."

Nance climbed up beside him on the bedclothes and took her seat.

"What you goin' to do?" she asked in a business-like tone.

"Dunno." Dan did not turn his head to look at her, but he felt a dumb comfort in her presence. It was as if her position there beside him on the pillory made his humiliation less acute. He shifted the water pitcher, and jerked his thumb over his shoulder:

"They all want to divide the things an' take keer of 'em 'til she comes," he said, "but I ain't goin' to let 'em."

"I wouldn't neither," agreed Nance. "Old man Smelts an' Mr. Gorman'd have what they took in hock before mornin'. There's a coal shed over to Slap Jack's ain't full. Why can't you put yer things in there for to-night?"

"He wouldn't let me. He's a mean old Dutchman."

"He ain't, neither! He's the nicest man in the alley, next to Uncle Jed an' that there old man with the fiddle. Mr. Jack an' me's friends. He gives me pretzels all the time. I'll go ast him."

A faint hope stirred in Dan as she slid down from her perch and darted into the saloon next door. She had wasted no time in conjecture or sympathy; she had plunged at once into action. When she returned, the fat saloonkeeper lumbered in her wake:

"Dose tings is too many, already," he protested. "I got no place to put my coal once de cold vedder comes."

"It ain't come yet," said Nance. "Besides his mother'll be here to-morrow, I 'spect."

"Mebbe she vill, und mebbe she von't," said the saloonkeeper astutely. "I don't want dat I should mess up myself mid dis here piziness."

"The things ain't goin' to hurt your old coal shed none!" began Nance, firing up; then with a sudden change of tactics, she slipped her hand into Mr. Jack's fat, red one, and lifted a pair of coaxing blue eyes. "Say, go on an' let him, Mr. Jack! I told him you would. I said you was one of the nicest men in the alley. You ain't goin' to make me out a liar, are you?"

"Vell, I leave him put 'em in for to-night," said the saloonkeeper grudgingly, his Teuton caution overcome by Celtic wile.

The conclave of women assembled in the hall of Number One, to carry out Mrs. Snawdor's threat of "taking a hand," were surprised a few minutes later, to see the objects under discussion being passed over the fence by Mr. Jack and Dan under the able generalship of the one feminine member of the alley whose counsel had been heeded.

When the last article had been transferred to the shed, and a veteran padlock had been induced to return to active service, the windows of the tenement were beginning to glow dully, and the smell of cabbage and onions spoke loudly of supper.

Nance, notwithstanding the fourth peremptory summons from aloft, to walk herself straight home that very minute, still lingered with Dan.

"Come on home with me," she said. "You can sleep in Uncle Jed's bed 'til five o'clock."

"I kin take keer of myself all right," he said. "It was the things that pestered me."

"But where you goin' to git yer supper?"

"I got money," he answered, making sure that his nickel was still in his pocket. "Besides, my mother might come while I was there."

"Well, don't you fergit that to-morrow we go to Mis' Purdy's."

Dan looked at her with heavy eyes.

"Oh! I ain't got time to fool around with that business. I don't know where I'll be at by to-morrow."

"You'll be right here," said Nance firmly, "and I ain't goin' to budge a step without you if I have to wait all afternoon."

"Well, I ain't comin'," said Dan.

"I'm goin' to wait," said Nance, "an' if I git took up fer not reportin', it'll be your fault."

Dan slouched up to the corner and sat on the curbstone where he could watch the street cars. As they stopped at the crossing, he leaned forward eagerly and scanned the passengers who descended. In and out of the swinging door of the saloon behind him passed men, singly and in groups. There were children, too, with buckets, but they had to go around to the side. He wanted to go in himself and buy a sandwich, but he didn't dare. The very car he was waiting for might come in his absence.

At nine o'clock he was still waiting when two men came out and paused near him to light their cigars. They were talking about Skeeter Newson, the notorious pickpocket, who two days before had broken jail and had not yet been found. Skeeter's exploits were a favorite topic of the Calvary Micks, and Dan, despite the low state of his mind, pricked his ears to listen.

"They traced him as far as Chicago," said one of the men, "but there he give 'em the slip."

"Think of the nerve of him taking that Lewis woman with him," said the other voice. "By the way, I hear she lives around here somewhere."

"A bad lot," said the first voice as they moved away.

Dan sat rigid with his back to the telegraph pole, his feet in the gutter, his mouth fallen open, staring dully ahead of him. Then suddenly he reached blindly for a rock, and staggered to his feet, but the figures had disappeared in the darkness. He sat down again, while his breath came in short, hard gasps. It was a lie! His mother was not bad! He knew she was good. He wanted to shriek it to the world. But even as he passionately defended her to himself, fears assailed him.

Why had they always lived so differently from other people? Why was he never allowed to ask questions or to answer them or to know where his mother went or how they got their living? What were the parcels she always kept locked up in the trunk in the closet? Events, little heeded at the time of occurrence, began to fall into place, making a hideous and convincing pattern. Dim memories of men stole out of the past and threw distorted shadows on his troubled brain. There was Bob who had once given him a quarter, and Uncle Dick who always came after he was in bed, and Newt— his neck stiffened suddenly. Newt, whom his mother used always to be talking about, and whose name he had not heard now for so long that he had almost forgotten it. Skeeter Newson—Newt—"The Lewis Woman." He saw it all in a blinding flash, and in that awful moment of realization he passed out of his childhood and entered man's estate.

Choking back his sobs, he fled from the scene of his disgrace. In one alley and out another he stumbled, looking for a hole in which he could crawl and pour out his pent-up grief. But privacy is a luxury reserved for the rich, and Dan and his kind cannot even claim a place in which to break their hearts.

It was not until he reached the river bank and discovered an overturned hogshead that he found a refuge. Crawling in, he buried his face in his arms and wept, not with the tempestuous abandonment of a lonely child, but with the dry, soul-racking sobs of a disillusioned man. His mother had been the one beautiful thing in his life, and he had worshiped her as some being from another world. Other boys' mothers had coarse, red hands and loud voices; his had soft, white hands and a sweet, gentle voice that never scolded.

Sometimes when she stayed at home, they had no money, and then she would lie on the bed and cry, and he would try to comfort her. Those were the times when he would stay away from school and go forth to sell things at the pawn shop. The happiest nights he could remember were the ones when he had come home with money in his pocket, to a lighted lamp in the window, and a fire on the hearth and his mother's smile of welcome. But those times were few and far between; he was much more used to darkened windows, a cold hearth, and an almost empty larder. In explanation of these things he had accepted unconditionally his mother's statement that she was a lady.

As he fought his battle alone there in the dark, all sorts of wild plans came to him. Across the dark river the shore lights gleamed, and down below at the wharf, a steamboat was making ready to depart. He had heard of boys who slipped aboard ships and beat their way to distant cities. A fierce desire seized him to get away, anywhere, just so he would not have to face the shame and disgrace that had come upon him. There was no one to care now where he went or what became of him. He would run away and be a tramp where nobody could ask questions.

With quick decision he started up to put his plan into action when a disturbing thought crossed his mind. Had Nance Molloy meant it when she said she wouldn't report to the probation officer if he didn't go with her? Would she stand there in the alley and wait for him all afternoon, just as he had waited so often for some one who did not come? His reflections were disturbed by a hooting noise up the bank, followed by a shower of rocks. The next instant a mongrel pup scurried down the levee and dropped shivering at his feet.

The yells of the pursuers died away as Dan gathered the whimpering beast into his arms and examined its injuries.

"Hold still, old fellow. I ain't goin' to hurt you," he whispered, tenderly wiping the blood from one dripping paw. "I won't let 'em git you. I'll take care of you."

The dog lifted a pair of agonized eyes to Dan's face and licked his hands.

"You lemme tie it up with a piece of my sleeve, an' I'll give you somethin' to eat," went on Dan. "Me an' you'll buy a sandich an' I'll eat the bread an' you can have the meat. Me an you'll be partners."

Misery had found company, and already life seemed a little less desolate. But the new-comer continued to yelp with pain, and Dan examined the limp leg dubiously.

"I b'lieve it's broke," he thought. Then he had an inspiration.

"I know what I'll do," he said aloud, "I'll carry you out to the animal man when me an' Nance go to report to-morrow."

CHAPTER VIII
AMBITION STIRS

After Nance Molloy's first visit to Butternut Lane, life became a series of thrilling discoveries. Hitherto she had been treated collectively. At home she was "one of the Snawdor kids"; to the juvenile world beyond the corner she was "a Calvary Alley mick"; at school she was "a pupil of the sixth grade." It remained for little Mrs. Purdy to reveal the fact to her that she was an individual person.

Mrs. Purdy had the most beautiful illusions about everything. She seemed to see her fellow-men not as they were, but as God intended them to be. She discovered so many latent virtues and attractions in her new probationers that they scarcely knew themselves.

When, for instance, she made the startling observation that Nance had wonderful hair, and that, if she washed it with an egg and brushed it every day, it would shine like gold, Nance was interested, but incredulous. Until now hair had meant a useless mass of tangles that at long intervals was subjected to an agonizing process of rebraiding. The main thing about hair was that it must never on any account be left hanging down one's back. Feuds had been started and battles lost by swinging braids. The idea of washing it was an entirely new one to her; but the vision of golden locks spurred her on to try the experiment. She carefully followed directions, but the egg had been borrowed from Mrs. Smelts who had borrowed it some days before from Mrs. Lavinski, and the result was not what Mrs. Purdy predicted.

"If ever I ketch you up to sech fool tricks again," scolded Mrs. Snawdor, who had been called to the rescue, "I'll skin yer hide off! You've no need to take yer hair down except when I tell you. You kin smooth it up jus' like you always done."

Having thus failed in her efforts at personal adornment, Nance turned her attention to beautifying her surroundings. The many new features observed in the homely, commonplace house in Butternut Lane stirred her ambition. Her own room, to be sure, possessed architectural defects that would have discouraged most interior decorators. It was small and dark, with only one narrow opening into an air-shaft. Where the plaster had fallen off, bare laths were exposed, and in rainy weather a tin tub occupied the center of the floor to catch the drippings from a hole in the roof. For the rest, a slat bed, an iron wash-stand, and a three-legged chair comprised the furniture.

But Nance was not in the least daunted by the prospect. With considerable ingenuity she evolved a dresser from a soap box and the colored supplements of the Sunday papers, which she gathered into a valance, in imitation of Mrs. Purdy's bright chintz. In the air-shaft window she started three potato vines in bottles, but not satisfied with the feeble results, she pinned red paper roses to the sickly white stems. The nearest substitutes she could find for pictures were labels off tomato cans, and these she tacked up with satisfaction, remembering Mrs. Purdy's admired fruit pictures.

"'Tain't half so dark in here as 'tis down in Smeltses," she bragged to Fidy, who viewed her efforts with pessimism. "Once last summer the sun come in here fer purty near a week. It shined down the shaft. You ast Lobelia if it didn't."

Nance was nailing a pin into the wall with the heel of her slipper, and the loose plaster was dropping behind the bed.

"Mis' Purdy says if I don't say no cuss words, an' wash meself all over on Wednesdays and Sat'days, she's goin' to help me make myself a new dress!"

"Why don't she give you one done made?" asked Fidy.

"She ain't no charity lady!" said Nance indignantly. "Me an' her's friends. She said we was."

"What's she goin' to give Dan?" asked Fidy, to whom personages from the upper world were interesting only when they bore gifts in their hands.

"She ain't givin' him nothin', Silly! She's lettin' him help her. He gits a quarter a hour, an' his dinner fer wheelin' Mr. Walter in the park."

"They say Mr. Jack's give him a room over the saloon 'til his maw comes back."

"I reckon I know it. I made him! You jus' wait 'til December when Dan'll be fourteen. Once he gits to work he won't have to take nothin' offen nobody!"

School as well as home took on a new interest under Mrs. Purdy's influence. Shoes and textbooks appeared almost miraculously, and reports assumed a new and exciting significance. Under this new arrangement Dan blossomed into a model of righteousness, but Nance's lapses from grace were still frequent. The occasional glimpses she was getting of a code of manners and morals so different from those employed by her stepmother, were not of themselves sufficient to reclaim her. On the whole she found being good rather stupid and only consented to conform to rules when she saw for herself the benefit to be gained.

For instance, when she achieved a burning desire to be on the honor roll and failed on account of being kept at home, she took the matter into her own small hands and reported herself to the once despised truant officer. The result was a stormy interview between him and her stepmother which removed all further cause of jealousy on the part of Mr. Snawdor, and gave Nance a record for perfect attendance.

Having attained this distinction, she was fired to further effort. She could soon glibly say the multiplication tables backward, repeat all the verses in her school reader, and give the names and length of the most important rivers in the world. On two occasions she even stepped into prominence. The first was when she electrified a visiting trustee by her intimate knowledge of the archipelagos of the eastern hemisphere. The fact that she had not the remotest idea of the nature of an archipelago was mercifully not divulged. The second had been less successful. It was during a visit of Bishop Bland's to the school. He was making a personal investigation concerning a report, then current, that public school children were underfed. Bishop Bland was not fond of children, but he was sensitive to any slight put upon the stomach, and he wished very much to be able to refute the disturbing rumor.

"Now I cannot believe," he said to the sixth grade, clasping his plump hands over the visible result of many good dinners, "that any one of you nice boys and girls came here this morning hungry. I want any boy in the room who is not properly nourished at home to stand up."

Nobody rose, and the bishop cast an affirmative smile on the principal.

"As I thought," he continued complacently. "Now I'm going to ask any little girl in this room to stand up and tell us just exactly what she had for breakfast. I shall not be in the least surprised if it was just about what I had myself."

There was a silence, and it began to look as if nobody was going to call the bishop's bluff, when Nance jumped up from a rear seat and said at the top of her voice:

"A pretzel and a dill pickle!"

The new-found enthusiasm for school might have been of longer duration had it not been for a counter-attraction at home. From that first night when old "Mr. Demry," as he had come to be called, had played for her to dance, Nance had camped on his door-step. Whenever the scrape of his fiddle was heard from below, she dropped whatever she held, whether it was a hot iron or the baby, and never stopped until she reached the ground floor. And by and by other children found their way to him, not only the children of the tenement, but of the whole neighborhood as well. It was soon noised abroad that he knew how to coax the fairies out of the woods and actually into the shadows of Calvary Alley where they had never been heard of before. With one or two children on his knees and a circle on the floor around him, he would weave a world of dream and rainbows, and people it with all the dear invisible deities of childhood. And while he talked, his thin cheeks would flush, and his dim eyes shine with the same round wonder as his listeners.

But some nights when the children came, they found him too sleepy to tell stories or play on the fiddle. At such times he always emptied his pockets of small coins and sent the youngsters scampering away to find the pop-corn man. Then he would stand unsteadily at the door and watch them go, with a wistful, disappointed look on his tired old face.

Nance overheard her elders whispering that "he took something," and she greatly feared that he would meet a fate similar to that of Joe Smelts. In Joe's case it was an overcoat, and he had been forced to accept the hospitality of the State for thirty days. Nance's mind was greatly relieved to find that it was only powders that Mr. Demry took—powders that made him walk queer and talk queer and forget sometimes where he lived. Then it was that the children accepted him as their special charge. They would go to his rescue wherever they found him and guide his wandering footsteps into the haven of Calvary Alley.

"He's a has-benn," Mrs. Snawdor declared to Uncle Jed. "You an' me are never-wases, but that old gent has seen better days. They tell me that settin' down in the orchestry, he looks fine. That's the reason his coat's always so much better'n his shoes an' pants; he dresses up the part of him that shows. You can tell by the way he acts an' talks that he's different from us."

Perhaps that was the reason, that while Nance loved Uncle Jed quite as much, she found Mr. Demry far more interesting. Everything about him was different, from his ideas concerning the proper behavior of boys and girls, to his few neatly distributed belongings. His two possessions that most excited her curiosity and admiration, were the violin and its handsome old rosewood case, which you were not allowed to touch, and a miniature in a frame of gold, of a beautiful pink and white girl in a pink and white dress, with a fair curl falling over her bare shoulder. Nance would stand before the latter in adoring silence; then she would invariably say:

"Go on an' tell me about her, Mr. Demry!"

And standing behind her, with his fine sensitive hands on her shoulders, Mr. Demry would tell wonderful stories of the little girl who had once been his. And as he talked, the delicate profile in the picture became an enchanting reality to Nance, stirring her imagination and furnishing an object for her secret dreams.

Hitherto Birdie Smelts had been her chief admiration. Birdie was fourteen and wore French heels and a pompadour and had beaux. She had worked in the ten-cent store until her misplaced generosity with the glass beads on her counter resulted in her being sent to a reformatory. But Birdie's bold attractions suffered in comparison with the elusive charm of the pink and white goddess with the golden curl.

This change marked the dawn of romance in Nance's soul. Up to this time she had demanded of Mr. Demry the most "scareful" stories he knew, but from now on Blue Beard and Jack, the Giant-Killer had to make way for Cinderella and the Sleeping Beauty. She went about with her head full of dreams, and eyes that looked into an invisible world. It was not that the juvenile politics of the alley were less interesting, or the street fights or adventures of the gang less thrilling. It was simply that life had become absorbingly full of other things.

As the months passed Mrs. Snawdor spent less and less time at home. She seemed to think that when she gave her nights on her knees for her family, she was entitled to use the remaining waking hours for recreation. This took the form of untiring attention to other people's business. She canvassed the alley for delinquent husbands to admonish, for weddings to arrange, for funerals to supervise—the last being a specialty, owing to experience under the late Mr. Yager.

Upon one of the occasions when she was superintending the entrance of a neighboring baby into the world, her own made a hurried exit. A banana and a stick of licorice proved too stimulating a diet for him, and he closed his eyes permanently on a world that had offered few attractions.

It was Nance who, having mothered him from his birth, worked with him through the long night of agony; and who, when the end came, cut the faded cotton flowers from her hat to put in the tiny claw-like hand that had never touched a real blossom; and it was Nance's heart that broke when they took him away.

It is doubtful whether any abstract moral appeal could have awakened her as did the going out of that little futile life. It stirred her deepest sympathies and affections, and connected her for the first time with the forces that make for moral and social progress.

"He wouldn't a-went if we'd treated him right!" she complained bitterly to Mr. Snawdor a week later. "He never had no sunshine, nor fresh air, nor nothin'. You can't expect a baby to live where a sweet-potato vine can't!"

"He's better off than me," said Mr. Snawdor, "what with the funeral, an' the coal out, an' the rent due, I'm at the end of my rope. I told her it was comin'. But she would have a white coffin an' six hacks. They'll have to set us out in the street fer all I can see!"

Nance looked at him apprehensively.

"Well, we better be doin' somethin'," she said. "Can't Uncle Jed help us?"

"I ain't goin' to let him. He's paid my rent fer the last time."

This unexpected flare of independence in Mr. Snawdor was disturbing. The Snawdor family without Uncle Jed was like a row of stitches from which the knitting needle has been withdrawn.

"If I was two years older, I could go to work," said Nance, thinking of Dan, who was now on the pay-roll of Clarke's Bottle Factory.

"It ain't right to make you stop school," said Mr. Snawdor. "It ain't bein' fair to you."

"I'd do it all right," said Nance, fired by his magnanimity, "only they're on to me now I've reported myself. Ain't you makin' any money at the shop?"

Mr. Snawdor shook his head.

"I might if I was willin' to buy junk. But you know where them boys gets their stuff."

Nance nodded wisely.

"The gang bust into a empty house last night an' cut out all the lead pipes. I seen 'em comin' home with it."

Mr. Snawdor rose and went to the window.

"There ain't no chance fer a honest man," he said miserably. "I'm sick o' livin', that's whut I am. I am ready to quit."

When Mrs. Snawdor arrived, she swept all domestic problems impatiently aside.

"Fer goodness' sake don't come tellin' me no more hard-luck tales. Ain't I got troubles enough of my own? Nance, soon 's you git through, go git me a bucket of beer, an' if you see any of the Gormans, say I'll stop in this evenin' on my way to work."

"I ain't goin' fer the beer no more," announced Nance.

"An' will ye tell me why?" asked Mrs. Snawdor.

"'Cause I ain't," said Nance, knowing the futility of argument.

Mrs. Snawdor lifted her hand to strike, but changed her mind. She was beginning to have a certain puzzled respect for her stepdaughter's decision of character.

After the children had been put to bed and Nance had cried over the smallest nightgown, no longer needed, she slipped down to the second floor and, pausing before the door behind which the sewing-machines were always whirring, gave a peculiar whistle. It was a whistle possible only to a person who boasted the absence of a front tooth, and it brought Ike Lavinski promptly to the door.

Ikey was a friend whom she regarded with mingled contempt and admiration—contempt because he was weak and undersized, admiration because he was the only person of her acquaintance who had ever had his name in the newspaper. On two occasions he had been among the honor students at the high school, and his family and neighbors regarded him as an intellectual prodigy.

"Say, Ikey," said Nance, "if you was me, an' had to make some money, an' didn't want to chuck school, what would you do?"

Ikey considered the matter. Money and education were the most important things in the world to him, and were not to be discussed lightly.

"If you were bigger," he said, sweeping her with a critical eye, "you might try sewing pants."

"Could I do it at night? How much would it pay me? Would yer pa take me on?" Nance demanded all in a breath.

"He would if he thought they wouldn't get on to it."

"I'd keep it dark," Nance urged. "I could slip down every night after I git done my work, an' put in a couple of hours, easy. I'm a awful big child fer my age—feel my muscle! Go on an' make him take me on, Ikey, will you?"

And Ikey condescendingly agreed to use his influence.

CHAPTER IX
BUTTONS

The Lavinskis' flat on the second floor had always possessed a mysterious fascination for Nance. In and out of the other flats she passed at will, but she had never seen beyond the half-open door of the Lavinskis'. All day and far into the night, the sewing-machines ran at high pressure, and Mr. Lavinski shuffled in and out carrying huge piles of pants on his head. The other tenants stopped on the stairs to exchange civilities or incivilities with equal warmth; they hung out of windows or dawdled sociably in doorways. But summer and winter alike the Lavinskis herded behind closed doors and ran their everlasting sewing-machines.

Mrs. Snawdor gave her ready consent to Nance trying her hand as a "home finisher."

"We got to git money from somewheres," she said, "an' I always did want to know how them Polocks live. But don't you let on to your Uncle Jed what you're doing."

"I ain't goin' to let on to nobody," said Nance, thrilled with the secrecy of the affair.

The stifling room into which Ikey introduced her that night was supposed to be the Lavinskis' kitchen, but it was evident that the poor room had long ago abandoned all notions of domesticity. The tea-kettle had been crowded off the stove by the pressing irons; a wash-tub full of neglected clothes, squeezed itself into a distant corner, and the cooking utensils had had to go climbing up the walls on hooks and nails to make way on the shelves for sewing materials.

On one corner of the table, between two towering piles of pants, were the remains of the last meal, black bread, potatoes, and pickled herring. Under two swinging kerosene lamps, six women with sleeves rolled up and necks bared, bent over whirring machines, while Mr. Lavinski knelt on the floor tying the finished garments into huge bundles.

"Here's Nance Molloy, Pa" said Ikey, raising his voice above the noise of the machines and tugging at his father's sleeve.

Mr. Lavinski pushed his derby hat further back on his perspiring brow, and looked up. He had a dark, sharp face, and alert black eyes, exactly like Ikey's, and a black beard with two locks of black hair trained down in front of his ears to meet it. Without pausing in his work he sized Nance up.

"I von't take childern anny more. I tried it many times already. De inspector git me into troubles. It don't pay."

"But I'll dodge the inspectors," urged Nance.

"You know how to sew, eh?"

"No; but you kin learn me. Please, Mr. Lavinski, Ikey said you would."

Mr. Lavinski bestowed a doting glance on his son.

"My Ikey said so, did he? He thinks he own me, that boy. I send him to high school. I send him to Hebrew class at the synagogue at night. He vill be big rich some day, that boy; he's got a brain on him."

"Cut it out, Pa," said Ikey, "Nance is a smart kid; you won't lose anything on her."

The result was that Nance was accorded the privilege of occupying a stool in the corner behind the hot stove and sewing buttons on knee pantaloons, from eight until ten P.M. At first the novelty of working against time, with a room full of grown people, and of seeing the great stacks of unfinished garments change into great stacks of finished ones, was stimulation in itself. She was proud of her cushion full of strong needles and her spool of coarse thread. She was pleased with the nods of approval gentle Mrs. Lavinski gave her work in passing, and of the slight interest with which she was regarded by the other workers.

But as the hours wore on, and the air became hotter and closer, and no enlivening conversation came to relieve the strain, her interest began to wane. By nine o'clock her hands were sore and stained, and her back ached. By a quarter past, the buttons were slipping through her fingers, and she could not see to thread her needle.

"You vill do better to-morrow night," said Mrs. Lavinski kindly, in her wheezing voice. "I tell Ikey you do verra good."

Mrs. Lavinski looked shriveled and old. She wore a glossy black wig and long ear-rings, and when she was not coughing, she smiled pleasantly over her work. Once Mr. Lavinski stopped pressing long enough to put a cushion at her back.

"My Leah is a saint," he said. "If effra'boddy was so good as her, the Messiah would come."

Nance dreamed of buttons that night, and by the next evening her ambition to become a wage-earner had died completely.

But a family conclave at the supper table revealed such a crisis in the family finances that she decided to keep on at the Lavinskis' for another week. Uncle Jed was laid up with the rheumatism, and Mr. Snawdor's entire stock in trade had been put in a wheelbarrow and dumped into the street, and a strange sign already replaced his old one of "Bungs and Fawcetts."

Things seemed in such a bad way that Nance had about decided to lay the matter before Mrs. Purdy, when Dan brought the disconcerting news that Mrs. Purdy had taken her brother south for the rest of the winter, and that there would be no more visits to the little house in Butternut Lane.

So Nance, not knowing anything better to do, continued to sit night after night on her stool behind the hot stove, sewing on buttons. Thirty-six buttons meant four cents, four cents meant a loaf of bread—a stale loaf, that is.

"Your little fingers vill git ofer bein' sore," Mrs. Lavinski assured her. "I gif you alum water to put on 'em. Dat makes 'em hard."

They not only became hard; they became quick and accurate, and Nance got used to the heat and the smell, and she almost got used to the backache. It was sitting still and being silent that hurt her more than anything else. Mr. Lavinski did not encourage conversation,—it distracted the workers,— and Nance's exuberance, which at first found vent in all sorts of jokes and capers, soon died for lack of encouragement. She learned, instead, to use all her energy on buttons and, being denied verbal expression, she revolved many things in her small mind. The result of her thinking was summed up in her speech to her stepmother at the end of the first week.

"Gee! I'm sick of doin' the same thing! I ain't learnin' nothin'. If anybody was smart, they could make a machine to put on two times as many buttons as me in half the time. I want to begin something at the beginning and make it clean through. I'm sick an' tired of buttons. I'm goin' to quit!"

But Mrs. Snawdor had come to a belated realization of the depleted state of the family treasury and she urged Nance to keep on for the present.

"We better cut all the corners we kin," she said, "till Snawdor gits over this fit of the dumps. Ain't a reason in the world he don't go into the junk business. I ain't astin' him to drive aroun' an' yell 'Old iron!' I know that's tryin' on a bashful man. All I ast him is to set still an' let it come to him. Thank the Lord, I *have* known husbands that wasn't chicken-hearted!"

So Nance kept on reluctantly, even after Mr. Snawdor got a small job collecting. Sometimes she went to sleep over her task and had to be shaken awake, but that was before she began to drink black coffee with the other workers at nine o'clock.

One thing puzzled her. When Ikey came from night school, he was never asked to help in the work, no matter how much his help was needed. He was always given the seat by the table nearest the lamp, and his father himself cleared a place for his books.

"Ikey gits the education," Mr. Lavinski would say, with a proud smile. "The Rabbi says he is the smartest boy in the class. He takes prizes over big boys. Ve vork fer him now, an' some day he make big money an' take care of us!"

Education as seen through Mr. Lavinski's eyes took on a new aspect for Nance. It seemed that you did not get rich by going to work at fourteen, but by staying at school and in some miraculous way skipping the factory altogether. "I vork with my hands," said Mr. Lavinski; "my Ikey, he vorks with his head."

Nance fell into the way of bringing her school books downstairs at night and getting Ike to help her with her lessons. She would prop the book in front of her and, without lessening the speed of her flying fingers, ply him with the questions that had puzzled her during the day.

"I wisht I was smart as you!" she said one night.

"I reckon you do!" said Ike. "I work for it."

"You couldn't work no more 'n whut I do!" Nance said indignantly.

"There's a difference between working and being worked," said Ike, wisely. "If I were you, I'd look out for number one."

"But who would do the cookin' an' lookin' after the kids, an' all?"

"They are nothing to you," said Ike; "none of the bunch is kin to you. Catch me workin' for them like you do!"

Nance was puzzled, but not convinced. Wiser heads than hers have struggled with a similar problem in vain. She kept steadily on, and it was only when the squeak of Mr. Demry's fiddle came up from below that her fingers fumbled and the buttons went rolling on the floor. Six nights in the week, when Mr. Demry was in condition, he played at the theater, and on Sunday nights he stayed at home and received his young friends. On these occasions Nance became so restless that she could scarcely keep her prancing feet on the floor. She would hook them resolutely around the legs of the stool and even sit on them one at a time, but despite all her efforts, they would respond to the rhythmic notes below.

"Them tunes just make me dance settin' down," she declared, trying to suit the action to the words.

Sometimes on a rainy afternoon when nobody was being born, or getting married, or dying, Mrs. Snawdor stayed at home. At such times Nance seized the opportunity to shift her domestic burden.

There was a cheap theater, called "The Star," around the corner, where a noisy crowd of boys and girls could always be found in the gallery. It was a place where you ate peanuts and dropped the shells on the heads of people below, where you scrapped for your seat and joined in the chorus and shrieked over the antics of an Irishman, a darkey, or a Jew. But it was a luxury seldom indulged in, for it cost the frightful sum of ten cents, not including the peanuts.

For the most part Nance's leisure half-hours were spent with Mr. Demry, discussing a most exciting project. He was contemplating the unheard-of festivity of a Christmas party, and the whole alley was buzzing with it. Even the big boys in Dan's gang were going to take part. There were to be pirates and fairies and ogres, and Nance was to be the princess and do a fancy dance in a petticoat trimmed with silver paper, and wear a tinsel crown.

Scrubbing the floor, figuring on the blackboard, washing dishes, or sewing on buttons, she was aware of that tinsel crown. For one magic night it was going to transform her into a veritable princess, and who knew but that a prince in doublet and hose and sweeping plume might arrive to claim her? But when Nance's imagination was called upon to visualize the prince, a hateful image came to her of a tall, slender boy, clad in white, with a contemptuous look in his handsome brown eyes.

"I don't know what ails Nance these days," Mrs. Snawdor complained to Uncle Jed. "She sasses back if you look at her, an' fergits everything, an' Snawdor says she mutters an' jabbers something awful in her sleep."

"Seems to me she works too hard," said Uncle Jed, still ignorant of her extra two hours in the sweat-shop. "A growin' girl oughtn't to be doin' heavy washin' an' carryin' water an' coal up two flights."

"Why, Nance is strong as a ox," Mrs. Snawdor insisted, "an' as fer eatin'! Why it looks like she never can git filled up."

"Well, what ails her then?" persisted Uncle Jed.

"I bet I know!" said Mrs. Snawdor darkly. "It's that there vaccination. Las' time I hid the other childern from the inspector she had to come out an' argue with him fer herself. She got paid up proper fer givin' in to him. Her arm was a plumb sight."

"Do you suppose it's the poison still workin' on her?" Uncle Jed asked, watching Nance in the next room as she lifted a boiler filled with the washing water from the stove.

"Why, of course, it is! Talk to me about yer State rules an' regerlations! It does look like us poor people has got troubles enough already, without rich folks layin' awake nights studyin' up what they can do to us next."

CHAPTER X
THE PRINCESS COMES TO GRIEF

And bring her rose-winged fancies,
From shadowy shoals of dream
To clothe her in the wistful hour
When girlhood steals from bud to flower;
Bring her the tunes of elfin dances,
Bring her the faery Gleam.—BURKE.

Christmas fell on a Saturday and a payday, and this, together with Mr. Demry's party, accounts for the fact that the holiday spirit, which sometimes limps a trifle languidly past tenement doors, swaggered with unusual gaiety this year in Calvary Alley. You could hear it in the cathedral chimes which began at dawn, in the explosion of fire-crackers, in the bursts of noisy laughter from behind swinging doors. You could smell it in the whiffs of things frying, broiling, burning. You could feel it in the crisp air, in the crunch of the snow under your feet, and most of all you could see it in the happy, expectant faces of the children, who rushed in and out in a fever of excitement.

Early in the afternoon Nance Molloy, with a drab-colored shawl over her head and something tightly clasped in one bare, chapped fist, rushed forth on a mysterious mission. When she returned, she carried a pasteboard box hugged to her heart. The thought of tripping her fairy measure in worn-out shoes tied on with strings, had become so intolerable to her that she had bartered her holiday for a pair of white slippers. Mr. Lavinski had advanced the money, and she was to work six hours a day, instead of two, until she paid the money back.

But she was in no mood to reckon the cost, as she prepared for the evening festivities. So great was her energy and enthusiasm, that the contagion spread to the little Snawdors, each of whom submitted with unprecedented meekness to a "wash all over." Nance dressed herself last, wrapping her white feet and legs in paper to keep them clean until the great hour should arrive.

"Why, Nance Molloy! You look downright purty!" Mrs. Snawdor exclaimed, when she came up after assisting Mr. Demry with his refreshments. "I never would 'a' believed it!"

Nance laughed happily. The effect had been achieved by much experimenting before the little mirror over her soap box. The mirror had a wave in it which gave the beholder two noses, but Nance had kept her pink and white ideal steadily in mind, and the result was a golden curl over a bare shoulder. The curl would have been longer had not half of it remained in a burnt wisp around the poker.

But such petty catastrophes have no place in a heart overflowing with joy. Nance did not even try to keep her twinkling feet from dancing; she danced through the table-setting and through the dish-washing, and between times she pressed her face to the dirty pane of the front window to see if the hands on the big cathedral clock were getting any nearer to five.

"They're goin' to have Christmas doin's over to the cathedral, too," she cried excitedly. "The boards is off the new window, an' it's jus' like the old one, an' ever'thing's lit up, an' it's snowin' like ever'thing!"

Mr. Demry's party was to take place between the time he came home from the matinee and the time he returned for the evening performance. Long before the hour appointed, his guests began to arrive, dirty-faced and clean, fat and thin, tidy and ragged, big and little, but all wearing in their eyes that gift of nature to the most sordid youth, the gift of expectancy. There were fairies and ogres and pirates and Indians in costumes that needed only the proper imagination to make them convincing. If by any chance a wistful urchin arrived in his rags alone, Mr. Demry promptly evolved a cocked hat from a newspaper, and a sword from a box top, and transformed him into a prancing knight.

The children had been to Sunday-school entertainments where they had sat in prim rows and watched grown people have all the fun of fixing the tree and distributing the presents, but for most of them this was the first Christmas that they had actually helped to make. Every link in the colored paper garlands was a matter of pride to some one.

What the children had left undone, Mr. Demry had finished. All the movables had been put out of sight as if they were never to be wanted again. From the ceiling swung two glowing paper lanterns that threw soft, mysterious, dancing lights on things. In the big fireplace a huge fire crackled and roared, and on the shelf above it were stacks of golden oranges, and piles of fat, brown doughnuts. Across one corner, on a stout cord, hung some green branches with small candles twinkling above them. It was not exactly a Christmas tree, but it had evidently fooled Santa Claus, for on every branch hung a trinket or a toy for somebody.

And nobody thought, least of all Mr. Demry, of how many squeaks of the old fiddle had gone into the making of this party, of the bread and meat that had gone into the oranges and doughnuts, of the fires that should have warmed Mr. Demry's chilled old bones for weeks to come, that went roaring up the wide chimney in one glorious burst of prodigality.

When the party was in full swing and the excitement was at its highest, the guests were seated on the floor in a double row, and Mr. Demry took his stand by the fireplace, with his fiddle under his chin, and began tuning up.

Out in the dark hall, in quivering expectancy, stood the princess, shivering with impatience as she waited for Dan to fling open the door for her triumphant entrance. Every twang of the violin strings vibrated in her heart, and she could scarcely wait for the signal. It was the magic moment when buttons ceased to exist and tinsel crowns became a reality.

The hall was dark and very cold, and the snow drifting in made a white patch on the threshold. Nance, steadying her crown against the icy draught, lifted her head suddenly and listened. From the room on the opposite side of the hall came a woman's frightened cry, followed by the sound of breaking furniture. The next instant the door was flung open, and Mrs. Smelts, with her baby in her arms, rushed forth. Close behind her rolled Mr. Smelts, his shifted ballast of Christmas cheer threatening each moment to capsize him.

"I'll learn ye to stop puttin' cures in my coffee!" he bellowed. "Spoilin' me taste fer liquor, are ye? I'll learn ye!"

"I never meant no harm, Jim," quailed Mrs. Smelts, cowering in the corner with one arm upraised to shield the baby. "I seen the ad in the paper. It claimed to be a whisky-cure. Don't hit me, Jim—don't—" But before she could finish, Mr. Smelts had struck her full in the face with a brutal fist and had raised his arm to strike again. But the blow never fell.

The quick blood that had made Phil Molloy one of the heroes of Chickasaw Bluffs rose in the veins of his small granddaughter, and she suddenly saw red. Had Jim Smelts been twice the size he was, she would have sprung at him just the same and rained blow after stinging blow upon his befuddled head with her slender fairy wand.

"Git up the steps!" she shrieked to Mrs. Smelts. "Fer God's sake git out of his way! Dan! Dan Lewis! Help! Help!"

Mr. Smelts, infuriated at the interference, had pinioned Nance's arms behind her and was about to beat her crowned head against the wall when Dan rushed into the hall.

"Throw him out the front door!" screamed Nance. "Help me push him down the steps!"

Mr. Smelts' resistance was fierce, but brief. His legs were much drunker than his arms, and when the two determined youngsters flung themselves upon him and shoved him out of the door, he lost his balance and fell headlong to the street below.

By this time the party had swarmed into the hall and out on the steps and Mr. Demry's gentle, frightened face could be seen peering over their decorated heads. The uproar had brought other tenants scurrying from the upper floors, and somebody was dispatched for a police. Dense and denser grew the crowd, and questions, excuses, accusations were heard on every side.

"They've done killed him," wailed a woman's voice above the other noises. It was Mrs. Smelts who, with all the abandonment of a bereft widow, cast herself beside the huddled figure lying motionless in the snow.

"What's all this row about?" demanded Cockeye, forcing his way to the front and assuming an air of stern authority.

"They've killed my Jim!" wailed Mrs. Smelts. "I'm goin' to have the law on 'em!"

The policeman, with an impolite request that she stop that there caterwauling, knelt on the wet pavement and made a hasty diagnosis of the case.

"Leg's broke, and head's caved in a bit. That's all I can see is the matter of him. Who beat him up?"

"Him an' her!" accused Mrs. Smelts hysterically, pointing to Dan and Nance, who stood shivering beside Mr. Demry on the top step.

"Well, I'll be hanged if them ain't the same two that was had up last summer!" said the policeman in profound disgust. "It's good-by fer them all right."

"But we was helpin' Mis' Smelts!" cried Nance in bewilderment. "He was beatin' her. He was goin' to hit the baby—"

"Here comes the Black Maria!" yelled an emissary from the corner, and the crowd parted as the long, narrow, black patrol-wagon clanged noisily into the narrow court.

Mr. Smelts was lifted in, none too gently, and as he showed no signs of returning consciousness, Cock-eye paused irresolute and looked at Dan.

"You best be comin' along, too," he said with sudden decision. "The bloke may be hurt worse 'rn I think. I'll just drop you at the detention home 'til over Sunday."

"You shan't take Dan Lewis!" cried Nance in instant alarm. "He was helpin' me, I tell you! He ain't done nothin' bad—" Then as Dan was hustled down the steps and into the wagon, she lost her head completely. Regardless of consequences, she hurled herself upon the law. She bit it and scratched it and even spat upon it.

Had Mrs. Snawdor or Uncle Jed been there, the catastrophe would never have happened; but Mrs. Snawdor was at the post-office, and Uncle Jed at the signal tower, and the feeble protests of Mr. Demry were as futile as the twittering of a sparrow.

"I'll fix you, you little spitfire!" cried the irate officer, holding her hands and lifting her into the wagon. "Some of you women put a cloak around her, and be quick about it."

Nance, refusing to be wrapped up, continued to fight savagely.

"I ain't goin' in the hurry-up wagon!" she screamed. "I ain't done nothin' bad! Let go my hands!"

But the wagon was already moving out of the alley, and Nance suddenly ceased to struggle. An accidental combination of circumstances, too complicated and overwhelming to be coped with, was hurrying her away to some unknown and horrible fate. She looked at her mud-splashed white slippers that were not yet paid for, and then back at the bright window behind which the party was waiting. In a sudden anguish of disappointment she flung herself face downward on the long seat and sobbed with a passion that was entirely too great for her small body.

Sitting opposite, his stiff, stubby hair sticking out beneath his pirate hat, Dan Lewis, forgetting his own misfortune, watched her with dumb compassion, and between them, on the floor, lay a drunken hulk of a man with blood trickling across his ugly, bloated face, his muddy feet resting on all that remained of a gorgeous, tinsel crown.

It was at this moment that the Christmas spirit fled in despair from Calvary Alley and took refuge in the big cathedral where, behind the magnificent new window, a procession of white-robed choir-boys, led by Mac Clarke, were joyously proclaiming:

"Hark! the herald angels sing
Glory to the new-born King;"

CHAPTER XI
THE STATE TAKES A HAND

The two reformatories to which the children, after various examinations, were consigned, represented the worst and the best types of such institutions.

Dan Lewis was put behind barred windows with eight hundred other young "foes of society." He was treated as a criminal, and when he resented it, he was put under a cold shower and beaten with a rattan until he fainted. Outraged, humiliated, bitterly resentful, his one idea was to escape. At the end of a month of cruelty and injustice he was developing a hatred against authority that would ultimately have landed him in the State prison had not a miraculous interference from without set him free and returned him to his work in Clarke's Bottle Factory.

It all came about through a letter received by Mrs. Purdy, who was wintering in Florida—a tear-stained, blotted, misspelled letter that had been achieved with great difficulty. It ran:

Dear Mis Purdy, me and Dan Lewis is pinched again. But I ain't a Dellinkent. The jedge says theres a diffrunce. He says he was not puting me in becose I was bad but becose I was not brot upright. He says for me to be good and stay here and git a education. He says its my chanct. I was mad at first, but now I aint. What Im writing you fer is to git Dan Lewis out. He never done nothink what was wrong and he got sent to the House of Refuse. Please Mis Purdy you git him off. He aint bad. You know he aint. You ast everbody at home, and then go tell the Jedge and git him off. I can't stan fer him to be in that ole hole becose it aint fair. Please don't stop at nothink til you git him out. So good-by, loveingly, NANCE.

This had been written a little at a time during Nance's first week at Forest Home. She had arrived in such a burning state of indignation that it required the combined efforts of the superintendent and the matron to calm her. In fact her spirit did not break until she was subjected to a thorough scrubbing from head to foot, and put to bed on a long porch between cold, clean sheets. She was used to sleeping in her underclothes in the hot close air of Snawdor's flat, with Fidy and Lobelia snuggled up on each side. This icy isolation was intolerable! Her hair, still damp, felt strange and uncomfortable; her eyes smarted from the recent application of soap. She lay with her knees drawn up to her chin and shivered and cried to go home.

Hideous thoughts tormented her. Who'd git up the coal, an' do the washin'? Would Mr. Snawdor fergit an' take off Rosy's aesophedity bag, so she'd git the measles an' die like the baby? What did Mr. Lavinski think of her fer not comin' to work out the slipper money? Would Dan ever git his place back at the factory after he'd been in the House of Refuse? Was Mr. Smelts' leg broke plum off, so's he'd have to hobble on a peg-stick?

She cowered under the covers. "God aint no friend of mine," she sobbed miserably.

When she awoke the next morning, she sat up and looked about her. The porch in which she lay was enclosed from floor to ceiling in glass, and there were rows of small white beds like her own, stretching away on each side of her. The tip of her nose was very cold, but the rest of her was surprisingly warm, and the fresh air tasted good in her mouth. It was appallingly still and strange, and she lay down and listened for the sounds that did not come.

There were no factory whistles, no clanging of car bells, no lumbering of heavy wagons. Instead of the blank wall of a warehouse upon which she was used to opening her eyes, there were miles and miles of dim white fields. Presently a wonderful thing happened. Something was on fire out there at the edge of the world—something big and round and red. Nance held her breath and for the first time in her eleven years saw the sun rise.

When getting-up time came, she went with eighteen other girls into a big, warm dressing-room.

"This is your locker," said the girl in charge.

"My whut?" asked Nance.

"Your locker, where you put your clothes."

Nance had no clothes except the ones she was about to put on, but the prospect of being the sole possessor of one of those little closets brought her the first gleam of consolation.

The next followed swiftly. The owner of the adjoining locker proved to be no other than Birdie Smelts. Whatever fear Nance had of Birdie's resenting the part she had played in landing Mr. Smelts in the city hospital was promptly banished.

"You can't tell me nothing about paw," Birdie said at the end of Nance's recital. "I only wish it was his neck instead of his leg that was broke."

"But we never aimed to hurt him," explained Nance, to whom the accident still loomed as a frightful nightmare. "They didn't have no right to send me out here."

"It ain't so worse," said Birdie indifferently. "You get enough to eat and you keep warm and get away from rough-housin'; that's something."

"But I don't belong here!" protested Nance, hotly.

"Aw, forget it," advised Birdie, with a philosophical shrug of her shapely shoulders. Birdie was not yet fifteen, but she had already learned to take the course of least resistance. She was a pretty, weak-faced girl, with a full, graceful figure and full red lips and heavy-lidded eyes that always looked sleepy.

"I wouldn't keer so much if it wasn't fer Dan Lewis," Nance said miserably. "He was inside Mr. Demry's room, an' never knowed a thing about it 'til I hollered."

"Say, I believe you are gone on Dan!" said Birdie, lifting a teasing finger.

"I ain't either!" said Nance indignantly, "but I ain't goin' to quit tryin' 'til I git him out!"

In the bright airy dining-room where they went for breakfast, Nance sat at a small table with five other girls and scornfully refused the glass of milk they offered her as a substitute for the strong coffee to which she was accustomed. She had about decided to starve herself to death, but changed her mind when the griddle-cakes and syrup appeared.

In fact, she changed her mind about many things during those first days. After a few acute attacks of homesickness, she began despite herself to take a pioneer's delight in blazing a new trail. It was the first time she had ever come into contact for more than a passing moment, with decent surroundings and orderly living, and her surprises were endless.

"Say, do these guys make you put on airs like this all the time?" she asked incredulously of her table-companion.

"Like what?"

"Like eatin' with a fork, an' washin' every day, an' doin' yer hair over whether it needs it or not?"

"If I had hair as grand as yours, they wouldn't have to make me fix it," said the close-cropped little girl enviously.

Nance looked at her suspiciously. Once before she had been lured by that bait, and she was wary. But the envy in the eyes of the short-haired girl was genuine.

Nance took the first opportunity that presented itself to look in a mirror. To her amazement, her tight, drab-colored braids had become gleaming bands of gold, and there were fluffy little tendrils across her forehead and at the back of her neck. It was unbelievable, too, how much more becoming one nose was to the human countenance than two.

A few days later when one of the older girls said teasingly, "Nance Molloy is stuck on her hair!" Nance answered proudly, "Well, ain't I got a right to be?"

At the end of the first month word came from Mrs. Purdy that she had succeeded in obtaining Dan's release, and that he was back at work at Clarke's, and on probation again. This news, instead of making Nance restless for her own freedom, had quite the opposite effect. Now that her worry over Dan was at an end, she resigned herself cheerfully to the business of being reformed.

The presiding genius of Forest Home was Miss Stanley, the superintendent. She did not believe in high fences or uniforms or bodily punishment. She was tall, handsome, and serene, and she treated the girls with the same grave courtesy with which she treated the directors.

Nance regarded her with something of the worshipful awe she had once felt before an image of the Virgin Mary.

"She don't make you 'fraid exactly," she confided to Birdie. "She makes you 'shamed."

"You can tell she's a real lady the way she shines her finger-nails," said Birdie, to whom affairs of the toilet were of great importance.

"Another way you can tell," Nance added, trying to think the thing out for herself, "is the way she takes slams. You an' me sass back, but a real lady knows how to hold her jaw an' make you eat dirt just the same."

They were standing side by side at a long table in a big, clean kitchen, cutting out biscuit for supper. Other white-capped, white-aproned girls, all intent upon their own tasks, were flitting about, and a teacher sat at a desk beside the window, directing the work. The two girls had fallen into the habit of doing their chores together and telling each other secrets. Birdie's had mostly to do with boys, and it was not long before Nance felt called upon to make a few tentative observations on the same engrossing subject.

"The prettiest boy I ever seen—" she said, "I mean I have ever saw"—then she laughed helplessly. "Well, anyhow, he was that Clarke feller. You know, the one that got pinched fer smashin' the window the first time we was had up?"

"Mac Clarke? Sure, I know him. He's fresh all right."

Birdie did not go into particulars, but she looked important.

"Say, Birdie," Nance asked admiringly, "when you git out of here, what you goin' to do?"

"I'll tell you what I *ain't* going to do," said Birdie, impressively, in a low voice, "I ain't going to stand in a store, and I ain't going out to work, and I ain't going to work at Clarke's!"

"But what else is left to do?"

"Swear you won't tell?"

Nance crossed her heart with a floury finger.

"I'm going to be a actress," said Birdie.

It was fortunate for Nance that Birdie's term at the home soon ended. She was at that impressionable age which reflects the nearest object of interest, and shortly after Birdie's departure she abandoned the idea of joining her on the professional boards, and decided instead to become a veterinary surgeon.

This decision was reached through a growing intimacy with the lame old soldier who presided over the Forest Home stables. "Doc" was a familiar character in the county, and his advice about horses was sought far and near. Next to horses he liked children, and after them dogs. Adults came rather far down the line, excepting always Miss Stanley, whom he regarded as infallible.

On the red-letter Sunday when Uncle Jed had tramped the ten miles out from town to assure himself of Nance's well-being, he discovered in Doc an old comrade of the Civil War. They had been in the same company, Uncle Jed as a drummer boy, and Doc in charge of the cavalry horses.

"Why, I expect you recollict this child's grandpaw," Uncle Jed said, with his hand on Nance's head, "Molloy, 'Fightin' Phil,' they called him. Went down with the colors at Chickasaw Bluffs."

Doc did remember. Fighting Phil had been one of the idols of his boyhood.

Miss Stanley found in this friendship a solution of Nance's chief difficulty. When a person of eleven has been doing practical housekeeping for a family of eight, she naturally resents the suggestion that there is anything in domestic science for her to learn. Moreover, when said person is anemic and nervous from overwork, and has a tongue that has never known control, it is perilously easy to get into trouble, despite heroic efforts to be good.

The wise superintendent saw in the girl all sorts of possibilities for both good and evil. For unselfish service and passionate sacrifice, as well as obstinate rebellion and hot-headed folly.

At those unhappy times when Nance threatened to break over the bounds, she was sent out to the stables to spend an afternoon with Doc.

No matter how sore her grievance, it vanished in the presence of the genial old veterinarian. She never tired of hearing him tell of her fighting Irish grandfather and the pranks he played on his messmates, of Uncle Jed and the time he lost his drumsticks and marched barefoot in the snow, beating his drum with the heels of his shoes.

Most of all she liked the horses. She learned how to put on bandages and poultices and to make a bran mash. Doc taught her how to give a sick horse a drink out of a bottle without choking him, how to hold his tongue with one hand and put a pill far down his throat with the other. The nursing of sick animals seemed to come to her naturally, and she found it much more interesting than school work and domestic science.

"She's got a way with critters," Doc confided proudly to Miss Stanley. "I've seen a horse eat out of her hand when it wouldn't touch food in the manger."

As the months slipped into years, the memory of Calvary Alley grew dim, and Nance began to look upon herself as an integral part of this orderly life which stretched away in a pleasant perspective of work and play. It was the first time that she had ever been tempted to be good, and she fell. It was not Miss Stanley's way to say "don't." Instead, she said, "do," and the "do's" became so engrossing that the "don'ts" were crowded out.

At regular, intervals Mrs. Snawdor made application for her dismissal, and just as regularly a probation officer visited the Snawdor flat and pronounced it unfit.

"I suppose if I had a phoneygraf an' lace curtains you'd let her come home," Mrs. Snawdor observed caustically during one of these inspections. "You bet I'll fix things up next time if I know you are comin'!"

The State was doing its clumsy best to make up to Nance for what she had missed. It was giving her free board, free tuition, and protection from harmful influences. But that did not begin to square the State's account, nor the account of society. They still owed her something for that early environment of dirt and disease. The landlord in whose vile tenement she had lived, the saloon-keeper who had sold her beer, the manufacturer who had bought the garments she made at starvation wages, were all her debtors. Society exists for the purpose of doing justice to its members, and society had not begun to pay its debt to that youthful member whose lot had been cast in Calvary Alley.

One Saturday afternoon in the early spring of Nance's fourth year at Forest Home, Miss Stanley stood in the school-house door, reading a letter. It was the kind of a day when heaven and earth cannot keep away from each other, but the fleecy clouds must come down to play in the sparkling pools, and white and pink blossoms must go climbing up to the sky to flaunt their sweetness against the blue. Yet Miss Stanley, reading her letter, sighed.

Coming toward her down the hillside, plunged a noisy group of children, and behind them in hot pursuit came Nance Molloy, angular, long-legged, lithe as a young sapling and half mad with the spring.

"Such a child still!" sighed Miss Stanley, as she lifted a beckoning hand.

The children crowded about her, all holding out hot fists full of faded wild flowers.

"Look!" cried one breathlessly. "We found 'em in the hollow. And Nance says if you'll let her, she'll take us next Saturday to the old mill where some yellow vi'lets grow!"

Miss Stanley looked down at the flushed, happy faces; then she put her arm around Nance's shoulder.

"Nancy will not be with us next Saturday," she said regretfully. "She's going home."

CHAPTER XII
CLARKE'S

Nance Molloy came out of Forest Home, an independent, efficient girl, with clear skin, luminous blue eyes, and shining braids of fair hair. She came full of ideals and new standards and all the terrible wisdom of sixteen, and she dumped them in a mass on the family in Calvary Alley and boldly announced that "what she was going to do was a-plenty!"

But like most reformers, she reckoned too confidently on cooperation. The rest of the Snawdor family had not been to reform school, and it had strong objections to Nance's drastic measures. Her innovations met with bitter opposition from William J., who indignantly declined to have the hitherto respected privacy of his ears and nose invaded, to Mrs. Snawdor, who refused absolutely to sleep with the windows open.

"What's the sense in working your fingers off to buy coal to heat the house if you go an' let out all the hot air over night?" she demanded. "They've filled up yer head with fool notions, but I tell you right now, you ain't goin' to work 'em off on us. You kin just tell that old maid Stanley that when she's had three husbands and five children an' a step, an' managed to live on less'n ten dollars a week, it'll be time enough fer her to be learnin' me tricks!"

"But don't all this mess ever get on your nerves? Don't you ever want to clear out and go to the country?" asked Nance.

"Not me!" said Mrs. Snawdor. "I been fightin' the country all my life. It's bad enough bein' dirt pore, without goin' an' settin' down among the stumps where there ain't nothin' to take yer mind off it."

So whatever reforms Nance contemplated had to be carried out slowly and with great tact. Mrs. Snawdor, having put forth one supreme effort to make the flat sufficiently decent to warrant Nance's return, proposed for the remainder of her life to rest on her laurels. As for the children, they had grown old enough to have decided opinions of their own, and when Nance threw the weight of her influence on the side of order and cleanliness, she was regarded as a traitor in the camp. It was only Mr. Snawdor who sought to uphold her, and Mr. Snawdor was but a broken reed.

Meanwhile the all-important question of getting work was under discussion. Miss Stanley had made several tentative suggestions, but none of them met with Mrs. Snawdor's approval.

"No, I ain't goin' to let you work out in private families!" she declared indignantly. "She's got her cheek to ast it! Did you tell her yer pa was a Molloy? An' Mr. Burks says yer maw was even better born than what Bud was. I'm goin' to git you a job myself. I'm goin' to take you up to Clarke's this very evenin'."

"I don't want to work in a factory!" Nance said discontentedly, looking out of the window into the dirty court below.

"I suppose you want to run a beauty parlor," said Mrs. Snawdor, with scornful reference to Nance's improved appearance. "You might just as well come off them high stilts an' stop puttin' on airs, Dan Lewis has been up to Clarke's goin' on four years now. I hear they're pushin' him right along."

Nance stopped drumming on the window-pane and became suddenly interested. The one thing that had reconciled her to leaving Miss Stanley and the girls at the home was the possibility of seeing Dan again. She wondered what he looked like after these four years, whether he would recognize her, whether he had a sweetheart? She had been home three days now and had caught no glimpse of him.

"We never see nothin' of him," her stepmother told her. "He's took up with the Methodists, an' runs around to meetin's an' things with that there Mis' Purdy."

"Don't he live over Slap Jack's?" asked Nance.

"Yes; he's got his room there still. I hear his ma died las' spring. Flirtin' with the angels by now, I reckon."

The prospect of seeing Dan cheered Nance amazingly. She spent the morning washing and ironing her best shirt-waist and turning the ribbon on her tam-o'-shanter. Every detail of her toilet received scrupulous attention.

It was raining dismally when she and Mrs. Snawdor picked their way across the factory yard that afternoon. The conglomerate mass of buildings known as "Clarke's" loomed somberly against the dull sky. Beside the low central building a huge gas-pipe towered, and the water, trickling down it, made a puddle through which they had to wade to reach the door of the furnace room.

Within they could see the huge, round furnace with its belt of small fiery doors, from which glass-blowers, with long blow-pipes were deftly taking small lumps of moulten glass and blowing them into balls.

"There's Dan!" cried Mrs. Snawdor, and Nance looked eagerly in the direction indicated.

In the red glare of the furnace, a big, awkward, bare-armed young fellow was just turning to roll his red-hot ball on a board. There was a steady look in the gray eyes that scowled slightly under the intense glare, a sure movement of the hands that dropped the elongated roll into the mold. When he saw Mrs. Snawdor's beckoning finger, he came to the door.

"This here is Nance Molloy," said Mrs. Snawdor by way of introduction. "She's about growed up sence you seen her. We come to see about gittin' her a job."

Nance, looking at the strange, stern face above her, withdrew the hand she had held out. Dan did not seem to see her hand any more than he saw her fresh shirt-waist and the hat she had taken so much pains to retrim. After a casual nod he stood looking at the floor and rubbing the toe of his heavy boot against his blow-pipe.

"Sure," he said slowly, "but this is no fit place for a girl, Mrs. Snawdor."

Mrs. Snawdor bristled immediately.

"I ain't astin' yer advice, Dan Lewis. I'm astin' yer help."

Dan looked Nance over in troubled silence.

"Is she sixteen yet?" he asked as impersonally as if she had not been present.

"Yes, an' past. I knowed they'd be scarin' up that dangerous trade business on me next. How long before the foreman'll be here?"

"Any time now," said Dan. "I'll take you into his office."

With a sinking heart, Nance followed them into the crowded room. The heat was stifling, and the air was full of stinging glass dust. All about them boys were running with red hot bottles on big asbestos shovels. She hated the place, and she hated Dan for not being glad to see her.

"They are the carrying-in boys," Dan explained, continuing to address all of his remarks to Mrs. Snawdor. "That's where I began. You wouldn't believe that those kids often run as much as twenty-two miles a day. Watch out there, boy! Be careful!"

But his warning came too late. One of the smaller youngsters had stumbled and dropped his shovel, and a hot bottle had grazed his leg, burning away a bit of the stocking.

"It's all right, Partner," cried Dan, springing forward, "You're not much hurt. I'll fix you up."

But the boy was frightened and refused to let him remove the stocking.

"Let me do it," begged Nance. "I can get it off without hurting him."

And while Dan held the child's leg steady, she bathed and bound it in a way that did credit to Doc's training. Only once daring the process did she look up, and then she was relieved to see instead of the stern face of a strange young man, the compassionate, familiar face of the old Dan she used to know.

The interview with the foreman was of brief duration. He was a thick-set, pimply-faced person whom Dan called Mr. Bean. He swept an appraising eye over the applicant, submitted a few blunt questions to Dan in an undertone, ignored Mrs. Snawdor's voluble comments, and ended by telling Nance to report for work the following week.

As Mrs. Snawdor and Nance took their departure, the former, whose thoughts seldom traveled on a single track, said tentatively:

"Dan Lewis has got to be real nice lookin' sence you seen him, ain't he?"

"Nothin' to brag on," said Nance, still smarting at his indifference. But as she turned the corner of the building, she stole a last look through the window to where Dan was standing at his fiery post, his strong, serious face and broad, bare chest lighted up by the radiance from the glory-hole.

It was with little enthusiasm that Nance presented herself at the factory on Monday morning, ready to enlist in what Bishop Bland called "the noble service of industry." Her work was in the finishing room where a number of girls were crowded at machines and tables, filing, clipping, and packing bottles. Her task was to take the screw-neck bottles that came from the leer, and chip and file their jagged necks and shoulders until all the roughness was removed. It was dirty work, and dangerous for unskilled hands, and she found it difficult to learn.

"Say, kid," said the ugly, hollow-chested girl beside her, "if I'm goin' to be your learner, I want you to be more particular. Between you an' this here other girl, you're fixin' to put my good eye out."

Nance glanced up at the gaunt face with its empty eye socket and then looked quickly away.

"Say," said the other new girl, complainingly, "is it always hot like this in here? I'm most choking."

"We'll git the boss to put in a 'lectric fan fer you," suggested the hollow-chested one, whose name was Mag Gist.

Notwithstanding her distaste for the work, Nance threw herself into it with characteristic vehemence. Speed seemed to be the quality above all others that one must strive for, and speed she was determined to have, regardless of consequences.

"When you learn how to do this, what do you learn next?" she asked presently.

Mag laughed gruffly.

"There ain't no next. If you'd started as a wrapper, you might 'a' worked up a bit, but you never would 'a' got to be a chuck-grinder. I been at this bench four years an' if I don't lose my job, I'll be here four more."

"But if you get to be awful quick, you can make money, can't you?"

"You kin make enough to pay fer two meals a day if yer appetite ain't too good."

Nance's heart sank. It was a blow to find that Mag, who was the cleverest girl in the finishing room, had been filing bottle necks for four years. She stole a glance at her stooped shoulders and sallow skin and the hideous, empty socket of her left eye. What was the good of becoming expert if it only put one where Mag was?

By eleven o'clock there was a sharp pain between her shoulder-blades, and her feet ached so that she angrily kicked off first one shoe, then the other. This was the signal for a general laugh.

"They're kiddin' you fer sheddin' yer shoes," explained Mag, who had laughed louder than anybody. "Greenhorns always do it first thing. By the time you've stepped on a piece of glass onct or twict, you'll be glad enough to climb back into 'em."

After a while one of the girls started a song, and one by one the others joined in. There were numerous verses, and a plaintive refrain that referred to "the joy that ne'er would come again to you and I."

When no more verses could be thought of, there were stories and doubtful jokes which sent the girls into fits of wild laughter.

"Oh, cheese it," said Mag after one of these sallies, "You all orter to behave more before these kids."

"They don't know what we are talkin' about," said a red-haired girl.

"You bet I do," said Nance, with disgust, "but you all give me a sick headache."

When the foreman made his rounds, figures that had begun to droop were galvanized into fresh effort. At Mag's bench he paused.

"How are the fillies making it?" he asked, with a familiar hand on the shoulder of each new girl. Nance's companion dropped her eyes with a simpering smile, but Nance jerked away indignantly.

The foreman looked at the back of the shining head and frowned.

"You'll have to push up the stroke," he said. "Can't you see you lose time by changing your position so often? What makes you fidget so?"

Nance set her teeth resolutely and held her tongue. But her Irish instinct always suffered from restraint and by the time the noon whistle blew, she was in a state of sullen resentment. The thought of her beloved Miss Stanley and what she would think of these surroundings brought a lump into her throat.

"Come on over here," called Mag from a group of girls at the open window. "Don't you mind what Bean says. He's sore on any girl that won't eat outen his dirty hand. You 're as smart again as that other kid. I can tell right off if a girl's got gumption, an' if she's on the straight.

"Chuck that Sunday-school dope," laughed a pretty, red-haired girl named Gert. "You git her in wrong with Bean, an' I wouldn't give a nickel fer her chance."

"You ought to know," said Mag, drily.

The talk ran largely to food and clothes, and Nance listened with growing dismay. It seemed that most of the girls lived in rooming houses and took their meals out.

"Wisht I had a Hamberger," said Mag. "I ain't had a bite of meat fer a month. I always buy my shoes with meat money."

"I git my hats with breakfasts," said another girl. "Fourteen breakfasts makes a dollar-forty. I kin buy a hat fer a dollar-forty-nine that's swell enough fer anybody."

"I gotta have my breakfast," said Mag. "Four cups of coffee ain't nothin' to me."

Gert got up and stretched herself impatiently.

"I'm sick an' tired of hearin' you all talk about eatin'. Mag's idea of Heaven is a place where you spend ten hours makin' money an' two eatin' it up. Some of us ain't built like that. We got to have some fun as we go along, an' we're goin' to git it, you bet your sweet life, one way or the other."

Soon after work was resumed, word was passed around that a big order had come in, and nobody was to quit work until it was made up. A ripple of sullen comment followed this announcement, but the girls bent to their tasks with feverish energy.

At two o'clock the other new girl standing next to Nance grew faint, and had to be stretched on the floor in the midst of the broken glass.

"She's a softie!" whispered Mag to Nance. "This ain't nothin' to what it is in hot weather."

The pain between Nance's shoulders was growing intolerable, and her cut fingers and aching feet made her long to cast herself on the floor beside the other girl and give up the fight. But pride held her to her task. After what seemed to her an eternity she again looked at the big clock over the door. It was only three. How was she ever to endure three more hours when every minute now was an agony?

Mag heard her sigh and turned her head long enough to say:

"Hang yer arms down a spell; that kind of rests 'em. You ain't goin' to flop, too, are you?"

"Not if I can hold out."

"I knowed you was game all right," said Mag, with grim approval.

By six o'clock the last bottle was packed, and Nance washed the blood and dirt off her hands and forced her swollen, aching feet into her shoes. She jerked her jacket and tam-o'-shanter from the long row of hooks, and half blind with weariness, joined the throng of women and girls that jostled one another down the stairs. Every muscle of her body ached, and her whole soul was hot with rebellion. She told herself passionately that nothing in the world could induce her to come back; she was through with factory work forever.

As she limped out into the yard, a totally vanquished little soldier on the battle-field of industry, she spied Dan Lewis standing beside the tall gas-pipe, evidently waiting for somebody. He probably had a sweetheart among all these trooping girls; perhaps it was the pretty, red-haired one named Gert. The thought, dropping suddenly into a surcharged heart, brimmed it over, and Nance had to sweep her fingers across her eyes to brush away the tears.

And then:

"I thought I'd missed you," said Dan, quite as a matter of course, as he caught step with her and raised her umbrella.

Nance could have flung her tired arms about him and wept on his broad shoulder for sheer gratitude. To be singled out, like that, before all the girls on her first day, to have a beau, a big beau, pilot her through the crowded streets and into Calvary Alley where all might see, was sufficient to change the dullest sky to rose and lighten the heart of the most discouraged.

On the way home they found little to say, but Nance's aching feet fairly tripped beside those of her tall companion, and when they turned Slap Jack's corner and Dan asked in his slow, deliberate way, "How do you think you are going to like the factory?" Nance answered enthusiastically, "Oh, I like it splendid!"

CHAPTER XIII
EIGHT TO SIX

Through that long, wet spring Nance did her ten hours a day, six days in the week and on the seventh washed her clothes and mended them. Her breaking in was a hard one, for she was as quick of tongue as she was of fingers, and her tirades against the monotony, the high speed, and the small pay were frequent and vehement. Every other week when Dan was on the night shift, she made up her mind definitely that she would stand it no longer.

But on the alternate weeks when she never failed to find him waiting at the gas-pipe to take her home, she thought better of it. She loved to slip in under his big cotton umbrella, when the nights were rainy, and hold to his elbow as he shouldered a way for her through the crowd; she liked to be a part of that endless procession of bobbing umbrellas that flowed down the long, wet, glistening street; best of all she liked the distinction of having a "steady" and the envious glances it brought her from the other girls.

Sometimes when they paused at a shop window, she caught her reflection in a mirror, and smiled approval at the bright face under the red tam. She wondered constantly if Dan thought she was pretty and always came to the conclusion that he did not.

From the time they left the factory until they saw the towering bulk of the cathedral against the dusk, Nance's chatter never ceased. She dramatized her experiences at the factory; she gave a lively account of the doings of the Snawdor family; she wove tales of mystery around old Mr. Demry. She had the rare gift of enhancing every passing moment with something of importance and interest.

Dan listened with the flattering homage a slow, taciturn nature often pays a quick, vivacious one. It was only when problems concerning the factory were touched upon that his tongue lost its stiffness. Under an unswerving loyalty to his employers was growing a discontent with certain existing conditions. The bad lighting system, the lack of ventilation, the employment of children under age, were subjects that rendered him eloquent. That cruel month spent in the reformatory had branded him so deeply that he was supersensitive to the wrongs of others, and spent much of his time in planning ways and means to better conditions.

"Don't you ever want a good time, Dan?" Nance asked. "Don't you ever want to sort of let go and do something reckless?"

"No; but I'll tell you what I do want. I want a' education. I've a good mind to go to night school and try to pick up some of the things I didn't get a chance to learn when I was a kid."

Nance scoffed the idea; school was almost invisible to her from the giddy height of sixteen. "Let's go on a bat," she urged. "Let's go out and see something."

So on the four following Sundays Dan took her to see the library, the reservoir, the city hall, and the jail. His ideas of recreation had not been cultivated.

The time in the week to which she always looked forward was Saturday afternoon. Then they got out early, and if the weather was fine, they would stop in Post-Office Square and, sitting on one of the iron benches, watch the passing throng. There was something thrilling in the jostling crowds, and the electric signs flashing out one by one down the long gay thoroughfare.

Post-Office Square, at the end of the day, was always littered with papers and trash. In its center was a battered, weather kiosk, and facing it, was a huge electric advertisement which indulged in the glittering generality, that "You get what you pay for."

It was not a place to inspire romance, yet every Saturday its benches were crowded with boys and girls who had no place to visit except on the street.

Through the long spring dusks, with their tender skies and silver stars, Nance and Dan kept company, unconcerned with the past or the future, wholly content with the May-time of the present. At a word or touch from Dan, Nance's inflammable nature would have taken fire but Dan, under Mrs. Purdy's influence, was passing through an acute stage of religious conversion, and all desires of the flesh were sternly repressed by that new creed to which he was making such heroic efforts to conform. With the zeal of a new convert, he considered it his duty to guard his small companion against all love-making, including his own.

Nance at an early age had developed a protective code that even without Dan's forbidding looks and constant surveillance might have served its purpose. Despite the high spirits and free speech that brought her so many admiring glances from the boys in the factory, it was soon understood that the "Molloy kid" was not to be trifled with.

"Say, little Sister, I like your looks," Bean had said to her one morning when they were alone in the hall. "It's more than I do yours," Nance had answered coolly, with a critical glance at his pimply nose.

As summer came on, the work, which at first was so difficult, gradually became automatic, and while her shoulders always ached, and her feet were always tired, she ceased for the most part to think of them. It was the confinement that told upon her, and when the long bright days came, and she thought of Forest Home and its woods and streams, her restlessness increased. The stifling finishing room, the endless complaints of the girls, and the everlasting crunching of glass under foot were at times almost unendurable.

One day when the blue of the sky could not be dimmed even by factory smoke, and the air was full of enticement, Nance slipped out at the noon hour, and, watching her chance, darted across the factory yard out through the stables, to the road beyond. A decrepit old elm-tree, which had evidently made heroic effort to keep tryst with the spring, was the one touch of green in an otherwise barren landscape. Scrambling up the bank, Nance flung herself on the ground beneath its branches, and between the bites of a dry sandwich, proceeded to give vent to some of her surplus vitality.

"Arra, come in, Barney McKane, out of the rain," she sang at the top of her voice.

"And sit down until the moon comes out again,
Sure a cup of tay I'll brew, just enough for me and you,
We'll snuggle up together, and we'll talk about the weather,
Do you hear? Barney dear, there's a queer
Sort of feelin' round me heart, that gives me pain,
And I think the likes o' me could learn to like the likes o' ye,
Arra, come in, Barney McKane, out of the rain!"

So absorbed was she in trying operatic effects that she did not notice an approaching automobile until it came to a stop in the road below.

"Hi there, Sembrich!" commanded a fresh young voice, the owner of which emphasized his salute with his horn, "are you one of the factory kids?"

Nance rose to a sitting posture.

"What's it to you?" she asked, instantly on the defensive.

"I want to know if Mr. Clarke's come in. Have you seen him?"

"No, indeed," said Nance, to whom Mr. Clarke was as vague as the Deity; then she added good-naturedly, "I'll go find out if you want me to."

The young man shut off his engine and, transferring two struggling pigeons from his left hand to his right, dismounted.

"Never mind," he said. "I'll go myself. Road's too rotten to take the machine in." Then he hesitated, "I say, will you hold these confounded birds 'til I come back? Won't be gone a minute. Just want to speak to the governor."

Nance scrambled down the bank and accepted the fluttering charges, then watched with liveliest interest the buoyant figure in the light suit go swinging up the road. There was something tantalizingly familiar in his quick, imperious manner and his brown, irresponsible eyes. In her first confusion of mind she thought he must be the prince come to life out of Mr. Demry's old fairy tale. Then she caught her breath.

"I believe it's that Clarke boy!" she thought, with rising excitement, "I wonder if he'd remember the fight? I wonder if he'd remember me?"

She went over to the automobile and ran her fingers over the silver initials on the door.

"M.D.C," she repeated. "It is him! It is!"

In the excitement of her discovery she relaxed her grasp on the pigeons, and one of them escaped. In vain she whistled and coaxed; it hopped about in the tree overhead and then soared away to larger freedom.

Nance was aghast at the catastrophe. She did not wait for the owner's return, but rushed headlong down the road to meet him.

"I let one of 'em go!" she cried in consternation, as he vaulted the fence and came toward her. "I wouldn't 'a' done it for anything in the world. But I'll pay you for it, a little each week. Honest I will!"

The handsome boyish face above her clouded instantly.

"You let it go?" he repeated furiously. "You little fool you! How did you do it?"

Nance looked at him for a moment; then she deliberately lifted the other pigeon as high as she could reach and opened her hand.

"Like that!" she cried.

Mac Clarke watched his second bird wheel into space; then his amazed glance dropped to the slim figure of the young girl in her short gingham dress, with the sunlight shining on her hair and on her bright, defiant eyes.

"You've got your nerve!" he said with a short laugh; then he climbed into his car and, with several backward glances of mingled anger and amusement, drove away.

Nance related the incident with great gusto to Dan that night on the way home.

"He never recognized me, but I knew him right off. Same old Smart Aleck, calling people names."

"I was up in the office when he come in," said Dan. "He'd been held up for speeding and wanted his father to pay his fine."'

"Did he do it?"

"Of course. Mac always gets what he wants. He told Bean he wasn't going to stay at that school in Virginia if he had to make 'em expel him. Sure enough they did. Wouldn't I like to have his chance though!"

"I don't blame him for not wanting to go to school," said Nance. Then she added absently, "Say, he's got to be a awful swell-looker, hasn't he?"

That night, for the first time, she objected to stopping in Post-Office Square.

"It ain't any fun to hang around there," she said impatiently. "I'm sick of doing tame things all the time."

The next time Nance saw Mac Clarke was toward the close of the summer. Through the long sweltering hours of an interminable August morning she had filed and chipped bottles with an accuracy and speed that no longer gave cause for criticism. The months of confinement were beginning to tell upon her; her bright color was gone, and she no longer had the energy at the noon hour to go down the road to the elm-tree. She wanted above all things to stretch out at full length and rest her back and relax all those tense muscles that were so reluctantly learning to hold one position for hours at a time.

At the noon hour she had the unexpected diversion of a visit from Birdie Smelts. Birdie had achieved her cherished ambition of going on the stage, and was now a chorus girl in the "Rag Time Follies." Meager news of her had reached the alley from time to time, but nobody was prepared for the very pretty and sophisticated young person who condescended to accept board and lodging from her humble parents during the interval between her engagements. Nance was genuinely glad to see her and especially gratified by the impression her white coat-suit and black picture hat made on the finishing room.

"It must be grand to be on the stage," said Gert enviously.

"Well, it's living," said Birdie, airily. "That's more than you can claim for this rotten grind."

She put a high-heeled, white-shod foot on the window ledge to adjust its bow, and every eye in the room followed the process.

"I bet I make more money in a week," she continued dramatically, "than you all make in a month. And look at your hands! Why, they couldn't pay me enough to have my hands scarred up like that!"

"It ain't my hands that's worryin' me," said another girl. "It's my feet. Say, the destruction on your shoes is somethin' fierce! You orter see this here room some nights at closin' time; it's that thick with glass you don't know where to step."

"I'd know," said Birdie. "I'd step down and out, and don't you forget it."

Nance had been following the conversation in troubled silence.

"I don't mind the work so awful much," she said restlessly. "What gets me is never having any fun. I haven't danced a step since I left Forest Home, Birdie."

"You'd get your fill of it if you was with me," Birdie said importantly. "Seven nights a week and two matinées."

"'Twouldn't be any too much for me," said Nance. "I could dance in my sleep."

Birdie was sitting in the window now, ostensibly examining her full red lips in a pocket-mirror, but in reality watching the factory yard below.

"There goes your whistle!" she said, getting up suddenly. "Say, Nance, can't you scare up an excuse to hook off this afternoon? I'll take you to a show if you will!"

Nance's pulses leapt at the thought, but she shook her head and went reluctantly back to her bench. For the next ten minutes her fingers lagged at their task, and she grew more and more discontented. All the youth in her clamored suddenly for freedom. She was tired of being the slave of a whistle, a cog in a machine. With a sudden rash impulse she threw down her tools and, slipping her hat from its peg, went in swift pursuit of Birdie.

At the foot of the narrow stairs she came to a sudden halt. Outside the door, in the niche made by the gas-pipe and the adjoining wall, stood Mac Clarke and Birdie. He had his arms about her, and there was a look in his face that Nance had never seen in a man's face before. Of course it was meant for the insolent eyes under the picture hat, but instead it fell on Nance standing in the doorway. For a full minute his ardent gaze held her captive; then he dropped his arms in sudden embarrassment, and she melted out of the doorway and fled noiselessly up the stairway.

On the upper landing she suffered a head-on collision with the foreman, who demanded in no gentle tones what in the devil she was doing out there with her hat on at that hour.

"None of your business," said Nance, recklessly.

Bean looked at her flashing eyes and flushed face, and laughed. She was the youngest girl in the factory and the only one who was not afraid of him.

"See here," he said, "I am going to kiss you or fire you. Which'll you have?"

Nance dodged his outstretched hand and reached the top step.

"You won't do neither!" she cried fiercely. "You can't fire me, because I fired myself ten minutes ago, and I wouldn't kiss you to stay in heaven, let alone a damned old bottle factory!"

It was the Nance of the slums who spoke—the Nance whose small bare fists had fought the world too long for the knuckles to be tender. She had drifted a long way from the carefully acquired refinements of Forest Home, but its influence, like a dragging anchor, still sought to hold her against the oncoming gales of life.

CHAPTER XIV
IDLENESS

When one has a famishing thirst for happiness, one is apt to gulp down diversions wherever they are offered. The necessity of draining the dregs of life before the wine is savored does not cultivate a discriminating taste. Nance saw in Birdie Smelts her one chance of escape from the deadly monotony of life, and she seized it with both hands. Birdie might not be approved of her seniors, but she was a disturbingly important person to her juniors. To them it seemed nothing short of genius for a girl, born as they were in the sordid environs of Calvary Alley, to side-step school and factory and soar away into the paradise of stage-land. When such an authority gives counsel, it is not to be ignored. Birdie's advice had been to quit the factory, and Nance had taken the plunge without any idea of what she was going to put in its place.

For some reason best known to herself, she never mentioned that episode in the factory yard to either Birdie or Dan Lewis. There were many things about Birdie that she did not like, and she knew only too well what Miss Stanley would have said. But then Miss Stanley wouldn't have approved of Mr. Demry and his dope, or Mrs. Snawdor and her beer, or Mag Gist, with her loud voice and coarse jokes. When one lives in Calvary Alley, one has to compromise; it is seldom the best or the next best one can afford, even in friends.

When Mrs. Snawdor heard that Nance had quit work, she was furious. Who was Nance Molloy, she wanted to know, to go and stick up her nose at a glass factory? There wasn't a bloomin' thing the matter with Clarke's. *She'd* begun in a factory an' look at her! What was Nance a-goin' to do? Run the streets with Birdie Smelts? It was bad enough, God knew, to have Snawdor settin' around like a tombstone, an' Fidy a-havin' a fit if you so much as looked at her, without havin' Nance eatin' 'em out of house an' home an' not bringin' in a copper cent. If she stayed at home, she'd have to do the work; that was all there was to it!

"Anybody'd think jobs happened around as regerlar as the rent man," she ended bitterly. "You'll see the day when you're glad enough to go back to the factory."

Before the month was over, Nance began to wonder if Mrs. Snawdor was right. With unabating zeal she tramped the streets, answering advertisements, applying at stores, visiting agencies. But despite the fact that she unblushingly recommended herself in the highest terms, nobody seemed to trust so young and inexperienced an applicant.

Meanwhile Birdie Smelts's thrilling prospect of joining her company at an early date threw other people's sordid possibilities into the shade. Every night she practised gymnastics and dance steps, and there being no room in the Smelts' flat, she got into the habit of coming up to Nance's room.

One of the conditions upon which Nance had been permitted to return to Calvary Alley, was that she should not sleep in the same bed with Fidy Yager, a condition which enraged Mrs. Snawdor more than all the rest.

"Annybody'd think Fidy's fits was ketchin'," she complained indignantly to Uncle Jed.

"That there front room of mine ain't doin' anybody no good," suggested Uncle Jed. "We might let Nance have that."

So to Nance's great joy she was given a big room all to herself. The slat bed, the iron wash-stand, the broken-legged chair, and the wavy mirror were the only articles that Mrs. Snawdor was willing to part with, but Uncle Jed donated a battered stove, which despite its rust-eaten top and sagging door, still proclaimed itself a "Little Jewel".

No bride, adorning her first abode, ever arranged her possessions with more enthusiasm than did Nance. She scrubbed the rough floor, washed the windows, and polished the "Little Jewel" until it shone. The first money she could save out of her factory earnings had gone to settle that four-year-old debt to Mr. Lavinski for the white slippers; the next went for bedclothes and cheese-cloth window curtains. Her ambition was no longer for the chintz hangings and gold-framed fruit pieces of Mrs. Purdy's cottage, but looked instead toward the immaculate and austere bedroom of Miss Stanley, with its "Melodonna" over the bed and a box of blooming plants on the window-sill.

Such an ideal of classic simplicity was foredoomed to failure. Mrs. Snawdor, like nature, abhorred a vacuum. An additional room to her was a sluice in the dyke, and before long discarded pots and pans, disabled furniture, the children's dilapidated toys, and, finally, the children themselves were allowed to overflow into Nance's room. In vain Nance got up at daybreak to make things tidy before going to work. At night when she returned, the washing would be hung in her room to dry, or the twins would be playing circus in the middle of her cherished bed.

"It's lots harder when you know how things ought to be, than when you just go on living in the mess, and don't know the difference," she complained bitterly to Birdie.

"I've had my fill of it," said Birdie, "I kiss my hand to the alley for good this time. What do you reckon the fellers would think of me if they knew I hung out in a hole like this?"

"Does he know?" asked Nance in an unguarded moment.

"Who?"

"Mac Clarke."

Birdie shot a glance of swift suspicion at her.

"What's he got to do with me?" she asked coldly.

"Ain't he one of your fellers?"

"Well, if he is, it ain't anybody's business but mine." Then evidently repenting her harshness, she added, "I got tickets to a dance-hall up-town to-night. I'll take you along if you want to look on. You wouldn't catch me dancing with any of those roughnecks."

Nance found looking on an agonizing business. Not that she wanted to dance with the roughnecks any more than Birdie did. Their common experience at Forest Home had given them certain standards of speech and manner that lifted them just enough above their kind to be scornful. But to sit against the wall watching other people dance was nothing short of agony to one of Nance's temperament.

"Come on and have a try with me, Birdie," she implored. "I'll pay the dime." And Birdie, with professional disdain, condescended to circle the room with her a few times.

That first dance was to Nance what the taste of blood is to a young tiger. For days after she could think of nothing else.

"Never you mind," Birdie promised her. "When I get back on the road, I'm going to see what I can do for you. Somebody's always falling out of the chorus, and if you keep up this practising with me, you'll be dancing as good as any of 'em. Ask old man Demry; he played in the orchestra last time we was at the Gaiety."

But when Nance threw out a few cautious remarks to Mr. Demry, she met with prompt discouragement:

"No, no, my dear child," he said uneasily. "You must put that idea out of your head. The chorus is no place for a nice girl."

"That's what Dan says about the factory, and what Mrs. Snawdor says about housework, and what somebody says about everything I start to do. Looks like being a nice girl don't pay!"

Mr. Demry took her petulant little chin in his thin old hand, and turned her face up to his.

"Nancy," he said, "these old eyes have seen a good deal over the fiddle strings. I would rather see you go back to the glass factory, bad as it is, than to go into the chorus."

"But I do dance as good as some of the girls, don't I, Mr. Demry?" she teased, and Mr. Demry, whose pride in an old pupil was considerable, had to acknowledge that she did.

Uncle Jed's attitude was scarcely more encouraging.

"No; I wouldn't be willin' to see you a playactor," he said, "walkin' round in skin tights, with your face all painted up."

Nance knew before asking that Dan would disapprove, but she couldn't resist mentioning the matter to him.

"That Birdie Smelts has been putting notions in your head," he said sternly. "I wish you'd quit runnin' with girls older than you. Besides, Birdie ain't your kind."

"I'd like to know why?" Nance challenged him in instant loyalty to her friend. "Besides, who else have I got to run with? Maybe you think it ain't stupid drudging around home all day and never having a cent to call my own. I want to get out and do something."

Dan looked down at her in troubled silence.

"Mrs. Purdy's always asking me why I don't bring you to some of the meetings at the church. They have real nice socials."

"I don't want to pray and sing silly old hymns!" cried Nance. "I want to dance."

"I don't believe in dancing," said Dan, firmly; then with a side-glance at her unhappy face, he added, "I can't take you to the swimming school, because they don't allow girls, but I might take you to the new skating-rink some Saturday."

In an instant Nance was all enthusiasm.

"Will you, Dan? I'm just crazy about skating. We used to do it out at the home. You ought to see Birdie and me do a Dutch roll. Say, let's take her along. What do you say?"

Dan was not at all in favor of it, but Nance insisted.

"I think we ought to be nice to Birdie on account of Mr. Smelts' stiff leg. Not that it ever did him any good when it was limber, but I always feel mean when I see it sticking out straight when he sits down."

This was a bit of feminine wile on Nance's part, and it had the desired effect. Dan, always vulnerable when his sympathy was roused, reluctantly included Birdie in the invitation.

On the Saturday night appointed, the three of them set out for the skating rink. Dan, with his neck rigid in a high collar and his hair plastered close to his head, stalked somberly beside the two girls, who walked arm in arm and giggled immoderately at each other's witticisms.

"Wake up, Daniel!" said Birdie, giving his hat a tilt. "We engaged you for a escort, not a pallbearer."

The rink was in an old armory, and the musicians sat at one end of the room on a raised platform under two drooping flags. It was dusty and noisy, and the crowd was promiscuous, but to Nance it was Elysium. When she and Birdie, with Dan between them, began to circle the big room to the rhythm of music, her joy was complete.

"Hullo! Dan Lewis is carrying two," she heard some one say as they circled past the entrance. Glancing back, she saw it was one of the boys from the factory. A sudden impulse seized her to stop and explain the matter to him, but instead she followed quite a contrary purpose and detaching herself from her companions, struck out boldly for herself.

Before she had been on the floor ten minutes people began to watch her. Her plain, neat dress setting off her trim figure, and her severe, black sailor hat above the shining bands of fair hair, were in sharp contrast to the soiled finery and draggled plumes of the other girls. But it was not entirely her appearance that attracted attention. It was a certain independent verve, a high-headed indifference, that made her reject even the attentions of the rink-master, a superior person boasting a pompadour and a turquoise ring.

No one could have guessed that behind that nonchalant air Nance was hiding a new and profoundly disturbing emotion. The sight of Birdie, clinging in affected terror to Dan Lewis, filled her with rage. Couldn't Dan see that Birdie was pretending? Didn't he know that she could skate by herself quite as well as he could? Never once during the evening did Dan make his escape, and never once did Nance go to his rescue.

When they were taking off their skates to go home, Birdie whispered to her:

"I believe I got old slow-coach going. Watch me make him smoke up for a treat!"

"No, you sha'n't," Nance said. "Dan's spent enough on us for one night."

"Another quarter won't break him," said Birdie. "I'm as dry as a piece of chalk."

Ten minutes later she landed the little party in a drug store and entered into a spirited discussion with the soda-water boy as to the comparative merits of sundry new drinks.

"Me for a cabaret fizz," she said. "What'll you have, Nance?"

"Nothing," said Nance, sullenly, turning and taking up her stand at the door.

"What do you want, Dan?" persisted Birdie, adding, with a mischievous wink at the white-coated clerk, "Give him a ginger ale; he needs stimulating."

While Birdie talked for the benefit of the clerk, and Dan sat beside her, sipping his distasteful ginger, Nance stood at the door and watched the people pouring out of the Gaiety Theater next door. Ordinarily the bright evening wraps, the glimpses of sparkling jewels, the gay confusion of the scene would have excited her liveliest interest, but to-night she was too busy hating Birdie Smelts to think of anything else. What right had she to monopolize Dan like that and order him about and laugh at him? What right had she to take his arm when they walked, or put her hand on his shoulder as she was doing this minute?

Suddenly Nance started and leaned forward. Out there in the crowded street a tall, middle-aged man, with grizzled hair and mustache, was somewhat imperiously making way for a pretty, delicate-looking lady enveloped in white furs, and behind them, looking very handsome and immaculate in his evening clothes, walked Mac Clarke.

Nance's eager eyes followed the group to the curbing; she saw the young man glance at her with a puzzled expression; then, as he stood aside to allow the lady to enter the motor, he looked again. For the fraction of a second their eyes held each other; then an expression of amused recognition sprang into his face, and Nance met it instantly with a flash of her white teeth.

The next instant the limousine swallowed him; a door slammed, and the car moved away. But Nance, utterly forgetful of her recent discomfort, still stood in the door of the drug store, tingling with excitement as she watched a little red light until it lost itself in the other moving lights on the broad thoroughfare.

CHAPTER XV
MARKING TIME

Early in the autumn Birdie took flight from the alley, and Nance found herself hopelessly engulfed in domestic affairs. Mr. Snawdor, who had been doing the work during her long absence, took advantage of her return to have malarial fever. He had been trying to have it for months, but could never find the leisure hour in which to indulge in the preliminary chill. Once having tasted the joys of invalidism he was loathe to forego them, and insisted upon being regarded as a chronic convalescent. Nance might have managed Mr. Snawdor, however, had it not been for the grave problem of Fidy Yager.

"Ike Lavinski says she ought to be in a hospital some place," she urged Mrs. Snawdor. "He says she never is going to be any better. He says it's epilepsy."

"Wel he ain't tellin' me anything' I don't know," said Mrs. Snawdor, "but I ain't goin' to put her away, not if she th'ows a fit a minute!"

It was not maternal solicitude alone that prompted this declaration. The State allowed seventy-live dollars a year to parents of epileptic children, and Mrs. Snawdor had found Fidy a valuable asset. Just what her being kept at home cost the other children was never reckoned.

"Well, I'll take care of her on one condition," stipulated Nance. "You got to keep Lobelia at school. It ain't fair for her to have to stay home to nurse Fidy."

"Well, if she goes to school, she's got to work at night. You was doin' your two hours at Lavinski's long before you was her age."

"I don't care if I was. Lobelia ain't strong like me. I tell you she ain't goin' to do home finishing, not while I'm here."

"Well, somebody's got to do it," said Mrs. Snawdor. "You can settle it between you."

Nance held out until the middle of January; then in desperation she went back to the Lavinskis. The rooms looked just as she had left them, and the whirring machines seemed never to have stopped. The acrid smell of hot cloth still mingled with the odor of pickled herrings, and Mr. Lavinski still came and went with his huge bundles of clothes.

Nance no longer sewed on buttons. She was promoted to a place under the swinging lamp where she was expected to make an old decrepit sewing-machine forget its ailments and run the same race it had run in the days of its youth. As she took her seat on the first night, she looked up curiously. A new sound coming regularly from the inner room made her pause.

"Is that a type-writer?" she asked incredulously.

Mr. Lavinski, pushing his derby from his shining brow, smiled proudly.

"Dat's vat it is," he said. "My Ike, he's got a scholarship offen de high school. He's vorking his vay through de medical college now. He'll be a big doctor some day. He vill cure my Leah."

Nance's ambition took fire at the thought of that type-writer. It appealed to her far more than the sewing-machine.

"Say, Ike," she said at her first opportunity, "I wish you'd teach me how to work it."

"What'll you give me?" asked Ike, gravely. He had grown into a tall, thin youth, with the spectacled eyes and stooped shoulders of a student.

"Want me to wash the dishes for your mother?" Nance suggested eagerly. "I could do it nights before I begin sewing."

"Very well," Ike agreed loftily. "We'll begin next Sunday morning at nine o'clock. Mind you are on time!"

Knowledge to Ike was sacred, and the imparting of it almost a religious rite. He frowned down all flippancy on the part of his new pupil, and demanded of her the same diligence and perseverance he exacted of himself. He not only taught her to manipulate the type-writer, but put her through an elementary course of stenography as well.

"Certainly you can learn it," he said sternly at her first sign of discouragement. "I got that far in my second lesson. Haven't you got any brains?"

Nance by this time was not at all sure she had, but she was not going to let Ike know it. Stung by his smug superiority, she often sat up far into the night, wrestling with the arbitrary signs until Uncle Jed, seeing her light under the door, would pound on the wall for her to go to bed.

She saw little of Dan Lewis these days. The weather no longer permitted them to meet in Post-Office Square, and conditions even less inviting kept them from trying to see each other in Snawdor's kitchen. Sometimes she would wait at the corner for him to come home, but this had its disadvantages, for there was always a crowd of loafers hanging about Slap Jack's, and now that Nance was too old to stick out her tongue and call names, she found her power of repartee seriously interfered with.

"I ain't coming up here to meet you any more," she declared to Dan on one of these occasions. "I don't see why we can't go to Gorman's Chili Parlor of an evening and set down and talk to each other, right."

"Gorman's ain't a nice place," insisted Dan. "I wish you'd come on up to some of the church meetings with me. I could take you lots of times if you'd go."

But Nance refused persistently to be inveigled into the religious fold. The very names of Epworth League, and prayer meeting made her draw a long face.

"You don't care whether we see each other or not!" she accused Dan, hotly.

"I do," he said earnestly, "but it seems like I never have time for anything. The work at the factory gets heavier all the time. But I'm getting on, Nance; they give me another raise last month."

"Everybody's getting on," cried Nance bitterly, "but me! You and Ike and Birdie! I work just as hard as you all do, and I haven't got a blooming thing to show for it. What I make sewing pants don't pay for what I eat. Sometimes I think I'll have to go back to the finishing room."

"Not if I can help it!" said Dan, emphatically. "There must be decent jobs somewhere for girls. Suppose I take you out to Mrs. Purdy's on Sunday, and see if she knows of anything. She's all the time asking me about you."

The proposition met with little enthusiasm on Nance's part. It was Mrs. Purdy who had got Dan into the church and persuaded him not to go to the theater or learn how to dance. It was Mrs. Purdy who took him home with her to dinner every Sunday after church and absorbed the time that used to be hers. But the need for a job was too pressing for Nance to harbor prejudices. Instead of sewing for the Lavinskis that night, she sewed for herself, trying to achieve a costume from the old finery bequeathed her by Birdie Smelts.

You would scarcely have recognized Dan that next Sunday in his best suit, with his hair plastered down, and a very red tie encircling a very high collar. To be sure Dan's best was over a year old, and the brown-striped shirt-front was not what it seemed, but his skin was clean and clear, and there was a look in his earnest eyes that bespoke an untroubled conscience.

Mrs. Purdy received them in her cozy fire-lit sitting-room and made Nance sit beside her on the sofa, while she held her hand and looked with mild surprise at her flaring hat and cheap lace collar.

"Dan didn't tell me," she said, "how big you had grown or—or how pretty."

Nance blushed and smiled and glanced consciously at Dan. She had felt dubious about her costume, but now that she was reassured, she began to imitate Birdie's tone and manner as she explained to Mrs. Purdy the object of her visit.

"Deary me!" said Mrs. Purdy, "Dan's quite right. We can't allow a nice little girl like you to work in a glass factory! We must find some nice genteel place for you. Let me see."

In order to see Mrs. Purdy shut her eyes, and the next moment she opened them and announced that she had the very thing.

"It's Cousin Lucretia Bobinet!" she beamed. "She is looking for a companion."

"What's that?" asked Nance.

"Some one to wait on her and read to her and amuse her. She's quite advanced in years and deaf and, I'm afraid, just a little peculiar."

"I'm awful good at taking care of sick people," said Nance complacently.

"Cousin Lucretia isn't ill. She's the most wonderfully preserved woman for her years. But her maid, that she's had for so long, is getting old too. Why, Susan must be seventy. She can't see to read any more, and she makes mistakes over cards. By the way, I wonder if you know how to play card games."

"Sure," said Nance. "Poker? seven-up?"

"Isn't there another game called penuchle?" Mrs. Purdy ventured, evidently treading unfamiliar ground.

"Yes!" cried Nance. "That's Uncle Jed's game. We used to play it heaps before Rosy cut up the queens for paper dolls."

"Now isn't it too wonderful that you should happen to know that particular game?" said Mrs. Purdy, with the gentle amazement of one who sees the finger of Providence in everything. "Not that I approve of playing cards, but Cousin Lucretia was always a bit worldly minded, and playing penuchle seems to be the chief diversion of her declining years. How old are you, my child?"

"I'm seventeen. And I ain't a bit afraid of work, am I, Dan?"

"I am sure you are not," said Mrs. Purdy. "Dan often tells me what a fine girl you are. Only we wish you would come to some of our services. Dan is getting to be one of our star members. So conscientious and regular! We call him our model young man."

"I expect it's time we was going," said Dan, greatly embarrassed. But owing to the fact that he wanted very much to be a gentleman, and didn't quite know how, he stayed on and on, until Nance informed him it was eleven o'clock.

At the door Mrs. Purdy gave final instructions about the new position, adding in an undertone:

"It might be just as well, dearie, for you to wear a plainer dress when you apply for the place, and I believe—in fact I am quite sure—Cousin Lucretia would rather you left off the ear-rings."

"Ain't ear-rings stylish?" asked Nance, feeling that she had been misinformed.

"Not on a little companion," said Mrs. Purdy gently.

Nance's elation over the prospect of a job was slightly dashed by the idea of returning to the wornout childish garb in which she had left the home.

"Say, Dan," she said, as they made their way out of Butternut Lane, "do you think I've changed so much—like Mrs. Purdy said?"

"You always look just the same to me," Dan said, as he helped her on with her coat and adjusted the collar with gentle, painstaking deference.

She sighed. The remark to a person who ardently desired to look different was crushing.

"I think Mrs. Purdy's an awful old fogey!" she said petulantly by way of venting her pique.

Dan looked at her in surprise, and the scowl that rarely came now darkened his face.

"Mrs. Purdy is the best Christian that ever lived," he said shortly.

"Well, she ain't going to be a Christian offen me!" said Nance.

The next morning, in a clean, faded print, and a thin jacket, much too small for her, Nance went forth to find Miss Lucretia Bobinet in Cemetery Street. It was a staid, elderly street, full of staid, elderly houses, and at its far end were visible the tall white shafts which gave it its name. At the number corresponding to that on Nance's card, she rang the bell. The door was opened by a squinting person who held one hand behind her ear and with the other grasped the door knob as if she feared it might be stolen.

"Who do you want to see?" she wheezed.

"Miss Bobinet."

"Who?"

"Miss Bobinet!" said Nance, lifting her voice.

"Stop that hollering at me!" said the old woman. "Who sent you here?"

"Mrs. Purdy."

"What for?"

Nance explained her mission at the top of her voice and was grudgingly admitted into the hall.

"You ain't going to suit her. I can tell you that," said the squint-eyed one mournfully, "but I guess you might as well go in and wait until she wakes up. Mind you don't bump into things."

Nance felt her way into the room indicated and cautiously let herself down into the nearest chair. Sitting facing her was an imposing old lady, with eyes closed and mouth open, making the most alarming noises in her throat. She began with a guttural inhalation that increased in ferocity until it broke in a violent snort, then trailed away in a prolonged and somewhat plaintive whistle. Nance watched her with amazement. It seemed that each recurrent snort must surely send the old wrinkled head, with its elaborately crimped gray wig, rolling away under the stiff horse-hair sofa.

The room was almost dark, but the light that managed to creep in showed a gloomy black mantelpiece, with vases of immortelles, and somber walnut chairs with crocheted tidies that made little white patches here and there in the dusk. Everything smelled of camphor, and from one of the corners came the slow, solemn tick of a clock.

After Nance had recovered from her suspense about Miss Bobinet's head, and had taken sufficient note of the vocal gymnastics to be able to reproduce them later for the amusement of the Snawdors, she began to experience great difficulty in keeping still. First one foot went to sleep, then the other. The minutes stretched to an hour. She had hurried off that morning without her breakfast, leaving everything at sixes and sevens, and she wanted to get back and clean up before Mrs. Snawdor got up. She stirred restlessly, and her chair creaked.

The old lady opened one eye and regarded her suspiciously.

"I am Nance Molloy," ventured the applicant, hopefully. "Mrs. Purdy sent me."

Miss Bobinet gazed at her in stony silence, then slowly closed her eye, and took up her snore exactly where she had left it off. This took place three times before she succeeded in getting her other eye open and becoming aware of Nance's presence.

"Well, well," she asked testily, in a dry cracked voice, "what are you sitting there staring at me for?"

Nance repeated her formula several times before she remembered that Miss Bobinet was deaf; then she got up and shouted it close to the old lady's ear.

"Lida Purdy's a fool," said Miss Bobinet, crossly. "What do I want with a chit of a girl like you?"

"She thought I could wait on you," screamed Nance, "and read to you and play penuchle." The only word that got past the grizzled fringe that bordered Miss Bobinet's shriveled ear was the last one.

"Penuchle?" she repeated. "Can you play penuchle?"

Nance nodded.

"Get the table," ordered the old lady, peremptorily.

Nance tried to explain that she had not come to stay, that she would go home, and get her things and return in the afternoon, but Miss Bobinet would brook no delay. Without inviting Nance to remove her hat and jacket, she ordered her to lift the shade, sit down, and deal the cards.

They were still playing when the squinting person hobbled in with a luncheon tray, and Miss Bobinet promptly transferred her attention from royal marriages to oyster stew.

"Have her come back at three," she directed Susan; then seeing Nance's eyes rest on the well filled tray, she added impatiently, "Didn't I tell you to stop staring? Any one would think you were watching the animals feed in the zoo."

Nance fled abashed. The sight of the steaming soup, the tempting bird, and dainty salad had made her forget her manners.

"I reckon I'm engaged," she said to Mrs. Snawdor, when she reached home and had cut herself a slice of dry bread to eat with the warmed-over coffee. "She never said what the pay was to be, but she said to come back."

"What does she look like?" asked Mrs. Snawdor, curiously.

"A horse," said Nance. "And she's deaf as anything. If I stay with her, she'll have to get her an ear-trumpet or a new wig before the month's out. I swallow a curl every time I speak to her."

"Well," said Mrs. Snawdor, "companions ain't in my line, but I got sense enough to know that when a woman's so mean she's got to pay somebody to keep her company, the job ain't no cinch."

CHAPTER XVI
MISS BOBINET'S

Nance's new duties, compared with those at the bottle factory, and the sweat-shop seemed, at first, mere child's play. She arrived at eight o'clock, helped Susan in the basement kitchen, until Miss Bobinet awoke, then went aloft to officiate at the elaborate process of that lady's toilet. For twenty years Susan had been chief priestess at this ceremony, but her increasing deafness infuriated her mistress to such an extent that Nance was initiated into the mysteries. The temperature of the bath, the choice of underclothing, the method of procedure were matters of the utmost significance, and the slightest mistake on the part of the assistant brought about a scene. Miss Bobinet would shriek at Susan, and Susan would shriek back; then both would indulge in scathing criticism of the other in an undertone to Nance.

The final rite was the most critical of all. Miss Bobinet would sit before her dresser with a towel about her neck, and take a long breath, holding it in her puffed-out cheeks, while rice powder was dusted over the corrugated surface of her face. She held the theory that this opened the pores of the skin and allowed them to absorb the powder. The sight of the old lady puffed up like a balloon was always too much for Nance, and when she laughed, Miss Bobinet was obliged to let her breath go in a sharp reprimand, and the performance had to start all over again.

"You laugh too much anyhow," she complained irritably.

When the toilet and breakfast were over, there followed two whole hours of pinochle. Nance came to regard the queen of spades and the jack of diamonds with personal animosity. Whatever possible interest she might have taken was destroyed by the fact that Miss Bobinet insisted upon winning two out of every three games. It soon became evident that while she would not cheat on her own behalf, she expected her opponent to cheat for her. So Nance dutifully slipped her trump cards back in the deck and forgot to declare while she idly watched the flash of diamonds on the wrinkled yellow hands, and longed for the clock to strike the next hour.

At lunch she sat in the kitchen opposite Susan and listened to a recital of that melancholy person's woes. Susan and her mistress, being mutually dependent, had endured each other's exclusive society for close upon twenty years. The result was that each found the other the most stimulating of all subjects of conversation. When Nance was not listening to tirades against Susan up-stairs, she was listening to bitter complaints against Miss Bobinet down-stairs.

In the afternoon she was expected to read at the top of her voice from "The Church Guide," until Miss Bobinet got sleepy; then it was her duty to sit motionless in the stuffy, camphor-laden room, listening to an endless succession of vocal gymnastics until what time the old lady saw fit to wake up.

If Nance had been a provident young person, she might have improved those idle hours during that interminable winter by continuing her study of stenography. But, instead, she crouched on the floor by the window, holding her active young body motionless, while her thoughts like distracted imprisoned things flew round their solid walls of facts, frantically seeking some loophole of escape. Day after day she crouched there, peeping out under the lowered shade with hungry eyes. The dreary street below offered no diversion; sometimes a funeral procession dragged its way past, but for the most part there was nothing to see save an occasional delivery wagon or a staid pedestrian.

She was at that critical time of transition between the romance of childhood, when she had become vaguely aware of the desire of the spirit, and the romance of youth, when she was to know to the full the desires of the flesh. It was a period of sudden, intense moods, followed by spells of languor. Something new and strange and incommunicable was fermenting within her, and nothing was being done to direct those mysterious forces. She was affectionate, with no outlet for her affection; romantic, with nothing for romance to feed upon.

The one resource lay in the bookcase that rose above the old-fashioned secretary in Miss Bobinet's front hall. She had discovered it on the day of her arrival and, choosing a volume at random, had become so engrossed in the doings of one of Ouida's heroes, that she had failed to hear Miss Bobinet's call. From that time on she was forbidden to take any books away from the bookcase, an order which she got around by standing beside it and eagerly devouring bits at a time.

The monotony of the days she might have endured if there had been any relief at the close of them. But when she returned home there was always endless work to be done. Her four years' absence at Forest Home had separated her from the young people she had known, and she had had no time to make new friends. The young bar-keeper at Slap Jack's, who always watched for her to pass in the morning, the good-looking delivery boy who sometimes brought parcels to Cemetery Street, the various youths with whom she carried on casual flirtations on her way to and from work, were her nearest approach to friends.

Dan, to be sure, still came for her every Saturday afternoon, but Cemetery Street was across the city from Clarke's, and their time together was short. Nance lived for these brief interviews, and then came away from them more restless and dissatisfied than before. Dan didn't look or talk or act like the heroes in the novels she was reading. He never "rained fervent kisses on her pale brow," or told her that she was "the day-star of his secret dreams." Instead he talked of eight-hour laws, and minimum wage, and his numerous church activities. He was sleeping at Mrs. Purdy's now, looking after the place while she was away with her brother, and Nance was jealous of his new interests and new opportunities.

As the long weeks stretched into long months, her restlessness grew into rebellion. So this was the kind of job, she told herself bitterly, that nice girls were supposed to hold. This was what Miss Stanley and Mrs. Purdy and Mr. Demry approved. But they were old. They had forgotten. Dan Lewis wasn't old. Why couldn't he understand? What right had he to insist upon her sticking it out when he knew how lonesome and unhappy she was? Dan didn't care, that was the trouble; he thought more of his old church and the factory than he thought of her.

She remembered, with sudden understanding, what red-haired Gert had said in the finishing room; some people weren't content with a good job; they had to have a good time with it. She told herself that she was one of these; she wanted to be good and do what was expected of her; she wanted fervently to please Dan Lewis, but she couldn't go on like this, she couldn't, she couldn't!

And yet she did. With a certain dogged commonsense, she stayed at her post, suppressing herself in a thousand ways, stifling her laughter, smothering the song on her lips, trying to make her prancing feet keep pace with the feeble steps of age. She lived through each day on the meager hope that something would happen at the end of it, that elusive "something" that always waits around the corner for youth, with adventure in one hand and happiness in the other and limitless promise in its shining eyes.

Almost a year crawled by before her hope was realized. Then one Tuesday morning as she was coming to work, she spied a bill poster announcing the appearance of the "Rag-Time Follies." Rows upon rows of saucy girls in crimson tights and gauzy wings smiled down upon her, smiled and seemed to beckon.

Since Birdie's departure from the alley, eighteen months ago, Nance had heard no word of her. Long ago she had given up the hope of escape in that direction. But the knowledge that she was in the city and the possibility of seeing her, wakened all manner of vague hopes and exciting possibilities.

Whatever happened Nance must see the play! She must be on hand to-morrow night when the curtain went up; perhaps she could wait outside for Birdie, and speak to her after the performance!

If only Dan would take her, and they could sit together and share the fun! But the very thought of Dan in connection with those frisky girls made her smile. No; if she went, she would have to go alone.

The all-important question now was how to get the ticket. Miss Bobinet could never be induced to advance a penny on the week's wages, and Susan, while ready to accept financial favors, was adamant when it came to extending them.

By six o'clock Nance had exhausted every resource but one. On her way home she visited a small shop which was all too familiar to the residents of Calvary Alley. When she emerged, the beloved locket, which usually dangled on the velvet ribbon around her neck, was no longer there, but tied in the corner of her handkerchief was a much desired silver coin.

In high spirits she rushed home only to be confronted on the threshold by a serious domestic complication. Mrs. Snawdor, with her hat on, was standing by the bed in the dark inside room that used to be Nance's, futilely applying a mustard plaster to whatever portion of Fidy's anatomy happened to be exposed.

"How long has she been like this?" cried Nance, flinging her jacket off and putting the tea kettle on the stove.

"Lord knows," said Mrs. Snawdor in a tone that implied a conspiracy on the part of poor Fidy and her Maker to interfere with her plans. "When I come in ten minutes ago, she was tryin' to eat the sheet."

"Didn't you give her the medicine the doctor left last time?"

"There ain't a drop left. Mr. Snawdor took every bit of it."

"Where's the bottle? We must get it filled."

"What's the use? It ain't no good. I was handlin' Fidy's fits before that there young dispensary doctor was out of knee pants. Besides I ain't got fifty cents in the house."

Nance stood for a moment irresolute. She looked at the writhing figure on the bed; then she snatched up her hat and jacket.

"Quick! Where's the bottle?" she cried. "I got the money."

But after the medicine had been bought, and Fidy had grown quiet under its influence, Nance went across the hall to her own cold, barren room and flung herself across her narrow bed. The last chance of seeing the play had vanished. The only light of hope that had shone on her horizon for months had gone out.

When she got up, cold and miserable, and lighted the gas, she saw on the floor, where it had evidently been slipped under the door, a mysterious pink envelope. Tearing it open, she found, written in a large, loose scrawl:

"Dear Nance. We have just struck town. Reckon you thought I was a quitter, but I ain't. You be at the Gaiety to-morrow morning at nine A.M. Maybe I can land you something. Don't say a word to anybody about it, and make yourself look as pretty as you can, and don't be late. Don't tell my folks I'm here. I got a room down-town.

"Bye bye,
"B.S."

Nance's breath caught in her throat. The bubble was so radiant, so fragile, so unbelievable, that she was afraid to stir for fear of breaking it. She waited until she heard Mrs. Snawdor's heavy feet descending the stairs, and then she crept across the hall and sat on the side of Fidy's bed, waiting to give her the next dose of medicine. Her eyes were fixed on the bare lathes over the headboard where she had once knocked the plaster off tacking up a tomato-can label. But she did not see the hole or the wall. Calvary Alley and Cemetery Street had ceased to exist for her. She was already transported to a region of warmth and gaiety and song. All that was ugly and old and sordid lay behind her, and she told herself, with a little sob of joy, that at last the beautiful something for which she had waited so long was about to happen.

CHAPTER XVII
BEHIND THE TWINKLING LIGHTS

The gaiety, with its flamboyant entrance, round which the lights flared enticingly at night, had always seemed to Nance an earthly paradise into which the financially blessed alone were privileged to enter. At the "Star" there were acrobats and funny Jews with big noses and Irishmen who were always falling down; but the Gaiety was different. Twice Nance had passed that fiery portal, and she knew that once inside, you drifted into states of beatitude, which eternity itself was too short to enjoy. The world ceased to exist for you, until a curtain, as relentless as fate, descended, and you reached blindly for your hat and stumbled down from the gallery to the balcony, and from the balcony to the lobby, and thence out into the garish world, dazed, bewildered, unreconciled to reality, and not knowing which way to turn to go home.

But to-day as she passed the main entrance and made her way through a side-passage to the stage-door, she tingled with a keener thrill than she had ever felt before.

"Is Miss Smelts here?" she asked a man who was going in as she did.

"Smelts?" he repeated. "What does she do?"

"She dances."

He shook his head.

"Nobody here by that name," he said, and hurried on.

Nance stood aside and waited, with a terrible sinking of the heart. She waited a half hour, then an hour, while people came and went. Just as she was about to give up in despair, she saw a tall, handsome girl hurry up the steps and come toward her. She had to look twice before she could make sure that the imposing figure was Birdie.

"Hello, kid," was Birdie's casual greeting. "I forgot all about you. Just as cute looking as ever, eh! Where did you get that hat?"

"Ten-cent store," said Nance, triumphantly.

"Can you beat that?" said Birdie. "You always did have a style about you. But your hair's fixed wrong. Come on down to the dressing-room while I change. I'll do it over before you see Reeser."

Nance followed her across a barn of a place where men in shirt-sleeves were dragging scenes this way and that.

"Mind the steps; they are awful!" warned Birdie, as they descended into a gas-lit region partitioned off into long, low dressing-rooms.

"Here's where I hang out. Sit down and let me dude you up a bit. You always did wear your hair too plain. I'll fix it so's it will make little Peroxide Pierson green with envy."

Nance sat before the mirror and watched Birdie's white fingers roll and twist her shining hair into the elaborate style approved at the moment.

"Gee! it looks like a horse-collar!" she said, laughing at her reflection. "What you going to do to me next?"

"Well, I haven't got much to do on," said Birdie, "but you just wait till I get you over to my room! I could fit you out perfect if you were just a couple of sizes bigger."

She was putting on a pair of bloomers herself as she spoke, and slipping her feet into her dancing slippers, and Nance watched every movement with admiring eyes.

"Come on now," Birdie said hurriedly. "We got to catch Reeser before rehearsal. He's the main guy in this company. What Reeser says goes."

At the head of the steps they encountered a gaunt, raw-boned man, with an angular, expressive face, and an apple in his long neck that would have embarrassed Adam himself.

"Well! Well!" he shouted at them, impatiently, "come on or else go back! Don't stand there in the way."

"Mr. Reeser, please, just a minute," called Birdie, "It's a new girl wants to get in the chorus."

The stage-manager paused and looked her over with a critical eye.

"Can she sing?"

"No," said Nance, "but I can dance. Want to see me?"

"Well, I think I can live a few minutes without it," said Reeser dryly. "Ever been on before?"

"No; but everybody's got to start some time." Then she added with a smile, "I wish you'd give me a chance."

"She's a awful cute little dancer," Birdie recommended. "She knows all the steps in the Red-Bird chorus. I taught her when I was here before. If you'd say a word to Mr. Pulatki he might try her out at rehearsal this morning."

Nance held her breath while Reeser's quizzical eyes continued to study her.

"All right!" he said suddenly. "She's pretty young, but we'll see what she can do. Now clear the way. Lower that drop a little, boys. Hurry up with the second set."

The girls scurried away to the wings where they found a narrow space in which Nance was put through the half-forgotten steps.

"It's all in the team work," Birdie explained. "You do exactly what I do, and don't let old Spagetti rattle you. He goes crazy at every rehearsal. Keep time and grin. That's all there is to it"

"I can do it!" cried Nance radiantly. "It's easy as breathing!"

But it proved more difficult than she thought, when in a pair of property bloomers she found herself one of a party of girls advancing, retreating, and wheeling at the arbitrary command of an excitable little man in his shirt-sleeves, who hammered out the time on a rattling piano.

Pulatki was a nervous Italian with long black hair and a drooping black mustache, both of which suffered harsh treatment in moments of dramatic frenzy. His business in life was to make forty lively, mischievous girls move and sing as one. The sin of sins to him, in a chorus girl, was individuality.

"You! new girl!" he screamed the moment he spied Nance, "you are out of ze line. Hold your shoulders stiff, so! Ah, *Dio!* Can you not move wiz ze rest?"

The girls started a stately number, diagonal from down-stage left toward upper center.

"Hold ze pose!" shouted the director. Then he scrambled up on the stage and seized Nance roughly by the arm. "You are too quick!" he shouted. "You are too restless. We do not want that you do a solo! Can you not keep your person still?"

And to Nance's untold chagrin she found that she could not. The moment the music started, it seemed to get into her tripping feet, her swinging arms, her nodding head; and every extra step and unnecessary gesture that she made evoked a storm from the director.

Just when his irritation was at his height, Reeser joined him from the wings.

"Here's a howdy-do!" he exclaimed. "Flossy Pierson's sprained her ankle."

"Ze leetle bear?" shrieked Pulatki; then he clutched his hair in both hands and raved maledictions on the absent Flossy.

"See here," said Reeser, "this is no time for fireworks. Who in the devil is to take her place?"

"Zere is none," wailed Pulatki. "She make her own part. I cannot teach it."

"It's not the part that bothers me," said Reeser. "It's the costume. We've got to take whoever will fit it. Who's the smallest girl in the chorus?"

The eyes of the two men swept the double column of girls until they rested on the one head that, despite its high coiffure, failed to achieve the average height.

"Come here!" called Reeser to Nance.

"But, no!" protested the director, throwing up his hands. "She is impossible. A cork on ze water! A leaf in ze wind! I cannot teach her. I vill not try!"

"It's too late to get anybody else for to-night," said Reeser, impatiently. "Let her walk through the part, and we'll see what can be done in the morning." Then seeing Nance's indignant eyes on the director, he added with a comical twist of his big mouth, "Want to be a bear?"

"Sure!" said Nance, with spirit, "if the Dago can't teach me to dance, maybe he can teach me to growl."

The joke was lost upon the director, but it put Reeser into such a good humor that he sent her down to the dressing-room to try on the costume. Ten minutes later, a little bear, awkward but ecstatic, scrambled madly up the steps, and an excited voice called out:

"Look, Mr. Reeser, it fits! it fits!"

For the rest of the morning Nance practised her part, getting used to the clumsy suit of fur, learning to adjust her mask so that she could see through the little, round, animal eyes, and keeping the other girls in a titter of amusement over her surreptitious imitation of the irascible Pulatki.

When the rehearsal was over there was much good-natured hustling and raillery as the girls changed into their street costumes. At Birdie's invitation Nance went with her to the rooming-house around the corner, where you had to ring a bell to get in, a convention which in itself spelt elegance, and up one flight, two flights, three flights of carpeted steps to a front-hall bedroom on the fourth floor.

"Gee, it's a mess!" said Birdie, tossing some beribboned lingerie from a chair into an open trunk. "There's a bag of rolls around here some place. We can make some tea over the gas."

Nance darted from one object to another with excited cries of admiration. Everything was sweet and wonderful and perfectly grand! Suddenly she came to a halt before the dresser, in the center of which stood a large, framed photograph.

"That's my High Particular," said Birdie, with an uneasy laugh, "recognize him?"

"It's Mac Clarke!" exclaimed Nance, incredulously, "how on earth did you ever get his picture?"

"He give it to me. How do you reckon? I hadn't laid eyes on him for a couple of years 'til I ran across him in New York about a month ago."

"Where'd you see him?"

"At the theater. He come in with a bunch of other college fellows and recognized me straight off. He stayed in New York two or three days, and maybe we didn't have a peach of a time! Only he got fired from college for it when he went back."

"Where's he now?"

"Here in town. Liable to blow in any minute. If he does, you don't want to let on you ever saw him before. He won't remember you if you don't remind him. He never thinks of anybody twice."

Nance, poring over every detail of the photograph, held her own counsel. She was thinking of the night she had stood in the drug-store door, and he had kept the motor waiting while he smiled at her over his shoulder. That was a smile that remembered!

"You want to be careful what you say to anybody," Birdie continued, "there ain't any use airing it around where you live, or what you been doing. There ain't a girl in the chorus knows my real name, or where I come from."

The allusion to home stirred Nance's conscience, and reminded her that over there beyond the cathedral spire, dimly visible from the window, lay a certain little alley which still had claims upon her.

"I ain't said a thing to 'em at home about this," she said. "Suppose they don't let me do it?"

"Let nothing!" said Birdie. "Write a note to Mrs. Snawdor, and tell her you are spending the night down-town with me. You'll know by morning whether Reeser is going to take you on or not. If he does, you just want to announce the fact that you are going, and go."

Nance looked at her with kindling eyes. This high-handed method appealed to her. After all wasn't she past eighteen? Birdie hadn't been that old when she struck out for herself.

"What about Miss Bobinet?" she asked ruefully.

"The wiggy old party up in Cemetery Street? Let her go hang. You've swallowed her frizzes long enough."

Nance laughed and gave the older girl's arm a rapturous squeeze. "And you think maybe Mr. Reeser'll take me on?" she asked for the sixteenth time.

"Well, Flossie Pierson has been shipped home, and they've got to put somebody in her place. It's no cinch to pick up a girl on the road, just the right size, who can dance even as good as you can. If Reeser engages you, it's fifteen per for the rest of the season, and a good chance for next."

"All right, here goes!" cried Nance, recklessly, seizing paper and pen.

When the hard rolls and strong tea which composed their lunch had been disposed of, Nance curled herself luxuriously on the foot of the bed and munched chocolate creams, while Birdie, in a soiled pink kimono that displayed her round white arms and shapely throat, lay stretched beside her. They found a great deal to talk about, and still more to laugh about. Nance loved to laugh; all she wanted was an excuse, and everything was an excuse to-day; Birdie's tales of stage-door Johnnies, the recent ire of old Spagetti, her own imitation of Miss Bobinet and the ossified Susan. Nance loved the cozy intimacy of the little room; even the heavy odor of perfumes and cosmetics was strange and fascinating; she thought Birdie was the prettiest girl she had ever seen. A thrilling vista of days like this, spent with her in strange and wonderful cities, opened before her.

"I'll rig you up in some of my clothes, until you get your first pay," Birdie offered, "then we can fit you out right and proper. You got the making of an awful pretty girl in you."

Nance shrieked her derision. Her own charms, compared with Birdie's generous ones, seemed absurdly meager, as she watched the older girl blow rings from the cigarette which she held daintily between her first and second finger.

Nance had been initiated into smoking and chewing tobacco before she was ten, but neither appealed to her. Watching Birdie smoke, she had a sudden desire to try it again.

"Give us a puff, Birdie," she said.

Birdie tossed the box over and looked at her wrist-watch.

"We ought to be fixing something for you to wear to-night," she said. "Like as not Mac and Monte 'll turn up and ask us to go somewhere for supper."

"Who is Monte?" asked Nance with breathless interest.

"He's a fat-headed swell Mac runs with. Spends dollars like nickels. No rarebit and beer for him; it's champagne and caviar every time. You cotton to him, Nance; he'll give you anything you want."

"I don't want him to give me anything," said Nance stoutly. "Time I'm earning fifteen dollars a week, I'll be making presents myself."

Birdie lifted her eyebrows and sighed.

"You funny kid!" she said, "you got a heap to learn."

During the early part of the afternoon the girls shortened one of Birdie's dresses and tacked in its folds to fit Nance's slender figure. Birdie worked in fits and starts; she listened every time anything stopped in the street below, and made many trips to the window. By and by her easy good humor gave place to irritability. At five o'clock she put on her hat, announcing that she had to go over to the drug store to do some telephoning.

"Lock the door," she counseled, "and if anybody knocks while I'm gone, don't answer."

Nance, left alone, sewed on for a while in a flutter of happy thoughts; then she got up and turned her chair so she would not have to crane her neck to see the photograph on the dresser.

"The making of an awful pretty girl!" she whispered; then she got up and went over to the mirror. Pulling out the hairpins that held the elaborate puffs in place, she let her shining mass of hair about her shoulders and studied her face intently. Her mouth, she decided, was too big, her eyes too far apart, her neck too thin. Then she made a face at herself and laughed:

"Who cares?" she said.

By and by it got too dark to sew; the match box refused to be found, and she decided it was time to stop anyhow. She opened the window and, gaily humming the music of the Little Bear dance, leaned across the sill, while the cool evening air fanned her hot cheeks.

Far away in the west, over the housetops, she could see the stately spire of the cathedral, a brown silhouette against a pale, lemon sky. Down below, through the dull, yellow dusk, faint lights were already defining the crisscross of streets. The whispers of the waking city came up to her, eager, expectant, like the subdued murmur of a vast audience just before the curtain ascends. Then suddenly, written on the twilight in letters of fire, came the familiar words, "You get what you pay for."

Nance's fingers ceased to drum on the window-sill. It was the big sign facing Post-Office Square, old Post-Office Square, with its litter of papers, its battered weather kiosk, and the old green bench where she and Dan had sat so many evenings on their way home from the factory. Dan! A wave of remorse swept over her. She had forgotten him as completely as if he had never existed. And now that she remembered what was she to do? Go to him and make a clean breast of it? And run the risk of having him invoke the aid of Mrs. Purdy and possibly of Miss Stanley? Not that she was afraid of their stopping her. She repeated to herself the words of defiance with which she would meet their objections and the scorn which she would fling at their "nice girl jobs." No; it was Dan himself she was afraid of. Her imagination quailed before his strong, silent face, and his deep, hurt eyes. She had always taken Dan's part in everything, and something told her she would take it now, even against herself.

The only safe course was to keep away from him, until the great step was taken, and then write him a nice long letter. The nicest she had ever written to anybody. Dear old Dan—dear, dear old Dan.

A long, low whistle from the sidewalk opposite made her start, and look down. At first no one was visible; then a match was struck, flared yellow for a second, and went out, and again that low, significant whistle. Nance dropped on her knees beside the window and watched. A man's figure emerged from the gloom and crossed the street. A moment later she heard the ringing of the doorbell. Could Dan have heard of her escapade and come after her? But nobody knew where she was; the note to Mrs. Snawdor still lay on the corner of the dresser.

She heard a step on the stairs, then three light taps on the door. She scrambled to her feet before she remembered Birdie's caution, then stood motionless, listening.

Again the taps and, "I say, Bird!" came in a vibrant whisper from without.

It seemed to Nance that whoever it was must surely hear the noisy beating of her heart. Then she heard the steps move away and she sighed with relief.

Birdie, coming in later, dismissed the matter with gay denial.

"One of your pipe-dreams, Nance! It must have been one of the other boarders, or the wash woman. Stop your mooning over there by the window and get yourself dressed; we got just thirty-five minutes to get down to the theater."

Nance shook off her misgivings and rushed headlong into her adventure. It was no time to dream of Dan and the letter she was going to write him, or to worry about a disturbing whistle in the street, or a mysterious whisper on the other side of the door. Wasn't it enough that she, Nance Molloy, who only yesterday was watching funerals crawl by in Cemetery Street, was about to dance to real music, on a real stage, before a great audience? She had taken her first mad plunge into the seething current of life, and in these first thrilling, absorbing moments she failed to see the danger signals that flashed across the darkness.

CHAPTER XVIII
THE FIRST NIGHT

At a quarter-past eight in the dressing-rooms of the Gaiety, pandemonium reigned. Red birds, fairies, gnomes, will-o'-the-wisps flitted about, begging, borrowing, stealing articles from each other in good-humored confusion. In and out among them darted the little bear, slapping at each passerby with her furry paws, practising steps on her cushioned toes, and rushing back every now and then to Birdie, who stood before a mirror in red tights, with a towel around her neck, putting the final touches on her make-up.

It was hot and stuffy, and the air reeked with grease paint. There was a perpetual chatter with occasional outbursts of laughter, followed by peremptory commands of "Less noise down there!" In the midst of the hub-bub a call-boy gave the signal for the opening number of the chorus; the chatter and giggling ceased, and the bright costumes settled into a definite line as the girls filed up the stairs.

Nance, left alone, sat on a trunk and waited for her turn in a fever of impatience. She caught the opening strains of the orchestra as it swung into the favorite melody of the day; she could hear the thud of dancing feet overhead. She was like a stoker shut up in the hold of the vessel while a lively skirmish is in progress on deck.

As she sat there the wardrobe woman, a matronly-looking, Irish person, came up and ordered her peremptorily to get off the trunk. Nance not only complied, but she offered her assistance in getting it out of the passage.

"May ye have some one as civil as ye are to wait on ye when ye are as old as I am!" said the woman. "It's your first night, eh?"

"Yep. Maybe my last for all I know. They 're trying me out."

"Good luck to ye," said the woman. "Well I mind the night I made me first bow."

"You!"

"No less. I'd a waist on me ye could span wid yer two hands. And legs! well, it ain't fer me to be braggin', but there ain't a girl in the chorus kin stack up alongside what I oncet was! Me an' a lad named Tim Moriarty did a turn called 'The Wearing of the Green,' — 'Ryan and Moriarty' was the team. I kin see the names on the bill-board now! We had 'em laughin' an' cryin' at the same time, 'til their tears run into their open mouths!"

"Wisht I could've seen you," said Nance. "I bet it was great."

The wardrobe woman, unused to such a sympathetic listener, would have lingered indefinitely had not a boy handed Nance a box which absorbed all her attention.

"Miss Birdie La Rue," was inscribed on one side of the card that dangled from it on a silver cord, and on the other was scribbled, "Monte and I will wait for you after the show. Bring another girl. M.D.C."

"And I'm the other girl!" Nance told herself rapturously.

There was a flurry in the wings above and the chorus overflowed down the stairs.

"It's a capacity house," gasped Birdie, "but a regular cold-storage plant. We never got but one round. Spagetti is having spasms."

"What's a round?" demanded Nance, but nobody had time to enlighten her.

It was not until the end of the second act that her name was called, and she went scampering up the stairs as fast as her clumsy suit would permit. The stage was set for a forest scene, with gnarled trees and hanging vines and a transparent drop that threw a midnight blue haze over the landscape.

"Crawl up on the stump there!" ordered Reeser, attending to half a dozen things at once. "Put you four paws together. Head up! Hold the pose until the gnomes go off. When I blow the whistle, get down and dance. I'll get the will-o'-the-wisps on as quick as I can. Clear the stage everybody! Ready for the curtain? Let her go!"

Nance, peering excitedly through the little round holes of her mask, saw the big curtain slowly ascend, revealing only a dazzling row of footlights beyond. Then gradually out of the dusk loomed the vast auditorium with its row after row of dim white faces, reaching back and up, up further than she dared lift her head to see. From down below somewhere sounded the weird tinkle of elfin music, and tiptoeing out from every tree and bush came a green-clad gnome, dancing in stealthy silence in the sleeping forest. Quite unconsciously Nance began to keep time. It was such glorious fun playing at being animals and fairies in the woods at night. Without realizing what she was doing, she dropped into what she used to call in the old sweat-shop days, "dancin' settin' down."

A ripple of amusement passed through the audience, and she looked around to see what the gnomes were up to, but they were going off the stage, and the suppressed titter continued. A soft whistle sounded in the wings, and with a furiously beating heart, she slid down from her high stump and ambled down to the footlights.

All might have gone well, had not a sudden shaft of white light shot toward her from the balcony opposite, making a white spot around the place she was standing. She got out of it only to find that it followed her, and in the bewilderment of the discovery, she lost her head completely. All her carefully practised steps and poses were utterly forgotten; she could think of nothing but that pursuing light, and her mad desire to get out of it.

Then something the director had said at the rehearsal flashed across the confusion. "She makes her own part," he had said of Flossy Pierson, and Nance, with grim determination, decided to do the same. A fat man in the left hand box had laughed out when she discovered the spotlight. She determined to make him laugh again. Simulating the dismay that at first was genuine, she began to play tag with the shaft of light, dodging it, jumping over it, hiding from it behind the stump, leading it a merry chase from corner to corner. The fat man grew hysterical. The audience laughed at him, and then it began to laugh at Nance. She threw herself into the frolic with the same mad abandonment with which she used to dance to the hand-organ in front of Slap Jack's saloon. She cut as many fantastic capers as a frisky kitten playing in the twilight; she leapt and rolled and romped, and the spectators, quick to feel the contagion of something new and young and joyful, woke up for the first time during the evening, and followed her pranks with round after round of applause.

When at last the music ceased, she scampered into the wings and sank gasping and laughing into a chair.

"They want you back!" cried Reeser, excitedly beckoning to her. "Go on again. Take the call."

"The what?" said Nance, bewildered. But before she could find out, she was thrust forward and, not being able to see where she was going, she tripped and fell sprawling upon the very scene of her recent triumph.

In the confusion of the moment she instinctively snatched off her mask, and as she did so the sea of faces merged suddenly into one. In the orchestra below, gazing at her with dropped jaw over his arrested fiddle-bow, was old Mr. Demry, with such a comical look of paralyzed amazement on his face that Nance burst into laughter.

There was something in her glowing, childish face, innocent of make-up, and in her seeming frank enjoyment of the mishap that took the house by storm. The man in the box applauded until his face was purple; gloved hands in the parquet tapped approval; the balcony stormed; the gallery whistled.

She never knew how she got off the stage, or whether the director shouted praise or blame as she darted through the wings. It was not until she reached the dressing-room, and the girls crowded excitedly around her that she knew she had scored a hit.

She came on once more at the end of the last act in the grand ballet, where all the dancers performed intricate manoeuvers under changing lights. Every time the wheeling figures brought her round to the footlights, there was a greeting from the front, and, despite warnings, she could not suppress a responsive wag of the head or a friendly wave of the paw.

"She is so fresh, so fresh!" groaned Pulatki from the wings.

"She's alive," said Reeser. "She'll never make a show girl, and she's got no voice to speak of. But she's got a personality that climbs right over the footlights. I'm going to engage her for the rest of the season."

When the play was over, Nance, struggling into Birdie's complicated finery in the dressing-room below, wondered how she could ever manage to exist until the next performance. Her one consolation was the immediate prospect of seeing Mac Clarke and the mysterious Monte to whom Birdie had said she must be nice. As she pinned on a saucy fur toque in place of her own cheap millinery, she viewed herself critically in the glass. Beside the big show girls about her, she felt ridiculously young and slender and insignificant.

"I believe I'll put on some paint!" she said.

Birdie laughed.

"What for, Silly? Your cheeks are blazing now. You'll have time enough to paint 'em when you've been dancing a couple of years."

They were among the last to leave the dressing-room, and when they reached the stage entrance, Birdie spied two figures.

"There they are!" she whispered to Nance, "the fat one is Monte, the other—"

Nance had an irresistible impulse to run away. Now that the time had come, she didn't want to meet those sophisticated young men in their long coats and high hats. She wouldn't know how to act, what to say. But Birdie had already joined them, and was turning to say airily:

"Shake hands with my friend Miss Millay, Mr. Clarke—and, I say, Monte, what's your other name?"

The older of the young men laughed good-naturedly.

"Monte'll do," he said. "I'm that to half the girls in town."

Mac's bright bold eyes scanned Nance curiously. "Where have I seen you before?" he asked instantly.

"Don't you recognize her?" said Monte. "She's the little bear! I'd know that smile in ten thousand!"

Nance presented him with one on the spot, out of gratitude for the diversion. She was already sharing Birdie's wish that no reference be made to Calvary Alley or the factory. They had no place in this rose-colored world.

Monte and the two girls had descended the steps to the street when the former looked over his shoulder.

"Why doesn't Mac come on?" he asked. "Who is the old party he is arguing with?"

"Oh, Lord! It's old man Demry," exclaimed Birdie in exasperation. "He plays in the orchestra. Full of dope half of the time. Why don't Mac come on and leave him?"

But the old musician was not to be left. He pushed past Mac and, staggering down the steps, laid his hand on Nance's arm.

"You must come home with me, Nancy," he urged unsteadily. "I want to talk to you. Want to tell you something."

"See here!" broke in Mac Clarke, peremptorily, "is this young lady your daughter?"

Mr. Demry put his hand to his dazed head and looked from one to the other in troubled uncertainty.

"No," he said incoherently. "I had a daughter once. But she is much older than this child. She must be nearly forty by now, and to think I haven't seen her face for twenty-two years. I shouldn't even know her if I should see her. I couldn't make shipwreck of her life, you know—shipwreck of one you love best in the world!"

"Oh, come ahead!" called Birdie from below. "He don't know what he's babbling about."

But the old man's wrinkled hand still clung to Nance's arm. "Don't go with them!" he implored. "I know. I've seen. Ten years playing for girls to dance. Stage no place for you, Nancy. Come home with me, child. Come!" He was trembling with earnestness and his voice quavered.

"Let go of her arm, you old fool!" cried Mac, angrily. "It's none of your business where she goes!"

"Nor of yours, either!" Nance flashed back instantly. "You keep your hands off him!"

Then she turned to Mr. Demry and patiently tried to explain that she was spending the night with Birdie Smelts; he remembered Birdie—used to live across the hall from him? She was coming home in the morning. She would explain everything to Mrs. Snawdor. She promised she would.

Mr. Demry, partly reassured, relaxed his grasp.

"Who is this young man, Nancy?" he asked childishly. "Tell me his name."

"It's Mr. Mac Clarke," said Nance, despite Birdie's warning glance.

A swift look of intelligence swept the dazed old face; then terror gathered in his eyes.

"Not—not—Macpherson Clarke?" he stammered; then he sat down in the doorway. "O my God!" he sobbed, dropping his head in his hands.

"He won't go home 'til morning!" hummed Monte, catching Birdie by the arm and skipping down the passage. Nance stood for a moment looking down at the maudlin old figure muttering to himself on the door-step; then she, too, turned and followed the others out into the gay midnight throng.

CHAPTER XIX
PREPARATIONS FOR FLIGHT

What a radically different place the world seems when one doesn't have to begin the day with an alarm clock! There is a hateful authority in its brassy, peremptory summons that puts one on the defensive immediately. To be sure, Nance dreamed she heard it the following day at noon, and sprang up in bed with the terrifying conviction that she would be late at Miss Bobinet's. But when she saw where she was, she gave a sigh of relief, and snuggled down against Birdie's warm shoulder, and tried to realize what had happened to her.

The big theater, the rows of smiling faces, the clapping hands—surely they must have all been a dream? And Mr. Demry? Why had he sat on the steps and cried into a big starchy handkerchief? Oh, yes; she remembered now, but she didn't like to remember, so she hurried on.

There was a café, big and noisy, with little tables, and a woman who stood on a platform, with her dress dragging off one shoulder, and sang a beautiful song, called "I'm A-wearying for You." Mr. Monte didn't think it was pretty; he had teased her for thinking so. But then he had teased her for not liking the raw oysters, and for saying the champagne made her nose go to sleep. They had all teased her and laughed at everything she said. She didn't care; she liked it. They thought she was funny and called her "Cubby." At least Mr. Monte did. Mr. Mac didn't call her anything. He talked most of the time to Birdie, but his eyes were all for *her*, with a smile that sort of remembered and sort of forgot, and—

"Say, Birdie!" She impulsively interrupted her own confused reflections. "Do you think they liked me—honest?"

"Who?" said Birdie, drowsily, "the audience?"

"No. Those fellows last night. I haven't got any looks to brag on, and I'm as green as a string-bean!"

"That's what tickles 'em," said Birdie. "Besides, you can't ever tell what makes a girl take. You got a independent way of walking and talking, and

Monte's crazy 'bout your laugh. But you're a funny kid; you beckon a feller with one hand and slap his face with the other."

"Not unless he gets nervy!" said Nance.

After what euphemistically might be termed a buffet breakfast, prepared over the gas and served on the trunk, Nance departed for Calvary Alley, to proclaim to the family her declaration of independence. She was prepared for a battle royal with all whom it might concern, and was therefore greatly relieved to find only her stepmother at home. That worthy lady surrendered before a gun was fired.

"Ain't that Irish luck fer you?" she exclaimed, almost enviously. "Imagine one of Yager's and Snawdor's childern gittin' on the stage! If Bud Molloy hadn't taken to railroading he could 'a' been a end man in a minstrel show! You got a lot of his takin' ways, Nance. It's a Lord's pity you ain't got his looks!"

"Oh, give me time!" said Nance, whose spirits were soaring.

"I sort 'er thought of joining the ballet onct myself," said Mrs. Snawdor, with a conscious smile. "It was on account of a scene-shifter I was runnin' with along about the time I met your pa."

"You!" exclaimed Nance. "Oh! haven't I got a picture of you dancing. Wait 'til I show you!" And ably assisted by the bolster and the bedspread, she gave a masterly imitation of her stout stepmother that made the original limp with laughter. Then quite as suddenly, Nance collapsed into a chair and grew very serious.

"Say!" she demanded earnestly, "honest to goodness now! Do you think there's any sin in me going on the stage?"

"Sin!" repeated Mrs. Snawdor. "Why, I think it's elegant. I was sayin' so to Mrs. Smelts only yesterday when she was takin' on about Birdie's treatin' her so mean an' never comin' to see her or writin' to her. 'Don't lay it on the stage,' I says to her. 'Lay it on Birdie; she always was a stuck-up piece.'"

Nance pondered the matter, her chin on her palm. Considering the chronic fallibility of Mrs. Snawdor's judgment, she would have been more comfortable if she had met with some opposition.

"Mr. Demry thinks it's wrong," said Nance, taking upon herself the role of counsel for the prosecution. "He took on something fierce when he saw me last night."

"He never knowed what he was doin'," Mrs. Snawdor said. "They tell me he can play in the orchestry, when he's full as a nut."

"And there's Uncle Jed," continued Nance uneasily. "What you reckon he's going to say?"

"You leave that to me," said Mrs. Snawdor, darkly. "Mr. Burks ain't goin' to git a inklin' 'til you've went. There ain't nobody I respect more on the face of the world than I do Jed Burks, but some people is so all-fired good that livin' with 'em is like wearin' new shoes the year round."

"'T ain't as if I was doing anything wicked," said Nance, this time counsel for the defense.

"Course not," agreed Mrs. Snawdor. "How much they goin' to pay you?"

The incredible sum was mentioned, and Mrs. Snawdor's imagination took instant flight.

"You'll be gittin' a autymobile at that rate. Say, if I send Lobelia round to Cemetery Street and git yer last week's pay, can I have it?"

Nance was counting on that small sum to finish payment on her spring suit, but in the face of imminent affluence she could ill afford to be niggardly.

"I'll buy Rosy V. some shoes, an' pay somethin' on the cuckoo clock," planned Mrs. Snawdor, "an' I've half a mind to take another policy on William J. That boy's that venturesome it wouldn't surprise me none to see him git kilt any old time!"

Nance, who had failed to convince herself, either as counsel for the defense or counsel for the prosecution, assumed the prerogative of judge and dismissed the case. If older people had such different opinions about right and wrong, what was the use in her bothering about it? With a shrug of her shoulders she set to work sorting her clothes and packing the ones she needed in a box.

"The gingham dresses go to Fidy," she said with reckless generosity, "the blue skirt to Lobelia, and my Madonna—" Her eyes rested wistfully on her most cherished possession. "I think I'd like Rosy to have that when she grows up."

"All right," agreed Mrs. Snawdor. "There ain't no danger of anybody takin' it away from her."

Nance was kneeling on the floor, tying a cord about her box when she heard steps on the stairs.

"Uncle Jed?" she asked in alarm.

"No. Just Snawdor. He won't ast no questions. He ain't got gumption enough to be curious."

"I hate to go sneaking off like this without telling everybody good-by," said Nance petulantly, "Uncle Jed, and the children, and the Levinskis, and Mr. Demry, and—and—Dan."

"You don't want to take no risks," said Mrs. Snawdor, importantly. "There's a fool society for everything under the sun, an' somebody'll be tryin' to git out a injunction. I don't mind swearin' to whatever age you got to be, but Mr. Burks is so sensitive about them things."

"All right," said Nance, flinging on her hat and coat, "tell 'em how it was when I'm gone. I'll be sending you money before long."

"That's right," whispered Mrs. Snawdor, hanging over the banister as Nance felt her way down the stairs. "You be good to yerself an' see if you can't git me a theayter ticket for to-morrow night. Git two, an' I'll take Mis' Gorman."

Never had Nance tripped so lightly down those dark, narrow stairs— the stairs her feet had helped to wear away in her endless pilgrimages with buckets of coal and water and beer, with finished and unfinished garments, and omnipresent Snawdor babies. She was leaving it all forever, along with the smell of pickled herrings and cabbage and soapsuds. But she was not going to forget the family! Already she was planning munificent gifts from that fabulous sum that was henceforth to be her weekly portion.

At Mr. Demry's closed door she paused; then hastily retracing her steps, she slipped back to her own room and got a potted geranium, bearing one dirty-faced blossom. This she placed on the floor outside his door and then, picking up her big box, she slipped quickly out of the house, through the alley and into the street.

It was late when she got back to Birdie's room, and as she entered, she was startled by the sound of smothered sobbing.

"Birdie!" she cried in sudden alarm, peering into the semi-darkness, "what's the matter? Are you fired?"

Birdie started up hastily from the bed where she had been lying face downward, and dried her eyes.

"No," she said crossly. "Nothing's the matter, only I got the blues."

"The blues!" repeated Nance, incredulously. "What for?"

"Oh, everything. I wish I was dead."

"Birdie Smelts, what's happened to you?" demanded Nance in alarm, sitting by her on the bed and trying to put her arm around her.

"Whoever said anything had happened?" asked the older girl, pushing her away. "Stop asking fool questions and get dressed. We'll be late as it is."

For some time they went about their preparations in silence; then Nance, partly to relieve the tension, and partly because the matter was of vital interest, asked:

"Do you reckon Mr. Mac and Mr. Monte will come again to-night?"

"You can't tell," said Birdie. "What do they care about engagements? We are nothing but dirt to them—just dirt under their old patent-leather pumps!"

This bitterness on Birdie's part was so different from her customary superiority where men were concerned, that Nance gasped.

"If they *do* come," continued Birdie vindictively, "you just watch me teach Mac Clarke a thing or two. He needn't think because his folks happen to be swells, he can treat me any old way. I'll make it hot for him if he don't look out, you see if I don't."

Once back at the Gaiety, Nance forgot all about Birdie and her love affairs. Her own small triumph completely engrossed her. A morning paper had mentioned the fantastic dance of the little bear, and had given her three lines all to herself. Reeser was jubilant, the director was mollified, and even the big comedian whose name blazed in letters of fire outside, actually stopped her in the wings to congratulate her.

"Look here, young person," he said, lifting a warning finger, "you want to be careful how you steal my thunder. You'll be taking my job next!"

Whereupon Nance had the audacity to cross her eyes and strike his most famous pose before she dodged under his arm and scampered down the stairs.

It seemed incredible that the marvelous events of the night before could happen all over again; but they did. She had only to imitate her own performance to send the audience into peals of laughter. It would have been more fun to try new tricks, but on this point Pulatki was adamant.

"I vant zat you do ze same act, no more, no less, see?" he demanded of her, fiercely.

When the encore came, and at Reeser's command she snatched off her bear's head and made her funny, awkward, little bow, she involuntarily glanced down at the orchestra. Mr. Demry was not there, but in the parquet she encountered a pair of importunate eyes that set her pulses bounding. They sought her out in the subsequent chorus and followed her every movement in the grand march that followed.

"Mr. Mac's down there," she whispered excitedly to Birdie as they passed in the first figure, but Birdie tossed her head and flirted persistently with the gallery which was quite unused to such marked attention from the principal show girl.

There was no supper after the play that night, and it was only after much persuasion on Mac's part, reinforced by the belated Monte, that Birdie was induced to come out of her sulks and go for a drive around the park.

"Me for the front seat!" cried Nance hoydenishly, and then, as Mac jumped in beside her and took the wheel, she saw her mistake.

"Oh! I didn't know—" she began, but Mac caught her hand and gave it a grateful squeeze.

"Confess you wanted to sit by me!" he whispered.

"But I didn't!" she protested hotly. "I never was in a automobile before and I just wanted to see how it worked!"

She almost persuaded herself that this was true when they reached the long stretch of parkway, and Mac let her take the wheel. It was only when in the course of instruction Mac's hand lingered too long on hers, or his gay, careless face leaned too close, that she had her misgivings.

"Say! this is great!" she cried rapturously, with her feet braced and her eyes on the long road ahead. "When it don't get the hic-cups, it beats a horse all hollow!"

"What do you know about horses?" teased Mac, giving unnecessary assistance with the wheel.

"Enough to keep my hands off the reins when another fellow's driving!" she said coolly—a remark that moved Mac to boisterous laughter.

When they were on the homeward way and Mac had taken the wheel again, they found little to say to each other. Once he got her to light a cigarette for him, and once or twice she asked a question about the engine. In Calvary Alley one talked or one didn't as the mood suggested, and Nance was unversed in the fine art of making conversation. It disturbed her not a whit that she and the handsome youth beside her had no common topic of interest. It was quite enough for her to sit there beside him, keenly aware that his arm was pressing hers and that every time she glanced up she found him glancing down.

It was a night of snow and moonshine, one of those transitorial nights when winter is going and spring is coming. Nance held her breath as the car plunged headlong into one mass of black shadows after another only to emerge triumphant into the white moonlight. She loved the unexpected revelations of the headlights, which turned the dim road to silver and lit up the dark turf at the wayside. She loved the crystal-clear moon that was sailing off and away across those dim fields of virgin snow. And then she was not thinking any longer, but feeling—feeling beauty and wonder and happiness and always the blissful thrill of that arm pressed against her own.

Not until they were nearing the city did she remember the couple on the back seat.

"Wake up there!" shouted Mac, tossing his cap over his shoulder. "Gone to sleep?"

"I am trying to induce Miss Birdie to go to the carnival ball with me to-morrow night," said Monte. "It's going to be no end of a lark."

"Take me, too, Birdie, please!" burst out Nance with such childish vehemence that they all laughed.

"What's the matter with us all going?" cried Mac, instantly on fire at the suggestion. "Mother's having a dinner to-morrow night, but I can join you after the show. What do you say, Bird?"

But Birdie was still in the sulks, and it was not until Mac had changed places with Monte and brought the full battery of his persuasions to bear upon her that she agreed to the plan.

That night when the girls were tucked comfortably in bed and the lights were out, they discussed ways and means.

"I'm going to see if I can't borrow a couple of red-bird costumes off Mrs. Ryan," said Birdie, whose good humor seemed completely restored. "We'll buy a couple of masks. I don't know what Monte's letting us in for, but I'll try anything once."

"Will there be dancing, Birdie?" asked Nance, her eyes shining in the dark.

"Of course, Silly! Nothing but. Say, what was the matter with you and Mac to-night? You didn't seem to hit it off."

"Oh! we got along pretty good."

"I never heard you talking much. By the way, he's going to take me to-morrow night, and you are going with Monte."

"Any old way suits me!" said Nance, "just so I get there." But she lay awake for a time staring into the dark, thinking things over.

"Does he always call you 'Bird'?" she asked after a long silence.

"Who, Mac? Yes. Why?"

"Oh! Nothing," said Nance.

The next day being Saturday, there were two performances, beside the packing necessary for an early departure on the morrow. But notwithstanding the full day ahead of her, Birdie spent the morning in bed, languidly directing Nance, who emptied the wardrobe and bureau drawers and sorted and folded the soiled finery. Toward noon she got up and, petulantly declaring that the room was suffocating, announced that she was going out to do some shopping.

"I'll come, too," said Nance, to whom the purchasing of wearing apparel was a new and exciting experience.

"No; you finish up here," said Birdie. "I'll be back soon."

Nance went to the window and watched for her to come out in the street below. She was beginning to be worried about Birdie. What made her so restless and discontented? Why wouldn't she go to see her mother? Why was she so cross with Mac Clarke when he was with her and so miserable when he was away? While she pondered it over, she saw Birdie cross the street and stand irresolute for a moment, before she turned her back on the shopping district and hastened off to the east where the tall pipes of the factories stood like exclamation points along the sky-line.

Already the noon whistles were blowing, and she recognized, above the rest, the shrill voice of Clarke's Bottle Factory. How she used to listen for that whistle, especially on Saturdays. Why, *this* was Saturday! In the exciting rush of events she had forgotten completely that Dan would be waiting for her at five o'clock at the foot of Cemetery Street. Never once in the months she had been at Miss Bobinet's had he failed to be there on Saturday afternoon. If only she could send him some word, make some excuse! But it was not easy to deceive Dan, and she knew he would never rest until he got at the truth of the matter. No; she had better take Mrs. Snawdor's advice and run no risks. And yet that thought of Dan waiting patiently at the corner tormented her as she finished the packing.

When the time arrived to report at the theater, Birdie had not returned, so Nance rushed off alone at the last minute. It was not until the first chorus was about to be called that the principal show girl, flushed and tired, flung herself into the dressing-room and made a lightning change in time to take her place at the head of the line.

There was a rehearsal between the afternoon and evening performances, and the girls had little time for confidences.

"Don't ask me any questions!" said Birdie crossly, as she sat before her dressing-table, wearily washing off the make-up of the afternoon in order to put on the make-up of the evening. "I'm so dog tired I'd lots rather be going to bed than to that carnival thing!"

"Don't you back out!" warned Nance, to whom it was ridiculous that any one should be tired under such exhilarating circumstances.

"Oh, I'll go," said Birdie, "if it's just for the sake of getting something decent to eat. I'm sick of dancing on crackers and ice-water."

That night Nance, for the first time, was reconciled to the final curtain. The weather was threatening and the audience was small, but that was not what took the keen edge off the performance. It was the absence in the parquet of a certain pair of pursuing eyes that made all the difference. Moreover, the prospect of the carnival ball made even the footlights pale by comparison.

The wardrobe woman, after much coaxing and bribing, had been induced to lend the girls two of the property costumes, and Nance, with the help of several giggling assistants, was being initiated into the mysteries of the red-bird costume. When she had donned the crimson tights, and high-heeled crimson boots, and the short-spangled slip with its black gauze wings, she gave a half-abashed glance at herself in the long mirror.

"I can't do it, Birdie!" she cried, "I feel like a fool. You be a red bird, and let me be a bear!"

"Don't we all do it every night?" asked Birdie. "When we've got on our masks, nobody 'll know us. We'll just be a couple of 'Rag-Time Follies' taking a night off."

"Don't she look cute with her cap on?" cried one of the girls. "I'd give my head to be going!"

Nance put on a borrowed rain-coat which was to serve as evening wrap as well and, with a kiss all around and many parting gibes, ran up the steps in Birdie's wake.

The court outside the stage entrance was a bobbing mass of umbrellas. Groups of girls, pulling their wraps on as they came, tripped noisily down the steps, greeting waiting cavaliers, or hurrying off alone in various directions.

"That's Mac's horn," said Birdie, "a long toot and two short ones. I'd know it in Halifax!"

At the curbing the usual altercation arose between Mac and Birdie as to how they should sit. The latter refused to sit on the front seat for fear of getting wet, and Mac refused to let Monte drive.

"Oh, I don't mind getting wet!" cried Nance with a fine show of indifference. "That's what a rain-coat's for."

When Mac had dexterously backed his machine out of its close quarters, and was threading his way with reckless skill through the crowded streets, he said softly, without turning his head:

"I think I rather like you, Nance Molloy!"

CHAPTER XX
WILD OATS

The tenth annual carnival ball, under the auspices of a too-well-known political organization, was at its midnight worst. It was one of those conglomerate gatherings, made up of the loose ends of the city—ward politicians, girls from the department stores, Bohemians with an unsated thirst for diversion, reporters, ostensibly looking for copy, women just over the line of respectability, sometimes on one side, sometimes on the other, and the inevitable sprinkling of well-born youths who regard such occasions as golden opportunities for seeing that mysterious phantom termed "life."

It was all cheap and incredibly tawdry, from the festoons of paper roses on the walls to the flash of paste jewels in make-believe crowns. The big hall, with its stage flanked by gilded boxes, was crowded with a shifting throng of maskers in costumes of flaunting discord. Above the noisy laughter and popping of corks, rose the blaring strains of a brass band. Through the odor of flowers came the strong scent of musk, which, in turn, was routed by the fumes of beer and tobacco which were already making the air heavy.

On the edge of all this stood Nance Molloy, in that magic hour of her girlhood when the bud was ready to burst into the full-blown blossom. Her slender figure on tiptoe with excitement, her eyes star-like behind her mask, she stood poised, waiting with all her unslaked thirst for pleasure, to make her plunge into the gay, dancing throng. She no longer cared if her skirts were short, and her arms and neck were bare. She no longer thought of how she looked or how she acted. There was no Pulatki in the wings to call her down for extra flourishes; there was no old white face in the orchestra to disturb her conscience. Her chance for a good time had come at last, and she was rushing to meet it with arms outstretched.

"They are getting ready for the grand march!" cried Monte, who, with Mac, represented the "two *Dromios*." "We separate at the end of the hall, and when the columns line up again, you dance with your vis-à-vis."

"My who-tee-who?" asked Nance.

"Vis-à-vis—fellow opposite. Come ahead!"

Down the long hall swung the gay procession, while the floor vibrated to the rhythm of the prancing feet. The columns marched and countermarched and fell into two long lines facing each other. The leader of the orchestra blew a shrill whistle, and Nance, marking time expectantly, saw one of the *Dromios* slip out of his place and into the one facing her. The next moment the columns flowed together, and she found herself in his arms, swinging in and out of the gay whirling throng with every nerve tingling response to the summoning music.

Suddenly a tender pressure made her glance up sharply at the white mask of her companion.

"Why—why, I thought it was Mr. Monte," she laughed.

"Disappointed?" asked Mac.

"N-no."

"Then why are you stopping?"

Nance could not tell him that in her world a "High Particular" was not to be trifled with. In her vigil of the night before she had made firm resolve to do the square thing by Birdie Smelts.

"Where are the others?" she asked in sudden confusion.

"In the supper room probably. Aren't you going to finish this with me?"

"Not me. I'm going to dance with Mr. Monte."

"Has he asked you?"

"No; I'm going to ask him." And she darted away, leaving Mac to follow at his leisure.

After supper propriety, which up to now had held slack rein on the carnival spirit, turned her loose. Masks were flung aside, hundreds of toy balloons were set afloat and tossed from hand to hand, confetti was showered from the balcony, boisterous song and laughter mingled with the music. The floor resembled some gigantic kaleidoscope, one gay pattern following another in rapid succession. And in every group the most vivid note was struck by a flashing red bird. Even had word not gone abroad that the girls in crimson and black were from the "Rag Time Follies", Birdie's conspicuous charms would have created instant comment and a host of admirers.

Nance, with characteristic independence, soon swung out of Birdie's orbit and made friends for herself. For her it was a night of delirium, and her pulses hammered in rhythm to the throbbing music. In one day life had caught her up out of an abyss of gloom and swung her to a dizzy pinnacle of delight, where she poised in exquisite ecstasy, fearing that the next turn of the wheel might carry her down again. Laughter had softened her lips and hung mischievous lights in her eyes; happiness had set her nerves tingling and set roses blooming in cheeks and lips. The smoldering fires of self-expression, smothered so long, burst into riotous flame. With utter abandonment she flung herself into the merriment of the moment, romping through the dances with any one who asked her, slapping the face of an elderly knight who went too far in his gallantries, dancing a hornpipe with a fat clown to the accompaniment of a hundred clapping hands. Up and down the crowded hall she raced, a hoydenish little tom-boy, drunk with youth, with freedom, and with the pent-up vitality of years.

Close after her, snatching her away from the other dancers only to have her snatched away from him in turn, was Mac Clarke, equally flushed and excited, refusing to listen to Monte's insistent reminder that a storm was brewing and they ought to go home.

"Hang the storm!" cried Mac gaily. "I'm in for it with the governor, anyhow. Let's make a night of it!"

At the end of a dance even wilder than the rest, Nance found herself with Mac at the entrance to one of the boxes that flanked the stage.

"I've got you now!" he panted, catching her wrists and pulling her within the curtained recess. "You've got to tell me why you've been running away from me all evening."

"I haven't," said Nance, laughing and struggling to free her hands.

"You have, too! You've given me the slip a dozen times. Don't you know I'm crazy about you?"

"Much you are!" scoffed Nance. "Go tell that to Birdie."

"I'll tell it to Birdie and every one else if you like," Mac cried. "It was all up with me the first time I saw you."

With his handsome, boyish face and his frilled shirt, he looked so absurdly like the choir boy, who had once sat on the fence flinging rocks at her, that she threw back her head and laughed.

"You don't even know the first time you saw me," she challenged him.

"Well, I know I've seen you somewhere before. Tell me where?"

"Guess!" said Nance, with dancing eyes.

"Wait! I know! It was on the street one night. You were standing in a drug store. A red light was shining on you, and you smiled at me."

"I smiled at you because I knew you. I'd seen you before that. Once when you didn't want me to. In the factory yard—behind the gas-pipe—"

"Were you the little girl that caught me kissing Bird that day?"

"Yes! But there was another time even before that."

He searched her face quizzically, still holding her wrists.

Nance, no longer trying to free her hands, hummed teasingly, half under her breath:

"Do ye think the likes of ye
Could learn to like the likes o' me?
Arrah, come in, Barney McKane, out of the rain!"

A puzzled look swept his face; then he cried exultantly:

"I've got it. It was you who let my pigeons go! You little devil! I'm going to pay you back for that!" and before she knew it, he had got both of her hands into one of his and had caught her to him, and was kissing her there in the shadow of the curtain, kissing her gay, defiant eyes and her half-childish lips.

And Nance, the independent, scoffing, high-headed Nance, who up to this time had waged successful warfare, offensive as well as defensive, against the invading masculine, forgot for one transcendent second everything in the world except the touch of those ardent lips on hers and the warm clasp of the arm about her yielding shoulders.

In the next instant she sprang away from him, and in dire confusion fled out of the box and down the corridor.

At the door leading back into the ball-room a group of dancers had gathered and were exchanging humorous remarks about a woman who was being borne, feet foremost, into the corridor by two men in costume.

Nance, craning her neck to see, caught a glimpse of a white face with a sagging mouth, and staring eyes under a profusion of tumbled red hair. With a gasp of recognition she pushed forward and impulsively seized one of the woman's limp hands.

"Gert!" she cried, "what's the matter? Are you hurt?"

The monk gave a significant wink at Mac, who had joined them, and the by-standers laughed.

"She's drunk!" said Mac, abruptly, pulling Nance away. "Where did you ever know that woman?"

"Why, it's Gert, you know, at the factory! She worked at the bench next to mine!"

Her eyes followed the departing group somberly, and she lingered despite Mac's persuasion.

Poor Gert! Was this what she meant by a good time? To be limp and silly like that, with her dress slipping off her shoulder and people staring at her and laughing at her?

"I don't want to dance!" she said impatiently, shaking off Mac's hand.

The steaming hall, reeking with tobacco smoke and stale beer, the men and women with painted faces and blackened eyes leering and languishing at each other, the snatches of suggestive song and jest, filled her with sudden disgust.

"I'm going home," she announced with determination.

"But, Nance!" pleaded Mac, "you can't go until we've had our dance."

But for Nance the spell was broken, and her one idea was to get away. When she found Birdie she became more insistent than ever.

"Why not see it out?" urged Mac. "I don't want to go home."

"You are as hoarse as a frog now," said Monte.

"Glad of it! Let's me out of singing in the choir to-morrow—I mean to-day! Who wants another drink?"

Birdie did, and another ten minutes was lost while they went around to the refreshment room.

The storm was at its height when at four o'clock they started on that mad drive home. The shrieking wind, the wet, slippery streets, the lightning flashing against the blurred wind-shield, the crashes of thunder that drowned all other sounds, were sufficient to try the nerves of the steadiest driver. But Mac sped his car through it with reckless disregard, singing, despite his hoarseness, with Birdie and Monte, and shouting laughing defiance as the lightning played.

Nance sat very straight beside him with her eyes on the road ahead. She hated Birdie for having taken enough wine to make her silly like that; she hated the boys for laughing at her. She saw nothing funny in the fact that somebody had lost the latch-key and that they could only get in by raising the landlady, who was sharp of tongue and free with her comments.

"You girls better come on over to my rooms," urged Monte. "We'll cook your breakfast on the chafing-dish, won't we, Mac?"

"Me for the couch!" said Birdie. "I'm cross-eyed, I'm so sleepy."

"I'm not going," said Nance, shortly.

"Don't be a short-sport, Nance," urged Birdie, peevishly. "It's as good as morning now. We can loaf around Monte's for a couple of hours and then go over to my room and change our clothes in time to get to the station by seven. Less time we have to answer questions, better it'll be for us."

"I tell you I ain't going!" protested Nance, hotly.

"Yes, you are!" whispered Mac softly. "You are going to be a good little girl and do whatever I want you to."

Nance grew strangely silent under his compelling look, and under the touch of his hand as it sought hers in the darkness. Why wasn't she angry with Mr. Mac as she was with the others? Why did she want so much to do whatever he asked her to? After all perhaps there was no harm in going to Mr. Monte's for a little while, perhaps—

She drew in her breath suddenly and shivered. For the first time in her life she was afraid, not of the storm, or the consequences of her escapade, but of herself. She was afraid of the quick, sweet shiver that ran over her whenever Mac touched her, of the strange weakness that came over her even now, as his hands claimed hers.

"Say, I'm going to get out," she said suddenly.

"Stop the car! Don't you hear me? I want to get out!"

"Nonsense!" said Mac, "you don't even know where you are! You are coming with us to Monte's; that's what you are going to do."

But Nance knew more than he thought. In the last flash of lightning she had seen, back of them on the left, startlingly white for the second against the blackness, the spire of Calvary Cathedral. She knew that they were rapidly approaching the railroad crossing where Uncle Jed's signal tower stood, beyond which lay a region totally unfamiliar to her.

She waited tensely until Mac had sped the car across the gleaming tracks, just escaping the descending gates. Then she bent forward and seized the emergency brake. The car came to a halt with a terrific jerk, plunging them all forward, and under cover of the confusion Nance leapt out and, darting under the lowered gate, dashed across the tracks. The next moment a long freight train passed between her and the automobile, and when it was done with its noisy shunting backward and forward, and had gone ahead, the street was empty.

Watching her chance between the lightning flashes, she darted from cover to cover. Once beyond the signal tower she would be safe from Uncle Jed's righteous eye, and able to dash down a short cut she knew that led into the street back of the warehouse and thence into Calvary Alley. If she could get to her old room for the next two hours, she could change her clothes and be off again before any one knew of her night's adventure.

Just as she reached the corner, a flash more blinding than the rest ripped the heavens. A line of fire raced toward her along the steel rails, then leapt in a ball to the big bell at the top of the signal tower. There was a deafening crash; all the electric lights went out, and Nance found herself cowering against the fence, apparently the one living object in that wild, wet, storm-racked night.

The only lights to be seen were the small red lamps suspended on the slanting gates. Nance waited for them to lower when the freight train that had backed into the yards five minutes before, rushed out again. But the lamps did not move.

She crept back across the tracks, watching with fascinated horror the dark windows of the signal tower. Why didn't Uncle Jed light his lantern? Why hadn't he lowered the gates? All her fear of discovery was suddenly swallowed up in a greater fear.

At the foot of the crude wooden stairway she no longer hesitated.

"Uncle Jed!" she shouted against the wind, "Uncle Jed, are you there?"

There was no answer.

She climbed the steep steps and tried the door, which yielded grudgingly to her pressure. It was only when she put her shoulder to it and pushed with all her strength that she made an opening wide enough to squeeze through. There on the floor, lying just as he had fallen, was the old gate-tender, his unseeing eyes staring up into the semi-darkness.

Nance looked at him in terror, then at the signal board and the levers that controlled the gates. A terrible trembling seized her, and she covered her eyes with her hands.

"God tell me quick, what must I do?" she demanded, and the next instant, as if in answer to her prayer, she heard herself gasp, "Dan!" as she fumbled wildly for the telephone.

CHAPTER XXI
DAN

The shrill whistle that at noon had obtruded its discord into Nance Molloy's thoughts had a very different effect on Dan Lewis, washing his hands under the hydrant in the factory yard. *He* had not forgotten that it was Saturday. Neither had Growler, who stood watching him with an oblique look in his old eye that said as plain as words that he knew what momentous business was brewing at five o'clock.

It was not only Saturday for Dan, but the most important Saturday that ever figured on the calendar. In his heroic efforts to conform to Mrs. Purdy's standard of perfection he had studied the advice to young men in the "Sunday Echo." There he learned that no gentleman would think of mentioning love to a young lady until he was in a position to marry her. To-day's pay envelope would hold the exact amount to bring his bank account up to the three imposing figures that he had decided on as the minimum sum to be put away.

As he was drying his hands on his handkerchief and whistling softly under his breath, he was summoned to the office.

For the past year he had been a self-constituted buffer between Mr. Clarke and the men in the furnace-room, and he wondered anxiously what new complication had arisen.

"He's got an awful grouch on," warned the stenographer as Dan passed through the outer office.

Mr. Clarke was sitting at his desk, tapping his foot impatiently.

"Well, Lewis," he said, "you've taken your time! Sit down. I want to talk to you."

Dan dropped into the chair opposite and waited.

"Is it true that you have been doing most of the new foreman's work for the past month?"

"Well, I've helped him some. You see, being here so long, I know the ropes a bit better than he does."

"That's not the point. I ought to have known sooner that he could not handle the job. I fired him this morning, and we've got to make some temporary arrangement until a new man is installed."

Dan's face grew grave.

"We can manage everything but the finishing room. Some of the girls have been threatening to quit."

"What's the grievance now?"

"Same thing—ventilation. Two more girls fainted there this morning. The air is something terrible."

"What do they think I am running?" demanded Mr. Clarke, angrily, "a health resort?"

"No, sir," said Dan, "a death trap."

Mr. Clarke set his jaw and glared at Dan, but he said nothing. The doctor's recent verdict on the death of a certain one-eyed girl, named Mag Gist, may have had something to do with his silence.

"How many girls are in that room now?" he asked after a long pause.

Dan gave the number, together with several other disturbing facts concerning the sanitary arrangements.

"Well, what's to be done?" demanded Mr. Clarke, fiercely. "We can't get out the work with fewer girls, and there is no way of enlarging that room."

"Yes, sir, there is," said Dan. "Would you mind me showing you a way?"

"Since you are so full of advice, go ahead."

With crude, but sure, pencil strokes, Dan got his ideas on paper. He had done it so often for his own satisfaction that he could have made them with his eyes shut. Ever since those early days when he had seen that room through Nance Molloy's eyes, he had persisted in his efforts to better it.

Mr. Clarke, with his fingers thrust through his scanty hair, watched him scornfully.

"Absolutely impractical," he declared. "The only feasible plan would be to take out the north partition and build an extension like this."

"That couldn't be done," said Dan, "on account of the projection."

Whereupon, such is the power of opposition, Mr. Clarke set himself to prove that it could. For over an hour they wrangled, going into the questions of cost, of time, of heating, of ventilation, scarcely looking up from the plans until a figure in a checked suit flung open the door, letting in a draught of air that scattered the papers on the desk.

"Hello, Dad," said the new-comer, with a friendly nod to Dan, "I'm sorry to disturb you, but I only have a minute."

"Which I should accept gratefully, I suppose, as my share of your busy day?" Mr. Clarke tried to look severe, but his eyes softened.

"Well, I just got up," said Mac, with an ingratiating smile, as he smoothed back his shining hair before the mirror in the hat-rack.

"Running all night, and sleeping half the day!" grumbled Mr. Clarke. "By the way, what time did you get in last night?"

Mac made a wry face.

"*Et tu, Brute?*" he cried gaily. "Mother's polished me off on that score. I have not come here to discuss the waywardness of your prodigal son. Mr. Clarke, I have come to talk high finance. I desire to negotiate a loan."

"As usual," growled his father. "I venture to say that Dan Lewis here, who earns about half what you waste a year, has something put away."

"But Dan's the original grinder. He always had an eye for business. Used to win my nickel every Sunday when we shot craps in the alley back of the cathedral. Say, Dan, I see you've still got that handsome thoroughbred cur of yours! By George, that dog could use his tail for a jumping rope!"

Dan smiled; he couldn't afford to be sensitive about Growler's beauty.

"Is that all, Mr. Clarke?" he asked of his employer.

"Yes. I'll see what can be done with these plans. In the meanwhile you try to keep the girls satisfied until the new foreman comes. By the way I expect you'd better stay on here to-night."

Dan paused with his hand on the door-knob. "Yes, sir," he said in evident embarrassment, "but if you don't mind—I 'd like to get off for a couple of hours this afternoon."

"Who's the girl, Dan?" asked Mac, but Dan did not stop to answer.

As he hurried down the hall, a boy appeared from around the corner and beckoned to him with a mysterious grin.

"Somebody's waiting for you down in the yard."

"Who is he?"

"'T ain't a he. It's the prettiest girl you ever seen!"

Dan, whose thoughts for weeks had been completely filled with one feminine image, sprang to the window. But the tall, stylish person enveloped in a white veil, who was waiting below, in no remote way suggested Nance Molloy.

A call from a lady was a new experience, and a lively curiosity seized him as he descended the steps, turning down his shirt sleeves as he went. As he stepped into the yard, the girl turned toward him with a quick, nervous movement.

"Hello, Daniel!" she said, her full red lips curving into a smile. "Don't remember me, do you?"

"Sure, I do. It's Birdie Smelts."

"Good boy! Only now it's Birdie La Rue. That's my stage name, you know. I blew into town Thursday with 'The Rag Time Follies.' Say, Dan, you used to be a good friend of mine, didn't you?"

Dan had no recollection of ever having been noticed by Birdie, except on that one occasion when he had taken her and Nance to the skating-rink. She was older than he by a couple of years, and infinitely wiser in the ways of the world. But it was beyond masculine human nature not to be flattered by her manner, and he hastened to assure her that he had been and was her friend.

"Well, I wonder if you don't want to do me a favor?" she coaxed. "Find out if Mac Clarke's been here, or is going to be here. I got to see him on particular business."

"He's up in the office now," said Dan; then he added bluntly "Where did you ever know Mac Clarke?"

Birdie's large, white lids fluttered a moment.

"I come to see him for a friend of mine," she said.

A silence fell between them which she tried to break with a rather shame faced explanation.

"This girl and Mac have had a quarrel. I'm trying to patch it up. Wish you'd get him down here a minute."

"It would be a lot better for the girl," said Dan, slowly, "if you didn't patch it up."

"What do you mean?"

Dan looked troubled.

"Clarke's a nice fellow all right," he said, "but when it comes to girls—" he broke off abruptly. "Do you know him?"

"I've seen him round the theater," she said.

"Then you ought to know what I mean."

Birdie looked absently across the barren yard.

"Men are all rotten," she said bitterly, then added with feminine inconsistency, "Go on, Dan, be a darling. Fix it so I can speak to him without the old man catching on."

Strategic manoeuvers were not in Dan's line, and he might have refused outright had not Birdie laid a white hand on his and lifted a pair of effectively pleading eyes. Being unused to feminine blandishments, he succumbed.

Half an hour later a white veil fluttered intimately across a broad, checked shoulder as two stealthy young people slipped under the window of Mr. Clarke's private office and made their way to the street.

Dan gave the incident little further thought. He went mechanically about his work, only pausing occasionally at his high desk behind the door to pore over a sheet of paper. Had his employer glanced casually over his shoulder, he might have thought he was still figuring on the plans of the new finishing room; but a second glance would have puzzled him. Instead of one large room there were several small ones, and across the front was a porch with wriggly lines on a trellis, minutely labeled, "honeysuckle."

At a quarter of five Dan made as elaborate a toilet as the washroom permitted. He consumed both time and soap on the fractious forelock, and spent precious moments trying to induce a limp string tie to assume the same correct set that distinguished Mac Clarke's four-in-hand.

Once on his way, with Growler at his heels, he gave no more thought to his looks. He walked very straight, his lips twitching now and then into a smile, and his gaze soaring over the heads of the ordinary people whom he passed. For twenty-one years the book of life had proved grim reading, but to-day he had come to that magic page whereon is written in words grown dim to the eyes of age and experience, but perennially shining to the eyes of youth: "And then they were married and lived happily ever after."

"Take care there! Look where you are going!" exclaimed an indignant pedestrian as he turned the corner into Cemetery Street.

"Why, hello, Bean!" he said in surprise, bringing his gaze down to a stout man on crutches. "Glad to see you out again!"

"I ain't out," said the ex-foreman. "I'm all in. I've got rheumatism in every corner of me. This is what your old bottle factory did for me."

"Tough luck," said Dan sympathetically, with what attention he could spare from a certain doorway half up the square. "First time you've been out?"

"No; I've been to the park once or twice. Last night I went to a show." He was about to limp on when he paused. "By the way, Lewis, I saw an old friend of yours there. You remember that Molloy girl you used to run with up at the factory?"

Dan's mouth closed sharply. Bean's attitude toward the factory girls was an old grievance with him and had caused words between them on more than one occasion.

"Well, I'll be hanged," went on Bean, undaunted, "if she ain't doing a turn up at the Gaiety! She's a little corker all right, had the whole house going."

"You got another guess coming your way," said Dan, coldly, "the young lady you're talking about's not on the stage. She's working up here in Cemetery Street. I happen to be waiting for her now."

Bean whistled.

"Well, the drinks are on me. That girl at the Gaiety is a dead ringer to her. Same classy way of handling herself, same—" Something in Dan's eyes made him stop. "I got to be going," he said. "So long."

Dan waited patiently for ten minutes; then he looked at his watch. What could be keeping Nance? He whistled to Growler, who was making life miserable for a cat in a neighboring yard, and strolled past Miss Bobinet's door; then he returned to the corner. Bean's words had fallen into his dream like a pebble into a tranquil pool. What business had Bean to be remembering the way Nance walked or talked. Restlessly, Dan paced up and down the narrow sidewalk. When he looked at his watch again, it was five-thirty.

Only thirty more minutes in which to transact the most important business of his life! With a gesture of impatience he strode up to Miss Bobinet's door and rang the bell.

A wrinkled old woman, with one hand behind her ear, opened the door grudgingly.

"Nance Molloy?" she quavered in answer to his query. "What you want with her?"

"I'd like to speak with her a minute," said Dan.

"Are you her brother?"

"No."

"Insurance man?"

"No."

The old woman peered at him curiously.

"Who be you?" she asked.

"My name's Lewis."

"Morris?"

"No, Lewis!" shouted Dan, with a restraining hand on Growler, who was sniffing at the strange musty odors that issued from the half-open door.

"Well, she ain't here," said the old woman. "Took herself off last Wednesday, without a word to anybody."

"Last Wednesday!" said Dan, incredulously. "Didn't she send any word?"

"Sent for her money and said she wouldn't be back. You dog, you!" This to Growler who had insinuated his head inside the door with the fixed determination to run down that queer smell if possible.

Dan went slowly down the steps, and Growler, either offended at having had the door slammed in his face, or else sensing, dog-fashion, the sudden change in his master's mood, trotted soberly at his heels. There was no time now to go to Calvary Alley to find out what the trouble was. Nothing to do but go back to the factory and worry through the night, with all sorts of disturbing thoughts swarming in his brain. Nance had been all right the Saturday before, a little restless and discontented perhaps, but scarcely more so than usual. He remembered how he had counseled patience, and how hard it had been for him to keep from telling her then and there what was in his heart. He began to wonder uneasily if he had done right in keeping all his plans and dreams to himself. Perhaps if he had taken her into his confidence and told her what he was striving and saving for, she would have understood better and been happy in waiting and working with him. For the first time he began to entertain dark doubts concerning those columns of advice to young men in the "Sunday Echo."

Once back at the factory, he plunged into his work with characteristic thoroughness. It was strangely hot and still, and somewhere out on the horizon was a grumbling discontent. It was raining hard at eleven o'clock when he boarded a car for Butternut Lane, and by the time he reached the Purdy's corner, the lightning was playing sharply in the northwest.

He let himself in the empty house and felt his way up to his room, but he did not go to bed. Instead, he sat at his table and with stiff awkward fingers wrote letter after letter, each of which he tossed impatiently into the waste-basket. They were all to Nance, and they all tried in vain to express the pent-up emotion that had filled his heart for years. Somewhere downstairs a clock struck one, but he kept doggedly at his task. Four o'clock found him still seated at the table, but his tired head had dropped on his folded arms, and he slept.

Outside the wind rose higher and higher, and the lightning split the heavens in blinding flashes. Suddenly a deafening crash of thunder shook the house, and Dan started to his feet. A moment later the telephone bell rang.

Half dazed, he stumbled down-stairs and took up the receiver.

"Hello, hello! Yes, this is Dan Lewis. What? I can't hear you. Who?" Then his back stiffened suddenly, and his voice grew tense, "Nance! Where are you? Is he dead? Who's with you? Don't be scared, I'm coming!" and, leaving the receiver dangling on the cord, he made one leap for the door.

CHAPTER XXII
IN THE SIGNAL TOWER

It seemed an eternity to Dan, speeding hatless, coatless, breathless through the storm, before he spied the red lights on the lowered gates at the crossing. Dashing to the signal tower, he took the steps two at a time. The small room was almost dark, but he could see Nance kneeling on the floor beside the big gatekeeper.

"Dan! Is it you?" she cried. "He ain't dead yet. I can feel him breathing. If the doctor would only come!"

"Who'd you call?"

"The first one in the book, Dr. Adair."

"But he's the big doctor up at the hospital; he won't come."

"He will too! I told him he had to. And the gates, I got 'em down. Don't stop to feel his heart, Dan. Call the doctor again!"

"The first thing to do is to get a light," said Dan. "Ain't there a lantern or something?"

"Strike matches, like I did. They are on the window-sill—only hurry—Dan, hurry!"

Dan went about his task in his own way, taking time to find an oil lamp on the shelf behind the door and deliberately lighting it before he took his seat at the telephone. As he waited for the connection, his puzzled, troubled eyes dwelt not on Uncle Jed, but on the crimson boots and fantastic cap of Uncle Jed's companion.

"Dr. Adair is on the way," he said quietly, when he hung up the receiver, "and a man is coming from the yards to look after the gates. Is he still breathing?"

"Only when I make him!" said Nance, pressing the lungs of the injured man. "There, Uncle Jed," she coaxed, "take another deep breath, just one time. Go on! Do it for Nance. One time more! That's right! Once more!"

But Uncle Jed was evidently very tired of trying to accommodate. The gasps came at irregular intervals.

"How long have you been doing this?" asked Dan, kneeling beside her.

"I don't know. Ever since I came."

"How did you happen to come?"

"I saw the lightning strike the bell. Oh, Dan! It was awful, the noise and the flash! Seemed like I'd never get up the steps. And at first I thought he was dead and—"

"But who was with you? Where were you going?" interrupted Dan in bewilderment.

"I was passing—I was going home—I—" Her excited voice broke in a sob, and she impatiently jerked the sleeve of her rain-coat across her eyes.

In a moment Dan was all tenderness. For the first time he put his arm around her and awkwardly patted her shoulder.

"There," he said reassuringly, "don't try to tell me now. See! He's breathing more regular! I expect the doctor'll pull him through."

Nance's hands, relieved of the immediate necessity for action, were clasping and unclasping nervously.

"Dan," she burst out, "I got to tell you something! Birdie Smelts has got me a place in the 'Follies.' I been on a couple of nights. I'm going away with 'em in the morning."

Dan looked at her as if he thought the events of the wild night had deprived her of reason.

"You!" he said, "going on the stage?" Then as he took it in, he drew away from her suddenly as if he had received a lash across the face. "And you were going off without talking it over or telling me or anything?"

"I was going to write you, Dan. It was all so sudden."

His eyes swept her bedraggled figure with stern disapproval.

"Were you coming from the theater at this time in the morning?"

Uncle Jed moaned slightly, and they both bent over him in instant solicitude. But there was nothing to do, but wait until the doctor should come.

"Where had you been in those crazy clothes?" persisted Dan.

"I'd been to the carnival ball with Birdie Smelts," Nance blurted out. "I didn't know it was going to be like that, but I might 'a' gone anyway. I don't know. Oh, Dan, I was sick to death of being stuck away in that dark hole, waiting for something to turn up. I told you how it was, but you couldn't see it. I was bound to have a good time if I died for it!"

She dropped her head on her knees and sobbed unrestrainedly, while the wind shrieked around the shanty, and the rain dashed against the gradually lightening window-pane. After a while she flung back her head defiantly.

"*Stop* looking at me like that, Dan. Lots of girls go on the stage and stay good."

"I wasn't thinking about the stage," said Dan. "I was thinking about to-night. Who took you girls to that place?"

Nance dried her tears.

"I can't tell you that," she said uneasily.

"Why not?"

"It wouldn't be fair."

Dan felt the hot blood surge to his head, and the muscles of his hands tighten involuntarily. He forgot Uncle Jed; he forgot to listen for the doctor, or to worry about traffic that would soon be held up in the street below. The only man in the world for him at that moment was the scoundrel who had dared to take his little Nance into that infamous dance hall.

Nance caught his arm and, with a quick gesture, dropped her head on it.

"Dan," she pleaded, "don't be mad at me. I promise you I won't go to any more places like that. I knew it wasn't right all along. But I got to go on with the 'Follies,' It's the chance I been waiting for all these months. Maybe it's the only one that'll ever come to me! You ain't going to stand in my way, are you, Dan?"

"Tell me who was with you to-night!"

"No!" she whispered. "I can't. You mustn't ask me. I promise you I won't do it again. I don't want to go away leaving you thinking bad of me."

His clenched hands suddenly began to tremble so violently that he had to clasp them tight to keep her from noticing.

"I better get used to—to not thinking 'bout you at all," he said, looking at her with the stern eyes of a young ascetic.

For a time they knelt there side by side, and neither spoke. For over a year Dan had been like one standing still on the banks of a muddy stream, his eyes blinded to all but the shining goal opposite, while Nance was like one who plunges headlong into the current, often losing sight of the goal altogether, but now and again catching glimpses of it that sent her stumbling, fighting, falling forward.

At the sound of voices below they both scrambled to their feet. Dr. Adair and the man from the yards came hurriedly up the steps together, the former drawing off his gloves as he came. He was a compact, elderly man whose keen observant eyes swept the room and its occupants at a glance. He listened to Nance's broken recital of what had happened, cut her short when he had obtained the main facts, and proceeded to examine the patient.

"The worst injury is evidently to the right arm and shoulder; you'll have to help me get his shirt off. No—not that way!"

Dan's hands, so eager to serve, so awkward in the service, fumbled over their task, eliciting a groan from the unconscious man.

"Let me do it!" cried Nance, springing forward. "You hold him up, Dan, I can get it off."

"It's a nasty job," warned the doctor, with a mistrustful glance at the youthful, tear-stained face. "It may make you sick."

"What if it does?" demanded Nance, impatiently.

It was a long and distressing proceeding, and Dan tried not to look at her as she bent in absorbed detachment over her work. But her steady finger-touch, and her anticipation of the doctor's needs amazed him. It recalled the day at the factory, when she, little more than a child herself, had dressed the wounds of the carrying-in boy. Once she grew suddenly white and had to hurry to the door and let the wind blow in her face. He started up to follow her, but changed his mind. Instead he protested with unnecessary vehemence against her resuming the work, but she would not heed him.

"That's right!" said the doctor, approvingly. "Stick it out this time and next time it will not make you sick. Our next move is to get him home. Where does he live?"

"In Calvary Alley," said Dan, "back of the cathedral."

"Very good," said the doctor, "I'll run him around there in my machine as soon as that last hypodermic takes effect. Any family?"

Dan shook his head.

"He has, too!" cried Nance. "We're his family!"

The doctor shot an amused glance at her over his glasses; then he laid a kindly hand on her shoulder.

"I congratulate him on this part of it. You make a first class little nurse."

"Is he going to get well?" Nance demanded.

"It is too early to say, my dear. We will hope for the best. I will have one of the doctors come out from the hospital every day to see him, but everything will depend on the nursing."

Nance cast a despairing look at the bandaged figure on the floor; then she shot a look of entreaty at Dan. One showed as little response to her appeal as the other. For a moment she stood irresolute; then she slipped out of the room and closed the door behind her.

For a moment Dan did not miss her. When he did, he left Dr. Adair in the middle of a sentence and went plunging down the steps in hot pursuit.

"Nance!" he called, splashing through the mud. "Aren't you going to say good-by?"

She wheeled on him furiously, a wild, dishevelled, little figure, strung to the breaking point:

"No!" she cried, "I am not going to say good-by! Do you suppose I could go away with you acting like that? And who is there to nurse Uncle Jed, I'd like to know, but me? But I want to tell you right now, Dan Lewis, if ever another chance comes to get out of that alley, I'm going to take it, and there can't anybody in the world stop me!"

CHAPTER XXIII
CALVARY CATHEDRAL

"I don't take no stock in heaven havin' streets of gold," said Mrs. Snawdor. "It'll be just my luck to have to polish 'em. You needn't tell me if there's all that finery in heaven, they won't keep special angels to do the dirty work!"

She and Mrs. Smelts were scrubbing down the stairs of Number One, not as a matter of cleanliness, but for the social benefit to be derived therefrom. It was a Sunday morning institution with them, and served quite the same purpose that church-going does for certain ladies in a more exalted sphere.

"I hope the Bible's true," said Mrs. Smelts, with a sigh. "Where it says there ain't no marryin' nor givin' in marriage."

"Oh, husbands ain't so worse if you pick 'em right," Mrs. Snawdor said with the conviction of experience. "As fer me, I ain't hesitatin' to say I like the second-handed ones best."

"I suppose they are better broke in. But no other woman but me would 'a' looked at Mr. Smelts."

"You can't tell," said Mrs. Snawdor. "Think of me takin' Snawdor after bein' used to Yager an' Molloy! Why, if you'll believe me, Mr. Burks, lyin' there in bed fer four months now, takes more of a hand in helpin' with the childern than Snawdor, who's up an' around."

"Kin he handle hisself any better? Mr. Burks, I mean."

"Improvin' right along. Nance has got him to workin' on a patent now. It's got somethin' to do with a engine switch. Wisht you could see the railroad yards she's rigged up on his bed. The childern are plumb crazy 'bout it."

"Nance is gittin' awful pretty," Mrs. Smelts said. "I kinder 'lowed Dan Lewis an' her'd be makin' a match before this."

Mrs. Snawdor gathered her skirts higher about her ankles and transferred her base of operations to a lower step.

"You can't tell nothin' at all 'bout that girl. She was born with the bit 'tween her teeth, an' she keeps it there. No more 'n you git her goin' in one direction than she turns up a alley on you. It's night school now. There ain't a spare minute she ain't peckin' on that ole piece of a type-writer Ike Lavinski loaned her."

"She's got a awful lot of energy," sighed Mrs. Smelts.

"Energy! Why it's somethin' fierce! She ain't content to let nothin' stay the way it is. Wears the childern plumb out washin' 'em an' learnin' 'em lessons, an' harpin' on their manners. If you believe me, she's got William J. that hacked he goes behind the door to blow his nose!"

"It's a blessin' she didn't go off with them 'Follies,'" said Mrs. Smelts. "Birdie lost her job over two months ago, an' the Lord knows what she's livin' on. The last I heard of her she was sick an' stranded up in Cincinnati, an' me without so much as a dollar bill to send her!" And Mrs. Smelts sat down in a puddle of soap-suds and gave herself up to the luxury of tears.

At this moment a door on the third floor banged, and Nance Molloy, a white figure against her grimy surroundings, picked her way gingerly down the slippery steps. Her cheap, cotton skirt had exactly the proper flare, and her tailor-made shirtwaist was worn with the proud distinction of one who conforms in line, if not in material, to the mode of the day.

"Ain't she the daisy?" exclaimed Mrs. Snawdor, gaily, and even Mrs. Smelts dried her eyes, the better to appreciate Nance's gala attire.

"We're too swell to be Methodist any longer!" went on Mrs. Snawdor, teasingly. "We're turned 'Piscopal!"

"You ain't ever got the nerve to be goin' over to the cathedral," Mrs. Smelts asked incredulously.

"Sure, why not?" said Nance, giving her hat a more sophisticated tilt. "Salvation's as free there as it is anywhere."

It was not salvation, however, that was concerning Nance Molloy as she took her way jauntily out of the alley and, circling the square, joined the throng of well-dressed men and women ascending the broad steps of the cathedral.

From that day when she had found herself back in the alley, like a bit of driftwood that for a brief space is whirled out of its stagnant pool, only to be cast back again, she had planned ceaselessly for a means of escape. During the first terrible weeks of Uncle Jed's illness, her thoughts flew for relief sometimes to Dan, sometimes to Mac. And Dan answered her silent appeal in person, coming daily with his clumsy hands full of necessities, his strong arms ready to lift, his slow speech quickened to words of hope and cheer. Mac came only in dreams, with gay, careless eyes and empty, useless hands, and lips that asked more than they gave. Yet it was around Mac's shining head that the halo of romance oftenest hovered.

It was not until Uncle Jed grew better, and Dan's visits ceased, that Nance realized what they had meant to her. To be sure her efforts to restore things to their old familiar footing had been fruitless, for Dan refused stubbornly to overlook the secret that stood between them, and Nance, for reasons best known to herself, refused to explain matters.

But youth reckons time by heart-throbs, and during Uncle Jed's convalescence Nance found the clock of life running ridiculously slow. Through Ike Lavinski, whose favor she had won by introducing him to Dr. Adair, she learned of a night school where a business course could be taken without expense. She lost no time in enrolling and, owing to her thorough grounding of the year before, was soon making rapid progress. Every night on her way to school, she walked three squares out of her way on the chance of meeting Dan coming from the factory, and coming and going, she watched the cathedral, wondering if Mac still sang there.

One Sunday, toward the close of summer, she followed a daring impulse, and went to the morning service. She sat in one of the rear pews and held her breath as the procession of white-robed men and boys filed into the choir. Mac Clarke was not among them, and she gave a little sigh of disappointment, and wondered if she could slip out again.

On second thought she decided to stay. Even in the old days when she had stolen into the cathedral to look for nickels under the seats, she had been acutely aware of "the pretties." But she had never attended a service, or seen the tapers lighted, and the vast, cool building, with its flickering lights and disturbing music, impressed her profoundly.

Presently she began to make discoveries: the meek apologetic person tip-toeing about lowering windows was no other than the pompous and lordly Mason who had so often loomed over her as an avenging deity. In the bishop, clad in stately robes, performing mysterious rites before the altar, she recognized "the funny old guy" with the bald head, with whom she had compared breakfast menus on a historical day at the graded school.

So absorbed was she in these revelations that she did not notice that she was sitting down while everybody else was standing up, until a small black book was thrust over her shoulder and a white-gloved finger pointed to the top of the page. She rose hastily and tried to follow the service. It seemed that the bishop was reading something which the people all around her were beseeching the Lord to hear. She didn't wonder that the Lord had to be begged to listen. She wasn't going to listen; that was one thing certain.

Then the organ pealed forth, and voices caught up the murmuring words and lifted them and her with them to the great arched ceiling. As long as the music lasted, she sat spell-bound, but when the bishop began to read again, this time from a book resting on the out-stretched wings of a big brass bird, her attention wandered to the great stained glass window above the altar. The reverse side of it was as familiar to her as the sign over Slap Jack's saloon. From the alley it presented opaque blocks of glass above the legend that had been one of the mysteries of her childhood. Now as she looked, the queer figures became shining angels with lilies in their hands, and she made the amazing discovery that "Evol si dog," seen from the inside, spelled "God is Love."

She sat quite still, pondering the matter. The bishop and the music and even Mac were for the time completely forgotten. Was the world full of things like that, puzzling and confused from the outside, and simple and easy from within? Within what? Her mind groped uncertainly along a strange path. So God was love? Why hadn't the spectacled lady told her so that time in the juvenile court instead of writing down her foolish answer? But love had to do with sweethearts and dime novels and plays on the stage. How could God be that? Maybe it meant the kind of love Mr. Demry had for his little daughter, or the love that Dan had for his mother, or the love she had for the Snawdor baby that died. Maybe the love that was good was God, and the love that was bad was the devil, maybe—

Her struggle with these wholly new and perplexing problems was interrupted by the arrival of a belated worshiper, who glided into the seat beside her and languidly knelt in prayer. Nance's attention promptly leaped from moral philosophy to clothes. Her quick eyes made instant appraisal of the lady's dainty costume, then rested in startled surprise on her lowered profile. The straight delicate features, slightly foreign, the fair hair rippling from the neck, were disconcertingly familiar. But when Nance saw her full face, with the petulant mouth and wrinkled brow, the impression vanished.

After a long time the service came to an end, and just as Nance was waiting to pass out, she heard some one say:

"When do you expect your son home, Mrs. Clarke? We miss him in the choir."

And the fair-haired lady in front of her looked up and smiled, and all her wrinkles vanished as she said:

"We expect him home before next Sunday, if the naughty boy doesn't disappoint us again!"

Nance waited to hear no more, but fled into the sunlight and around the corner, hugging her secret. She was not going to let Mr. Mac see her, she assured herself; she was just going to see him, and hear him sing.

When the next Sunday morning came, it found her once more hurrying up the broad steps of the cathedral. She was just in time, for as she slipped into a vacant pew, the notes of the organ began to swell, and from a side door came the procession of choir boys, headed by Mac Clarke carrying a great cross of gold.

Nance, hiding behind the broad back of the man in front of her, watched the procession move into the chancel, and saw the members of the choir file into their places. She had no interest now in the bishop's robes or the lighted tapers or cryptic inscriptions. Throughout the long service her attention was riveted on the handsome, white-robed figure which sat in a posture of bored resignation, wearing an expression of Christian martyrdom.

When the recessional sounded, she rose with the rest of the congregation, still keeping behind the protecting back of the man in front. But when she saw Mac lift the shining cross and come toward her down the chancel steps at the head of the singing procession, something made her move suddenly to the end of the pew, straight into the shaft of light that streamed through the great west window.

Mac, with his foot on the lowest step, paused for the fraction of a second, and the cross that he held swayed slightly. Then he caught step again and moved steadily forward.

Nance hurried away before the benediction. She was never going to do it again, she promised herself repeatedly. And yet, how wonderful it had been! Straight over the heads of the congregation for their eyes to meet like that, and for him to remember as she was remembering!

For three weeks she kept her promise and resolutely stayed away from the cathedral. One would have to be "goin' on nineteen" and live in Calvary Alley to realize the heroic nature of her moral struggle. Victory might have been hers in the end, had not Dan Lewis for the first time in years, failed one Saturday to spend his half-holiday with her. He had come of late, somber and grimly determined to give her no peace until he knew the truth. But Dan, even in that mood, was infinitely better than no Dan at all. When he sent her word that he was going with some of the men from the factory up the river for a swim, she gave her shoulders a defiant shrug, and set to work to launder her one white dress and stove-polish her hat, with the pleasing results we have already witnessed through the eyes of Mrs. Snawdor and Mrs. Smelts.

There is no place where a flirtation takes quicker root or matures more rapidly than in ecclesiastical soil. From the moment Nance entered the cathedral on that third Sunday, she and Mac were as acutely aware of each other's every move as if they had been alone together in the garden of Eden.

At first she tried to avert her eyes, tried not to see his insistent efforts to attract her attention, affected not to know that he was singing to her, and watching her with impatient delight.

Then the surging notes of the organ died away, the bishop ascended the pulpit, and the congregation settled down to hear the sermon. From that time on Nance ceased to be discreet. There was glance for glance, and smile for smile, and the innumerable wireless messages that youth has exchanged since ardent eyes first sought each other across forbidden spaces.

It was not until the end of the sermon that Nance awoke to the fact that it was high time for Cinderella to be speeding on her way. Seizing a moment when the choir's back was turned to the congregation, she slipped noiselessly out of the cathedral and was fleeing down the steps when she came face to face with Monte Pearce.

"Caught at last!" he exclaimed, planting himself firmly in her way. "I've been playing watchdog for Mac for three Sundays. What are you doing in town?"

"In town?"

"Yes; we thought you were on the road with the 'Follies.' When did you get back?"

"You're seeking information, Mr. Monte Carlo," said Nance, with a smile. "Let me by. I've got to go home."

"I'll go with you. Where do you live?"

"Under my hat."

"Well, I don't know a nicer place to be." Monte laughed and looked at her and kept on laughing, until she felt herself blushing up to the roots of her hair.

"Honest, Mr. Monte, I got to go on," she said appealingly. "I'm in no end of a hurry."

"I can go as fast as you can," said Monte, his cane tapping each step as he tripped briskly down beside her. "I've got my orders from Mac. I'm to stay with you, if you won't stay with me. Which way?"

In consternation for fear the congregation should be dismissed before she could get away, and determined not to let him know where she lived, she jumped aboard a passing car.

"So be it!" said her plump companion, settling himself comfortably on the back seat beside her. "Now tell your Uncle Monte all about it!"

"There's nothing to tell!" declared Nance, with the blush coming back. She was finding it distinctly agreeable to be out alone like this with a grandly sophisticated young gentleman who wore a light linen suit with shoes to match, and whose sole interest seemed to center upon her and her affairs.

"But you know there is!" he persisted. "What made you give us the shake that night of the ball?"

Nance refused to say; so he changed the subject.

"How's Miss Birdie?"

"Give it up. Haven't seen her since you have."

"What? Didn't you go on with the show that next morning?"

"No."

"And you've been in town all summer?"

She nodded, and her companion gave a low, incredulous whistle.

"Well, I'll be darned!" he said. "And old Mac sending letters and telegrams every few minutes and actually following the 'Follies' to Boston!"

"Birdie was with 'em up to two months ago," said Nance.

"Mac wasn't after Birdie!" said Monte. "He hasn't had but one idea in his cranium since that night of the carnival ball. I never saw him so crazy about a girl as he is about you."

"Yes, he is!" scoffed Nance, derisively, but she let Monte run on at length, painting in burning terms the devastating extent of Mac's passion, his despair at losing her, his delight at finding her again, and his impatience for an interview.

When Monte finished she looked at him sidewise out of her half-closed eyes.

"Tell him I've gone on a visit to my rich aunt out to the sea-shore in Kansas."

"Give him another show," coaxed Monte. "We were all a bit lit up that night at the ball."

"No, we weren't either!" Nance flashed. "I hadn't had a thing, but one glass of beer, and you know it! I hate your old fizz-water!"

"Well, make it up with Mac. He's going back to college next month, and he's wild to see you."

"Tell him I haven't got time. Tell him I'm studying instrumental."

Nance was fencing for time. Her cool, keen indifference gave little indication of the turmoil that was going on within. If she could manage to see Mac without letting him know where she lived, without Dan's finding it out—

The car compassed the loop and started on the return trip.

"Where do we get off?" asked Monte.

"I'm not getting off anywhere until after you do."

"I've got lots of nickels."

"I've got lots of time!" returned Nance, regardless of her former haste.

At Cathedral Square, Monte rang the bell.

"Have it your own way," he said good-naturedly. "But do send a message to Mac."

Nance let him get off the back platform; then she put her head out of the window.

"You tell him," she called, "that he can't kill two birds with one stone!"

CHAPTER XXIV
BACK AT CLARKE'S

The promotion of Uncle Jed from the bed to a pair of crutches brought about two important changes in the house of Snawdor. First, a financial panic caused by the withdrawal of his insurance money, and, second, a lightening of Nance's home duties that sent her once more into the world to seek a living.

By one of those little ironies in which life seems to delight, the only opportunity that presented itself lay directly in the path of temptation. A few days after her interview with Monte Pearce, Dan came to her with an offer to do some office work at the bottle factory. The regular stenographer was off on a vacation, and a substitute was wanted for the month of September.

"Why, I thought you'd be keen about it," said Dan, surprised at her hesitation.

"Oh! I'd like it all right, but—"

"You needn't be afraid to tackle it," Dan urged. "Mr. Clarke's not as fierce as he looks; he'd let you go a bit slow at first."

"He wouldn't have to! I bet I've got as much speed now as the girl he's had. It's not the work."

"I know how you feel about the factory," said Dan, "and I wouldn't want you to go back in the finishing room. The office is different. You take my word for it; it's as nice a place as you could find."

They were standing on the doorless threshold of Number One, under the fan-shaped arch through which the light had failed to shine for twenty years. From the room on the left came the squeak of Mr. Demry's fiddle and the sound of pattering feet, synchronizing oddly with the lugubrious hymn in which Mrs. Smelts, in the room opposite, was giving vent to her melancholy.

Nance, eager for her chance, yearning for financial independence, obsessed by the desire to escape from the dirt and disorder and confusion about her, still hesitated.

"If you're afraid I'm going to worry you," said Dan, fumbling with his cap, "I can keep out of your way all right."

In an instant her impulsive hand was on his arm.

"You shut up, Dan Lewis!" she said sharply. "What makes me want to take the job most is our coming home together every night like we used to."

Dan's eyes, averted until now, lifted with sudden hope.

"But I got a good reason for not coming," she went on stubbornly. "It hasn't got anything to do with you or the work."

"Can't you tell me, Nance?"

The flicker of hope died out of his face as she shook her head. He looked down the alley for a moment; then he turned toward her with decision:

"See here, Nance," he said earnestly, "I don't know what your reason is, but I know that this is one chance in a hundred. I want you to take this job. If I come by for you to-morrow morning, will you be ready?"

Still she hesitated.

"Let me decide it for you," he insisted, "will you, Nance?"

She looked up into his earnest eyes, steadfast and serious as a collie's.

"All right!" she said recklessly, "have it your own way!"

The first day in Mr. Clarke's office was one of high tension. Added to the trepidation of putting her newly acquired business knowledge to a practical test, was the much more disturbing possibility that at any moment Mac might happen upon the scene. Just what she was going to do and say in such a contingency she did not know. Once when she heard the door open cautiously, she was afraid to lift her eyes. When she did, surprise took the place of fear.

"Why, Mrs. Smelts!" she cried. "What on earth are you doing here?"

Birdie's mother, faded and anxious, and looking unfamiliar in bonnet and cape, was evidently embarrassed by Nance's unexpected presence.

"He sent for me," she said, nervously, twitching at the fringe on her cape. "I wrote to his wife, but he sent word fer me to come here an' see him at ten o'clock. Is it ten yet?"

"Mr. Clarke sent for *you*?" Nance began incredulously; then remembering that a stenographer's first business is to attend to her own, she crossed the room with quite a professional manner and tapped lightly on the door of the inner office.

For half an hour the usually inaccessible president of the bottle factory and the scrub woman from Calvary Alley held mysterious conclave; then the door opened again, and Mrs. Smelts melted into the outer passage as silently as she had come.

Nance, while frankly curious, had little time to indulge in idle surmise. All her faculties were bent on mastering the big modern type-writer that presented such different problems from the ancient machine on which she had pounded out her lessons. She didn't like this sensitive, temperamental affair that went off half-cocked at her slightest touch, and did things on its own account that she was in the habit of doing herself.

Her first dictation left her numb with terror. She heard Mr. Clarke repeating with lightning rapidity phrases which she scarcely comprehended: "Enclose check for amount agreed upon." "Matter settled once and for all." "Any further annoyance to be punished to full extent of the law."

"Shall I address an envelope?" she asked, glancing at the "Dear Madam" at the top of the page.

"No," said Mr. Clarke, sharply, "I'll attend to that."

Other letters followed, and she was soon taking them with considerable speed. When mistakes occurred they could usually be attributed to the graded school which, during its brief chance at Nance, had been more concerned in teaching her the names and the lengths of the rivers of South America than in teaching her spelling.

At the noon hour Mr. Clarke departed, and she stood by the window eating her lunch and watching the men at work on the new wing. The old finishing room was a thing of the past, and Dan's dream of a light, well-ventilated workroom for the girls was already taking definite form. She could see him now in the yard below, a blue-print in his hand, explaining to a group of workmen some detail of the new building. One old glass-blower, peering at the plan through heavy, steel-rimmed spectacles, had his arm across Dan's shoulder. Nance smiled tenderly. Dear Dan! Everybody liked him—even those older men from the furnace-room who had seen him promoted over their heads. She leaned forward impulsively and called to him.

"Danny!" she cried, "here's an apple. Catch!"

He caught it dexterously in his left hand, gave her a casual nod, then went gravely on with the business in hand. Nance sighed and turned away from the window.

In the afternoon the work went much easier. She was getting used to Mr. Clarke's quick, nervous speech and abrupt manner. She was beginning to think in sentences instead of words. All was going famously when a quick step sounded in the passage without, followed by a gaily whistled tune, and the next instant the door behind her was flung open.

Mr. Clarke went steadily on with his dictation, but the new stenographer ceased to follow. With bent head and lips caught between her teeth, she made futile efforts to catch up, but she only succeeded in making matters worse.

"That will do for this afternoon," said Mr. Clarke, seeing her confusion. "Make a clear copy of that last letter and put it on my desk." Then he turned in his chair and glared over his shoulder. "Well, Mac!" he said, "I've waited for you just one hour and thirty-five minutes."

"Dead sorry, Dad. Didn't know it was so late," said the new-comer, blithely. "How long before you are going home?"

"Ten minutes. I've got to go over to the new building first. Don't go until I return. There's something I want to see you about."

Nance heard the door close as Mr. Clarke went out; then she waited in a tremor, half trepidation, half glee, for Mac to recognize her. He was moving about restlessly, first in one office, then in the other, and she could feel his bright inquisitive eyes upon her from different angles. But she kept her face averted, changing her position as he changed his. Presently he came to a halt near her and began softly to whistle the little-bear dance from the "Rag-Time Follies." She smiled before she knew it, and the next instant he was perched on the corner of her desk, demanding rapturously to know what she was doing there, and swearing that he had recognized her the moment he entered the room.

"Let go my hand, Mr. Mac!" she implored in laughing confusion.

"I'm afraid to! You might give me the slip again. I've been scouring the town for you and to think I should find you here!"

"Look out!" warned Nance. "You're upsetting the ink-bottle!"

"What do I care? Gee, this is luck! You ought to see my new racer, a regular peach! Will you come out with me sometime?"

"Will you let me run it?"

"I'll let you do anything you like with anything I've got," he declared with such ardor that she laughed and regretted it the next moment.

"Now look here, Mr. Mac!" she said, severely, "you touch me again, and I quit to-night. See?"

"I'll be good. I'll do anything you say if you'll just stay and play with me."

"Play nothing! I've got work to do."

"Work be hanged! Do you suppose when I haven't seen you for four months that I'm not going to claim my inning?"

"Well, I want to tell you right here," she said, shaking a warning pencil in his face, "that I mean what I say about your behaving yourself."

Mac caught the end of the pencil and held it while their eyes challenged each other.

"So be it!" he said. "I promise to be a model of discretion. Nance, I've been mad about you! Did Monte tell you—"

"Mr. Monte didn't tell me anything I wanted to hear," she said in her cool, keen way, as she got the imperiled ink-well to a place of safety, and straightened the other articles on the desk.

"You wouldn't be so down on a fellow if you knew how hard hit I am," persisted Mac. "Besides, I'm in for an awful row with the governor. You may see my scalp fly past the window in less than ten minutes."

"What's the row about?"

"Same old thing. I am the original devil for getting found out." For the space of a minute he gloomily contemplated a spot in the carpet; then he shrugged his shoulders, rammed his hands in his pockets, and began to whistle.

"The governor'll fork out," he said. "He always does. Say, Nance, you haven't said a word about my moustache."

"Let's see it," said Nance in giggling derision. "Looks like a baby's eyebrow. Does it wash off?"

A step in the hall sent them flying in opposite directions, Nance back to her desk, and Mac into the inner office, where his father found him a moment later, apparently absorbed in a pamphlet on factory inspection.

When Nance started home at six o'clock, she found Dan waiting at his old post beside the gas-pipe.

"It's like old times," he said happily, as he piloted her through the outpouring throng. "I remember the first night we walked home together. You weren't much more than a kid. You had on a red cap with a tassel to it. Three years ago the tenth of last May. Wouldn't think it, would you?"

"Think what?" she asked absently.

"Tired?" he asked anxiously. "Is the work going to be too heavy?"

She shook her head impatiently.

"No, the work's all right. But—but I wish you hadn't made me come back, Dan."

"Stick it out for a week," he urged, "and then if you want to stop, I won't say a word."

She looked up at him quizzically and gave a short enigmatic laugh.

"That's my trouble," she said, "if I stick it out for a week, I won't be wanting to quit!"

CHAPTER XXV
MAC

Nance's prophecy regarding herself was more than fulfilled. Whatever scruples had assailed her at the start were soon overthrown by the on-rushing course of events. That first month in Mr. Clarke's office proved to be a time of delightful madness. There were daily meetings with Mac at the noon hour, stolen chats on street corners, thrilling suppers with him and Monte at queer cafes, and rides after dark in that wonderful racer that proved the most enticing of playthings.

Dan was as busy as Mac was idle; Mr. Clarke was gloomy and preoccupied; Mrs. Snawdor was in bed when Nance left home in the morning, and gone to work when she returned in the evening. The days flashed by in a glorious succession of forbidden joys, with nobody to interrupt the furious progress of affairs.

Half of her salary Nance gave to her stepmother, and the other half she spent on clothes. She bought with taste and discrimination, measuring everything by the standard set up by her old idol, Miss Stanley at Forest Home. The result was that she soon began to look very much like the well-dressed women with whom she touched elbows on the avenue.

She had indeed got the bit between her teeth, and she ran at full tilt, secure in the belief that she had full control of the situation. As long as she gave satisfaction in her work, she told herself, and "behaved right," she could go and come as she liked, and nobody would be the worse for it.

She did not realize that her scoffing disbelief in Mac's avowals, and her gay indifference were the very things that kept him at fever heat. He was not used to being thwarted, and this high-handed little working-girl, with her challenging eyes and mocking laugh, who had never heard of the proprieties, and yet denied him favors, was the first person he had ever known who refused absolutely to let him have his own way. With a boy's impetuous desire he became obsessed by the idea of her. When he was not with her, he devised schemes to remind her of him, making love to her by proxy in a dozen foolish, whimsical ways. When it was not flowers or candy, it was a string of nonsense verses laid between the pages of her type-writer paper, sometimes a clever caricature of himself or Monte, and always it was love notes in the lining of her hat, in her gloves, in her pocket-book. She was afraid to raise her umbrella for fear a rain of tender missives would descend therefrom. Once he gave her a handsome jeweled bracelet which she wore under her sleeve. But he got hard up before the week was over and borrowed it back and pawned it.

Of two things Nance succeeded in keeping him in ignorance. During all their escapades he never discovered where she lived, and he never suspected her friendship for Dan Lewis. He was not one to concern himself with troublesome details. The pleasure of the passing moment was his sole aim in life.

And Nance, who ordinarily scorned subterfuge and hated a secret, succeeded not only in keeping him in ignorance of Dan; but with even greater strategy managed to keep Dan in complete ignorance of the whole situation. Dan, to be sure, took his unconscious revenge. His kind, puzzled eyes haunted her dreams, and the thought of him proved the one disturbing element in these halcyon days. In vain she told herself that he was an old fogy, that he had Sunday-school notions, that he wouldn't be able to see anything but wrong in a harmless flirtation that would end with Mac's return to college. But would it end? That was a question Nance was beginning to ask herself with curious misgiving.

The last of the month rolled round with incredible swiftness. It brought to Nance not only an end to all her good times, but the disheartening knowledge that she would soon be out of employment again with no money saved, and under the self-imposed necessity of making a clean breast of her misdeeds to Dan Lewis.

On the Saturday before Mac's intended departure, as she sat at her desk ruefully facing the situation, he rushed into the office.

"Has a mean-looking little Jew been in here this morning?" he demanded breathlessly.

"Nobody's been here," said Nance.

"Gloree!" said Mac, collapsing into a chair. "He gave me a scare! Wonder if he 'phoned!"

"Mr. Clarke's been out all morning. These are the people who called up."

Mac ran his eye hurriedly down the list and sighed with relief. Then he got up and went to the window and stood restlessly tapping the pane.

"I've a good notion to go East to-night," he said, half to himself, "no use waiting until Monday."

Nance glanced at him quickly.

"What's up?" she asked.

"Money, as usual," said Mac in an aggrieved tone. "Just let me get ready to leave town, and fellows I never heard of turn up with bills. I could stand off the little fellows, but Meyers is making no end of a stew. He holds a note of mine for five hundred and sixty dollars. It was due yesterday, and he swore that if I didn't smoke up by noon to-day, he'd come to the governor."

"Won't he give you an extension?"

"He's given me two already. It's the money I lost last spring at the races. That's the reason I can't get it out of the governor. It looks as if it were about time for little Willie to take to the tall timbers."

Nance got up from her desk and joined him at the window. There was something she had been burning to say to him for ten days, but it was something she found it very hard to say. He might tell her it was none of her business; he might even not like her any more.

"See here, Mr. Mac," she said, bracing herself for the ordeal, "did it ever strike you that you spend a lot of money that don't belong to you?"

"It'll all be mine some day," said Mac reassuringly. "If the governor would listen to mother, we'd never have these financial rackets. She knows that it takes a lot for a fellow to live right."

"It takes a lot more for him to live wrong," said Nance, stoutly. "You get a whacking big allowance; when you get to the end of it, why don't you do like some of the rest of us—go without the things you can't pay for?"

"I am going to," said Mac as if the idea was a new one. "Once I get squared up, you bet I'll stay so. But that doesn't help me out of this mess. The money has got to come from somewhere, and I tell you I haven't got a sou!"

Nance had never seen him so perturbed. He usually approached these conflicts with his father with a passing grimace, exhibited sufficient repentance to get what he wanted, and emerged more debonair than ever. It was disturbing to see him so serious and preoccupied.

"I bet your father'd help you if he thought you'd make a new start," she said.

Mac shook his head.

"He would have a month ago. But he's got it in for me now. He believes an idiotic story that was cocked up about me, and he's just waiting for my next slip to spring a mine on me. I got to keep him from finding out until I'm gone; that's all there is to it!"

He fumbled in his pocket for a match and instead drew out a bank-note.

"By George! here's a lonesome five-spot I didn't know I had! I believe I'll play it on the races and see what it'll do for me. Maybe it's a mascot."

His momentary depression was gone, and he was eager to be off. But Nance stood between him and the door, and there was a dangerous light in her eyes.

"Do you know," she said, "I've a good mind to tell you what I think of you?"

He caught her hand. "Do, Nance! And make it nice. It's going to be no end of a grind to leave you. Say something pretty that I can live on 'til Christmas. Tell me I'm the sweetest fellow that ever lived. Go on. Make love to me, Nance!"

"I think you are a short-sport!" she burst forth. "Any fellow that'll go on making debts when he can't pay his old ones, that'll get things in a muddle and run off and let somebody else face the racket is a coward—I think—"

"Help! Help!" cried Mac, throwing up an arm in pretended defense, and laughing at her flashing eyes and blazing cheeks. "By jinks, I don't know whether you look prettiest when you are mad or when you are glad. If you don't stop this minute I'll have to kiss you!"

The anger in Nance's face faded into exasperation. She felt suddenly hot and uncomfortable and a little ashamed of her violence. She had neither offended him nor humiliated him; she had simply amused him. Tears of chagrin sprang to her eyes, and she turned away abruptly.

"Nance!" Mac demanded, with quick concern, "you surely aren't crying? Why the very idea! It makes me perfectly miserable to see girls cry. You mustn't, you know. Look at me, Nance! Smile at me this minute!"

But Nance's head was down on her desk, and she was past smiling.

"I'll do anything you say!" cried Mac, dropping on his knees beside her. "I'll 'fess up to the governor. I'll go on the water-wagon. I'll cut out the races. I'll be a regular little tin god if you'll only promise to be good to me."

"Good to you nothing!" said Nance, savagely, lifting a tear-stained, earnest face. "What right have I got to be anything to you? Haven't I been letting you spend the money on me that wasn't yours? I've been as bad as you have, every bit."

"Oh, rot!" said Mac, hotly. "You've been an angel. There isn't another girl in the world that's as much fun as you are and yet on the square every minute."

"It isn't on the square!" contradicted Nance, twisting her wet handkerchief into a ball. "Sneaking around corners and doing things on the sly. I am ashamed to tell you where I live, or who my people are, and you are ashamed to have your family know you are going with me. Whenever I look at your father and see him worrying about you, or think of your mother—"

"Yes, you think of everybody but me. You hold me at arm's length and knock on me and say things to me that nobody else would dare to say! And the worse you treat me, the more I want to take you in my arms and run away with you. Can't you love me a little, Nance? Please!"

He was close to her, with his ardent face on a level with hers. He was never more irresistible than when he wanted something, especially a forbidden something, and in the course of his twenty-one years he had never wanted anything so much as he wanted Nance Molloy.

She caught her breath and looked away. It was very hard to say what she intended, with him so close to her. His eloquent eyes, his tremulous lips were very disconcerting.

"Mr. Mac," she whispered intently, "why don't you tell your father everything, and promise him some of the things you been promising me? Why don't you make a clean start and behave yourself and stop giving 'em all this trouble?"

"And if I do, Nance? Suppose I do it for you, what then?"

For a long moment their eyes held each other. These two young, undisciplined creatures who had started life at opposite ends of the social ladder, one climbing up and the other climbing down, had met midway, and the fate of each trembled in the balance.

"And if I do?" Mac persisted, hardly above his breath.

Nance's eyelids fluttered ever so slightly, and the next instant, Mac had crushed her to him and smothered her protests in a passion of kisses.

CHAPTER XXVI
BETWEEN TWO FIRES

When Mr. Clarke returned from luncheon, it was evident that he was in no mood to encourage a prodigal's repentance. For half an hour Nance heard his voice rising and falling in angry accusation; then a door slammed, and there was silence. She waited tensely for the next sound, but it was long in coming. Presently some one began talking over the telephone in low, guarded tones, and she could not be sure which of the two it was. Then the talking ceased; the hall door of the inner office opened and closed quietly.

Nance went to the window and saw Mac emerge from the passage below and hurry across the yard to the stables. His cap was over his eyes, and his hands were deep in his pockets. Evidently he had had it out with his father and was going to stay over and meet his difficulties. Her eyes grew tender as she watched him. What a spoiled boy he was, in spite of his five feet eleven! Always getting into scrapes and letting other people get him out! But he was going to face the music this time, and he was doing it for her! If only she hadn't let him kiss her! A wave of shame made her bury her hot cheeks in her palms.

She was startled from her reverie by a noise at the door. It was Dan Lewis, looking strangely worried and preoccupied.

"Hello, Nance," he said, without lifting his eyes. "Did Mr. Clarke leave a telegram for me?"

"Not with me. Perhaps it is on his table. Want me to see?"

"No, I'll look," Dan answered and went in and closed the door behind him.

Nance looked at the closed door in sudden apprehension. What was the matter with Dan? What had he found out? She heard him moving about in the empty room; then she heard him talking over the telephone. When he came out, he crossed over to where she was sitting.

"Nance," he began, still with that uneasy manner, "there's something I've got to speak to you about. You won't take it amiss?"

"Cut loose," said Nance, with an attempt at lightness, but her heart began to thump uncomfortably.

"You see," Dan began laboriously. "I'm sort of worried by some talk that's been going on 'round the factory lately. It hadn't come direct to me until to-day, but I got wind of it every now and then. I know it's not true, but it mustn't go on. There's one way to stop it. Do you know what it is?"

Nance shook her head, and he went on.

"You and I have been making a mess of things lately. Maybe it's been my fault, I don't know. You see a fellow gets to know a lot of things a nice girl don't know. And the carnival ball business—well—I was scared for you, Nance, and that's the plain truth."

"I know, Dan," she said impatiently. "I was a fool to go that time, but I never did it again."

Dan fingered the papers on the desk.

"I ain't going to rag about that any more. But I can't have 'em saying things about you around the factory. You know how I feel about you—how I always have felt—Nance I want you to marry me."

Nance flashed a look at him, questioning, eager, uncertain; then her eyes fell. How could she know that behind his halting sentences a paean of love was threatening to burst the very confines of his inarticulate soul? She only saw an awkward young workman in his shirt sleeves, with a smudge across his cheek and a wistful look in his eyes, who knew no more about making love than he knew about the other graces of life.

"I've saved enough money," he went on earnestly, "to buy a little house in the country somewhere. That's what you wanted, wasn't it?"

Nance's glance wandered to the tall gas-pipe that had been their unromantic trysting place. Then she closed her eyes and pressed her fingers against them to keep back the stinging tears. If Dan loved her, why didn't he say beautiful things to her, why didn't he take her in his arms as Mac had done, and kiss away all those fears of herself and of the future that crowded upon her? With her head on his shoulder she could have sobbed out her whole confession and been comforted, but now—

"You care for me, don't you, Nance?" Dan asked with a sharp note of anxiety in his voice.

"Of course I care!" she said irritably. "But I don't want to get married and settle down. I want to get out and see the world. When you talk about a quiet little house in the country, I want to smash every window in it!"

Dan slipped the worn drawing he had in his hand back into his pocket. It was no time to discuss honeysuckle porches.

"We don't have to go to the country," he said patiently. "I just thought it was what you wanted. We can stay here, or we can go to another town if you like. All I want is to make you happy, Nance."

For a moment she sat with her chin on her palms, staring straight ahead; then she turned toward him with sudden resolution.

"What's the talk you been hearing about me?" she demanded.

"There's no use going into that," he said. "It's a lie, and I mean to stamp it out if I have to lick every man in the factory to do it."

"Was it—about Mac Clarke?"

"Who dared bring it to you?" he asked fiercely.

"What are they saying, Dan?"

"That you been seen out with him on the street, that you ride with him after night, and that he comes down here every day at the noon hour to see you."

"Is that all?"

"Ain't it enough?"

"Well, it's true!" said Nance, defiantly. "Every word of it. If anybody can find any real harm in what I've done, they are welcome to it!"

"It's true?" gasped Dan, his hands gripping a chair-back. "And you never told me? Has he—has he made love to you, Nance?"

"Why, he makes love to everybody. He makes love to his mother when he wants to get something out of her. What he says goes in one ear and out the other with me. But I like him and I ain't ashamed to say so. He's give me the best time I ever had in my life, and you bet I don't forget it."

"Will you answer me one thing more?" demanded Dan, sternly.

"Yes; I ain't afraid to answer any question you can ask."

"Was it Clarke that took you to the carnival ball?"

"Him and a fellow named Monte Pearce."

"Just you three?"

"No; Birdie Smelts was along."

Dan brushed his hand across his brow as if trying to recall something.

"Birdie come here that day," he said slowly. "She wanted to see Clarke for a friend of hers. Nance did he—did he ever ask you to kiss him?"

"Yes."

Dan groaned.

"Why didn't you tell me all this before, Nance? Why didn't you give me a chance to put you on your guard?"

"I *was* on my guard!" she cried, with rising anger. "I don't need anybody to take care of me!"

But Dan was too absorbed in his own thoughts to heed her.

"It's a good thing he's going away in a couple of days," he said grimly. "If ever the blackguard writes to you, or dares to speak to you again—"

Nance had risen and was facing him.

"Who's to stop him?" she asked furiously. "I'm the one to say the word, and not you!"

"And you won't let me take it up with him?"

"No!"

"And you mean to see him again, and to write to him?"

Nance had a blurred vision of an unhappy prodigal crossing the factory yard. He had kept his part of their compact; she must keep hers.

"I will if I want to," she said rather weakly.

Dan's face flushed crimson.

"All right," he said, "keep it up if you like. But I tell you now, I ain't going to stay here to see it. I'm going to clear out!"

He turned toward the door, and she called after him anxiously:

"Dan, come back here this minute. Where are you going?"

He paused in the doorway, his jaw set and a steady light in his eyes.

"I am going now," he said, "to apologize to the man I hit yesterday for telling the truth about you!"

That night Nance shed more tears than she had ever shed in the whole course of her life before; but whether she wept for Mac, or Dan, or for herself, she could not have said. She heard the sounds die out of the alley one by one, the clanging cars at the end of the street became less frequent; only the drip, drip, drip from a broken gutter outside her window, and the rats in the wall kept her company. All day Sunday she stayed in-doors, and came to the office on Monday pale and a bit listless.

Early as it was, Mr. Clarke was there before her, pacing the floor in evident perturbation.

"Come in here a moment, Miss Molloy," he said, before she had taken off her hat. "I want a word with you."

Nance followed him into the inner room with a quaking heart.

"I want you to tell me," he said, waiving all preliminaries, "just who was in this room Saturday afternoon after I left."

"Dan Lewis. And of course, Mr. Mac. You left him here."

"Who else?"

"Nobody."

"But there must have been," insisted Mr. Clarke, vehemently. "A man, giving my name, called up our retail store between two and two-thirty o'clock, and asked if they could cash a check for several hundred dollars. He said it was too late to go to the bank, and he wanted the money right away. Later a messenger brought my individual check, torn out of this checkbook, which evidently hasn't been off my desk, and received the money. The cashier thought the signature looked queer and called me up yesterday. I intend to leave no stone unturned until I get at the truth of the matter. You were the only person here all afternoon. Tell me, in detail, exactly what happened."

Nance recalled as nearly as she could, the incidents of the afternoon, with careful circuits around her own interviews with Mac and Dan.

"Could any one have entered the inner office between their visits, without your knowing it?" asked Mr. Clarke, who was following her closely.

"Oh, yes, sir; only there wasn't time. You see Mr. Mac was just going out the factory yard as Dan come in here."

"Did either of them use my telephone?"

"Both of them used it."

"Could you hear what was said?"

"No; the door was shut both times."

"Did Lewis enter through the other room, or through the hall?"

"He come through the other room and asked me if you had left a telegram for him."

"Then he came in here?"

"Yes, sir."

Mr. Clarke's brows were knitted in perplexity. He took up the telephone.

"Send Lewis up here to my office," he directed. "What? Hasn't come in yet?" he repeated incredulously. "That's strange," he said grimly, half to himself. "The first time I ever knew him to be late."

Something seemed to tighten suddenly about Nance's heart. Could it be possible that Mr. Clarke was suspecting Dan of signing that check? She watched his nervous hands as they ran over the morning mail. He had singled out one letter and, as he finished reading it, he handed it to her.

It was from Dan, a brief business-like resignation, expressing appreciation of Mr. Clarke's kindness, regret at the suddenness of his departure, and giving as his reason private affairs that took him permanently to another city.

When Nance lifted her startled eyes from the signature, she saw that Mr. Clarke was closely scrutinizing the writing on the envelope.

"It's incredible!" he said, "and yet the circumstances are most suspicious. He gives no real reason for leaving."

"I can," said Nance, resolutely. "He wanted me to marry him, and I wouldn't promise. He asked me Saturday afternoon, after he come out of here. We had a quarrel, and he said he was going away; but I didn't believe it."

"Did he ask you to go away with him? Out of town anywhere?"

"Yes; he said he would go anywhere I said."

A flash of anger burnt out the look of fear that had been lurking in Mr. Clarke's face.

"He's the last man I would have suspected! Of course I knew he had been in a reformatory at one time, but—"

The band that had been tightening around Nance's heart seemed suddenly to burst. She sprang to her feet and stood confronting him with blazing eyes.

"What right have you got to think Dan did it? There were two of them in this room. Why don't you send for Mr. Mac and ask him questions?"

"Well, for one reason he's in New York, and for another, my son doesn't have to resort to such means to get what money he wants."

"Neither does Dan Lewis! He was a street kid; he was had up in court three times before he was fourteen; he was a month at the reformatory; and he's knocked elbows with more crooks than you ever heard of; but you know as well as me that there ain't anybody living more honest than Dan!"

"All he's got to do is to prove it," said Mr. Clarke, grimly.

Nance looked at the relentless face of the man before her and thought of the money at his command to prove whatever he wanted to prove.

"See here, Mr. Clarke!" she said desperately, "you said a while ago that all the facts were against Dan. Will you tell me one thing?"

"What is it?"

"Did you give Mr. Mac the money to pay that note last Saturday?"

"What note?"

"The one the Meyers fellow was after him about?"

"Mac asked for no money, and I gave him none. In fact he told me that aside from his debts at the club and at the garage, he owed no bills. So you see your friend Meyers misinformed you."

Here was Nance's chance to escape; she had spoken in Dan's defense; she had told of the Meyers incident. To take one more step would be to convict Mac and compromise herself. For one miserable moment conflicting desires beat in her brain; then she heard herself saying quite calmly:

"No, sir, it wasn't Meyers that told me; it was Mr. Mac himself."

Mr. Clarke wheeled on her sharply.

"How did my son happen to be discussing his private affairs with you?"

"Mr. Mac and me are friends," she said. "He's been awful nice to me; he's given me more good times than I ever had in my whole life before. But I didn't know the money wasn't his or I wouldn't have gone with him."

"And I suppose you thought it was all right for a young man in Mac's position to be paying attention to a young woman in yours?"

Mr. Clarke studied her face intently, but her fearless eyes did not falter under his scrutiny.

"Are you trying to implicate Mac in this matter to spare Lewis, is that it?"

"No, sir. I don't say it was Mr. Mac. I only say it wasn't Dan. There are some people you just *know* are straight, and Dan's one of them."

Mr. Clarke got up and took a turn about the room, his hands locked behind him. Her last shot had evidently taken effect.

"Tell me exactly what Mac told you about this Meyers note," he demanded.

Nance recounted the facts in the case, ending with the promise Mac had made her to tell his father everything and begin anew.

"I wish I had known this Saturday!" Mr. Clarke said, sinking heavily into his chair. "I came down on the boy pretty severely on another score and gave him little chance to say anything. Did he happen to mention the exact amount of his indebtedness to Meyers?"

"He said it was five hundred and sixty dollars."

A sigh that was very like a groan escaped from Mr. Clarke; then he pulled himself together with an effort.

"You understand, Miss Molloy," he said, "that it is quite a different thing for my son to have done this, and for Lewis to have done it. Mac knows that what is mine will be his eventually. If he signed that check, he was signing his own name as well as mine. Of course, he ought to have spoken to me about it. I am not excusing him. He has been indiscreet in this as well as in other ways. I shall probably get a letter from him in a few days explaining the whole business. In the meanwhile the matter must go no further. I insist upon absolute silence. You understand?"

She nodded.

"And one thing more," Mr. Clarke added. "I forbid any further communication between you and Mac. He is not coming home at Christmas, and we are thinking of sending him abroad in June. I propose to keep him away from here for the next two or three years."

Nance fingered the blotter on the table absently. It was all very well for them to plan what they were going to do with Mac, but she knew in her heart that a line from her would set at naught all their calculations. Then her mind flew back to Dan.

"If he comes back—Dan, I mean,—are you going to take him on again?"

Mr. Clarke saw his chance and seized it.

"On one condition," he said. "Will you give me your word of honor not to communicate with Mac in any way?"

They were both standing now, facing each other, and Nance saw no compromise in the stern eyes of her employer.

"I'll promise if I've got to," she said.

"Very well," said Mr. Clarke. "That's settled."

CHAPTER XXVII
FATE TAKES A HAND

Some sinister fascination seems to hover about a bridge at night, especially for unhappy souls who have grappled with fate and think themselves worsted. Perhaps they find a melancholy pleasure in the company of ghosts who have escaped from similar defeats; perhaps they seek to read the riddle of the universe, as they stand, elbows on rail, studying the turbulent waters below.

On the third night after Dan's arrival in Cincinnati, the bridge claimed him. He had deposited his few belongings in a cheap lodging-house on the Kentucky side of the river, and then aimlessly paced the streets, too miserable to eat or sleep, too desperate even to look for work. His one desire was to get away from his tormenting thoughts, to try to forget what had happened to him.

A cold drizzle of rain had brought dusk on an hour before its time. Twilight was closing in on a sodden day. From the big Ohio city to the smaller Kentucky towns, poured a stream of tired humanity. Belated shoppers, business men, workers of all kinds hurried through the murky soot-laden air, each hastening to some invisible goal.

To Dan, watching with somber eyes from his niche above the wharf, it seemed that they were all going home to little lamp-lit cottages where women and children awaited them. A light in the window and somebody waiting! The old dream of his boyhood that only a few days ago had seemed about to come true!

Instead, he had been caught up in a hurricane and swept out to sea. His anchors had been his love, his work, and his religion, and none of them held. The factory, to which he had given the best of his brain and his body, for which he had dreamed and aspired and planned, was a nightmare to him. Mrs. Purdy and the church activities, which had loomed so large in his life, were but fleeting, unsubstantial shadows.

Only one thing in the wide universe mattered now to him, and that was Nance. Over and over he rehearsed his final scene with her, searching for some word of denial or contrition or promise for the future. She had never lied to him, and he knew she never would. But she had stood before him in angry defiance, refusing to defend herself, declining his help, and letting him go out of her life without so much as lifting a finger to stop him.

His heavy eyes, which had been following the shore lights, came back to the bridge, attracted by the movement of a woman leaning over one of the embrasures near him. He had been vaguely aware for the past five minutes of a disturbing sound that came to him from time to time; but it was only now that he noticed the woman was crying. She was standing with her back to him, and he could see her lift her veil every now and then and wipe her eyes.

With a movement of impatience, he moved further on. He had enough troubles of his own to-night without witnessing those of others. He had determined to stop fleeing from his thoughts and to turn and face them. A rich young fellow, like Mac Clarke, didn't go with a girl like Nance for nothing. Why, this thing must have been going on for months, perhaps long before the night he had found Nance at the signal tower. They had been meeting in secret, going out alone together; she had let him make love to her, kiss her.

The blood surged into his head, and doubts blacker than the waters below assailed him, but even as he stood there with his head in his hands and his cap pulled over his eyes, all sorts of shadowy memories came to plead for her. Memories of a little, tow-headed, independent girl coming and going in Calvary Alley, now lugging coal up two flights of stairs, now rushing noisily down again with a Snawdor baby slung over her shoulder, now to snatch her part in the play. Nance, who laughed the loudest, cried the hardest, ran the fastest, whose hand was as quick to help a friend as to strike a foe! He saw her sitting beside him on the mattress, sharing his disgrace on the day of the eviction, saw her standing before the bar of justice passionately pleading his cause. Then later and tenderer memories came to reinforce the earlier ones—memories of her gaily dismissing all other offers at the factory to trudge home night after night with him; of her sitting beside him in Post-Office Square, subdued and tender-eyed, watching the electric lights bloom through the dusk; of her nursing Uncle Jed, forgetting herself and her disappointment in ministering to him and helping him face the future.

A wave of remorse swept over him! What right had he to make her stay on and on in Cemetery Street when he knew how she hated it? Why had he forced her to go back to the factory? She had tried to make him understand, but he had been deaf to her need. He had expected her to buckle down to work just as he did. He had forgotten that she was young and pretty and wanted a good time like other girls. Of course it was wrong for her to go with Mac, but she was good, he *knew* she was good.

The words reverberated in his brain like a hollow echo, frightening away all the pleading memories. Those were the very words he had used about his mother on that other black night when he had refused to believe the truth. All the bitterness of his childhood's tragedy came now to poison his present mood. If Nance was innocent, why had she kept all this from him, why had she refused in the end to let him defend her good name?

He thought of his own struggle to be good; of his ceaseless efforts to be decent in every thought as well as deed for Nance's sake. Decent! His lip curled at the irony of it! That wasn't what girls wanted? Decency made fellows stupid and dull; it kept them too closely at work; it made them take life too seriously. Girls wanted men like Mac Clarke—men who snapped their fingers at religion and refused responsibilities, and laughed in the face of duty. Laughter! That was what Nance loved above everything! All right, let her have it! What did it matter? He would laugh too.

With a reckless resolve, he turned up his coat collar, rammed his hands in his pockets, and started toward the Kentucky shore. The drizzle by this time had turned into a sharp rain, and he realized that he was cold and wet. He remembered a swinging door two squares away.

As he left the bridge, he saw the woman in the blue veil hurry past him, and with a furtive look about her, turn and go down the steep levee toward the water. There was something so nervous and erratic in her movements, that he stopped to watch her.

For a few moments she wandered aimlessly along the bank, apparently indifferent to the pelting rain; then she succeeded, after some difficulty, in climbing out on one of the coal barges that fringed the river bank.

Dan glanced down the long length of the bridge, empty now save for a few pedestrians and a lumbering truck in the distance. In mid-stream the paddle of a river steamer was churning the water into foam, and upstream, near the dock, negro roustabouts could be heard singing. But under the bridge all was silent, and the levee was deserted in both directions. He strained his eyes to distinguish that vague figure on the barge from the surrounding shadows. He saw her crawling across the shifting coal; then he waited to see no more.

Plunging down the bank at full speed, he scrambled out on the barge and seized her by the arms. The struggle was brief, but fierce. With a cry of despair, she sank face downward on the coal and burst into hysterical weeping.

"Don't call a policeman!" she implored wildly. "Don't let 'em take me to a hospital!"

"I won't. Don't try to talk 'til you get hold of yourself," said Dan.

"But I'm chokin'! I can't breathe! Get the veil off!"

As Dan knelt above her, fumbling with the long veil, he noticed for the first time that she was young, and that her bare neck between the collar and the ripple of her black hair was very white and smooth. He bent down and looked at her with a flash of recognition.

"Birdie!" he cried incredulously, "Birdie Smelts!"

Her heavy white lids fluttered wildly, and she started up in terror.

"Don't be scared!" he urged. "It's Dan Lewis from back home. How did you ever come to be in this state?"

With a moan of despair she covered her face with her hands.

"I was up there on the bridge," Dan went on, almost apologetically. "I saw you there, but I didn't know it was you. Then when you started down to the water, I sorter thought—"

"You oughtn't 'a' stopped me," she wailed. "I been walkin' the streets tryin' to get up my courage all day. I'm sick, I tell you. I want to die."

"But it ain't right to die this way. Don't you know it's wicked?"

"Good and bad's all the same to me. I'm done for. There ain't a soul in this rotten old town that cares whether I live or die!"

Dan flushed painfully. He was much more equal to saving a body than a soul, but he did not flinch from his duty.

"God cares," he said. "Like as not He sent me out on the bridge a-purpose to-night to help you. You let me put you on the train, Birdie, and ship you home to your mother."

"Never! I ain't goin' home, and I ain't goin' to a hospital. Promise me you won't let 'em take me, Dan!"

"All right, all right," he said, with an anxious eye on her shivering form and her blue lips. "Only we got to get under cover somewhere. Do you feel up to walking yet?"

"Where'd I walk to?" she demanded bitterly. "I tell you I've got no money and no place to go. I been on the street since yesterday noon."

"You can't stay out here all night!" said Dan at his wit's end. "I'll have to get you a room somewhere."

"Go ahead and get it. I'll wait here."

But Dan mistrusted the look of cunning that leaped into her eyes and the way she glanced from time to time at the oily, black water that curled around the corner of the barge.

"I got a room a couple of squares over," he said slowly. "You might come over there 'til you get dried out and rested up a bit."

"I don't want to go anywhere. I'm too sick. I don't want to have to see people."

"You won't have to. It's a rooming house. The old woman that looks after things has gone by now."

It took considerable persuasion to get her on her feet and up the bank. Again and again she refused to go on, declaring that she didn't want to live. But Dan's patience was limitless. Added to his compassion for her, was the half-superstitious belief that he had been appointed by Providence to save her.

"It's just around the corner now," he encouraged her. "Can you make it?"

She stumbled on blindly, without answering, clinging to his arm and. breathing heavily.

"Here we are!" said Dan, turning into a dark entrance, "front room on the left. Steady there!"

But even as he opened the door, Birdie swayed forward and would have fallen to the floor, had he not caught her and laid her on the bed.

Hastily lighting the lamp on the deal table by the window, he went back to the bed and loosened the neck of her dripping coat and then looked down at her helplessly. Her face, startlingly white in its frame of black hair, showed dark circles under the eyes, and her full lips had lost not only their color, but the innocent curves of childhood as well.

Presently she opened her eyes wearily and looked about her.

"I'm cold," she said with a shiver, "and hungry. God! I didn't know anybody could be so hungry!"

"I'll make a fire in the stove," cried Dan; "then I'll go out and get you something hot to drink. You'll feel better soon."

"Don't be long, Dan," she whispered faintly. "I'm scared to stay by myself."

Ten minutes later Dan hurried out of the eating-house at the corner, balancing a bowl of steaming soup in one hand and a plate of food in the other. He was soaked to the skin, and the rain trickled from his hair into his eyes. As he crossed the street a gust of wind caught his cap and hurled it away into the wet night. But he gave no thought to himself or to the weather, for the miracle had happened. That dancing gleam in the gutter came from a lighted lamp in a window behind which some one was waiting for him.

He found Birdie shaking with a violent chill, and it was only after he had got off her wet coat and wrapped her in a blanket, and persuaded her to drink the soup that she began to revive.

"What time of night is it?" she asked weakly.

"After eleven. You're going to stay where you are, and I'm going out and find me a room somewhere. I'll come back in the morning."

All of Birdie's alarms returned.

"I ain't going to stay here by myself, Dan. I'll go crazy, I tell you! I don't want to live and I am afraid to die. What sort of a God is He to let a person suffer like this?"

And poor old Dan, at death-grips with his own life problem, wrestled in vain with hers; arguing, reassuring, affirming, trying with an almost fanatic zeal to conquer his own doubts in conquering hers.

Then Birdie, bent on keeping him with her, talked of herself, pouring out an incoherent story of misfortune: how she had fainted on the stage one night and incurred the ill-will of the director; how the company went on and left her without friends and without money; how matters had gone from bad to worse until she couldn't stand it any longer. She painted a picture of wronged innocence that would have wrung a sterner heart than Dan's.

"I know," he said sympathetically. "I've seen what girls are up against at Clarke's."

Birdie's feverish eyes fastened upon him.

"Have you just come from Clarke's?"

"Yes."

"Is Mac there?"

Dan's face hardened.

"I don't know anything about him."

"No; and you don't want to! If there's one person in this world I hate, it's Mac Clarke."

"Same here," said Dan, drawn to her by the attraction of a common antipathy.

"Thinks he can do what he pleases," went on Birdie, bitterly, "with his good looks and easy ways. He'll have a lot to answer for!"

Dan sat with his fists locked, staring at the floor. A dozen questions burned on his lips, but he could not bring himself to ask them.

A fierce gust of wind rattled the window, and Birdie cried out in terror.

"You stop being afraid and go to sleep," urged Dan, but she shook her head.

"I don't dare to! You'd go away, and I'd wake up and go crazy with fear. I always was like that even when I was a kid, back home. I used to pretty near die of nights when pa would come in drunk and get to breaking up things. There was a man like that down where I been staying. He'd fall against my door 'most every night. Sometimes I'd meet him out in the street, and he'd follow me for squares."

Dan drew the blanket about her shoulders.

"Go to sleep," he said. "I won't leave you."

"Yes; but to-morrow night, and next night! Oh, God! I'm smothering. Lift me up!"

He sat on the side of the bed and lifted her until she rested against his shoulder. A deathly pallor had spread over her features, and she clung to him weakly.

Through the long hours of the stormy night he sat there, soothing and comforting her, as he would have soothed a terror-stricken child. By and by her clinging hands grew passive in his, her rigid, jerking limbs relaxed, and she fell into a feverish sleep broken by fitful sobs and smothered outcries. As Dan sat there, with her helpless weight against him, and gently stroked the wet black hair from her brow, something fierce and protective stirred in him, the quick instinct of the chivalrous strong to defend the weak. Here was somebody more wretched, more desolate, more utterly lonely than himself—a soft, fearful, feminine somebody, ill-fitted to fight the world with those frail, white hands.

Hitherto he had blindly worshiped at one shrine, and now the image was shattered, the shrine was empty—so appallingly empty that he was ready to fill it at any cost. For the first time in three days he ceased to think of Nance Molloy or of Mac Clarke, whose burden he was all unconsciously bearing. He ceased, also, to think of the soul he had been trying so earnestly to save. He thought instead of the tender weight against his shoulder, of the heavy lashes that lay on the tear-stained cheeks so close to his, of the soft, white brow under his rough, brown fingers. Something older than love or religion was making its claim on Dan.

CHAPTER XXVIII
THE PRICE OF ENLIGHTENMENT

It was November of the following year that the bird of ill-omen, which had been flapping its wings over Calvary Alley for so long, decided definitely to alight. A catastrophe occurred that threatened to remove the entire population of the alley to another and, we trust, a fairer world.

Mrs. Snawdor insists to this day that it was the sanitary inspector who started the trouble. On one of his infrequent rounds he had encountered a strange odor in Number One, a suspicious, musty odor that refused to come under the classification of krout, kerosene, or herring. The tenants, in a united body, indignantly defended the smell.

"It ain't nothin' at all but Mis' Smelts' garbage," Mrs. Snawdor declared vehemently. "She often chucks it in a hole in the kitchen floor to save steps. Anybody'd think the way you was carryin' on, it was a murdered corpse!"

But the inspector persisted in his investigations, forcing a way into the belligerent Snawdor camp, where he found Fidy Yager with a well-developed case of smallpox. She had been down with what was thought to be chicken-pox for a week, but the other children had been sworn to secrecy under the threat that the doctor would scrape the skin off their arms with a knife if they as much as mentioned Fidy's name.

It was a culmination of a battle that had raged between Mrs. Snawdor and the health authorities for ten years, over the question of vaccination. The epidemic that followed was the visible proof of Mrs. Snawdor's victory.

Calvary Alley, having offered a standing invitation to germs in general, was loathe to regard the present one as an enemy. It resisted the inspector, who insisted on vaccinating everybody all over again; it was indignant at the headlines in the morning papers; it was outraged when Number One was put in quarantine.

Even when Fidy Yager, who "wasn't all there," and who, according to her mother, had "a fit a minute," was carried away to the pest-house, nobody was particularly alarmed. But when, twenty-four hours later, Mr.

Snawdor and one of the Lavinski helpers came down with it, the alley began to look serious, and Mrs. Snawdor sent for Nance.

For six months now Nance had been living at a young women's boarding home, realizing a life-long ambition to get out of the alley. But on hearing the news, she flung a few clothes into an old suitcase and rushed to the rescue.

Since that never-to-be-forgotten day a year ago when word had reached her of Dan's marriage to Birdie Smelts, a hopeless apathy had possessed her. Even in the first weeks after his departure, when Mac's impassioned letters were pouring in and she was exerting all her will power to make good her promise to his father, she was aware of a dull, benumbing anxiety over Dan. She had tried to get his address from Mrs. Purdy, from Slap Jack's, where he still kept some of his things, from the men he knew best at the factory. Nobody could tell her where he had gone, or what he intended to do.

Just what she wanted to say to him she did not know. She still resented bitterly his mistrust of her, and what she regarded as his interference with her liberty, but she had no intention of letting matters rest as they were. She and Dan must fight the matter out to some satisfactory conclusion.

Then came the news of his marriage, shattering every hope and shaking the very foundation of her being. From her earliest remembrance Dan had been the most dependable factor in her existence. Whirlwind enthusiasms for other things and other people had caught her up from time to time, but she always came back to Dan, as one comes back to solid earth after a flight in an aeroplane.

In her first weeks of chagrin and mortification she had sought refuge in thoughts of Mac. She had slept with his unanswered letters under her pillow and clung to the memory of his ardent eyes, his gay laughter, the touch of his lips on her hands and cheeks. Had Mac come home that Christmas, her doom would have been sealed. The light by which she steered had suddenly gone out, and she could no longer distinguish the warning coast lights from the harbor lights of home.

But Mac had not come at Christmas, neither had he come in the summer, and Nance's emotional storm was succeeded by an equally intolerable calm. Back and forth from factory to boarding home she trudged day by day, and on Sunday she divided her wages with Mrs. Snawdor, on the condition that she should have a vote in the management of family affairs. By this plan Lobelia and the twins were kept at school, and Mr. Snawdor's feeble efforts at decent living were staunchly upheld.

When the epidemic broke out in Calvary Alley, and Mrs. Snawdor signaled for help, Nance responded to the cry with positive enthusiasm. Here was something stimulating at last. There was immediate work to be done, and she was the one to do it.

As she hurried up the steps of Number One, she found young Dr. Isaac Lavinski superintending the construction of a temporary door.

"You can't come in here!" he called to her, peremptorily. "We're in quarantine. I've got everybody out I can. But enough people have been exposed to it already to spread the disease all over the city. Three more cases to-night. Mrs. Smelts' symptoms are very suspicious. Dr. Adair is coming himself at nine o'clock to give instructions. It's going to be a tussle all right!"

Nance looked at him in amazement. He spoke with more enthusiasm than he had ever shown in the whole course of his life. His narrow, sallow face was full of keen excitement. Little old Ike, who had hidden under the bed in the old days whenever a fight was going on, was facing death with the eagerness of a valiant soldier on the eve of his first battle.

"I'm going to help you, Ike!" Nance cried instantly. "I've come to stay 'til it's over."

But Isaac barred the way.

"You can't come in, I tell you! I've cleared the decks for action. Not another person but the doctor and nurse are going to pass over this threshold!"

"Look here, Ike Lavinski," cried Nance, indignantly, "you know as well as me that there are things that ought to be done up there at the Snawdors'!"

"They'll have to go undone," said Isaac, firmly.

Nance wasted no more time in futile argument. She waited for an opportune moment when Ike's back was turned; then she slipped around the corner of the house and threaded her way down the dark passage, until she reached the fire-escape. There were no lights in the windows as she climbed past them, and the place seemed ominously still.

At the third platform she scrambled over a wash-tub and a dozen plaster casts of Pocahontas,—Mr. Snawdor's latest venture in industry,— and crawled through the window into the kitchen. It was evident at a glance that Mrs. Snawdor had at last found that long-talked-of day off and had utilized it in cleaning up. The room didn't look natural in its changed condition. Neither did Mrs. Snawdor, sitting in the gloom in an attitude of deep dejection. At sight of Nance at the window, she gave a cry of relief.

"Thank the Lord, you've come!" she said. "Can you beat this? Havin' to climb up the outside of yer own house like a fly! They've done sent Fidy to the pest-house, an' scattered the other childern all over the neighborhood, an' they got me fastened up here, like a hen in a coop!"

"How is he?" whispered Nance, glancing toward the inner room.

"Ain't a thing the matter with him, but the lumbago. Keeps on complainin' of a pain in his back. I never heard of such a hullabaloo about nothin' in all my life. They'll be havin' me down with smallpox next. How long you goin' to be here?"

Nance, taking off her hat and coat, announced that she had come to stay.

Mrs. Snawdor heaved a sigh of relief.

"Well, if you'll sorter keep a eye on him, I believe I'll step down an' set with Mis' Smelts fer a spell. I ain't been off the place fer two days."

"But wait a minute! Where's Uncle Jed? And Mr. Demry?"

"They 're done bounced too! Anybody tell you 'bout yer Uncle Jed's patent? They say he stands to make as much as a hundern dollars offen it. They say—"

"I don't care what they say!" cried Nance, distractedly. "Tell me, did the children take clean clothes with 'em? Did you see if Uncle Jed had his sweater? Have you washed the bedclothes that was on Fidy's bed?"

Mrs. Snawdor shook her head impatiently.

"I didn't, an' I ain't goin' to! That there Ike Lavinski ain't goin' to run me! He took my Fidy off to that there pest-house where I bet they operate her. He'll pay up fer this, you see if he don't!"

She began to cry, but as Nance was too much occupied to give audience to her grief, she betook herself to the first floor to assist in the care of Mrs. Smelts. Illness in the abode of another has a romantic flavor that home-grown maladies lack.

When Dr. Adair and Isaac Lavinski made their rounds at nine o'clock, they found Nance bending over a steaming tub, washing out a heavy comfort.

"What are you doing here?" demanded Isaac in stern surprise.

"Manicuring my finger-nails," she said, with an impudent grin, as she straightened her tired shoulders. Then seeing Dr. Adair, she blushed and wiped her hands on her apron.

"You don't remember me, Doctor, do you? I helped you with Uncle Jed Burks at the signal tower that time when the lightning struck him."

He looked her over, his glance traveling from her frank, friendly face to her strong bare arms.

"Why, yes, I do. You and your brother had been to some fancy-dress affair. I remember your red shoes. It isn't every girl of your age that could have done what you did that night. Have you been vaccinated?"

"Twice. Both took."

"She's got no business being here, sir," Isaac broke in hotly. "I told her to keep out."

"Doctor! Listen at me!" pleaded Nance, her hand on his coat sleeve. Honest to goodness, I *got* to stay. Mrs. Snawdor don't believe it's smallpox. She'll slip the children in when you ain't looking and go out herself and see the neighbors. Don't you see that somebody's got to be here that understands?"

"The girl's right, Lavinski," said Dr. Adair. "She knows the ropes here, and can be of great service to us. The nurse downstairs can't begin to do it all. Now let us have a look at the patient."

Little Mr. Snawdor was hardly worth looking at. He lay rigid, like a dried twig, with his eyes shut tight, and his mouth shut tight, and his hands clenched tighter still. It really seemed as if this time Mr. Snawdor was going to make good his old-time threat to quit.

Dr. Adair gave the necessary instructions; then he turned to go. He had been watching Nance, as she moved about the room carrying out his orders, and at the door he laid a hand on her shoulder.

"How old are you, my girl?" he asked.

"Twenty."

"We need girls like you up at the hospital. Have you ever thought of taking the training?"

"Me? I haven't got enough spondulicks to take a street-car ride."

"That part can be arranged if you really want to go into the work. Think it over."

Then he and the impatient Isaac continued on their rounds, and Nance went back to her work. But the casual remark, let fall by Dr. Adair, had set her ambition soaring. Her imagination flared to the project. Snawdor's flat extended itself into a long ward; poor little Mr. Snawdor, who was hardly half a man, became a dozen; and Miss Molloy, in a becoming uniform, moved in and out among the cots, a ministering angel of mercy.

For the first time since Dan Lewis's marriage, her old courage and zest for life returned, and when Mrs. Snawdor came in at midnight, she found her sitting beside her patient with shining eyes full of waking dreams.

"Mis' Smelts is awful bad," Mrs. Snawdor reported, looking more serious than she had heretofore. "Says she wants to see you before the nurse wakes up. Seems like she's got somethin' on her mind."

Nance hurried into her coat and went out into the dark, damp hall. Long black roaches scurried out of her way as she descended the stairs. In the hall below the single gas-jet flared in the draught, causing ghostly shadows to leap out of corners and then skulk fearfully back again. Nance was not afraid, but a sudden sick loathing filled her. Was she never going to be able to get away from it all? Was that long arm of duty going to stretch out and find her wherever she went, and drag her back to this noisome spot? Were all her dreams and ambitions to die, as they had been born, in Calvary Alley?

Mrs. Smelts had been moved into an empty room across the hall from her own crowded quarters, and as Nance pushed open the door, she lifted a warning hand and beckoned.

"Shut it," she said in a hoarse whisper. "I don't want nobody to hear what I got to tell you."

"Can't it wait, Mrs. Smelts?" asked Nance, with a pitying hand on the feverish brow across which a long white scar extended.

"No. They're goin' to take me away in the mornin'. I heard 'em say so. It's about Birdie, Nance, I want to tell you. They've had to lock her up."

"It's the fever makes you think that, Mrs. Smelts. You let me sponge you off a bit."

"No, no, not yet. She's crazy, I tell you! She went out of her head last January when the baby come. Dan's kept it to hisself all this time, but now he's had to send her to the asylum."

"Who told you?"

"Dan did. He wrote me when he sent me the last money. I got his letter here under my pillow. I want you to burn it, Nance, so no one won't know."

Nance went on mechanically stroking the pain-racked head, as she reached under the pillow for Dan's letter. The sight of the neat, painstaking writing made her heart contract.

"You tell him fer me," begged Mrs. Smelts, weakly, "to be good to her. She never had the right start. Her paw handled me rough before she come, an' she was always skeery an' nervous like. But she was so purty, oh, so purty, an' me so proud of her!"

Nance wiped away the tears that trickled down the wrinkled cheeks, and tried to quiet her, but the rising fever made her talk on and on.

"I ain't laid eyes on her since a year ago this fall. She come home sick, an' nobody knew it but me. I got out of her whut was her trouble, an' I went to see his mother, but it never done no good. Then I went to the bottle factory an' tried to get his father to listen—"

"Whose father?" asked Nance, sharply.

"The Clarke boy's. It was him that did fer her. I tell you she was a good girl 'til then. But they wouldn't believe it. They give me some money to sign the paper an' not to tell; but before God it's him that's the father of her child, and poor Dan—"

But Mrs. Smelts never finished her sentence; a violent paroxysm of pain seized her, and at dawn the messenger that called for the patient on the third floor, following the usual economy practised in Calvary Alley, made one trip serve two purposes and took her also.

By the end of the month the epidemic was routed, and the alley, cleansed and chastened as it had never been before, was restored to its own. Mr. Snawdor, Fidy Yager, Mrs. Smelts, and a dozen others, being the unfittest to survive, had paid the price of enlightenment.

CHAPTER XXIX
IN TRAINING

One sultry July night four years later Dr. Isaac Lavinski, now an arrogant member of the staff at the Adair Hospital, paused on his last round of the wards and cocked an inquiring ear above the steps that led to the basement. Something that sounded very much like suppressed laughter came up to him, and in order to confirm his suspicions, he tiptoed down to the landing and, making an undignified syphon of himself, peered down into the rear passage. In a circle on the floor, four nurses in their nightgowns softly beat time, while a fifth, arrayed in pink pajamas, with her hair flying, gave a song and dance with an abandon that ignored the fact that the big thermometer in the entry registered ninety-nine.

The giggles that had so disturbed Dr. Lavinski's peace of mind increased in volume, as the dancer executed a particularly daring *passeul* and, turning a double somersault, landed deftly on her bare toes.

"Go on, do it again!" "Show us how Sheeny Ike dances the tango." "Sing Barney McKane," came in an enthusiastic chorus.

But before the encore could be responded to, a familiar sound in the court without, sent the girls scampering to their respective rooms.

Dr. Isaac, reluctantly relinquishing his chance for administering prompt and dramatic chastisement, came down the stairs and out to the entry.

An ambulance had just arrived, and behind it was a big private car, and behind that Dr. Adair's own neat runabout.

Dr. Adair met Dr. Isaac at the door.

"It's an emergency case," he explained hastily. "I may have to operate to-night. Prepare number sixteen, and see if Miss Molloy is off duty."

"She is, sir," said Isaac, grimly, "and the sooner she's put on a case the better."

"Tell her to report at once. And send an orderly down to lend a hand with the stretcher."

Five minutes later an immaculate nurse, every button fastened, every fold in place, presented herself on the third floor for duty. You would have had to look twice to make certain that that slim, trim figure in its white uniform was actually Nance Molloy. To be sure her eyes sparkled with the old fire under her becoming cap, and her chin was still carried at an angle that hinted the possession of a secret gold mine, but she had changed amazingly for all that. Life had evidently been busy chiseling away her rough edges, and from a certain poise of body and a professional control of voice and gesture, it was apparent that Nance had done a little chiseling on her own account.

As she stood in the dim corridor awaiting orders, she could not help overhearing a conversation between Dr. Adair and the agitated lady who stood with her hand on the door-knob of number sixteen.

"My dear madam," the doctor was saying in a tone that betokened the limit of patience, "you really must leave the matter to my judgment, if we operate—"

"But you won't unless it's the last resort?" pleaded the lady. "You know how frightfully sensitive to pain he is. But if you find out that you must, then I want you to promise me not to let him suffer afterward. You must keep him under the influence of opiates, and you will wait until his father can get here, won't you?"

"But that's the trouble. You've waited too long already. Appendicitis is not a thing to take liberties with."

"You don't mean it's too late? You don't think—"

"We don't think anything at present. We hope everything." Then spying Nance, he turned toward her with relief. "This is the nurse who will take charge of the case."

The perturbed lady uncovered one eye.

"You are sure she is one of your very best?"

"One of our best," said the doctor, as he and Nance exchanged a quizzical smile.

"Let her go in to him now. I can't bear for him to be alone a second. As I was telling you—"

Nance passed into the darkened room and closed the door softly. The patient was evidently asleep; so she tiptoed over to the window and slipped into a chair. On each side of the open space without stretched the vine-clad wings of the hospital, gray now under the starlight. Nance's eyes traveled reminiscently from floor to floor, from window to window. How many memories the old building held for her! Memories of heartaches and happiness, of bad times and good times, of bitter defeats and dearly won triumphs.

It had been no easy task for a girl of her limited education and undisciplined nature to take the training course. But she had gallantly stood to her guns and out of seeming defeat, won a victory. For the first time in her diversified career she had worked in a congenial environment toward a fixed goal, and in a few weeks now she would be launching her own little boat on the professional main.

Her eyes grew tender as she thought of leaving these protecting gray walls that had sheltered her for four long years; yet the adventure of the future was already calling. Where would her first case lead her?

A cough from the bed brought her sharply back to the present. She went forward and stooped to adjust a pillow, and the patient opened his eyes, stared at her in bewilderment, then pulled himself up on his elbow.

"Nance!" he cried incredulously. "Nance Molloy!"

She started back in dismay.

"Why, it's Mr. Mac! I didn't know! I thought I'd seen the lady before— no, please! Stop, they're coming! Please, Mr. Mac!"

For the patient, heretofore too absorbed in his own affliction to note anything, was covering her imprisoned hands with kisses and calling on Heaven to witness that he was willing to undergo any number of operations if she would nurse him through them.

Nance escaped from the room as Mrs. Clarke entered. With burning cheeks she rushed to Dr. Adair's office.

"You'll have to get somebody else on that case, Doctor," she declared impulsively. "I used to work for Mr. Clarke up at the bottle factory, and— and there are reasons why I don't want to take it."

Dr. Adair looked at her over his glasses and frowned.

"It is a nurse's duty," he said sternly, "to take the cases as they come, irrespective of likes or dislikes. Mr. Clarke is an old friend of mine, a man I admire and respect."

"Yes, sir, I know, but if you'll just excuse me this once—"

"Is Miss Rand off duty?"

"No, sir. She's in number seven."

"Miss Foster?"

"No, sir."

"Then I shall have to insist upon your taking the case. I must have somebody I can depend upon to look after young Clarke for the next twenty-four hours. It's not only the complication with his appendix; it's his lungs."

"You mean he's tubercular?"

"Yes."

Nance's eyes widened.

"Does he know it?"

"No. I shall wait and tell his father. I wouldn't undertake to break the news to that mother of his for a house and lot! You take the case to-night, and I'll operate in the morning—"

"No, no, please, Doctor! Mr. Clarke wouldn't want me."

"Mr. Clarke will be satisfied with whatever arrangement I see fit to make. Besides another nurse will be in charge by the time he arrives."

"But, Doctor—"

A stern glance silenced her, and she went out, closing the door as hard as she dared behind her. During her four years at the hospital the memory of Mac Clarke had grown fainter and fainter like the perfume of a fading flower. But the memory of Dan was like a thorn in her flesh, buried deep, but never forgotten.

To herself, her fellow-nurses, the young internes who invariably fell in love with her, she declared gaily that she was "through with men forever." The subject that excited her fiercest scorn was matrimony, and she ridiculed sentiment with the superior attitude of one who has weighed it in the balance and found it wanting.

Nevertheless something vaguely disturbing woke in her that night when she watched with Mrs. Clarke at Mac's bedside. Despite the havoc five years had wrought in him, there was the old appealing charm in his voice and manner, the old audacity in his whispered words when she bent over him, the old eager want in his eyes as they followed her about the room.

Toward morning he dropped into a restless sleep, and Mrs. Clarke, who had been watching his every breath, tiptoed over to the table and sat down by Nance.

"My son tells me you are the Miss Molloy who used to be in the office," she whispered. "He is so happy to find some one here he knows. He loathes trained nurses as a rule. They make him nervous. But he has been wonderfully good about letting you do things for him. It's a tremendous relief to me."

Nance made a mistake on the chart that was going to call for an explanation later.

"He's been losing ground ever since last winter," the doting mother went on. "He was really quite well at Divonne-les-Bains, but he lost all he gained when we reached Paris. You see he doesn't know how to take care of himself; that's the trouble."

Mac groaned and she hurried to him.

"He wants a cigarette, Miss Molloy. I don't believe it would hurt him," she said.

"His throat's already irritated," said Nance, in her most professional tone. "I am sure Dr. Adair wouldn't want him to smoke."

"But we can't refuse him anything to-night," said Mrs. Clarke, with an apologetic smile as she reached for the matches.

Nance looking at her straight, delicate profile thrown into sudden relief by the flare of the match, had the same disturbing sense of familiarity that she had experienced long ago in the cathedral.

But during the next twenty-four hours there was no time to analyze subtle impressions or to indulge in sentimental reminiscence. From the moment Mac's unconscious form was borne down from the operating room and handed over to her care, he ceased to be a man and became a critically ill patient.

"We haven't much to work on," said Dr. Adair, shaking his head. "He has no resisting power. He has burned himself out."

But Mac's powers of resistance were stronger than he thought, and by the time Mr. Clarke arrived the crisis was passed. Slowly and painfully he struggled back to consciousness, and his first demand was for Nance.

"It's the nurse he had when he first came," Mrs. Clarke explained to her husband. "You must make Dr. Adair give her back to us. She's the only nurse I've ever seen who could get Mac to do things. By the way, she used to be in your office, a rather pretty, graceful girl, named Molloy."

"I remember her," said Mr. Clarke, grimly. "You better leave things as they are. Miss Hanna seems to know her business."

"But Mac hates Miss Hanna! He says her hands make him think of bedsprings. Miss Molloy makes him laugh and helps him to forget the pain. He's taken a tremendous fancy to her."

"Yes, he had quite a fancy for her once before."

"Now, Macpherson, how can you?" cried Mrs. Clarke on the verge of tears. "Just because the boy made one slip when he was little more than a *child*, you suspect his every motive. I don't see how you can be so cruel! If you had seen his agony, if you had been through what I have—"

Thus it happened that instead of keeping Nance out of Mac's sight, Mrs. Clarke left no stone unturned to get her back, and Mr. Clarke was even persuaded to take it up personally with Dr. Adair.

Nance might have held out to the end, had her sympathies not been profoundly stirred by the crushing effect the news of Mac's serious tubercular condition had upon his parents. On the day they were told Mr. Clarke paced the corridor for hours with slow steps and bent head, refusing to see people or to answer the numerous inquiries over the telephone. As for Mrs. Clarke, all the fragile prettiness and girlish grace she had carried over into maturity, seemed to fall away from her within the hour, leaving her figure stooped and her face settled into lines of permanent anxiety.

The mother's chief concern now was to break the news of his condition to Mac, who was already impatiently straining at the leash, eager to get back to his old joyous pursuits and increasingly intolerant of restrictions.

"He refuses to listen to me or to his father," she confided to Nance, who had coaxed her down to the yard for a breath of fresh air. "I'm afraid we've lost our influence over him. And yet I can't bear for Dr. Adair to tell him. He's so stern and says such dreadful things. Do you know he actually was heartless enough to tell Mac that he had brought a great deal of this trouble on himself!"

Nance slipped her hand through Mrs. Clarke's arm, and patted it reassuringly. She had come to have a sort of pitying regard for this terror-stricken mother during these days of anxious waiting.

"I wonder if you would be willing to tell him?" Mrs. Clarke asked, looking at her appealingly. "Maybe you could make him understand without frightening him."

"I'll try," said Nance, with ready sympathy.

The opportunity came one day in the following week when the regular day nurse was off duty. She found Mac alone, propped up in bed, and tremendously glad to see her. To a less experienced person the brilliancy of his eyes and the color in his cheeks would have meant returning health, but to Nance they were danger signals that nerved her to her task.

"I hear you are going home next week," she said, resting her crossed arms on the foot of his bed. "Going to be good and take care of yourself?"

"Not on your life!" cried Mac, gaily, searching under his pillow for his cigarette case. "The lid's been on for a month, and it's coming off with a bang. I intend to shoot the first person that mentions health to me."

"Fire away then," said Nance. "I'm it. I've come to hand you out a nice little bunch of advice."

"You needn't. I've got twice as much now as I intend to use. Come on around here and be sociable. I want to make love to you."

Nance declined the invitation.

"Has Dr. Adair put you wise on what he's letting you in for?"

"Rather! Raw eggs, rest, and rust. Mother put him up to it. It's perfect rot. I'll be feeling fit as a fiddle inside of two weeks. All I need is to get out of this hole. They couldn't have kept me here this long if it hadn't been for you."

"And I reckon you're counting on going back and speeding up just as you did before?"

"Sure, why not?"

"Because you can't. The sooner you soak that in, the better."

He blew a succession of smoke rings in her direction and laughed.

"So they've taken you into the conspiracy, have they? Going to frighten me into the straight and narrow, eh? Suppose I tell them that I'm lovesick? That there's only one cure for me in the world, and that's you?"

The ready retort with which she had learned to parry these personalities was not forthcoming. She felt as she had that day five years ago in his father's office, when she told him what she thought of him. He smiled up at her with the same irresponsible light in his brown eyes, the same eager desire to sidestep the disagreeable, the old refusal to accept life seriously. He was such a boy despite his twenty-six years. Such a spoiled, selfish lovable boy!

With a sudden rush of pity, she went to him and took his hand:

"See here, Mr. Mac," she said very gravely, "I got to tell you something. Dr. Adair wanted to tell you from the first, but your mother headed him off."

He shot a swift glance at her.

"What do you mean, Nance?"

Then Nance sat on the side of his bed and explained to him, as gently and as firmly as she could, the very serious nature of his illness, emphasizing the fact that his one chance for recovery lay in complete surrender to a long and rigorous regime of treatment.

From scoffing incredulity, he passed to anxious skepticism and then to agonized conviction. It was the first time he had ever faced any disagreeable fact in life from which there was no appeal, and he cried out in passionate protest. If he was a "lunger" he wanted to die as soon as possible. He hated those wheezy chaps that went coughing through life, avoiding draughts, and trying to keep their feet dry. If he was going to die, he wanted to do it with a rush. He'd be hanged if he'd cut out smoking, drinking, and running with the boys, just to lie on his back for a year and perhaps die at the end of it!

Nance faced the bitter crisis with him, whipping up his courage, strengthening his weak will, nerving him for combat. When she left him an hour later, with his face buried in the pillow and his hands locked above his head, he had promised to submit to the doctor's advice on the one condition that she would go home with him and start him on that fight for life that was to tax all his strength and patience and self-control.

CHAPTER XXX
HER FIRST CASE

October hovered over Kentucky that year in a golden halo of enchantment. The beech-trees ran the gamut of glory, and every shrub and weed had its hour of transient splendor. A soft haze from burning brush lent the world a sense of mystery and immensity. Day after day on the south porch at Hillcrest Mac Clarke lay propped with cushions on a wicker couch, while Nance Molloy sat beside him, and all about them was a stir of whispering, dancing, falling leaves. The hillside was carpeted with them, the brook below the pergola was strewn with bits of color, while overhead the warm sunshine filtered through canopies of russet and crimson and green.

"I tell you the boy is infatuated with that girl," Mr. Clarke warned his wife from time to time.

"What nonsense!" Mrs. Clarke answered. "He is just amusing himself a bit. He will forget her as soon as he gets out and about."

"But the girl?"

"Oh, she's too sensible to have any hopes of that kind. She really is an exceptionally nice girl. Rather too frank in her speech, and frequently ungrammatical and slangy, but I don't know what we should do without her."

But even Mrs. Clarke's complacence was a bit shaken as the weeks slipped away, and Mac's obsession became the gossip of the household. To be sure, so long as Nance continued to regard the whole matter as a joke and refused to take Mac seriously, no harm would be done. But that very indifference that assured his adoring mother, at the same time piqued her pride. That an ordinary trained nurse, born and brought up, Heaven knew where, should be insensible to Mac's even transient attention almost amounted to an impertinence. Quite unconsciously she began to break down Nance's defenses.

"You must be very good to my boy, dear," she said one day in her gentle, coaxing way. "I know he's a bit capricious and exacting at times. But we can't afford to cross him now when he is just beginning to improve. He was terribly upset last night when you teased him about leaving."

"But I ought to go, Mrs. Clarke. He'd get along just as well now with another nurse. Besides I only promised—"

"Not another word!" implored Mrs. Clarke in instant alarm. "I wouldn't answer for the consequences if you left us now. Mac goes all to pieces when it is suggested. He has always been so used to having his own way, you know."

Yes, Nance knew. Between her unceasing efforts to get him well, and her grim determination to keep the situation well in hand, she had unlimited opportunity of finding out. The physicians agreed that his chances for recovery were one to three. It was only by the most persistent observance of certain regulations pertaining to rest, diet, and fresh air, that they held out any hope of arresting the malady that had already made such alarming headway. Nance realized from the first that it was to be a fight against heavy odds, and she gallantly rose to the emergency. Aside from the keen personal interest she took in Mac, and the sympathy she felt for his stricken parents, she had an immense pride in her first private case, on which she was determined to win her spurs.

For three months now she had controlled the situation. With undaunted perseverance she had made Mac submit to authority and succeeded in successfully combatting his mother's inclination to yield to his every whim. The gratifying result was that Mac was gradually putting on flesh and, with the exception of a continued low fever, was showing decided improvement. Already talk of a western flight was in the air.

The whole matter hinged at present on Mac's refusal to go unless Nance could be induced to accompany them. The question had been argued from every conceivable angle, and gradually a conspiracy had been formed between Mac and his mother to overcome her apparently absurd resistance.

"It isn't as if she had any good reason," Mrs. Clarke complained to her husband, with tears in her eyes. "She has no immediate family, and she might just as well be on duty in California as in Kentucky. I don't see how she can refuse to go when she sees how weak Mac is, and how he depends on her."

"The girl's got more sense than all the rest of you put together!" said Mr. Clarke. "She sees the way things are going."

"Well, what if Mac is in love with her?" asked Mrs. Clarke, for the first time frankly facing the situation. "Of course it's just his sick fancy, but he is in no condition to be argued with. The one absolutely necessary thing is to get her to go with us. Suppose you ask her. Perhaps that's what she is waiting for."

"And you are willing to take the consequences?"

"I am willing for anything on earth that will help me keep my boy," sobbed Mrs. Clarke, resorting to a woman's surest weapon.

So Mr. Clarke turned his ponderous batteries upon the situation, using money as the ammunition with which he was most familiar.

The climax was reached one night toward the end of October when the first heavy hoar-frost of the season gave premonitory threat of coming winter. The family was still at dinner, and Mac was having his from a tray before the library fire. The heavy curtains had been drawn against the chill world without, and the long room was a soft harmony of dull reds and browns, lit up here and there by rose-shaded lamps.

It was a luxurious room, full of trophies of foreign travel. The long walls were hung with excellent pictures; the floors were covered with rare rugs; the furniture was selected with perfect taste. Every detail had been elaborately and skilfully worked out by an eminent decorator. Only one insignificant item had been omitted. In the length and breadth of the library, not a book was to be seen.

Mac, letting his soup cool while he read the letter Nance had just brought him, gave an exclamation of surprise.

"By George! Monte Pearce is going to get married!"

Nance laughed.

"I've got a tintype of Mr. Monte settling down. Who's the girl?"

"A cousin of his in Honolulu. Her father is a sugar king; no end of cash. Think of old Monte landing a big fish like that!"

"That's what you'll be doing when you get out to your ranch."

"I intend to take my girl along."

"You'll have to get her first."

Mac turned on her with an invalid's fretfulness. "See here, Nance," he cried, "cut that out, will you? Either you go, or I stay, do you see? I know I'm a fool about you, but I can't help it. Nance, why don't you love me?"

Nance looked down at him helplessly. She had been refusing him on an average of twice a day for the past week, and her powers of resistance were weakening. The hardest granite yields in the end to the persistent dropping of water. However much the clear-headed, independent side of her might refuse him, to another side of her he was strangely appealing. Often when she was near him, the swift remembrance of other days filled her with sudden desire to yield, if only for a moment, to his insatiable demands. Despite her most heroic resolution, she sometimes relaxed her vigilance as she did to-night, and allowed her hand to rest in his.

Mac made the most of the moment.

"I don't ask you to promise me anything, Nance. I just ask you to come with me!" he pleaded, with eloquent eyes, "we can get a couple of ponies and scour the trails all over those old mountains. At Coronada there's bully sea bathing. And the motoring—why you can go for a hundred miles straight along the coast!"

Nance's eyes kindled, but she shook her head. "You can do all that without me. All I do is to jack you up and make you take care of yourself. I should think you 'd hate me, Mr. Mac."

"Well, I don't. Sometimes I wish I did. I love you even when you come down on me hardest. A chap gets sick of being mollycoddled. When you fire up and put your saucy little chin in the air, and tell me I sha'n't have a cocktail, and call me a fool for stealing a smoke, it bucks me up more than anything. By George, I believe I'd amount to something if you'd take me permanently in hand."

Nance laughed, and he pulled her down on the arm of his chair.

"Say you'll marry me, Nance," he implored. "You'll learn to care for me all right. You want to get out and see the world. I'll take you. We'll go out to Honolulu and see Monte. Mother will talk the governor over; she's promised. They'll give me anything I want, and I want you. Oh, Nance darling, don't leave me to fight through this beastly business alone!"

There was a haunted look of fear in his eyes as he clung to her that appealed to her more than his former demands had ever done. Instinctively her strong, tender hands closed over his thin, weak ones.

"Nobody expects you to fight it through alone," she reassured him, "but you come on down off this high horse! We'll be having another bad night the first thing you know."

"They'll all be bad if you don't come with me, Nance. I won't ask you to say yes to-night, but for God's sake don't say no!"

Nance observed the brilliancy of his eyes and the flush on his thin cheeks, and knew that his fever was rising.

"All right," she promised lightly. "I won't say no to-night, if you'll stop worrying. I'm going to fix you nice and comfy on the couch and not let you say another word."

But when she had got him down on the couch, nothing would do but she must sit on the hassock beside him and soothe his aching head. Sometimes he stopped her stroking hand to kiss it, but for the most part he lay with eyes half-closed and elaborated his latest whim.

"We could stay awhile in Honolulu and then go on to Japan and China. I want to see India, too, and Mandalay,

... somewhere east of Suez, where the best is like the worst,
And there aren't no Ten Commandments

—you remember Kipling's Mandalay?"

Nance couldn't remember what she had never known, but she did not say so. Since her advent at Hillcrest she had learned to observe and listen without comment. This was not her world, and her shrewd common-sense told her so again and again. Even the servants who moved with such easy familiarity about their talks were more at home than she. It had kept her wits busy to meet the situation. But now that she had got over her first awkwardness, she found the new order of things greatly to her liking. For the first time in her life she was moving in a world of beautiful objects, agreeable sounds, untroubled relations, and that starved side of her that from the first had cried out for order and beauty and harmony fed ravenously upon the luxury around her.

And this was what Mac was offering her,—her, Nance Molloy of Calvary Alley,—who up to four years ago had never known anything but bare floors, flickering gas-jets, noise, dirt, confusion. He wanted her to marry him; he needed her.

She ceased to listen to his rambling talk, her eyes rested dreamily on the glowing back-log. After all didn't every woman want to marry and have a home of her own, and later perhaps—Twenty-four at Christmas! Almost an old maid! And to think Mr. Mac had gone on caring for her all these years, that he still wanted her when he had all those girls in his own world to choose from. Not many men were constant like that, she thought, as an old memory stabbed her.

Then she was aware that her hand was held fast to a hot cheek, and that a pair of burning eyes were watching her.

"Nance!" Mac whispered eagerly, "you're giving in! You're going with me!"

A step in the hall made Nance scramble to her feet just before Mrs. Clarke came in from the dining-room.

"I thought we should never get through dinner!" said that lady, with an impatient sigh. "The bishop can talk of nothing else but his new hobby, and do you know he's actually persuaded your father to give one of the tenements back of the cathedral for the free clinic!"

Nance who was starting out with the tray, put it down suddenly.

"How splendid!" she cried. "Which house is it?"

"I don't know, I am sure. But they are going to put a lot of money into doing it over, and Dr. Adair has offered to take entire charge of it. For my part I think it is a great mistake. Just think what that money would mean to our poor mission out in Mukden! These shiftless people here at home have every chance to live decently. It's not our fault if they refuse to take advantage of their opportunities."

"But they don't know how, Mrs. Clarke! If Dr. Adair could teach the mothers—"

Mrs. Clarke lifted her hands in laughing protest.

"My dear girl, don't you know that mothers can't be taught? The most ignorant mother alive has more instinctive knowledge of what is good for her child than any man that ever lived! Mac, dearest, why didn't you eat your grapes?"

"Because I loathe grapes. Nance is going to work them off on an old sick man she knows."

"Some one at the hospital?" Mrs. Clarke asked idly.

"No," said Nance, "it's an old gentleman who lives down in the very place we're talking about. He's been sick for weeks. It's all right about the grapes?"

"Why, of course. Take some oranges, too, and tell the gardener to give you some flowers. The dahlias are going to waste this year. Mac, you look tired!"

He shook off her hand impatiently.

"No, I'm not. I feel like a two-year old. Nance thinks perhaps she may go with us after all."

"Of course she will!" said Mrs. Clarke, with a confident smile at the girl. "We are going to be so good to her that she will not have the heart to refuse."

Mrs. Clarke with her talent for self-deception had almost convinced herself that Nance was a fairy princess who had languished in a nether world of obscurity until Mac's magic smile had restored her to her own.

Nance evaded an answer by fleeing to the white and red breakfast-room where the butler was laying the cloth for her dinner. As a rule she enjoyed these tête-à-têtes with the butler. He was a solemn and pretentious Englishman whom she delighted in shocking by acting and talking in a manner that was all too natural to her. But to-night she submitted quite meekly to his lordly condescension.

She ate her dinner in dreamy abstraction, her thoughts on Mac and the enticing prospects he had held out. After all what was the use in fighting against all the kindness and affection? If they were willing to take the risk of her going with them, why should she hesitate? They knew she was poor and uneducated and not of their world, and they couldn't help seeing that Mac was in love with her. And still they wanted her.

California! Honolulu! Queer far-off lands full of queer people! Big ships that would carry her out of the sight and sound of Calvary Alley forever! And Mac, well and happy, making a man of himself, giving her everything in the world she wanted.

Across her soaring thoughts struck the voices from the adjoining dining-room, Mr. Clarke's sharp and incisive, the bishop's suave and unctious. Suddenly a stray sentence arrested her attention and she listened with her glass half-way to her lips.

"It is the labor question that concerns us more than the war," Mr. Clarke was saying. "I have just succeeded in signing up with a man I have been after for four years. He is a chap named Lewis, the only man in this part of the country who seems to be able to cope with the problem of union labor."

"A son of General Lewis?"

"No, no. Just a common workman who got his training at our factory. He left me five or six years ago without rhyme or reason, and went over to the Ohio Glass Works, where he has made quite a name for himself. I had a tussle to get him back, but he comes to take charge next month. He is one of those rare men you read about, but seldom find, a practical idealist."

Nance left her ice untouched, and slipped through the back entry and up to the dainty blue bedroom that had been hers now for three months. All the delicious languor of the past hour was gone, and in its place was a turmoil of hope and fear and doubt. Dan was coming back. The words beat on her brain. He cared nothing for her, and he was married, and she would never see him, but he was coming back.

She opened the drawer of her dressing table and took out a small faded photograph which she held to the silk-shaded lamp. It was a cheap likeness of an awkward-looking working-boy in his Sunday clothes, a stiff lock of unruly hair across his temple, and a pair of fine earnest eyes looking out from slightly scowling brows.

Nance looked at it long and earnestly; then she flung it back in the drawer with a sigh and, putting out the light, went down again to her patient.

CHAPTER XXXI
MR. DEMRY

The next afternoon, armed with her flowers and fruit, Nance was setting forth for Calvary Alley, when Mrs. Clarke called to her from an upper window.

"If you will wait ten minutes, I will take you down in the machine."

"But I want the walk," Nance insisted. "I need the exercise."

"Nonsense, you are on your feet nearly all the time. I won't be long."

Nance made a wry face at an unoffending sparrow and glanced regretfully at the long white road that wound invitingly in and out of the woods until it dropped sharply to the little station in the valley a mile below. She had been looking forward to that walk all morning. She wanted to get away from the hot-house atmosphere of the Clarke establishment, away from Mac's incessant appeals and his mother's increasing dependence. Aside from amusing her patient and seeing that he obeyed Dr. Adair's orders, her duties for the past few weeks had been too light to be interesting. The luxury that at first had so thrilled her was already beginning to pall. She wanted to be out in the open alone, to feel the sharp wind of reality in her face, while she thought things out.

"I am going to the cathedral," said Mrs. Clarke, emerging from the door, followed by a maid carrying coats and rugs. "But I can drop you wherever you say."

"I'll go there, too," said Nance as she took her seat in the car. "The old gentleman I'm taking the things to lives just back of there, in the very house Dr. Adair is trying to get for the clinic."

"Poor soul!" said Mrs. Clarke idly, as she viewed with approval Nance's small brown hat that so admirably set off the lights in her hair and the warm red tints of her skin.

"He's been up against it something fierce for over a year now," Nance went on. "We've helped him all he'd let us since he stopped playing at the theater."

"Playing?" Mrs. Clarke repeated the one word that had caught her wandering attention. "Is he an actor?"

"No; he is a musician. He used to play in big orchestras in New York and Boston. He plays the fiddle."

For the rest of the way into town Mrs. Clarke was strangely preoccupied. She sat very straight, with eyes slightly contracted, and looked absently out of the window. Once or twice she began a sentence without finishing it. At the cathedral steps she laid a detaining hand on Nance's arm.

"By the way, what did you say was the name of the old man you are going to see?"

"I never said. It's Demry."

"Demry—Never mind, I just missed the step. I'm quite all right. I think I will go with you to see this—this—house they are talking about."

"But it's in the alley. Mrs. Clarke; it's awfully dirty."

"Yes, yes, but I'm coming. Can we go through here?"

So impatient was she that she did not wait for Nance to lead the way, but hurried around the bishop's study and down the concrete walk to the gate that opened into the alley.

"Look out for your skirt against the garbage barrel," warned Nance. It embarrassed her profoundly to have Mrs. Clarke in these surroundings; she hated the mud that soiled her dainty boots, the odors that must offend her nostrils, the inevitable sights that awaited her in Number One. She only prayed that Mrs. Snawdor's curl-papered head might not appear on the upper landing.

"Which way?" demanded Mrs. Clarke, impatiently.

Nance led the way into the dark hall where a half-dozen ragged, dirty-faced children were trying to drag a still dirtier pup up the stairs by means of a twine string.

"In here, Mrs. Clarke," said Nance, pushing open the door at the left

The outside shutters of the big cold room were partly closed, but the light from between them fell with startling effect on the white, marble-like face of the old man who lay asleep on a cot in front of the empty fireplace. For a moment Mrs. Clarke stood looking at him; then with a smothered cry she bent over him.

"Father!" she cried sharply, "Oh, God! It's my father!"

Nance caught her breath in amazement; then her bewildered gaze fell upon a familiar object. There, in its old place on the mantel stood the miniature of a pink and white maiden in the pink and white dress, with the golden curl across her shoulder. In the delicate, beautiful profile Nance read the amazing truth.

Mr. Demry sighed heavily, opened his eyes with an effort and, looking past the bowed head beside him, held out a feeble hand for the flowers.

"Listen, Mr. Demry," said Nance, breathlessly. "Here's a lady says she knows you. Somebody you haven't seen for a long, long time. Will you look at her and try to remember?"

His eyes rested for the fraction of a minute on the agonized face lifted to his, then closed wearily.

"Can you not get the lady a chair, Nancy?" he asked feebly. "You can borrow one from the room across the hall."

"Father!" demanded Mrs. Clarke, "don't you know me? It is Elise. Your daughter, Elise Demorest!"

"Demorest," he repeated, and smiled. "How unnatural it sounds now! Demorest!"

"It's no use," said Nance. "His mind wanders most of the time. Let me take you back to the cathedral, Mrs. Clarke, until we decide what's got to be done."

"I am going to take him home," said Mrs. Clarke, wildly. "He shall have every comfort and luxury I can give him. Poor Father, don't you want to come home with Elise?"

"I live at Number One, Calvary Alley," said Mr. Demry, clinging to the one fact he had trained his mind to remember. "If you will kindly get me to the corner, the children will—"

"It's too late to do anything!" cried Mrs. Clarke, wringing her hands. "I knew something terrible would happen to him. I pleaded with them to help me find him, but they put me off. Then I got so absorbed in Mac that he drove everything else out of my mind. How long has he been in this awful place? How long has he been ill? Who takes care of him?"

Nance, with her arms about Mrs. Clarke, told her as gently as she could of Mr. Demry's advent into the alley fourteen years before, of his friendship with the children, his occasional lapses from grace, and the steady decline of his fortune.

"We must get him away from here!" cried Mrs. Clarke when she had gained control of herself. "Go somewhere and telephone Mr. Clarke. Telephone Dr. Adair. Tell him to bring an ambulance and another nurse and—and plenty of blankets. Telephone to the house for them to get a room ready. But wait—there's Mac—he mustn't know—"

It was the old, old mother-cry! Keep it from Mac, spare Mac, don't let Mac suffer. Nance seized on it now to further her designs.

"You go back to Mr. Mac, Mrs. Clarke. I'll stay here and attend to everything. You go ahead and get things ready for us."

And Mrs. Clarke, used to taking the easiest way, allowed herself to be persuaded, and after one agonized look at the tranquil face on the pillow, hurried away.

Nance, shivering with the cold, got together the few articles that constituted Mr. Demry's worldly possessions. A few shabby garments in the old wardrobe, the miniature on the shelf, a stack of well-worn books, and the violin in its rose-wood case. Everything else had been sold to keep the feeble flame alive in that wasted old form.

Nance looked about her with swimming eyes. She recalled the one happy Christmas that her childhood had known. The gay garlands of tissue paper, the swinging lanterns, the shelf full of oranges and doughnuts, and the beaming old face smiling over the swaying fiddle bow! And to think that Mrs. Clarke's own father had hidden away here all these years, utterly friendless except for the children, poor to the point of starvation, sick to the point of death, grappling with his great weakness in heroic silence, and going down to utter oblivion rather than obtrude his misfortune upon the one he loved best.

As the old man's fairy tales had long ago stirred Nance's imagination and wakened her to the beauty of invisible things, so now his broken, futile life, with its one great glory of renunciation, called out to the soul of her and roused in her a strange, new sense of spiritual beauty.

For one week he lived among the luxurious surroundings of his daughter's home. Everything that skill and money could do, was done to restore him to health and sanity. But he saw only the sordid sights he had been seeing for the past fourteen years; he heard only the sounds to which his old ears had become accustomed.

"You would better move my cot, Nancy," he would say, plucking at the silken coverlid. "They are scrubbing the floor up in the Lavinski flat. The water always comes through." And again he would say: "It is nice and warm in here, but I am afraid you are burning too much coal, dear. I cannot get another bucket until Saturday."

One day Mrs. Clarke saw him take from his tray, covered with delicacies, a half-eaten roll and slip it under his pillow.

"We must save it," he whispered confidentially, "save it for to-morrow." In vain they tried to reassure him; the haunting poverty that had stalked beside him in life refused to be banished by death.

Mrs. Clarke remained "the lady" to him to the end. When he spoke to her, his manner assumed a faint dignity, with a slight touch of gallantry, the unmistakable air of a gentleman of the old school towards an attractive stranger of the opposite sex.

His happiest hours were those when he fancied the children were with him.

"Gently! gently!" he would say; "there is room for everybody. This knee is for Gussie Gorman, this one for Joe, because they are the smallest, you know. Now are you ready?" And then he would whisper fairy stories, smiling at the ceiling, and making feeble gestures with his wasted old hands.

The end came one day after he had lain for hours in a stupor. He stirred suddenly and asked for his violin.

"I must go—to the—theater, Nancy," he murmured. "I—do not want—to be—a—burden."

They laid the instrument in his arms, and his fingers groped feebly over the strings; then his chin sank into its old accustomed place, and a great light dawned in his eyes. Mr. Demry, who was used to seeing invisible things, had evidently caught the final vision.

That night, worn with nursing and full of grief for the passing of her old friend, Nance threw a coat about her and slipped out on the terrace. Above her, nebulous stars were already appearing, and their twinkling was answered by responsive gleams in the city below. Against the velvety dusk two tall objects towered in the distance, the beautiful Gothic spire of the cathedral, and the tall, unseemly gas pipe of Clarke's Bottle Factory. Between them, under a haze of smoke and grime, lay Calvary Alley.

"I don't know which is worse," thought Nance fiercely, "to be down there in the mess, fighting and struggling and suffering to get the things you want, or up here with the mummies who haven't got anything left to wish for. I wish life wasn't just a choice between a little hard green apple and a rotten big one!"

She leaned her elbows on the railing and watched the new moon dodging behind the tree trunks and, as she watched, she grappled with the problem of life, at first bitterly and rebelliously, then with a dawning comprehension of its meaning. After all was the bishop, with his conspicuous virtues and his well-known dislike of children, any better than old Mr. Demry, with his besetting sin and his beautiful influence on every child with whom he came in contact? Was Mr. Clarke, working children under age in the factory to build up a great fortune for his son, very different from Mr. Lavinski, with his sweat-shop, hoarding pennies for the ambitious Ikey? Was Mrs. Clarke, shirking her duty to her father, any happier or any better than Mrs. Snawdor, shirking hers to her children? Was Mac, adored and petted and protected, any better than Birdie, now in the state asylum paying the penalty of their joint misdeed? Was the tragedy in the great house back of her any more poignant than the tragedy of Dan Lewis bound by law to an insane wife and burdened with a child that was not his own? She seemed to see for the first time the great illuminating truth that the things that make men alike in the world are stronger than the things that make them different. And in this realization an overwhelming ambition seized her. Some hidden spiritual force rose to lift her out of the contemplation of her own interests into something of ultimate value to her fellowmen.

After all, those people down there in Calvary Alley were her people, and she meant to stand by them. It had been the dream of her life to get out and away, but in that moment she knew that wherever she went, she would always come back. Others might help from the top, but she could help understandingly from the bottom. With the magnificent egotism of youth, she outlined gigantic schemes on the curtain of the night. Some day, somehow, she would make people like the Clarkes see the life of the poor as it really was, she would speak for the girls in the factories, in the sweatshops, on the stage. She would be an interpreter between the rich and the poor and make them serve each other.

"Nance!" called an injured voice from the music room behind her, "what in the mischief are you doing out there in the cold? Come on in here and amuse me. I'm half dead with the dumps!"

"All right, Mr. Mac. I'm coming," she said cheerfully, as she stepped in through the French window and closed it against her night of dreams.

CHAPTER XXXII
THE NEW FOREMAN

The Dan Lewis who came back to Clarke's Bottle Factory was a very different man from the one who had walked out of it five years before. He had gone out a stern, unforgiving, young ascetic, accepting no compromise, demanding perfection of himself and of his fellow-men. The very sublimity of his dream doomed it to failure. Out of the crumbling ideals of his boyhood he had struggled to a foothold on life that had never been his in the old days. His marriage to Birdie Smelts had been the fiery furnace in which his soul had been softened to receive the final stamp of manhood.

For his hour of indiscretion he had paid to the last ounce of his strength and courage. After that night in the lodging-house, there seemed to him but one right course, and he took it with unflinching promptness. Even when Birdie, secure in the protection of his name and his support, lapsed into her old vain, querulous self, he valiantly bore his burden, taking any menial work that he could find to do, and getting a sort of grim satisfaction out of what he regarded as expiation for his sin.

But when he became aware of Birdie's condition and realized the use she had made of him, the tragedy broke upon him in all of its horror. Then he, too, lost sight of the shore lights, and went plunging desperately into the stream of life with no visible and sustaining ideal to guide his course, but only the fighting necessity to get across as decently as possible.

After a long struggle he secured a place in the Ohio Glass Works, where his abilities soon began to be recognized. Instead of working now with tingling enthusiasm for Nance and the honeysuckle cottage, he worked doggedly and furiously to meet the increasing expense of Birdie's wastefulness and the maintenance of her child.

Year by year he forged ahead, gaining a reputation for sound judgment and fair dealing that made him an invaluable spokesman between the employer and the employed. He set himself seriously to work to get at the real conditions that were causing the ferment of unrest among the working classes. He made himself familiar with socialistic and labor newspapers; he attended mass meetings; he laid awake nights reading and wrestling with the problems of organized industrialism. His honest resentment against the injustice shown the laboring man was always nicely balanced by his intolerance of the haste and ignorance and misrepresentation of the labor agitators. He was one of the few men who could be called upon to arbitrate differences, whom both factions invariably pronounced "square." When pressure was brought to bear upon him to return to Clarke's, he was in a position to dictate his own terms.

It was the second week after his reinstatement that he came up to the office one day and unexpectedly encountered Nance Molloy. At first he did not recognize the tall young lady in the well-cut brown suit with the bit of fur at the neck and wrists and the jaunty brown hat with its dash of gold. Then she looked up, and it was Nance's old smile that flashed out at him, and Nance's old impulsive self that turned to greet him.

For one radiant moment all that had happened since they last stood there was swept out of the memory of each; then it came back; and they shook hands awkwardly and could find little to say to each other in the presence of the strange stenographer who occupied Nance's old place at the desk by the window.

"They told me you weren't working here," said Dan at length.

"I'm not. I've just come on an errand for Mrs. Clarke."

Dan's eyes searched hers in swift inquiry.

"I'm a trained nurse now," she said, determined to take the situation lightly. "You remember how crazy I used to be about doping people?"

He did not answer, and she hurried on as if afraid of any silence that might fall between them.

"It all started with the smallpox in Calvary Alley. Been back there, Dan?"

"Not yet."

"Lots of changes since the old days. Mr. Snawdor and Fidy and Mrs. Smelts and Mr. Demry all gone. Have you heard about Mr. Demry?"

Dan shook his head. He was not listening to her, but he was looking at her searchingly, broodingly, with growing insistence.

The hammering of the type-writer was the only sound that broke the ensuing pause.

"Tell me your news, Dan," said Nance in desperation. "Where you living now?"

"At Mrs. Purdy's. She's going to take care of Ted for me."

"Ted? Oh! I forgot. How old is he now?"

For the first time Dan's face lit up with his fine, rare smile.

"He's four, Nance, and the smartest kid that ever lived! You'd be crazy about him, I know. I wonder if you couldn't go out there some day and see him?"

Nance showed no enthusiasm over the suggestion; instead she gathered up her muff and gloves and, leaving a message for Mr. Clarke with the stenographer, prepared to depart.

"I am thinking about going away," she said. "I may go out to California next week."

The brief enthusiasm died out of Dan's face.

"What's taking you to California?" he asked dully, as he followed her into the hall.

"I may go with a patient. Have you heard of the trouble they're in at the Clarkes'?"

"No."

"It's Mr. Mac. He's got tuberculosis, and they are taking him out to the coast for a year. They want me to go along."

Dan's face hardened.

"So it's Mac Clarke still?" he asked bitterly.

His tone stung Nance to the quick, and she wheeled on him indignantly.

"See here, Dan! I've got to put you straight on a thing or two. Where can we go to have this business out?"

He led her across the hall to his own small office and closed the door.

"I'm going to tell you something," she said, facing him with blazing eyes, "and I don't care a hang whether you believe it or not. I never was in love with Mac Clarke. From the day you left this factory I never saw or wrote to him until he was brought to the hospital last July, and I was put on the case. I didn't have anything more to do with him than I did with you. I guess you know how much that was!"

"What about now? Are you going west with him?"

Dan confronted her with the same stern inquiry in his eyes that had shone there the day they parted, in this very place, five years ago.

"I don't know whether I am or not!" cried Nance, firing up. "They've done everything for me, the Clarkes have. They think his getting well depends on me. Of course that's rot, but that's what they think. As for Mr. Mac himself—"

"Is he still in love with you?"

At this moment a boy thrust his head in the door to say that Dr. Adair had telephoned for Miss Molloy to come by the hospital before she returned to Hillcrest.

Nance pulled on her gloves and, with chin in the air, was departing without a word, when Dan stopped her.

"I'm sorry I spoke to you like that, Nance," he said, scowling at the floor. "I've got no right to be asking you questions, or criticizing what you do, or where you go. I hope you'll excuse me."

"You *have* got the right!" declared Nance, with one of her quick changes of mood. "You can ask me anything you like. I guess we can always be friends, can't we?"

"No," said Dan, slowly, "I don't think we can. I didn't count on seeing you like this, just us two together, alone. I thought you'd be married maybe or moved away some place."

It was Nance's time to be silent, and she listened with wide eyes and parted lips.

"I mustn't see you—alone—any more, Nance," Dan went on haltingly. "But while we are here I want to tell you about it. Just this once, Nance, if you don't mind."

He crossed over and stood before her, his hands gripping a chair back.

"When I went away from here," he began, "I thought you had passed me up for Mac Clarke. It just put me out of business, Nance. I didn't care where I went or what I did. Then one night in Cincinnati I met Birdie, and she was up against it, too—and—"

After all he couldn't make a clean breast of it! Whatever he might say would reflect on Birdie, and he gave the explanation up in despair. But Nance came to his rescue.

"I know, Dan," she said. "Mrs. Smelts told me everything. I don't know another fellow in the world that would have stood by a girl like you did Birdie. She oughtn't have let you marry her without telling you."

"I think she meant to give me my freedom when the baby came," said Dan. "At least that was what she promised. I couldn't have lived through those first months of hell if I hadn't thought there was some way out. But when the baby came, it was too late. Her mind was affected, and by the law of the State I'm bound to her for the rest of her life."

"Do you know—who—who the baby's father is, Dan?"

"No. She refused from the first to tell me, and now I'm glad I don't know. She said the baby was like him, and that made her hate it. That was the way her trouble started. She wouldn't wash the little chap, or feed him, or look after him when he was sick. I had to do everything. For a year she kept getting worse and worse, until one night I caught her trying to set fire to his crib. Of course after that she had to be sent to the asylum, and from that time on, Ted and I fought it out together. One of the neighbors took charge of him in the day, and I wrestled with him at night."

"Couldn't you put him in an orphan asylum?"

Dan shook his head.

"No, I couldn't go back on him when he was up against a deal like that. I made up my mind that I'd never let him get lonesome like I used to be, with nobody to care a hang what became of him. He's got my name now, and he'll never know the difference if I can help it."

"And Birdie? Does she know you when you go to see her?"

"Not for two years now. It's easier than when she did."

There was silence between them; then Nance said:

"I'm glad you told me all this, Dan. I—I wish I could help you."

"You can't," said Dan, sharply. "Don't you see I've got no right to be with you? Do you suppose there's been a week, or a day in all these years that I haven't wanted you with every breath I drew? The rest was just a nightmare I was living through in order to wake up and find you. Nance—I love you! With my heart and soul and body! You've been the one beautiful thing in my whole life, and I wasn't worthy of you. I can't let you go! I—Oh, God! what am I saying? What right have I—Don't let me see you again like this, Nance, don't let me talk to you—"

He stumbled to a chair by the desk and buried his head in his arms. His breath came in short, hard gasps, with a long agonizing quiver between, and his broad shoulders heaved. It was the first time he had wept since that night, so long ago, when he had sat in the gutter in front of Slap Jack's saloon and broken his heart over an erring mother.

For one tremulous second Nance hovered over him, her face aflame with sympathy and almost maternal pity; then she pulled herself together and said brusquely:

"It's all right, Danny. I understand. I'm going. Good-by."

And without looking back, she fled into the hall and down the steps to the waiting motor.

CHAPTER XXXIII
NANCE COMES INTO HER OWN

For two hours Nance was closeted with Dr. Adair in his private office, and when she came out she had the look of one who has been following false trails and suddenly discovers the right one.

"Don't make a hasty decision," warned Dr. Adair in parting. "The trip with the Clarkes will be a wonderful experience; they may be gone a year or more, and they'll do everything and see everything in the approved way. What I am proposing offers no romance. It will be hard work and plenty of it. You'd better think it over and give me your answer to-morrow."

"I'll give it to you now," said Nance. "It's yes."

He scrutinized her quizzically; then he held out his hand with its short, thick, surgeon's fingers.

"It's a wise decision, my dear," he said. "Say nothing about it at present. I will make it all right with the Clarkes."

During the weeks that followed, Nance was too busy to think of herself or her own affairs. She superintended the shopping and packing for Mrs. Clarke; she acted as private secretary for Mr. Clarke; she went on endless errands, and looked after the innumerable details that a family migration entails.

Mac, sulking on the couch, feeling grossly abused and neglected, spent most of his time inveighing against Dr. Adair. "He's got to let you come out by the end of next month." he threatened Nance, "or I'll take the first train home. What's he got up his sleeve anyhow?"

"Ask him," advised Nance, over her shoulder, as she vanished into the hall.

Toward the end of November the Clarkes took their departure; father, mother, and son, two servants, and the despised, but efficient Miss Hanna. Nance went down to see them off, hovering over the unsuspecting Mac with feelings of mingled relief and contrition.

"I wish you'd let me tell him," she implored Mrs. Clarke. "He's bound to know soon. Why not get it over with now?"

Mrs. Clarke was in instant panic.

"Not a word, I implore you! We will break the news to him when he is better. Be good to him now, let him go away happy. Please, dear, for my sake!" With the strength of the weak, she carried her point.

For the quarter of an hour before the train started, Nance resolutely kept the situation in hand, not giving Mac a chance to speak to her alone, and keeping up a running fire of nonsense that provoked even Mr. Clarke to laughter. When the "All Aboard!" sounded from without, there was scant time for good-bys. She hurried out, and when on the platform, turned eagerly to scan the windows above her. A gust of smoke swept between her and the slow-moving train; then as it cleared she caught her last glimpse of a gay irresponsible face propped about with pillows and a thin hand that threw her kisses as far as she could see.

It was with a curious feeling of elation mingled with depression, that she tramped back to the hospital through the gloom of that November day. Until a month ago she had scarcely had a thought beyond Mac and the progress of his case; even now she missed his constant demands upon her, and her heart ached for the disappointment that awaited him. But under these disturbing thoughts something new and strange and beautiful was calling her.

Half mechanically she spent the rest of the afternoon reestablishing herself in the nurses' quarters at the hospital which she had left nearly four months before. At six o'clock she put on the gray cape and small gray bonnet that constituted her uniform, and leaving word that she would report for duty at nine o'clock, went to the corner and boarded a street car. It was a warm evening for November, and the car with its throng of home-going workers was close and uncomfortable. But Nance, clinging to a strap, and jostled on every side, was superbly indifferent to her surroundings. With lifted chin and preoccupied eyes, she held counsel with herself, sometimes moving her lips slightly as if rehearsing a part. At Butternut Lane she got out and made her way to the old white house midway of the square.

A little boy was perched on the gate post, swinging a pair of fat legs and trying to whistle. There was no lack of effort on his part, but the whistle for some reason refused to come. He tried hooking a small finger inside the corners of his mouth; he tried it with teeth together and teeth apart.

Nance, sympathizing with his thwarted ambition, smiled as she approached; then she caught her breath. The large brown eyes that the child turned upon her were disconcertingly familiar.

"Is this Ted?" she asked.

He nodded mistrustfully; then after surveying her gravely, evidently thought better of her and volunteered the information that he was waiting for his daddy.

"Where is Mrs. Purdy?" Nance asked.

"Her's making me a gingerbread man."

"I know a story about a gingerbread man; want to hear it?"

"Is it scareful?" asked Ted.

"No, just funny," Nance assured. Then while he sat very still on the gate post, with round eyes full of wonder, Nance stood in front of him with his chubby fists in her hands and told him one of Mr. Demry's old fairy tales. So absorbed were they both that neither of them heard an approaching step until it was quite near.

"Daddy!" cried Ted, in sudden rapture, scrambling down from the post and hurling himself against the new-comer.

But for once his daddy's first greeting was not for him. Dan seized Nance's outstretched hand and studied her face with hungry, inquiring eyes.

"I've come to say good-by, Dan," she said in a matter-of-fact tone.

His face hardened.

"Then you are going with the Clarkes? You've decided?"

"I've decided. Can't we go over to the summer-house for a few minutes. I want to talk to you."

They crossed the yard to the sheltered bower in its cluster of bare trees, while Ted trudged behind them kicking up clouds of dead leaves with his small square-toed boots.

"You run in to Mother Purdy, Teddykins," said Dan, but Nance caught the child's hand.

"Better keep him here," she said with an unsteady laugh. "I got to get something off my chest once and for all; then I'll skidoo."

But Ted had already spied a squirrel and gone in pursuit, and Nance's eyes followed him absently.

"When I met you in the office the other day," she said, "I thought I could bluff it through. But when I saw you all knocked up like that; and knew that you cared—" Her eyes came back to his. "Dan we might as well face the truth."

"You mean—"

"I mean I'm going to wait for you if I have to wait forever. You're not free now, but when you are, I'll come to you."

He made one stride toward her and swept her into his arms.

"Do you mean it, girl?" he asked, his voice breaking with the unexpected joy. "You are going to stand by me? You are going to wait?"

"Let me go, Dan!" she implored. "Where's Ted? I mustn't stay—I—"

But Dan held her as if he never meant to let her go, and suddenly she ceased to struggle or to consider right or wrong or consequences. She lifted her head and her lips met his in complete surrender. For the first time in her short and stormy career she had found exactly what she wanted.

For a long time they stood thus; then Dan recovered himself with a start.

He pushed her away from him almost roughly. "Nance, I didn't mean to! I won't again! Only I've wanted you so long, I've been so unhappy. I can't let you leave me now! I can't let you go with the Clarkes!"

"You don't have to. They've gone without me."

"But you said you'd come to say good-by. I thought you were starting to California."

"Well, I'm not. I am going to stay right here. Dr. Adair has asked me to take charge of the clinic—the new one they are going to open in Calvary Alley."

"And we're going to be near each other, able to see each other every day—"

But she stopped him resolutely.

"No, Dan, no. I knew we couldn't do that before I came to-night. Now I know it more than ever. Don't you see we got to cut it all out? Got to keep away from each other just the same as if I was in California and you were here?"

Dan's big strong hands again seized hers.

"It won't be wrong for us just to see each other," he urged hotly. "I promise never to say a word of love or to touch you, Nance. What's happened to-night need never happen again. We can hold on to ourselves; we can be just good friends until—"

But Nance pulled her hands away impatiently.

"You might. I couldn't. I tell you I got to keep away from you, Dan. Can't you see? Can't you understand? I counted on you to see the right of it. I thought you was going to help me!" And with an almost angry sob, she sat down suddenly on the leaf-strewn bench and, locking her arms across the railing, dropped her flaming face upon them.

For a long time he stood watching her, while, his face reflected the conflicting emotions that were fighting within him for mastery. Then into his eyes crept a look of dumb compassion, the same look he had once bent on a passion-tossed little girl lying on the seat of a patrol-wagon in the chill dusk of a Christmas night.

He straightened his shoulders and laid a firm hand on her bowed head.

"You must stop crying, Nance," he commanded with the stern tenderness he would have used toward Ted. "Perhaps you are right; God knows. At any rate we are going to do whatever you say in this matter. I promise to keep out of your way until you say I can come."

Nance drew a quivering breath, and smiled up at him through her tears.

"That's not enough, Dan; you got to keep away whether I say to come or not. You're stronger and better than what I am. You got to promise that whatever happens you'll make me be good."

And Dan with trembling lips and steady eyes made her the solemn promise.

Then, sitting there in the twilight, with only the dropping of a leaf to break the silence, they poured out their confidences, eager to reach a complete understanding in the brief time they had allotted themselves. In minute detail they pieced together the tangled pattern of the past; they poured out their present aims and ambitions, coming back again and again to the miracle of their new-found love. Of their personal future, they dared not speak. It was locked to them, and death alone held the key.

Darkness had closed in when the side door of the house across the yard was flung open, and a small figure came plunging toward them through the crackling leaves.

"It's done, Daddy!" cried an excited voice. "It's the cutest little gingerbread man. And supper's ready, and he's standing up by my plate."

"All right!" said Dan, holding out one hand to him and one to Nance. "We'll all go in together to see the gingerbread man."

"But, Dan—"

"Just this once; it's our good-by night, you know."

Nance hesitated, then straightening the prim little gray bonnet that would assume a jaunty tilt, she followed the tall figure and the short one into the halo of light that circled the open door.

The evening that followed was one of those rare times, insignificant in itself, every detail of which was to stand out in after life, charged with significance. For Nance, the warmth and glow of the homely little house, with its flowered carpets and gay curtains, the beaming face of old Mrs. Purdy in its frame of silver curls, the laughter of the happy child, and above all the strong, tender presence of Dan, were things never to be forgotten.

At eight o'clock she rose reluctantly, saying that she had to go by the Snawdors' before she reported at the hospital at nine o'clock.

"Do you mind if I go that far with you?" asked Dan, wistfully.

On their long walk across the city they said little. Their way led them past many familiar places, the school house, the old armory, Cemetery Street, Post-Office Square, where they used to sit and watch the electric signs. Of the objects they passed, Dan was superbly unaware. He saw only Nance. But she was keenly aware of every old association that bound them together. Everything seemed strangely beautiful to her, the glamorous shop-lights cutting through the violet gloom, the subtle messages of lighted windows, the passing faces of her fellow-men. In that gray world her soul burned like a brilliant flame lighting up everything around her.

As they turned into Calvary Alley the windows of the cathedral glowed softly above them.

"I never thought how pretty it was before!" said Nance, rapturously. "Say, Dan, do you know what 'Evol si dog' means?"

"No; is it Latin?"

She squeezed his arm between her two hands and laughed gleefully.

"You're as bad as me," she said, "I'm not going to tell you; you got to go inside and find out for yourself."

On the threshold of Number One they paused again. Even the almost deserted old tenement, blushing under a fresh coat of red paint, took on a hue of romance.

"You wait 'til we get it fixed up," said Nance. "They're taking out all the partitions in the Smelts' flat, and making a big consulting room of it. And over here in Mr. Demry's room I'm going to have the baby clinic. I'm going to have boxes of growing flowers in every window; and storybooks and—"

"Yes," cried Dan, fiercely, "you are going to be so taken up with all this that you won't need me; you'll forget about to-night!"

But her look silenced him.

"Dan," she said very earnestly, "I always have needed you, and I always will. I love you better than anything in the world, and I'm trying to prove it."

A wavering light on the upper landing warned them that they might be overheard. A moment later some one demanded to know who was there.

"Come down and see!" called Nance.

Mrs. Snawdor, lamp in hand, cautiously descended.

"Is that you, Nance?" she cried. "It's about time you was comin' to see to the movin' an' help tend to things. Who's that there with you?"

"Don't you know?"

"Well, if it ain't Dan Lewis!" And to Dan's great embarrassment the effusive lady enveloped him in a warm and unexpected embrace. She even held him at arm's length and commented upon his appearance with frank admiration. "I never seen any one improve so much an' yet go on favorin' theirselves."

Nance declined to go up-stairs on the score of time, promising to come on the following Sunday and take entire charge of the moving.

"Ain't it like her to go git mixed up in this here fool clinic business?" Mrs. Snawdor asked of Dan. "Just when she'd got a job with rich swells that would 'a' took her anywhere? Here she was for about ten years stewin' an' fumin' to git outen the alley, an' here she is comin' back again! She's tried about ever'thin' now, but gittin' married."

Dan scenting danger, changed the direction of the conversation by asking her where they were moving to.

"That's some more of her doin's," said Mrs. Snawdor. "She's gittin' her way at las' 'bout movin' us to the country. Lobelia an' Rosy V. is goin' to keep house, an' me an' William Jennings is going to board with 'em. You'd orter see that boy of mine, Dan. Nance got him into the 'lectric business an' he's doin' somethin' wonderful. He's got my brains an' his pa's manners. You can say what you please, Mr. Snawdor was a perfect gentleman!"

It was evident from the pride in her voice that since Mr. Snawdor's demise he had been canonized, becoming the third member of the ghostly firm of Molloy, Yager, and Snawdor.

"What about Uncle Jed?" asked Nance. "Where's he going?"

Mrs. Snawdor laughed consciously and, in doing so, exhibited to full advantage the dazzling new teeth that were the pride of her life.

"Oh, Mr. Burks is goin' with us," she said. "It's too soon to talk about it yet,—but—er—Oh, you know me, Nance!" And with blushing confusion the thrice-bereaved widow hid her face in her apron.

The clock in the cathedral tower was nearing nine when Nance and Dan emerged from Number One. They did not speak as they walked up to the corner and stood waiting for the car. Their hands were clasped hard, and she could feel his heart thumping under her wrist as he pressed it to his side.

Passers-by jostled them on every side, and an importunate newsboy implored patronage, but they seemed oblivious to their surroundings. The car turned a far corner and came toward them relentlessly.

"God bless you, Dan," whispered Nance as he helped her on the platform; then turning, she called back to him with one of her old flashing smiles. "And me too, a little bit!"